A FOOL'S TRIUMPH

G. S. ROCK

This is a work of fiction. All characters, names, places, incidents, organizations, and dialogue in this novel are the product of the author's imagination or are used fictitiously.

Copyright © 2015 by G. S. Rock
All rights reserved
ISBN: 0692545646
ISBN-13: 9780692545645
Library of Congress Control Number: 2015953704
The Post Oak Company, Fairfax, VA

To my family and friends whose kind encouragement was invaluable as I endeavored to complete this story

The best laid schemes o' mice and men gang aft a-gley

Robert Burns
To a Mouse, 1785

Standing in a clearing on the banks of the Potomac River, TD Adkins has no idea how many of the men he faces are armed. It's possible he's the only one here without a weapon. The men opposite him have proven they'll kill to get what they want. The only reason they're here is because they expect him to deliver it to them.

It was an error in judgment on his part that has brought them all here, a huge error. An error he has since magnified with additional mistakes. Everything now rides on his plan to settle the matter. Unfortunately, it appears that has turned out to be his final blunder.

MONDAY EVENING - FIVE DAYS EARLIER

S logging through the evening's ebbing rush hour west of Washington DC, two cars are moving toward the same destination. Only one of the drivers knows they're travelling together.

Tim Crane, handsome, in his early forties, is driving the car in front. Though quite successful, a couple of hours ago he checked-in to a cheap motel. Now he's returning there, but paying minimal attention to the road. Instead, he's constantly glancing at the young woman riding next to him, while his right hand lightly caresses her thigh.

Cyndi Reynolds doesn't mind the attention. A waitress, she met Tim a little over a month ago. This is their third date and she's enjoying the evening out. Like Tim, she's unaware another car is travelling with them three cars back.

It's a typically hot and muggy summer evening in Fairfax, a few miles west of the Beltway, DC's monument to endless traffic and political grid-lock. Besides his attention to Cyndi's leg, Tim ponders an important question: should he suggest a shower upon arrival, or get right down to the only reason he's frequenting a third-rate local motel. A motel that's less than a ten-mile drive from his home, where he lives with his wife of fourteen years and their two children. Either way, he'll have Cyndi's clothes off moments after entering the room. It's a simple problem. Nothing compared to the business challenges he faces as an Executive Vice-President for one of DC's myriad consulting firms.

With about a mile remaining to the motel, Tim decides the shower can wait. After they have sex, he'll shower first. If Cyndi wants, she can rinse off after him while he gets dressed and finishes the wine he put on ice when he checked in.

Tim likes the idea of wine, more than he enjoys its taste and pleasures. He has friends who talk about wine regularly, speaking with reverence of vineyards and vintages, Pinots versus Cab Savs. Tim knows enough about the subject to bluff a certain level of expertise, but the truth is he can't tell much difference between a good bottle and a great one. Unlike most of his friends, he prefers whites to reds. Earlier today, he purchased an $8.99 bottle of Chardonnay at a convenience store. He left it to chill in the small cooler he keeps handy in the trunk of his company-provided, midnight blue BMW.

While Cyndi showers, he'll call her a taxi and then dress for the third time today. He's currently wearing clothes he changed into at the gym. Later, he'll put back on the shirt, tie, and suit he was wearing when he left home this morning, clothes bearing no traces of his encounter with Cyndi.

For Tim, nothing beats a relaxing evening of casual sex away from his family and home. Listening to his wife talk is grating and for the most part unbearable. His kids are old enough that they're no longer especially thrilled if Daddy comes home early. An evening out doesn't set him back much either. The cost of dinner, a cheap motel room, and an occasional token gift for his dates are a bargain in exchange for the kicks and gratification he receives from his little adventures.

Tim's job often requires him to spend evenings out with potential clients or business partners. They attend sporting events or enjoy luxurious dinners, all financed with profits gleaned from their current customers. The activities usually include sufficient time for scheming, lobbying, and staying abreast of insider information. It's all a prerequisite for capturing a share of the next giant, multi-year, multi-million dollar project, drawn from the bottomless well of Federal government spending. Particularly choice are the long-term contracts, the five- and ten-year deals generating enough profits to support their lavish executive lifestyles while still leaving a modest payout for shareholders.

The corporate nights out provide an excellent cover story for his wife, Julia. As long as he's home by ten-thirty or so there's rarely any problem. Tonight should seem like any another evening spent with clients.

Tim limits his cheating to women he meets on a casual basis, usually within the context of their job, such as cashiers or waitresses. It isn't that he has a thing for waitresses specifically, or that other women don't interest him. It's more a way to keep his fun and games from overlapping with his professional and social circles. To minimize further chance of detection, he often ends the evenings at a cheap motel. One where his friends, colleagues, and out of town clients would never stay.

Despite his efforts to mask his affairs from home and work, there have been narrow escapes. Once, he was sure of exposure. He was hosting a senior staff dinner at the Capital Grille with Julia accompanying him for the evening. Suddenly one of his girlfriends appeared before them as one of the servers for the large party. Luckily, she stayed cool, avoiding overt recognition. She knew Tim occasionally gave personal gifts, so she played it smart, betting on a future reward.

She was correct. A week later, her discretion garnered a beautiful bracelet. It was no great cost to Tim, actually none at all. He always files for company reimbursement of his gifts, vaguely describing them as a client-related business development expense. He also moved on from their relationship soon after the encounter.

Tim thinks of himself as a smart operator. He has become completely comfortable with his extramarital affairs. Long ago, he convinced himself that Julia is clueless about his activities. His career success, coupled with his ability to avoid detection of his affairs, underlies a strong sense that he's a man in full control of an increasingly successful life, one he deserves.

Unfortunately, Tim couldn't be more wrong. He doesn't know, for example, that for some time Julia has had a good idea of the nature of his late evening outings. Or that she is carefully planning their end. She has spent no small amount of time calculating her share of a divorce settlement, one that will certainly be lucrative. She is also plotting to catch him red-handed, ensuring this particular waitress ends the parade of women with whom he has cheated.

The two things most important to Julia are keeping their multimillion-dollar Great Falls home and maintaining her image with the women she socializes with, many whose children attend the same private academy. Divorce is not uncommon in her circle. Of paramount importance is avoiding public knowledge of Tim's cheating, particularly with someone she would describe with the adjective 'common'. If Julia has her way, the costs of Tim's nights out are about to increase exponentially.

Tim is completely unaware of the car following him along his entire route this evening. He has been shadowed since the moment he left work under the guise of a late-afternoon client meeting. He also doesn't know that he has been tailed several times in this manner.

Tim also doesn't know that after tonight, he will never have another extramarital affair.

⅄

Unlike Tim, the driver of the second car in this evening's asphalt ballet is acutely aware of the other car and its passengers. TD Adkins is purposefully following Tim Crane.

He not only knows their destination, the Gateway Motor Inn on Fairfax Boulevard, but he checked-in there as well little over an hour ago. TD has a job to do. He has been tailing Tim Crane on and off for several weeks, all part of a contract he was hired to fulfill. He expects to finish that job tonight.

He resumed the tail this afternoon when Tim left work and followed him to the Fitness America gym. To facilitate his surveillance, TD had taken Fitness America up on their offer of a short-term trial membership. Today, he watched his subject from the low-impact equipment.

Tim often goes for solid workouts, but this afternoon's visit was not about building up his pecs. It was about having a place to shower and change clothes for his date. Even though TD has followed him inside the gym twice, he risks little chance of being noticed. Tim rarely shifts his eyes from their vigilant perusal of the female customers' bodies. It's unlikely he would ever glance TD's way.

After the workout, he followed Tim to the Gateway Motor Inn. He watched as Tim checked-in to Room 114 and then immediately left the motel for his date. In all the times he has followed him, the man has never shown an inkling he's being watched. Some of that is certainly due to TD's skill, but like so many others, Tim's completely self-centered view of the world makes it much easier.

TD Adkins is a private eye, a licensed private investigator as legally defined by the Code of the Commonwealth of Virginia. He's registered because the law requires it, though there are few hurdles to achieving this status. Virginia's licensing requirements call for only sixty hours of training.

TD completed the coursework and obtained a license, but he works independently and rarely has a job. He never advertises, has no website, and doesn't go to an office. There's little on his desk at home that indicates he does any work at all. He has no separate phone listing as an investigator. To contact him you need to use either his residential line or cell phone. It's certainly not easy to find or hire him in a professional capacity.

The few people who know TD well would tell you the situation is exactly as he prefers. He has floated through life with no purpose for over two years now. With sparse employment and little activity altogether, he is deeply mired in a kind of post-traumatic introspective funk.

TD is not rich, at least by the measures of those with real wealth, yet he does have a decent amount of money set aside. By no plan or effort of his own, he unexpectedly came into a large sum, an amount exceeding a million dollars. He knows if he manages it wisely, it could allow him certain small freedoms. He could easily cover the costs of relocating to live and work in any locale he chooses. He could pursue career choices that might be less financially rewarding, but more satisfying.

Yet, he has done none of that since the events resulting in his windfall. He has not invested the money, nor spent any of it. He did make several major changes but the results have not been an improvement. Unhappy and unfulfilled, his life has gone adrift.

He put the money into a separate account at the bank and let it sit. He also sold his home, realizing only a modest gain in a down market. Instead of leaving the area, he purchased a small, condominium apartment in suburban Northern Virginia, located only a few miles from where he already lived.

He left his career behind, but opted for none of the vocations he thought he might at one time pursue. He has shown no real interest in anything and his few friends worry about him. They have no idea what he does with all of his free time, except that he has taken to regularly hanging out at a local 'gentlemen's' club.

TD has no steady employment primarily because he's uninterested. He never seeks work and the only jobs he takes are the result of someone repeatedly attempting to contact him. When they finally get lucky and he answers his phone, they still have to get him to agree to their request.

It's such a rare occasion when TD takes on a piece of investigative work it would be generous to describe his efforts as part-time. He earns very little, certainly not enough to pay the bills. He's currently getting by living off the profits from his home sale. If he still needs income when that dwindling reserve is gone, he plans to draw on his personal savings, leaving the new money untouched.

At age forty-three, TD is in decent enough physical shape if you don't count the extra weight he added the last two years. At six-feet tall, there's no doubt he can stand to lose a few. It's been a long time since he's been on a scale, but he wouldn't be surprised if he were carrying just over two hundred pounds. He has finally learned to stay away from all-you-can-eat buffets, unless of course they're serving Chinese food. Surprisingly, he can still complete a five-mile jog in a reasonable time.

With sandy brown hair, TD is pleasant enough to look at. At certain times when he's lost in thought, he'll tilt his head up a little. He'll take on a distant look, with his hazel eyes squinting, and his solid jaw line set in determination. Oddly, those are among the few times a woman has ever told him he was handsome.

Upon graduating from college, if you had asked him where he would be in twenty years, it's unlikely he would have suggested anything resembling investigative work. Yet TD possesses some rather unique skills, skills that are the foundation of his being a top investigator.

He only recently became a private eye. Before that, he worked his entire career in the insurance industry. Within a few years of starting, he achieved recognition as an elite claims investigator with few peers. He spent almost two decades working for one of the nation's largest casualty and life insurance firms, handling their toughest and potentially costliest claims.

At their core, TD's skills are instinctual, manifesting themselves through an uncanny proficiency at deductive reasoning. He has an innate ability to understand what people are thinking. He reads people. He doesn't read their minds or random thoughts, but it's as if he knows their plans. He excels at predicting the choices people will make, especially if they're under pressure or trying to hide something. He almost always knows when someone is lying. This talent seemingly covers all kinds of lying: lying by omission, lying to others, even when people are lying to themselves.

Being a human lie detector isn't always a good thing. It can make both personal and professional interactions quite difficult at times. But it helped him become a top claims investigator, one with a pick of the most interesting cases. If something about a case seemed odd, or there was a higher potential for fraud, then TD was assigned. In addition to working only the most complex claims, he also found satisfaction in mentoring younger investigators.

All of that was before the events, before the 'accidents' precipitating his windfall. It was before his company began investigating a large death-benefit claim; a claim he did not investigate because he was the sole beneficiary. Before that investigation was completed, TD had resigned his position and ended his career. It was also a claim that was ultimately paid.

After a few months with almost no contact with anyone, TD began receiving calls from several colleagues in the industry, as well as a few private attorneys. Each encouraged him to obtain a private investigator's license. They weren't calling out of consideration for his personal happiness or career. They knew a time would come when they'd need a top pro to help crack a tough case. They wanted to be able contract for his services and they wanted him ready and legal. TD understood all that but he did nothing about it.

He finally consented, only because of his best friend's efforts. Phil Madrigal is an insurance agent for the same firm where TD had worked. Phil never gave up and regularly raised the topic. He finally convinced TD he'd eventually care about working again. When that time came, he'd be glad he had obtained a license. Phil counted on their long friendship and deep personal loyalty to win him over. He was only somewhat successful. TD got the license, but refused nearly every solicitation for cases.

Right now, he couldn't care less for the work or the money. Impassioned pleading by would-be clients, or offers of triple the going rate, rarely influence him to take a case. It usually comes down to the personal side of the equation. Every now and then he'll take one on, making an exception for one of a few colleagues he would hate to let down.

Even when the cases are interesting or complex, they never tempt him back into the game full-time. As soon as he finishes one, he immediately sinks back to wallowing in his funk, pondering whether anything or anyone can renew his interest in life more than briefly.

That he is working the Tim Crane adultery case is quite unusual. There's no big-time fraud, or monster fee, nor anything complex or intriguing. It's a straightforward tale of a cheating husband headed for an expensive divorce. It's rather childish, including his role as the snoop capturing the photographic evidence. He has never worked this kind of case. He only agreed to take it because Phil was the one asking. TD has never been able to turn down his friend.

Julia Crane, a sorority sister of Phil's wife Anne, had asked if Phil knew of a good, discreet private investigator. She believed her husband was cheating on her. She wanted to confront him, but only after, and Phil quoted her here, "I have his balls in a vise." Anne Madrigal promised to help her, and wore Phil down over several evenings of subtle nagging. Anne wanted Phil to convince TD to take the case; no one else would do.

Phil made the pitch face-to-face over beers one night, pleading with TD to accept the job. When TD agreed, Phil leaned across the table.

"Charge her double or more, TD," he urged. "The case is a piece of crap. A woman like Julia Crane should pay the price."

This evening, after Tim's first stop at the motel, TD had followed him to a mid-priced eatery where Cyndi was already waiting. Cute, in her early twenties, TD had learned she's a waitress and sometimes tends bar at a western-themed steakhouse.

As they crawl through heavy traffic, he wonders how guys like Tim get away with taking their dates to marginal restaurants and then still manage to score in an even dumpier motel. This is the third time in three weeks he has watched Tim come to the Gateway, the second time with Cyndi. TD is puzzled why a woman would put up with such treatment, yet it's obvious she doesn't mind. Along with some rather juvenile displays of affection on each of their dates, there's also an air of closeness to her body language.

Based on prior evenings, he guesses Tim will be in and out of the motel within an hour- and-a-half tops. Leaving the girl in the room, he'll take off before a taxi for her arrives. With the photos he'll get tonight, TD can finish assembling his album of Tim's most recent escapades. Tomorrow, he'll contact the wife and set up a meeting to deliver the results of the investigation. Then he'll be paid and finished with this sleazy assignment.

Even though the fees are great and the work isn't physically demanding, this particular case has been tediously boring. To help pass the time, he makes little bets with himself guessing every one of Tim's next moves. After checking the distance remaining to the motel, he quickly changes lanes, accelerates, and slides through the next intersection on a yellow light. Checking his mirror, he can see the BMW failed to make it through before the signal turned red.

TD has no fear he'll lose him. Tim is sharply focused on the girl and likely counting down the minutes until he'll have her in the room. The red light, along with a little aggressive driving on the last leg, should get TD back to the motel five to ten minutes earlier. When the BMW pulls in, he can get a great photo of them emerging from the car, maybe even giggling as they walk arm in arm to the room.

Passing the motel, TD pulls into the parking lot of a small regional bank. The branch contains little more than a tiny lobby, teller counter, and small vault, with an ATM and drive-through window tacked on the side. Closed for the evening, the small building sits like an island in a pond of asphalt, sandwiched between a McDonald's and the west side of the motel.

The location serves his purposes perfectly. He'll park there and walk the short distance back to the motel. His car cannot be seen from any of the rooms. The only time anyone might spot him is during the two seconds it takes to round the back corner of the motel and enter his room. TD grabs his camera off the front seat, stowing it in a backpack already containing a collapsible tripod. He should be finished in two hours.

TD believes he's smarter than the average person he investigates and his track record proves him right. With his skill at reading people and situations, he's rarely surprised. Despite that, he has absolutely no idea of the events that are unfolding around him.

He has no idea he's not the only person working a job at the Gateway Motor Inn tonight. He doesn't know that at this moment, there are men driving to that very motel, men pursuing goals that are in direct opposition to each other's. Men like him, and Tim Crane, who have no intention of spending the night there.

He also doesn't know that though this case will end tonight, he will never collect his fee.

⚔

Eddie King's work has also brought him to the motel this evening. When he arrived, he paid for the use of Room 112, something he does regularly. But unlike other guests, there's no record of Eddie having ever stayed in that room, or any other. According to the motel's records, Marvin Williams currently occupies Room 112. In this case, those records are accurate. Marvin has been living in that room for almost a year.

Built in the late 1950's, the Gateway Motor Inn served tourists arriving in the Washington area who didn't want to stay downtown. It also catered to those conducting business with the city or county governments based in Fairfax, twenty miles west of DC.

Today's thriving county seat is nothing like tiny Fairfax, circa 1960. Only a few blocks wide in either direction, there was little more to the town then a courthouse with two Civil War-era cannons on the lawn, a cluster of attorney's offices, and several administrative buildings. Now the city serves as the municipal hub of a vast county exceeding a million residents, with the courthouse and various city and county offices located on several modern campuses.

For its first thirty years, the Gateway Motor Inn was never successful, barely surviving while regularly changing ownership from one overly optimistic operator to another. The small motel consists of just twenty-four rooms. There's no restaurant, business center, or exercise room. A couple of aging, often empty vending machines are the sole amenity for guests. The rooms are of a decent size, but shabbily furnished. A cracked and crumbling concrete hole in the ground lies in front of the building masquerading as a pool 'under repair'.

Despite its complete lack of appeal, the motel became profitable in the early-Nineties and has generated a modest return for its owners ever since. Its occupancy rate rarely slips below seventy-five percent. The Gateway is a different type of lodging establishment when compared to low-end franchise chains. Along with several other similarly aging properties across the area, its success is based on the loyalty of one crucial customer, the county's Department of Social Services.

The rooms are leased as part of an assistance program providing basic housing for the working poor and other social service beneficiaries. Individuals, and in a few cases small families, live at highly subsidized rates, sometimes at no cost. They stay at the motel while getting back on their feet from whatever setbacks they've encountered, setbacks often self-inflicted. The residents have little chance of affording an apartment rental and might otherwise be homeless. They're often recovering addicts or victims of life's tougher breaks.

Marvin Williams is one of those recovering addicts. Just past his sixtieth birthday, he's trying to make a go at a normal life, having wrestled with drugs and alcohol for most of his adult years. Sober for over a year now, he has a part-time minimum wage job at a local car wash that the county helped him find.

One evening, Eddie King knocked on Marvin's door offering $100 to use the room for two hours, no questions asked. Marvin took it, walked up the street, and bought himself a steak dinner he couldn't otherwise afford. He didn't hesitate, nor worry about allowing a stranger in his room. He has few personal possessions, and certainly nothing worth $100. Besides, Eddie doesn't have the look of someone in need of anything Marvin owns.

The first three occasions, Eddie had someone tail Marvin after he left. He needed to make sure Marvin wasn't simply hanging around the motel waiting to return. He also might be curious as to why someone would pay him for a room you could legitimately procure for considerably less. Eddie learned Marvin is a creature of habit, routinely walking almost a mile to a local restaurant for dinner. He generally spends the entire time there enjoying a few pleasant hours away from his room.

Eddie was confident he had found what he needed at the motel. He felt sure Marvin would stay clear while he borrowed the room, if only out of respect for the hassle free source of cash. It was as much as he could earn in a couple of days work. Marvin proved him right each time, usually staying away longer than asked.

⅄

This evening, it's about a quarter after six when Eddie arrives in his silver Cadillac CTS-V Coupe. When Marvin answers the knock on his door, Eddie tells him that he needs the room for three hours tonight and offers an extra fifty dollars to cover any inconvenience. Stuffing the cash in his pocket, Marvin heads off with a smile in the same direction as always.

Minutes after Marvin's departure, Eddie returns to his car where he removes an oversized dark blue vinyl gym bag from the trunk, something he has done on each of his visits. The bags are popular with athletes and are large enough to hold a basketball, along with shoes and some clothing.

Back in the room, Eddie unzips the thin, but durable bag. Folded up inside is a second identical bag along with two sheets of paper. After placing the papers on the small desk, he spreads both bags open on the bed. He then slides the room's only chair next to the window and pulls back the curtains. He'll spend a good part of the next hour watching the limited comings and goings, establishing that this evening is safe to conduct his business.

There's never much traffic at the Gateway. Only five rooms are currently available for non-residential customers and it's a rare night when more than one is booked. Other than a simple yellow pages listing, the Gateway doesn't advertise. There's no online reservation system. A large blue and white sign that can be seen from the road hovers above the office, but it hasn't been lit for at least ten years.

Thanks to the contract with the county, the motel requires no ad hoc bookings to show a profit. That contract requires providing the residential guests with a limited, weekly room- cleaning service, including a change of towels and linens. In reality, the housekeeper comes through the room pushing a sufficiently noisy but ineffective vacuum cleaner over the carpet's main traffic, while using a free hand to wipe any uncluttered surface with a small towel, sprayed with a hint of Lysol. Add in a couple of minutes to wipe down the bathroom and the contract is fulfilled.

The entire operation runs with a single housekeeper and a few clerks to cover the office and answer the phone, deal with lost keys, and report any problems. The jobs are all part-time, pay minimum wage, and offer no benefits. The employees are mostly recent immigrants. A couple of them are students who find ample time to study while manning the desk.

Eddie King's 'business' at the motel is limited to receiving gym bags delivered by a series of couriers. Smaller than the bags he has in the room, these are loaded with cash. Eddie works for an organization that refers to itself as 'The Group'. Among its many illicit business concerns, The Group operates a thriving gambling network running from Baltimore, south through Richmond, and east to Norfolk.

The core of The Group's gambling business is sports betting. Their sportsbook offers its customers an attractive, slightly lower vig than available on internet gambling sites or even in Las Vegas. The small amount given up is easily recovered by allowing its players to gamble on credit; credit that generates short-term loans, repayable at prohibitive interest rates.

The Group also operates a dozen discreet, illegal gambling venues. All provide high-stakes poker games. Several offer blackjack and a few have craps. The gambling operations are naturally profitable and produce an abundance of cash, none of which can be dropped off at the local bank's night depository.

To protect its lifeblood and minimize the amount of money at risk, The Group's head of security designed a frequently executed collection procedure. Profits are regularly removed from the gaming sites but are still held locally at a secure location. The funds are then periodically transported to a central site where they are consolidated before being picked up for processing.

Eddie King has worked for The Group for several years with increasing responsibilities. He now sits near the top of the operational pyramid of collection activities. He is one of just three consolidators who manage the cash collections for the organization's entire network.

Approximately once a month, a consolidator completes a final harvest of cash. The date of the activity changes by a day or two each month as part of the security scheme. After the money is delivered, it winds its way through a complex series of manipulations and obfuscations before it ever sees the light of day or an accounting statement.

On the morning of a consolidation, Eddie receives a call setting the process in motion. He then notifies his couriers to bring in their accumulations, including a one-word code designating the general time to arrive at the drop site. The couriers leave well in advance and pre-position themselves nearby to avoid problems with the area's notorious traffic snarls.

Once there, each waits for his final call. The call either consists of the same one-word signal, indicating it's time to make their delivery, or a different word calling it off. Eddie is extremely careful, but has never needed to signal an abort.

Eddie views the motel as a perfect, easily controlled location for making the drops. Situated on the south side of a busy four lane divided road, you can only access the single driveway entrance heading eastbound. Cars have to slow considerably to make the sharp ninety-degree right-hand turn into a narrow driveway. They then immediately climb a short, steep hill before again turning right into the motel.

The building is T-shaped, with the long stem running parallel to the highway. The top leg runs perpendicular at the end opposite the entrance. The motel's office is at the bottom of the T. Parking is in front of the rooms along with a courtyard area on both sides of the building.

There are twelve rooms on each side: nine along the length of the building and three along the top leg of the T. The even-numbered rooms face the highway, as well as the derelict pool, covered with a torn sun-bleached tarp. The pool takes up most of the front courtyard, surrounded by a paved but gravelly oval that could handle overflow parking if there ever was any. Beyond that, a steep grassy hill runs down to Fairfax Boulevard.

One other business shares the motel's driveway, a Castle Guard self-storage facility. Located further up the hill behind the motel, the warehouse is enclosed by a security fence. Tenants use a passcode to operate an access gate. Due to the nature of the two businesses, Eddie can rely on very little vehicle traffic despite being next to a heavily travelled road.

After carefully scouting the property and watching the various residents, Eddie judged Marvin the best candidate to approach. His room is a little more than halfway down the front row with its window affording a complete view of the courtyard and parking area. As with all the rooms, the only drawback is no visibility of the entrance off the main road. The steep hill the driveway climbs blocks the view of any cars entering.

To address that problem on consolidation nights, Eddie positions a sentry at the Qwik Lube garage a few hundred yards away. The garage sits above street level, just past the motel, in the corner of the parking lot of an adjacent shopping center. From behind the garage, there's a clear view of the driveway entrance as well as two blocks up the street to the west. The sentry lets Eddie know whenever a car makes the turn off the main road. He can also determine if anyone follows one of their couriers' cars into the motel, critical information to have.

Eddie's primary concern is not the police. If the police are onto them and intent on making a bust, there's little he can do. His greatest fear is an attempt to hijack the cash. A considerable amount accumulates in Marvin's room before the pick-up driver arrives.

Eddie believes the odds of a hijacking are very low. Their security regime is solid, and who'd guess the shabby motel is the site of such a large cash handling activity. Additionally, the date of the consolidation changes each month. He can guess at it, but he never knows until he receives the call. Still, he maintains a professional approach. Each time he methodically works through a mental checklist of preparatory steps before signaling the couriers to arrive.

Everything appears straightforward this evening. There's been nobody walking about and only two other cars in the lot. He has already confirmed seeing each car on at least one prior visit, by checking a short list of models and plate numbers he keeps for that very purpose. With everything quiet, and not wanting to fill Marvin's room with smoke, he leaves the room and begins a slow walk around the pool while he enjoys a cigarette.

Eddie King stands out in a crowd wherever he goes. He's obviously particular about his appearance. Dressing sharply and enjoying fine things are essential to his self-image. Part of that image is the cigarettes he smokes, Davidoff Magnums. He derives as much satisfaction from smoking the niche brand, marketed primarily in Europe, as he does for their rich flavor.

At ease in most settings, Eddie is unaware of the anomaly he presents strolling the motel grounds wearing a bespoke sports coat, silk shirt with two buttons open, and Italian loafers. He'd also be unhappy if he knew what the guys working for him thought of his affectations. To them the cigarettes taste harsh and bitter. And they're convinced his clothes and shoes are a waste of money. Regardless, his crew takes him quite seriously as their boss. They respect him as their leader as well as the position he holds in the organization, one they're fiercely loyal to.

The stroll around the courtyard also provides Eddie the opportunity to inspect the windows of every room on this side of the motel. He isn't looking for something in particular, just changes. He likes that the motel's residents differ little from month to month. This evening, as almost always, the courtyard is silent and deserted. The few residents who aren't out working have their curtains shut tight.

The last thing on his list before moving forward with the consolidation this evening is a stop by the front office. Upon entering, he sees the desk clerk on duty is Bobby, the one he has worked with every time but once. This should be quick and easy.

⬥

Bobby Tomlin was on duty the first time Eddie came to the motel. Twenty-four years old, Bobby is a hard-working hustler with endless energy. Upon graduating from high school, he and his girlfriend Kristen began attending the local community college. That changed when she became pregnant at age twenty. They now have two children and been married for four years.

Bobby works nearly full-time at Home Depot, pulling a hodgepodge of shifts but mostly overnight stock work. He also works several evenings each week at the motel. On top of that, he takes two or three college courses each semester. At the current pace, it will take him a couple of more years to earn his degree in Economics. He rarely scores a full night's sleep, occasionally snagging a quick nap between classes and jobs, or catching a short snooze near the end of a shift at the motel.

Bobby hesitated when Eddie initially approached him, but he had a fabulous smile and a smooth friendly way about him. The first time he walked into the front office, Eddie already had his hand out as he introduced himself.

"My name is Eddie," he said, as he released the firm handshake. Looking directly at Bobby, he asked, "You work here every day?"

Bobby thought it was an odd question, one no guest had ever asked him. Despite that, he saw no harm in answering. He told the man the truth; he usually works Mondays through Wednesdays, from four in the afternoon until ten.

"Look, I'm wondering if you could help me out sometime."

"With a room?" Bobby thought the guy might be looking for a discount. Or maybe he wanted to pay cash without providing an ID or credit card. That was a common request from the few paying customers who used the motel.

"No. It's just that sometime soon I may stop by to see if anybody new has checked-in. You know, paying customers, not the regular residents." Eddie paused for a second before finishing. "Of course, I'd be very grateful, and sure to give you a generous gratuity for providing the information."

Bobby looked down at the book he had been studying and said nothing as he thought of how to politely decline. All the while, the guy stood there smiling at him. Before he could respond, Eddie spoke again.

"Look, I can tell you do a good job here, and you're a serious hardworking guy. Really, I'd never ask you to do anything that would put you in a tough spot. Listen, think about it. I'll check back sometime. And seriously, no matter what your answer is, I'll respect it."

Bobby liked the relaxed way Eddie put things; especially that he didn't demand an answer that moment. He looked up as Eddie stuck out his hand again to shake, smiling like a kid with a double dip ice cream cone. Eddie pressed something into Bobby's hand as they shook, winking as he turned away.

Bobby thought it would be money but he was still surprised by the denomination of the bill. He pocketed the hundred dollars knowing he'd try to help Eddie out if he ever could.

$$\blacktriangle$$

As he is doing tonight, Eddie has stopped in once a month to inquire if anyone had checked-in and was staying there that evening. Each visit, it was easy for Bobby to get past any ethical objections. That was because each time the answer was no, no one had checked-in. What harm could there be in telling someone that? And each time, Eddie shook his hand with that same splendid smile, slipping that hundred-dollar thank you note into his palm.

The problem for Bobby is this evening is different. For the first time, the answer to Eddie's question is yes. Actually, two customers have checked-in. One he put in Room 114. The other was all the way at the end in 124. Bobby feels he owes Eddie after all that he has been paid. Without waiting, he describes both men along with the cars they're driving. He also divulges their room numbers. Suddenly, Eddie isn't smiling and Bobby feels nervous.

Eddie shoots Bobby a quick "thanks", as he turns and exits the office without another word. Worse, he fails to give Bobby his customary handshake. Based on Eddie's quick exit and grim expression, Bobby knows he's not being tipped tonight. He also feels the first pangs of regret for having ever gotten involved with the man.

Eddie spends the next minute pacing in front of the motel office, then another staring out across the courtyard. Finally, he turns and re-enters the office. "Is there anything you can tell me about these guys? Were they alone, or did it seem like they were together? Where are their cars?"

Bobby responds nervously. "They both drove off after checking in, but they came at different times. I don't think they're together."

Pausing, Bobby looks up as he thinks about the two men. Then, with enthusiasm he says, "Wait! Yeah! I've seen one of them at least twice before. He checks-in, then he always comes a couple hours later with a girl."

"What about the other guy?"

Bobby thinks for a second before saying, "He looked sort of sad, but maybe he was just tired. He asked for a room near the end of the row. He said he needed as much quiet as possible so he could get a good night's sleep."

With something of a smile, Eddie holds hand is out with the usual gratuity. "Thanks my man. Catch you later."

Bobby is also smiling. He's happy to help such a nice guy, and relieved that he didn't let him down. And he's definitely happy to snag another hundred dollars. He's soon relaxed enough to return to studying.

Bobby never considers why Eddie wants such information or why he comes here every month. He knows Eddie hangs out in Marvin's room, and that on those nights a number of other cars stop by. But that's all he knows. Besides, Marvin has never caused a single problem. Nor for that matter, has Eddie.

Eddie's smile quickly disappears on the way back to Marvin's room. As he walks, he decides they've been using this place too long. It feels safe enough to proceed with tonight's consolidation, but it's time to scout for a new location.

Once inside the room, he speaks a single word into his phone letting the sentry know he's kicking things off. He then contacts the five couriers working for The Group tonight putting them on alert. They'll each now wait for their final one-word signal from Eddie to proceed with their delivery.

Eddie then makes one last call to a sixth courier. He will be the first to arrive. This courier doesn't work for The Group. Tonight's first courier works for Eddie personally.

Throughout his climb through The Group's collections operations, Eddie closely observed how the organization managed its growing activities. He admires their professional, yet hard-nosed manner of doing business. He also has specific knowledge of the location of every gambling site and other illicit operation The Group operates in his region. He also knows where they don't do business.

After a few years, Eddie started applying what he had learned. He took on a few lucrative betting customers and began running a couple of gambling sites. All on the side, off the books from The Group. He's very careful. He never competes with them for a betting customer, nor operates in one of their localities. Over time, he even mimicked several of their other activities, setting up a small fence to receive stolen goods, and providing modest loans and money laundering services.

This evening, Eddie is also running a consolidation of his own proceeds. It's the first time he's piggybacking on one of The Group's collections and he's tense about doing so. He almost bailed on the idea, but his revenues have really been taking off. Two of his heaviest sports bettors just went on a losing rampage during the NBA playoffs. It has also been almost two months since he last brought in his cash.

Eddie works with very little direct supervision and knows the chances The Group will discover his activities tonight are close to zero. Still, as an added layer of security, he had his consolidator merge his cash at a separate location. It's now all in one bag, to be delivered and stowed away before he starts the main consolidation.

Eddie sees himself as a smart guy. With the extra income he's generating, he's also becoming a fairly rich guy. He's not thinking about retiring any time soon, but if he's ever forced to get away quickly, he can at least do so in a little comfort.

Despite all of his security preparations, there are several critical things Eddie is unaware of this evening. Most importantly, just like TD Adkins, Eddie knows nothing about the other men whose work is bringing them to the motel. He understands that at some point, the two registered guests will return, but he has no clue there are more cars on the way. Or that they carry young men with a mission of their own.

Eddie also doesn't know the he is needlessly concerned about mixing his own business with that of The Group. Tonight will be his last consolidation for them.

⋏

Rafael Flores sits in the passenger seat of a black, 1985 Chevy Monte Carlo SS, parked at the McDonald's just two blocks west of the Gateway Motor Inn. His focus is solely on the steadily passing eastbound traffic as he keeps a lookout for a specific vehicle: a luxurious, black Mercedes S600 sedan with smoked-glass rear windows.

The Monte Carlo is Flores's personal car. Most days, one of his crew serves as his driver. Flores enjoys a feeling of self-importance when he's being chauffeured around. He also craves the respect he perceives it earns him. When it's only the two of them, he often rides in the back seat. If there are other passengers, he'll usually ride shotgun. Besides the ego-trip, not having to drive gives Flores extra time to think about his business.

The car is immaculate. Both the interior and body are nearly as sharp as when it left its first dealer. When he purchased it used two years ago, it was in decent enough condition but with relatively high mileage. Flores became its fifth owner and immediately began a total restoration.

The only major components remaining from the original vehicle are the frame and several sections of the body. The engine and transmission were swapped out along with many smaller parts. Every element of the car's interior has been refurbished or replaced. The replacement parts are always manufacturer original, often cannibalized from another '85 Flores purchased specifically for that purpose.

Rafael Flores likes to be called Raffi. He spends a lot of time in the Monte Carlo cruising the DC area, scouting for business opportunities while also keeping an eye out for police. Since Raffi's business is stealing things, the two activities closely intertwine.

⏶

Raffi came to the U.S. with his parents when he was young. They emigrated legally from El Salvador in the 1980's and settled in Annandale, Virginia. He got off to a tough start in school, speaking little English. It was going to take hard work to learn a new language at the same time as everything else, and Raffi has always had an aversion to hard work. Soon he was one, then two years behind the other students his age. During Ninth grade, he simply stopped attending school.

He could soon be found hanging around the edges of the area's Hispanic gang scene. Luckily, he had only a few minor encounters with the law, primarily in suburban Maryland. Only once did he come close to being arrested, but he was let go with a warning. He has never spent a night in jail.

Raffi is highly intelligent, but notoriously lazy. He found himself appalled by the frequency and ferocity of the inter-gang violence he witnessed. He was also disenchanted by the inability of the gangs to accumulate any sustainable wealth. It wasn't easy to do, but he turned away from his Maryland-based crew, striking out on his own. He hoped to find cleaner, yet still illegal ways to earn a living in Northern Virginia.

Not physically large, Raffi is fiercely handsome and athletically built. He's also quite skilled at parlaying his good looks with a knack for sweet talking women to get what he wants. Though he keeps a home base in the well-furnished basement of his parents' home, Raffi often stays with the women he dates; sometimes even for several months. Along with his accommodations, he's often the recipient of gifts of expensive clothing, dinners at fine restaurants, and even spending money.

Raffi's formula for success is based on exploiting short-term relationships. When he meets a woman he senses will serve his needs, he showers her with personal attention and carefully applied does of romance. As for the women, once the excitement of having a handsome, charming young man in their lives wanes, they soon resent his dependency on them.

As his taste for a wealthier lifestyle grew, Raffi needed a more consistent source of income. He constantly dreamt of ways to generate more cash without any consideration of legality. There were only a few limitations. A job should require little physical work. Neither should it require long hours, as he's easily bored and values leisure time over all else. Lastly, there must be a low risk of physical harm. Though not averse to using violence as a threat, he prefers minimizing the chances of such situations arising.

Several years ago, Raffi was attending a party. After picking up a woman there, he soon had them moving through the upstairs of the home looking for some privacy. Opening a bedroom door, he stumbled upon a guy he knew who just happened to be in the act of stealing jewelry from the party's host. Though exhilarated by what he witnessed, Raffi acted as if he had seen nothing. Apologizing for interrupting, he quickly moved on to another room.

Raffi contacted the guy the next day. Under the threat of disclosure, he agreed to coach Raffi on the ins and outs of burglary and petty theft. Raffi soon tried his hand. He knew he had found his calling the first time a fence paid him cash for a stolen necklace, no questions asked.

Raffi rapidly became an expert thief and supplier to the black market. The work satisfied every aspect of his criteria. His intelligence, intuition, and boldness are essential elements of the skill-set needed to succeed at his chosen occupation. Gaining access through easy break-ins, he initially stole only jewelry and cash from homes and apartments. Soon he added high-end electronics. More and more, he timed his burglaries during vacation and holiday seasons.

It's surprisingly easy to break into many older, nicer homes, particularly those without a security system. A home without an alarm is easy pickings for a thief. Raffi also gave himself another advantage. Investing untold hours driving through the region's dense suburban neighborhoods, he developed a considerable list of homes with large RVs parked in the driveway. Raffi knows that when an RV is gone, it usually leaves an empty home behind; and rarely just for the weekend. Once he discovered a missing RV, he'd conduct a break-in as soon as possible, maximizing the period before detection.

As his activities increased, Raffi rented a self-storage unit at the Castle Guard facility in Manassas, Virginia. There, he accumulated what he stole, holding certain items until they cooled off enough to find a buyer or to sell to a fence. He also added another wrinkle to his burglaries.

Many people leave unused checks laying in a desk drawer or file cabinet. Whenever Raffi located a box of spares, he'd steal several blank checks from the middle of the bottom pad. When they finally discover the break-in, owners are so relieved to see the box of checks they almost always fail to detect those missing from near the end of the series. Mixing and matching the checks with identification documents he also regularly stole, Raffi had himself another low-effort source of income.

Rafael Flores is sought by police in every Northern Virginia jurisdiction and several in Maryland; but only as a concept, not by name. Separately, the various law enforcement agencies have slowly reached the conclusion that they have a successful burglar or team of thieves operating in their area. Unfortunately, they don't have a single fingerprint or concrete lead of substance pointing toward a given suspect.

Since the crimes are non-violent and sometimes go undetected for days or weeks, the investigations are often non-starters, taking a back seat to crimes that are more serious. Raffi also operates at a level below inter-jurisdictional taskforces; units that might see the bigger picture and piece together a better profile of who they're after.

⬥

To take his activities to the next level, Raffi needed help. He slowly assembled a small, reliable crew to assist with transportation and security. His first move was to add a trusted friend, Cesar Ayala, as a driver. Ayala had been working part-time for an excavation company driving large dump trucks.

The day he was fired from his job, he was part of a small caravan hauling dirt away from a new housing development site. As they arrived at the site, he failed to brake and slow his truck sufficiently. Before he could stop, he plowed into the rear of another of the company's expensive trucks. The other driver was only slightly injured, but both vehicles were badly damaged.

Finding himself without a job, Cesar welcomed Raffi's offer to join him. Opportunity came their way a few months after they started working together. They struck the mother lode the Tuesday night before Thanksgiving.

It was just before nine and they were sitting in the Monte Carlo, parked behind the Best Buy store in the Fair Lakes area. They had stopped to smoke some pot Raffi had snagged on a recent burglary. Suddenly, they're forced to scrunch down in their seats, surprised by the headlights and roaring engine of an eighteen-wheel Best Buy truck coming around the back corner of the building.

Moving past their car, the truck begins its final maneuver as it backs up to the loading dock. It's already been a tough week for the driver. He's on his third run from the warehouse that day alone, as the company crams the stores with goods in preparation for the Black Friday Sale in just over two days.

Through the light haze of smoke, Raffi and Cesar watch the driver climb down from his rig and press a buzzer next to the delivery bay door. After waiting through multiple failed attempts for someone to open the door, he tries using his phone. Equally unsuccessful and increasingly frustrated, the driver curses loudly as he hops down from the loading dock and takes off on foot, circling around toward the front of the building.

Raffi decides to risk stealing the truck right there and then. He figures it can't be that much more difficult than driving a dump truck, so Cesar should have a decent chance at handling the big rig. Besides, it's worth the gamble. Whatever the contents of the load, a holiday season delivery to Best Buy has to be highly lucrative.

Raffi barks at Cesar to get out of the car as he shakes off some of the buzz from the pot. He tells him to climb up into the truck's cab and see if the keys are still there. If they are, he's to drive the truck out of there; they'll head west to Manassas.

Cesar quickly understands the opportunity. Finding the keys still in the ignition, it doesn't take him long to figure things out and get underway. With Raffi leading the way in the Monte Carlo, they clear the lot before the driver or anyone at the store knows what's happening.

Planning on the fly, Raffi quickly leads Cesar onto a nearby highway. He's taking them to an empty warehouse unit in a light industrial park. He's only aware of the location because he recently considered renting the space. Though he had liked that the building was in a lightly trafficked area, he decided it was larger than he needed and too expensive. They're able to break into the vacant unit with very little effort. By the time the police arrive at the Best Buy and sort out what has happened, Flores already has a small team rapidly unloading the truck.

While in route to the warehouse, Raffi had called in three extra guys. He's happy to steal the goods, but he certainly isn't going to start lifting a bunch of boxes. In great spirits, he laughs and jokes with his small team as they offload a treasure trove of computers, TVs, gaming consoles, and enough game discs and DVDs to stuff hundreds of stockings. Once the scores of shipping cartons are inside, they cover them with a few tarps retrieved from Raffi's nearby self-storage unit and re-secure the door.

With his guys on alert to meet him back there in the morning, Raffi and Cesar leave to dispose of the truck. After going only a few miles, Raffi brazenly leads them into the parking lot of a different Best Buy, this one in Manassas. Moments later, they leave the keys with the now empty truck and flee undetected.

Raffi never sleeps that night as he plans what he needs to do next. The first thing will be renting an additional storage unit. Then he needs to get the stolen goods out of the warehouse he broke into before someone notices. Leery of creating too much of a footprint at the storage facility he currently uses, he decides to use a different location.

Raffi decides to stick with the Castle Guard brand, primarily because they let him pay without a credit card. He finds what he's looking for in nearby Fairfax, roughly ten miles from the other unit. This one sits off a main road behind a cheap motel. With the idea of taking on more jobs like the one he just pulled off, Raffi chooses one of their largest units. He pays for six months' rent in advance, registering with a different name from the one he used for his other unit in Manassas.

Over the next few hours, Raffi supervises as the same crew from the night before shuttles the entire load to the new storage unit. Using a light pickup and a couple of work vans, they have the last load out of Manassas by just after Noon. That's about the same time the police located the empty truck. And that was only because the store manager called in the discovery of the pilfered rig parked on his front lot.

Within a week, the new storage unit is empty. Raffi's fence was so enthusiastic about the stolen goods that he paid the highest rate on the dollar Raffi had ever received. A valuable lesson was learned as well. You'll be paid quickly and profitably when you have products that move easily on the black market, particularly items like high-end consumer electronics during the holiday season.

Since that time, in addition to scouting for home burglaries, Raffi keeps an eye out for larger-scale opportunities like the Best Buy heist. He recently pulled off a similar job that netted a truckload full of cases of wine. He has also been using the storage unit in Fairfax more often.

Leaving his Fairfax storage unit one afternoon in early January, Raffi notices an attractive Latina woman walking up the driveway toward the motel. In her early twenties, she's wearing a dingy white parka with a faux fur-trimmed hood, looking cold and a little tired. Always on the lookout for women he might be able to exploit, Raffi tells his driver to stop.

Rolling down the window, he says, "Hi. Don't I know you?"

When she says she doesn't think so, Raffi quickly responds, "I think I would remember someone as sexy as you. Maybe we met at a party."

The young woman blushes as Raffi continues the banter. He has soon asked for her name, where she's going, and if he can give her a ride. She tells him her name is Carmela. Casting her eyes downward, she points up the driveway, seemingly ashamed. She tells him she's almost home. She has had some troubles recently and right now lives here at the motel.

Masking his disappointment, Raffi asks her out to dinner without skipping a beat. He's not sure why, but he doesn't have a date that night and there's something about her looks and demeanor that arouse him.

Carmela is a little shocked by his boldness, yet at the same time, there's something beguiling about him. He's also very handsome and riding in a great car. And she never gets such offers. She's living on county assistance, working as a part-time fast food cashier. Without taking long to think it over, she agrees. He can return in two hours to pick her up.

That evening, he takes her to the best restaurant she has ever been to. At the end of the evening, they return to her room at the Gateway Motor Inn; Room 110.

After that night, Raffi makes a habit of stopping by. He enjoys Carmela's company and the no-strings-attached sexual pleasure she enthusiastically provides. Occasionally he brings a carryout meal with him, substituting a small gift or a little cash instead of taking her out to dinner. Carmela doesn't mind at all. The meals and Raffi's company are a huge improvement over her endless parade of boring evenings, almost always spent alone.

▲

At the end of lazy afternoon and evening together at the motel, Raffi is pre-paring to leave when he hears a car pull up in front of the room. Assuming his driver has arrived a little early, he gave Carmela a quick kiss before go-ing to the door. Once there, he sees the car already pulling off. It wasn't his man after all.

He hears another car just a few minutes later. Before leaving the room, he looks out the window and is again surprised to see it isn't his driver. While keeping his attention on the car, he remarks to Carmela that he can't remember ever seeing this much traffic at the motel.

The driver is taking an unconventional route. After first circling around the far side of the abandoned pool, he has come back around in front of the rooms before stopping almost in front of Carmela's door. Once there, instead of pulling into a parking spot, he has stopped parallel to the rooms, pointing towards the exit. There's something Raffi likes about the maneuver. He reminds himself to tell his drivers he wants them to enter the courtyard this way when they bring him to the motel.

With no one other than the driver in the car, Raffi expects he's pick-ing up someone from one of the rooms. Instead, the driver leaves the car. Carrying a small bag, he quickly walks directly to the room next door. Raffi can hear the door open before anyone knocks and then close within just seconds. No words were audible. Almost immediately, the now empty-handed driver hops back into the car and drives off.

Raffi quickly calls his own driver and tells him to delay picking him up from the motel until he calls back later. Over the next fifteen minutes, he finds himself riveted to the activity outside as he watches a series of cars arrive and quickly depart. Each time, a solo driver pulls in and delivers a bag to someone in Room 112.

During all this, Carmela has been growing increasingly uncomfortable. When she asks Raffi to leave the window and sit next to her, he tells her to leave him alone and to stay where she is. He wants to focus on what he's witnessing, a series of events completely out of place for this rundown mo-tel. He's also intrigued to find out what will happen next.

Within another ten minutes, a large black Mercedes sedan arrives. Just like the other cars, it also circles the pool before stopping parallel to the room next door. This time though, there's one significant difference. As it sits with its engine idling, it becomes clear that no one is getting out of the vehicle.

A moment later, a man comes out of Room 112 carrying two large gym bags. After opening the trunk remotely, the driver of the Mercedes now also appears, though he does not move away from the car. Instead, he remains standing behind the driver's door. He then slowly scans the empty courtyard, seemingly ignoring the other man. Only after the bags have been hoisted into the trunk do the two men acknowledge each other by exchanging a glance and a nod. As the man from the room steps back and gives a casual salute, the driver re-enters the car and departs. The whole activity was executed without a word spoken.

Raffi is fascinated by what has played out in front of him. Obviously, he has witnessed a series of deliveries or exchanges followed by a pick-up. Though he can't be positive, it has to be drugs or money, and possibly both.

Only minutes later, when he hears the door to the room next door open, he rushes to the window again. He's just in time to see the same man climb into a silver Cadillac parked two spots away. Raffi continues watching for a while, even after he drives off.

After an extended period with no further action, Raffi finally decides to call his driver. As he's making the call, he sees an older man walking across the courtyard, appearing to have come out of nowhere. The man is walking directly toward the room, but then finally veers off a little as he produces a key from his pocket. He then uses it to enter the room next door that just received the deliveries.

Raffi turns toward Carmela on the bed and asks if she knows her neighbor.

"Yes. His name is Marvin. He's lived here since before I moved in."

"You're here a lot in the evenings. Have you seen ever this before? This thing with all the cars coming? You know. The guy with the deliveries next door."

He can hardly finish the last part before she quickly says no. He wouldn't have believed her even if she weren't clearly fidgety and nervous. With a hard edge to his voice, he looks into her eyes and says, "I don't like repeating myself. Why don't you just tell me what you know?"

Carmela quickly demurs with a burst of emotion, "It's none of my business, Rafael. And it should be none of yours."

Raffi glares at her intensely as he stands with his hands on his hips. Fearing his disappointment, Carmela breaks the silence. The words come out fast and he doesn't interrupt.

"About once a month, the same nice looking guy comes to the room. When he comes, Marvin leaves. I don't know where he goes, so don't ask. Then the guy walks around outside for a while and smokes. Soon the cars come by. The drivers come up to the door of the room but I don't think they go in. Then the big black car comes. After that, the guy leaves. Then Marvin returns. I swear to Mother Mary that's all I know, Raffi."

"How long has this been going on," Raffi asks, almost before she finishes.

Seeing him this intense, Carmela knows she can't lie. "At least since I started living here three or four months ago. Probably longer, but I just don't know."

Raffi smiles as he sits next to her on the bed. This relaxes Carmela. Regaining confidence, she tells him how she once tried asking Marvin about it. She tells Raffi how Marvin looked right at her and lied. He said he had no idea know what she was talking about. She knew the hard look he shot her meant to never to ask anything more about it. After that, she paid no more attention to any of it.

While she has been talking, Raffi has been watching her so closely he can tell it has unsettled her. Sensing her fear, he reassures her with a hug and a kiss. He also tells her they won't talk about it anymore that evening.

⋏

After that night, Raffi showers Carmela with even more attention and she loves it. He's handsome and affectionate and she knows a poor girl like her is lucky to have a man at all.

Over the next several weeks, Raffi often questions her about the man and the cars. As she gains confidence and becomes more devoted to him, she takes pride in providing the information he seeks. She chooses to ignore the reasons for his interest. Carefully, she begins noting the dates and times of the deliveries. Each time she describes all she sees. Each time it is exactly the same.

Now that he's certain the activities are a fixed routine, Raffi visits Carmela more frequently. They also go out far less, usually staying at the motel throughout the afternoon and evening. To keep their relationship strong, Raffi hints at helping her move out and paying for a nice apartment. It's something he has absolutely no intention of doing.

On a visit in April, he gets lucky and witnesses the ritual again. Nothing has changed. Nothing varies. That night, he decided he was going to take it down. He has Carmela promise to be even more watchful. She was to call him immediately the next time the deliveries begin.

Raffi puts a plan in place, spending more time preparing for a job than ever before. Unfortunately, he's too far from the motel to get there in time when the call from Carmela comes the next month. Still, it was a valuable exercise and they almost made it in time. They were waiting at a traffic signal just a block from the motel, close enough to see the Mercedes leaving, headed away from them.

Raffi wasn't interested in a pursuit or an ad hoc attack. Instead of following the car, he had his driver park across the road from the motel so they could watch the exit. Soon the man from Marvin's room appeared at the end of the driveway and pulled into traffic. As he passed by them, Raffi noticed he was driving slowly, using his cell phone, and turning his head several times. It seemed as if he was looking toward the Qwik Lube on his right.

Almost immediately, a car came from directly behind the Qwik Lube and pulled into traffic a few cars behind the Cadillac. Raffi ordered his driver to follow, and a few minutes later, they watched as both cars pulled into the parking lot of a local diner. After leaving their vehicles, the two men talked for a few minutes while they smoked a cigarette, before entering the restaurant together.

Though Raffi and his crew failed that night, they gained valuable information. They also spotted another member of the opposing crew, probably a sentry or back-up. Raffi has also been marking a calendar each time Carmela reported an event. Though they don't repeat the day or the date, the deliveries clearly occur once a month, and never on a weekend.

Raffi fine-tunes his plans over the next few weeks. He reworks his team, selecting the toughest members of his crew for the upcoming job. Even more prepared, this month he's going to keep them close to the motel on the likely dates of the exchange.

Raffi hates the idea of a violent confrontation, but he's talked himself into the need for going in heavily armed for this job. He hopes it can be avoided, but he reminds his crew they must be prepared to use their weapons. The guy taking the deliveries appears to be more of a casually dressed businessman than any kind of real muscle. He tells his crew the real potential for danger comes from the driver of the Mercedes who is probably armed.

In all the times he or Carmela watched, they've never seen any weapons. And it has always been only the two same participants in the final exchange: the pick-up driver and the guy carrying out the bags. Now they've also identified a likely sentry parked behind the Qwik Lube.

Getting past the sentry is a small issue, but to be safe, Raffi decides the sentry must be stopped. He must be stopped from acting as back up once the takedown starts, and also from following them afterwards. The extra month has given him time to create a better plan for addressing that issue as well.

⋏

This month Raffi was ready and nearby when he received the call from Carmela. He now waits with confidence, having assembled his crew just a block from the motel.

Raffi has every reason to be confident. Since becoming his own boss, he has never come close to being caught. He has never even seen the police or met any resistance from his victims during a job. From his perspective, the only difference between tonight and the truck heists is that he's going to have to point a gun at someone. If this job yields the cash he believes it will, it should set him up big time and be worth the greater risk.

Raffi's revised plan calls for one of his crew to use a car to ram the sentry at the Qwik Lube, immobilizing him and his vehicle. At the same time, Raffi's driver will navigate them into the motel parking lot at full speed. If they time it all right, they should arrive without warning and find the guy from the room out in the open, along with the bags.

They are driving stolen cars, both common mid-sized models almost ten years old. Stolen over a year ago, they've used them only a few times during residential heists. When it's time to roll, Raffi will quickly exit the comfort of his Monte Carlo and switch vehicles, leaving behind a driver to ferry his beloved car away from the scene.

The plan has them roaring into the motel loud and fast, pulling up close in front of the Mercedes. Hopping out of their car screaming, with guns raised, they hope to startle and freeze the driver and the man with the bags. Two others from Raffi's crew will arrive on foot from behind the building. They'll sprint onto the scene from the opposite direction of Raffi and his driver, encircling their targets.

Surrounded and outgunned, the driver and the man with the bags should put up no resistance. Raffi's driver will then knock them out with the butt of his gun. It should take only two to three minutes to fly in, grab the bags and leave. Simple, clean and quick, with minimal effort; the only way Raffi likes to work.

Raffi views himself as quite a smooth operator. He's savvier, and definitely better looking than most men. Women love him and he has never had to work an honest day in his life. When he carefully plans his jobs, they always come off smoothly. He also feels that luck is often on his side. He has never committed a violent crime, nor physically hurt anyone. There's no reason this evening has to be any different.

Despite his confidence, Raffi is unsure of several significant factors about this job. He isn't positive the driver, sentry, and bagman are the only men involved in the final exchange. And yet, he has no contingency if it turns out he's wrong. And although he hopes this will be his biggest score, he has no idea how high the stakes are that he's playing for this evening.

He also knows nothing about the men he's going up against, veteran members of a criminal organization. He greatly underestimates their loyalty and toughness, failing to consider that guys like Eddie King and the driver of the Mercedes are likely to be far more motivated to protect their goods than the average delivery-truck driver.

Raffi also doesn't know that after tonight's job, the police will finally know who he is.

▲

It's just before seven-thirty as Eddie King waits for the first courier. Summer evenings in the DC area can be oppressing muggy affairs, but today is different. It has turned relatively pleasant, thanks to a round of afternoon thunderstorms cleansing the air and erasing the blanket of humidity built up over a day of temperatures in the low-nineties.

Back inside the room after another cigarette, Eddie makes a mental note to adjust the time for next month's consolidation and slide it back an hour. He has forgotten how late it stays light during the summer. Sunset isn't for an hour and there will be plenty of twilight, even until nine. It's just too much light for conducting this kind of business as far as he's concerned.

The light isn't the only thing putting him on edge. The nicer weather has turned the normally deserted courtyard into a more active place. While he was outside smoking, he heard people in two different rooms pop open their long-closed windows, hoping to let in some fresh air. And the cute Latina girl from the next room opened her door and considered coming outside, before his hard stare forced a quick retreat.

Eddie is becoming increasingly anxious. This was never a big issue when it was darker and colder. But tonight, someone might inadvertently come outside at the wrong moment. He knows it isn't the end of the world if it happens. And he doesn't fear someone seeing him; they could always be watching from behind a curtained window. He just doesn't want to have to be looking over his shoulder at the very moment he's carrying more than a half a million dollars out to the pick-up car.

Eddie inherited his job and the process from the prior consolidation manager. His former boss ran the whole deal out of a warehouse in a light industrial park during the middle of the business day. The Group leased the property and legitimately used it to store equipment and vehicles. The place also came in handy for the occasional private meeting or rendezvous.

Eddie didn't like the location. For one thing, it made no sense to associate the cash operation directly with a property openly leased by The Group. A second issue was the amount of traffic. The industrial park housed multiple storefront businesses, including several showrooms, and was well covered by security cameras. As they drove through the complex on his first visit to the location, he had spotted what he was sure was a small brothel operating under the thin disguise of a massage parlor. They also passed an unmarked police car cruising the area.

When Eddie asked about the obvious risks, his boss claimed no one would worry about a few cars coming and going amid all the other activity. Eddie disagreed; there was too much going on. Between the cameras, the presence of the other businesses, and even occasional police surveillance, it was only a matter of time before someone began paying attention. No matter who that was, it wouldn't be good.

Before tonight, Eddie has always been satisfied with his decision to move the consolidation to the motel. Even though it's located in a busy area, the place has an almost vacant feel. No one would suspect a well-run criminal organization of using such a place for a critical operation involving such large sums of cash. Certainly not the long-term residents he views as little more than a collection of lost souls. When they're even around, they generally turn on the TV and tune out the real world.

During all the times he has conducted business here, he has always felt a sense of privacy, even isolation. It's also a huge plus that there's no apparent drug or sex traffic at the motel to attract police attention. Nor are there any security cameras, like those found at contemporary facilities.

But tonight there is a larger problem, and he has never felt as tense as he started a consolidation. The lingering daylight, the open windows, and the potential for people outside are simply irritants. The two guests who checked in earlier are what is making him most uncomfortable. Neither has shown up yet, making them a wild card.

ᐱ

Across the courtyard, TD Adkins peers around the front corner of the motel. Having just come from the bank parking lot, he's just in time to see a man tossing away a still smoldering cigarette as he leaves the area near the pool. He appears to be moving toward Room 112 where the door sits partially open.

TD notes the man is sharply attired, wearing far more expensive clothing than any of the motel's residents could afford. Along with an athletic build, he clearly cares about his appearance. And there's no mistaking the fragrance of a European cigarette. TD thinks the odds are pretty low this guy is actually staying at the motel tonight. He's probably here for the same reason as Tim.

As the man disappears behind his door, TD slips around the corner of the building and re-enters Room 124. The room is the last on the front side of the building, sitting at the end of the short row of three rooms making up the top of the motel's T shape. He had requested that room or one near it. Mumbling about being exhausted and wanting to avoid noise, he had paid with cash and tipped the clerk $10.

TD knows there are a limited number of vacancies at the motel and Tim had stayed in Room 114 on a prior visit. The end of the row provides a great view of that room. Unfortunately, if Tim ends up on the back row, or even next door, TD will have to either reposition himself somewhere outside or wait until another time to finish the job.

He'll soon know if he guessed correctly. If so, he has an unobstructed view of the parking area, as well as the doors and windows of every room along the front. At an angle, it's less than thirty yards across to the room where Tim last stayed.

TD quickly scans the courtyard from behind the faded curtains cling-ing to the window. After he peels them away so they hang straight down, the bottoms now brush the top of the noisy, vibrating air conditioning unit bolted to the wall below. In need of something to hold the curtains in posi-tion, he grabs an aging copy of the Yellow Pages from the bottom of the open-framed nightstand.

The phonebook serves the purpose perfectly, pinning the bottom of the curtains against the windowsill. TD then carefully re-positions them to suit his needs. Working along the outer edge, he leaves a small triangular gap at the lower left-hand corner of the window for viewing. He knows someone glancing at a window focuses on the center and rarely notices the corners.

Working quickly, TD removes a camera and tripod from the heavily worn backpack he carries. He has been using it for years as a combination briefcase and camera bag. After attaching the camera to the tripod, it sits roughly waist high, perfectly aligned with the gap he created in the corner of the curtains. Using the handle attached to the tripod's swivel base, TD slowly pans a shot across the courtyard, pausing briefly on the door of each room.

Moving away from the window, he takes the room's only chair from the small desk and positions it behind the tripod, before going to relieve himself in the cramped bathroom. From years of experience, he knows it's better to start with an empty bladder when settling in to wait and watch, even if he's anticipating a short job.

With the curtains covering the darkened room and no cars parked at the end of the row, there's nothing to indicate his room is currently occu-pied. Even looking directly at it, there's little chance anyone would be able to see him when he's sitting back from the window, recording the evidence he needs to finish this lame job.

⋏

During the brief time TD is away from the window, Eddie comes out of his room as a car enters the motel. His personal courier has arrived. After making the usual entrance lap, the car comes to a stop just past the trunk of his Cadillac.

Opening the rear door of his car, the driver pulls out a large gym bag. Though a slightly different edition, it's practically the same as the ones lying empty inside the room. While the two men exchange a few words, Eddie reaches into a pocket of his sports coat and uses a remote key to open the trunk of his car. As soon as there's enough clearance, the courier swings the bag into the trunk.

Eddie smiles as the driver pulls away. He then gives the lid of the trunk an almost loving double pat with the palm of his hand. With his personal business now out of the way, he pulls out a phone and makes a one word call.

It's the signal for the first of The Group's couriers to proceed.

Back from the bathroom, TD settles into the chair to adjust the camera just as Eddie finishes receiving his first delivery. TD has returned only in time to see a car leaving, and the man he had observed a few minutes earlier patting his hand on the trunk of a Cadillac coupe. From the looks of it, he just put something inside the car. As TD watches, the man then pulls out a phone and makes an abbreviated call.

When he's working, even on a job as simple as this one, TD's observation skills are on full throttle, his mind registering scores of minor details. Among other things, he noticed that the call the man just placed was extremely short, a word or two, but no more. He also spotted his smile. Based on his appearance and mannerisms, along with a noticeable sense of confidence, he gives the guy a nickname: Slick.

TD concludes he must have just missed witnessing some kind of transaction. He guesses the man's call was either a confirmation or maybe an indication of more to come. TD is also wearing a smile now. He's pleased to have something to observe while waiting for Tim to continue his cheap little motel affair.

As the man re-enters his room, TD says aloud, "Alright, Slick. Let's see if we can figure out what you're up to tonight."

The words are hardly out of his mouth before he sees Tim's BMW arriving. TD watches as it pulls into the empty space to the right of the Cadillac. Then, oddly, well over a minute passes and no one gets out. Now the car appears to be empty.

TD is confused. He wonders if he has just suffered some kind of un-explained lapse and missed them entering the room. Finally, he glimpses a flash of movement in the car's rear view mirror. With a twinge of disgust, he realizes Tim and his date have sunk down almost completely out of view and are making out in the front seat like two teenagers.

⚓

Inside Tim's BMW with the seats fully reclined, Tim and Cyndi are nearing a point of no return. Either they must break things off or they'll soon be having sex in the car.

Tim finally realizes he can't allow that to happen, definitely not in a car his wife rides in. Popping up in his seat, he enjoys a last lingering kiss be-fore gaining control of the situation. Saying nothing more than, "Let's go", he pushes away from Cyndi and exits the vehicle. He then waits impatiently at the front of the car, not bothering to come and open her door.

Cyndi can't leave the car until she reaches a minimal level of decency. Once she finishes rearranging her bunched up dress and taming her hair, she gets out and moves toward the room where Tim is already opening the door. It's Room 114, right beside where Eddie King awaits his next delivery.

⚓

TD knows he has caught a nice break; Tim is using the same room he stayed in before. His preliminary camera setup needs only the smallest ad-justment before he begins recording everything on video. With a high ca-pacity memory card, he can record and store all the images he needs.

Video allows TD to capture even the most subtle facial expressions, unavailable when attempting a single shot. Later, he can select the most damning freeze frames and produce several perfect images for his client. The short-lived public display of affection he just witnessed is an added bonus. The images of overtly sexual behavior will provide solid visual evidence of the nature of Tim's affair. With those in hand, his wife will have all the ammunition she needs to dictate the terms of their divorce.

When he first started the case, TD didn't care about the outcome. His only concerns were doing the job professionally and providing his client the results of fact-based investigation. That soon changed as he observed how Tim operated.

Along with the brazenness, TD was quickly disgusted by the man's cheapness and poor manners. Tonight, the man took his date to a mediocre restaurant and a cheap motel. Once they arrived, he didn't even open her car door or wait for her to join him before entering the room. Even worse, is that his methods apparently succeed, at least from Tim's point of view.

⋏

Once inside the room, Tim and Cyndi crash onto the bed, flushed from the arousal they generated in the car. Groping each other as they kiss, they begin pulling each other's clothes off with an almost violent frenzy. Suddenly, Tim stops and curses.

He forgot to turn on the air conditioner when he checked-in earlier. Now, augmented by their body heat, the hot and stuffy room is starting to feel like a sauna. He's already dripping sweat as he leaves the bed to start the bulky unit. Even on its max setting, he knows it won't cool things down quickly.

⋏

With little time to think, Eddie had been forced to make a critical decision. He had received the warning from his sentry as he was entering Marvin's room. A car had turned into the driveway and was entering the motel; the courier was only a few minutes out.

Initially he was horrified, simply because of the timing. He had to decide whether to wave off the delivery; something they had never had to do. His concern only grew when the car pulled in right next to his.

He immediately began to relax as he watched the couple's make out session. The only question had become how long they would stay at it. Soon after they came up for air and entered their room, Eddied decided to let the courier come ahead.

Thanks to the thin walls, Eddie had quickly learned his neighbor's first name. Though somewhat muffled, he could easily hear the woman almost incessantly moaning, "Tim, oh Tim." Most importantly, the sounds helped reassure Eddie about the couple's presence during the consolidation. He doubted there would be any threat from a lothario named Tim banging his girlfriend in a cheap motel.

Now, just minutes later, his phone rings again. This time the sentry gives the all-clear signal. The first courier has turned into the driveway. There are no other vehicles trailing.

Eddie nervously fiddles with the two bags on the bed, spreading them further open in preparation. Upon hearing the courier's car entering the gravelly parking area, he relaxes a little further. It appears everything will go smoothly after all.

Out in front, a man in his early thirties hops out of the car. Wearing a charcoal sport coat along with a black shirt and pants, he walks briskly toward the room. He's carrying a small gym bag by its strap, hanging it down by his knees instead of over a shoulder. The bag is clearly heavy and bulging a little.

Using the strap for leverage, the courier swings the bag forward just as the door to the room opens. His serious expression transforms into a broad smile as he releases the strap and the bag arcs perfectly into Eddie's waiting hands. Though this courier is one of his favorites, Eddie wishes he would handle the job more discreetly, with less joking around. Silently, he gives a small nod, acknowledged by a wink as the courier turns back towards his car.

Before closing the door to the room, Eddie makes the call to the next courier. He has set everything up to mimic an air traffic control pattern. Right now, the remaining couriers are circling in traffic in the immediate vicinity, waiting to be cleared for arrival. When they do finally come to the motel, they spend very little time there. The total time, including driving in an out of the courtyard and the drop-off, is less than two minutes. Unless someone is focusing specifically on that area as the car pulls in, they are likely to miss the entire event.

The carefully designed script is constructed to keep things moving, and Eddie definitely wants to keep it that way tonight. In between couriers, he quickly moves through the tasks that are his own part of the process.

Across the way, TD is relaxed and settling in for the wait. Though there's the possibility Tim could come out of his room at any time, TD knows it will be awhile before he finishes his tryst. Still, he keeps his eyes on the room through the viewfinder, the camera's lens peeking through the carefully positioned curtains. The camera is currently paused, but he can resume recording with the touch of a button.

Surveillance can span hours of nothingness. It took TD a while to learn how to pass the time while maintaining a focus. A voracious reader, he has always had the habit of carrying along various books, magazines, and newspapers wherever he goes, knocking of a few pages whenever a chance arises. He has a book and two magazines back in the car that he could be enjoying right now. Unfortunately, early in his career he realized the impracticality of reading anything while conducting a competent surveillance. Instead, he uses the time to ruminate over a topic he has read about recently.

Boredom isn't a problem this evening. The scene in front of him has been far from static. He may have missed a delivery to 'Slick' while he was in the bathroom, but he has just watched another car arrive and stop parallel to the same room. His attention drawn by the pattern of activity, TD decides to record the proceedings. He checks the image and pulls back on the zoom to get a wider view, but keeps the door to Tim's room in the frame.

As the driver returns to his car, TD sees Slick standing in the doorway of his room holding a gym bag. And just as occurred when the first car drove off, Slick immediately makes a phone call. With the phone in one hand, he shoulders the strap of the gym bag and turns back into the room, shutting the door with a kick of his heel.

TD is fascinated by what he is observing. Something interesting is going on with Room 112 and it all appears to be orchestrated.

⅄

Eddie removes the cash from the courier's bag using the bed as a workspace. Sorted and counted prior to delivery, the bills are in straps of one hundred, along with a tally sheet for the total amount. Each strap constitutes either $2,000 in twenties or $10,000 in hundreds. To process the bag, he neatly piles the cash on the bed and verifies the total. He then segregates the denominations into the two larger bags. After loading the cash, he updates the tally sheets for each of his bags.

Eddie helped refine the controls mechanisms for the consolidation process when he took over. Once that activity begins, it becomes very difficult for someone to skim anything off the top. He also handpicked the men for this work. There's never been a single discrepancy under his regime, and that's important.

With The Group, the penalties for malfeasance are far more severe than simply losing your job. Eddie's team is well aware of the work The Group's enforcers are occasionally required to perform. They're the guys called in to apply a little pressure on a slow-paying client or to administer discipline within the crew. On top of the respect and loyalty that are a natural part of working for such an organization, knowledge of the enforcers' existence goes a long way to minimizing losses.

When he finishes processing all of the drops, the tally sheets will indicate how much money from each courier is in the two larger bags, as well as the total for the entire consolidation. The task is easy enough and has become routine, leaving him enough time to do his job without rushing before the next courier arrives.

After processing a second drop, Eddie can tell this month's take is going to be exceptionally large. It will easily clear the $600,000 he manages in an average consolidation. The first two of The Group's couriers have each delivered over $150,000.

Eddie chooses to wait outside for the next car. Standing in front of his room, he chuckles to himself as he lights a cigarette. Lover boy Tim must be pounding away again. Even out here, he can hear his new neighbors, and Tim's date is obviously enjoying every second.

▲

TD has decided to continue video recording the deliveries. He'll watch it back later if he's unable to determine what's occurring by the time he leaves tonight. He'd like to figure it out, if only for the intellectual challenge.

He has now witnessed three deliveries. Everyone involved appears to be following an established routine, with a smooth, matter of fact manner. There's no way this is the first time they've used this location. He begins speculating what will come next. How many more drop-offs remain? Is the guy in 112 taking everything with him, or is there a final pick up?

When Slick steps out in front of his room to smoke, TD intensifies his focus on the man's demeanor. Once you get past the sharp, well-appointed exterior, there's clearly a toughness there, along with a sense of entitlement. He's definitely not someone to be trifled with.

Considering Slick's manner, and the probable nature of the deliveries, TD hopes Tim and his date don't choose the wrong moment to emerge from their room. At least he doesn't have to follow them. He knows Tim's routine. First, the girl will depart by taxi. Then, after changing back into the same clothes he was wearing this morning, Tim will drive directly home.

Over the next fifteen minutes, the deliveries continue. With three more handoffs, TD can now account for at least six. The only difference in the routine was with the first one. Based on what he witnessed then, he believes whatever was delivered is currently sitting inside the trunk of the Cadillac. There's also no suggestion that the deliveries are some kind of transaction or exchange. Slick never pays for anything and the couriers take nothing away. It's just a series of straightforward drops.

After a little more consideration, TD formulates his first hypothesis. This is not about drugs. He's witnessing a collection of cash. The money has been generated elsewhere at multiple locations and then delivered here. If he's correct, taking into account the size of the bags and the number of drops, a significant amount of money is accumulating here at the Gateway Motor Inn.

Finishing his thoughts, he notices it has now been a considerably longer interval since the last drop. That probably means it's the end of the series. After a few more minutes, TD concludes that his interesting distraction has come to an end. Reaching his arms over his head, he stretches his back and shoulders to relieve the ache from hunching over the camera. He the refocuses the view more tightly on the door to Tim's room and pauses the recording.

Despite having enjoyed the speculation about what's been occurring, he's glad the deliveries have ended. The end of all the activity increases the likelihood he'll get some clean shots of Tim and his date's departure. And it's now far less likely Tim will exit his room at a bad time. TD doesn't have to like the guy, but Tim doesn't deserve getting sideways with Slick.

As the motel returns to its normal dormant state, TD considers how well the location works for both Tim and Slick. The layout is perfect. With the pool and courtyard in front, the building sits well back from the road and the small hill blocks the remaining view from street level. With no visibility, there's little chance of someone seeing you or your car, unless, of course, they happen to be watching from inside one of the rooms.

⅄

Two blocks away, Raffi is dressed to impress. His expensive suede sports coat is trimmed with polished leather features on the collar and cuffs. He's also wearing a cream-colored open-neck dress shirt, black slacks, and fine-tooled leather boots. Raffi's attire reflects his original plans for the evening, a first date with a wealthy, attractive married woman he had recently met. With her husband out of town, the date presented the opportunity for both an intimate evening with a beautiful woman plus the bonus of scoping out a potential robbery target.

Everything changed when Carmela called, alerting him that the guy who took the deliveries had returned and was now in Marvin's room. When Raffi cancelled his date at the last minute, the woman was genuinely disappointed and made him promise to reschedule. He considers it another good omen for what's now ahead.

Raffi is quite superstitious. He also believes he is personally lucky. Prior to a job, he's always in search of good omens. Since the police have never come close to catching him, any portents of good fortune he unmasks always appear to have been true. Last night, two of his crew returned from a short trip to Las Vegas. Before leaving the parking area, they peeled off a couple of sets of license plates from cars parked in the airport's long-term lot. With any luck, their theft will go undiscovered for days. Presented with the stolen plates earlier today, Raffi declared it "the best of omens".

With everything falling into place, Raffi put out the alert and had his driver take him to the McDonald's, the rendezvous point for tonight's job. By the time he got there, the other three men had arrived. They were waiting inside one of the stolen cars being used tonight, a faded silver sedan wearing one of the sets of freshly stolen plates. The team looks eager and relatively sharp, despite having just shared a large joint. Raffi has no objections; he also likes to smoke a little pot to help him relax before a job.

For now, he stays in the Monte Carlo. When they're finally ready to head to the motel, he'll leave the car, which will immediately be driven away and parked in front of his house. It's something he has been doing lately on most jobs. If for some reason he needs an alibi, claiming to be at home with his car parked in plain view out front, just might help.

Javier, Raffi's most fearless wheelman, will drive him in the stolen car on the final leg to the motel. Along with Javier, Nelson and Marco will take part in the robbery. They all listen closely as Raffi again reviews how the job is to go down. First, he reminds them that Cesar will kick off the attack.

Raffi's closest friend is driving the other stolen vehicle. Parked with his engine idling, he is already in position behind a small shopping center just down the street, connected to the Qwik Lube via a short maze of curbing and asphalt. Cesar has easily spotted Eddie King's sentry. He was exactly where Raffi predicted, sitting in a car behind the lube shop. He has parked almost up against the building. Facing in the direction of the motel, he's parallel with one of the large service bay doors that are closed at this hour.

When the final pick-up car arrives, Raffi will signal Cesar. He'll then pull from behind the stores, navigate through the parking lot, and immobilize the sentry. Based on the position of the sentry's car, he's going to have to ram him broadside. As he has waited, Cesar has grown increasingly concerned that the crash will kill the sentry. He now greatly regrets his assignment, but his loyalty to his Raffi is everything. Raffi saved him from the gangs and Cesar is not about to let him down tonight. He'll do his job. If the sentry is meant to live, he will live.

At the McDonald's, Raffi has finished reviewing each individual's role when they reach the motel. Now as they wait, influenced by the pot, he spends a little time daydreaming. He imagines himself the leader of an elite commando unit, expertly positioning his men to unleash an ambush attack. In reality, his team stands slouched against their car, mildly buzzed, listening to music as they try to relax.

Tonight's job is a big step up and they can feel each other's tension. Their past efforts have been simple unopposed burglaries with an occasional hijacking mixed in. They've never gone up against anyone who might thwart them. They've also never carried so much weaponry. Each of them is armed with one of the fully loaded semi-automatic pistols Raffi provided.

Over the last month, he has repeatedly reassured them the job will be a pushover. They not only outnumber their targets two to one, but they also have surprise on their side. Again, as they waited this evening, he told them, "Remember, we're just ripping off a couple of middle-age businessmen. This one's going to be short and sweet."

Businessmen or not, he has rarely had anyone on his crew carry a gun. It's something they're simply not comfortable doing and it increases the pressure on them all. Still, as with Eddie King's team, Raffi's men are fiercely loyal. Despite displaying a few nerves, they remain ready to do whatever he asks.

Checking his watch, Raffi is becoming restless. It feels like it has been a long time since receiving a second call from Carmela confirming that the deliveries had started. And still, there's no sign of the pick-up car. His thoughts begin to race. Maybe they've changed vehicles, or changed their routine.

Then, as he begins to worry that tonight will end up being another blown opportunity, the Mercedes with smoked glass windows rolls past. Raffi feels his heart jump when he sees the car's brake lights flash as it slows to make the sharp turn into the motel.

Grabbing his phone as he leaps from the Monte Carlo, he sends a text message for Cesar to proceed. Marco and Nelson are also reacting quickly, pitching away their cigarettes. Even as Raffi is yelling at them to get moving, they are already running across the parking lot towards the motel.

With Raffi now in the passenger seat of the stolen car, Javier takes off, displaying excellent driving skills. In just a few moments, he maneuvers them out of the parking lot. As they are coming up to speed, they hear the sound Raffi has been waiting for. They can almost feel the scream of compressing metal from Cesar's crash two hundred yards ahead of them.

In the sudden silence following the collision, Raffi lets out a whooping scream of joy and excitement, badly startling Javier. Amidst the unfolding action of his own creation, Raffi is alternately screaming and laughing with excitement. So far, the job is running just smoothly as he planned it. Minutes from now, he's going to have the drugs or money he knows are just waiting to be taken. Then they'll stash their take and hide out for a few days while waiting for things to cool off.

As they close in on the turn for the motel, Raffi knows one thing for sure; this is exactly how he is meant to live his life. If this job is as lucrative as he hopes, he won't need to pull another one for some time. Maybe he'll take a real vacation somewhere.

Raffi is correct about one thing. He won't be working another job anytime soon.

▲

Several minutes earlier, Cyndi's clearly audible state of arousal finally ended. After riding Tim to a climax for both of them, she rolled onto her back leaving them dripping with sweat. With it too hot for any cuddling, Tim got up and poured them both a glass of wine.

After taking only a few short sips, he set his glass down and moved toward the shower. He only made it the first few steps before stopping, suddenly pushed aside. With an athletic leap from the bed, Cyndi has darted past him, grinning, and giggling as she closes the bathroom door behind her.

Waiting a minute and then finally hearing the toilet flush, Tim moves to the door. With a forceful tone he calls out, "Don't forget. I need to shower first."

"Uh huh," Cyndi quickly responds. "I hear you. Just give me a second, baby."

Tim knows she has tricked him when he hears the shower come on. He tries the doorknob and is surprised to find it locked. Rapping loudly on the thin door, with a whiny tone he lies to her, "C'mon, baby. You know I still need to get some work done tonight. I need to get rolling. Let me in there please."

Waiting for her to unlock the door, Tim figures that if she wants to, they can shower together. He can then quickly get dressed and leave while she finishes up.

Cyndi is having none of it and refuses to answer him. Instead, she focuses on generating a handful of lather from the hard thin bar of motel soap. The last time they hooked up, Tim had rudely left her with hardly a goodbye. After letting him shower first, she had taken her turn only to then come out to find him gone. There was a brief note with the words 'love you', on the back of a napkin, and twenty dollars for cab fare to get back to her car. A few minutes later, he called and mumbled some inane apology for having left so quickly. This time she's going to make him wait; she's positive he won't dare go home without showering, smelling of sweat and sex.

Cyndi knows Tim is married. That's a firm fixed fact, despite his oft-repeated claims of being divorced. She has seen too many obvious signs, including the pale indentation on his finger from the ring he must slip off before seeing her. Each time after sex, he has a lame excuse for why he has to leave, undoubtedly so he can return home at a reasonable hour. Surprising herself, she realizes that emotionally she doesn't care. The dinners and small gifts are nice and the sex is admittedly awesome. She isn't looking for a relationship right now and a night out with Tim beats the hell out of most anything else she might plan.

Still, she had decided tonight was going to be different. While showering, she reaffirms her determination to have him treat her with more respect. She'll be damned if he's going to leave her behind in a cheap motel like a toy tossed aside until he's ready to play with it again. No, tonight they're leaving together. He's going to end the evening like a gentleman, enough so to at least drive her back to her car.

She giggles more as Tim raps on the bathroom door again, now whining that he needs to use the toilet. Finally, he stops. She's enjoying the shower and feeling a glow of satisfaction from winning their little battle of wills. His surrender is complete when she hears him at the door one last time, telling her he's going out to his car for a cigarette. Of course, she knows he'll return with the change of clothes he always brings along, the most damning sign of his infidelity.

⋏

Next door, Eddie King is finally beginning to relax. The last delivery has come and gone and he has finished his own work. The cash has been sorted and placed in the two large bags, along with the final tally sheets he completed. After a quick check to make sure he didn't drop anything on the bed or the floor, he calls for the pick-up car to come in. From here, the money will be removed to a location even he doesn't know.

Eddie will then head to a local bar to hang out with a couple of the couriers. The ritual gatherings help him wind down from the evening's job while also contributing to the crew's morale. On the way to the bar, he plans to stop by his nearby apartment. There, he'll store his own cash inside a new fireproof safe he recently had installed.

While he waits for the pick-up car, he revisits the idea of moving the consolidation to a new location. He shouldn't have used this location for so long. Luckily, there have been zero problems. In all the months here, he never spotted a single cop. He has rarely encountered any of the motel's residents other than Marvin, or the young woman next door. There's no doubt the place has worked out well.

Leveraging the concept of utilizing low-end motels, he's reminded of several older properties lining Route 1, including a rundown former Howard Johnson he used a few times for an impromptu meeting. If he remembers correctly, it has a layout and traffic flow similar to the Gateway. Going forward, he plans to rotate to a different location every month or two. Who knows, he could even end up back here every now and then.

Eddie likes planning well in advance. Even if a couple of his precautions end up being unnecessary, the farther ahead he works a problem, the less he'll be unprepared. At times, he shares his thinking with a select few on his team. It helps to use them as a sounding board, and it has the benefit of preparing them as well. If they ever need to step up and take charge, at least they'll have an understanding of how he likes to handle certain situations.

He's definitely pleased nothing troublesome occurred this evening. Things have gone smoothly, particularly considering two unidentified extra guests had checked-in. And tonight would have been a particularly bad time to screw up; the consolidation was oversized as he had guessed. He put are over a hundred straps of cash into the two bags, totally $852,000. It's his highest monthly total ever, and as much as he handles over some two-month periods.

This past year, Eddie has paid close attention to the details of The Group's operations. Over time, the information he gleaned helped him evolve a deeper understanding of the business and its structure. For example, he knows his boss will be particularly happy with this month's proceeds. The plentiful haul will help carry The Group through July and August. Like many businesses, gambling slows down a bit in the summer. Poker players take vacations like anyone else. Other than baseball, there are no pro sports for bettors, along with a total absence of college games. Fortunately, it all begins percolating again in late August and business remains solid through to the next June.

Though Eddie can't take credit for the total of the monthly consolidation, the well-orchestrated collection from all the various sources is definitely due to his management skills. He reminds himself to come up with a way to point this out to his boss. Like so many others, he wants to move up in the organization he invests so much of his time and life in.

In some way, the increased revenue for The Group this month helps him feels less guilty about the relatively small business he's running on the side. His own take, waiting in the trunk of his car, approaches a quarter of a million. He remembers the jolt of excitement when his man delivered the bag and whispered the amount. Sure, his total covers a three-month period, but it's exciting to reach such a threshold.

At the same time, he has to consider whether to grow the business any further. There are huge risks generating so much cash out of sight of The Group. The amount he's earning on the side is definitely large enough to piss people off if they find out. He doesn't want to begin to think about their reaction if they learn he has set up shop to the tune of nearly a million dollars a year.

He also understands the considerable contradiction of running his own action on the sly, while at the same time striving to be rewarded with a promotion.

⼈

Continuing to sweat while he waits to shower, Tim has become increasingly upset with Cyndi. Her little stunt has him thinking she's more trouble than she's worth. Whenever a girlfriend creates a problem, or he simply becomes bored, he begins the process of finding a replacement. He won't dump the current girl until he finds the next, but the result is inevitable. As he leaves the room to go to his car, he's pretty sure the end is near for Cyndi.

Barefoot, and wearing only an undershirt with his slacks, he gingerly steps across the hot gravelly pavement to the rear of his car. Except for his nights out, he rarely gets a chance to smoke. His wife forbids it at home, even outside. Opening the trunk, he finds the pack he keeps in a gym bag that's anchoring a suit and dress shirt draped neatly across the trunk. Inside the bag, along with his workout clothes are the socks and underwear he wore earlier that day.

Tim snags the smokes and takes everything from the trunk. Inside the room, he pitches the bag onto the bed and hangs the suit on the back of the door. Then, stepping back outside into the parking area, he lights up as he leans against the trunk of his car.

TD has been anticipating Tim's re-appearance. Despite ending the recording when the deliveries stopped, he has been poised to start again. Based on his prior trysts, he expects Tim will show his face anytime. After noticing a slight movement of the curtains in Tim's room, TD resumes recording.

A few seconds later, the door opens. He's surprised to see Tim partly undressed; this is definitely a first. He's also noticeably sweating as he almost tiptoes to his car. Watching him move his suit and a bag to the room, and then return outside to light up, TD puts it together. Tim is waiting to shower. That means his date must have gotten first dibs. Knowing it never goes down this way, TD gives her a silent nod of respect.

When his phone chirps, Eddie snaps out of his reverie over his career prospects. It's the call from his sentry. He hears just two words. One indicates the arrival of the pick-up car, the other the all clear.

Moving the bags from the bed, he sets them on the floor, positioning one to each side of the door. He then opens the door and steps outside.

In his late fifties, and by far the oldest member of Eddie King's crew, Petey Bowman has worked in many capacities for The Group. Lately, his job pretty much consists of covering Eddie's back. That's all right with Petey; Eddie is a stand-up guy if you ask his opinion, and the work isn't hard. His current task is quite simple: he keeps a constant eye on the entrance off the main road and alerts Eddie any time a car that's not theirs turns in towards the motel. That has been a rare occurrence. The few times it has happened, the cars have always continued up the driveway to the storage facility behind the motel.

Petey's role takes on an elevated importance once a courier arrives. If the courier turns in with no one following, Petey calls in an 'all clear'. If any vehicle follows a courier's car off the main road, he will immediately alert Eddie with an abort code. He's to do the same, if someone turns in during the brief timeframe a courier is in the courtyard making their drop. Either way, he'll make the call and then haul ass to the motel on foot, ready to provide whatever backup is needed. As it stands, nothing like that has ever happened. Not while they've been here at the Gateway, or any other location they've used.

Tonight is no different. There has been no other traffic as the couriers have come and gone. He has passed the time in between deliveries by listening to a Washington Nationals' game on the radio. Finally, the pickup car has arrived. After it leaves the motel, he'll wait for Eddie to depart. Then he's planning to meet up with a few of the guys for beers.

Petey barely lifts his head as the black Mercedes passes and he calls in the 'all clear'. With his job all but finished, he nudges up the volume and reclines his seat a little further. He's old enough to remember listening to the old Washington Senators as a boy. Every season, the Senators lost far more games than they won but it hardly mattered. Like tonight, he finds a simple comfort in the act of listening to baseball on a summer evening.

As the Nats move a runner into scoring position, Petey is distracted by the sound of a car's engine, rapidly growing louder. Rising up in his seat to see what's going on, he spends the last seconds of his life in a state of total confusion. A driverless car is just the blink of an eye away from crashing straight into him.

⋏

Cesar sees he has scraped large amounts of skin off his arms as he picks himself up off the pavement. Both of his elbows and one entire forearm are raw and bleeding and feel like they're on fire. His left shoulder and hip are also now screaming with pain after absorbing the main impact when he landed. Despite his injuries, he feels a sense of satisfaction looking across at the wreckage; he completed his assignment exactly as Raffi planned.

He had jammed the accelerator to the floor as he lined up squarely with the sentry's car and then jumped from his car less than fifty feet before impact. He had never experienced such pain as when he hit the asphalt. After rolling over several times, he watched from the ground as his car closed the final distance. He couldn't have steered it better if he had stayed behind the wheel.

Even knowing what was about to happen, he still flinched as the momentum of his car slammed the parked vehicle sideways, smashing it into the garage door. The impact shattered the door's large plexiglass panels and buckled it almost completely off the frame. Stunned by the ferocity of the crash and the probable death of the sentry, it had been several moments before he found the willpower to stagger to his feet.

Finally turning away, he quickly retreats behind the stores where a second car is pre-positioned for his getaway. His next task is to drive to one of the parking lot exits. Once there, he'll wait for Raffi to pass and then pull in behind, acting as a rearguard if needed.

Sitting inside the motel office, Bobby Tomlin is startled by the sound of a car crash, so loud that it must be extremely close by. Fearing that someone might be hurt badly, his first reaction is to call 911. Then, changing his mind, he decides he should learn a little more before making a report.

As he reaches the door to the office, he first hears and then sees a car flying by as it screeches into the courtyard. He fears another crash is imminent, knowing that the Mercedes just drove past and has likely parked where it always does. As he steps outside, he can only hope the car is able to stop in time.

Carmella has been fretting and trembling with nervousness since calling Raffi, a call she now regrets making. Watching the drivers arrive and depart with their professional demeanor started her thinking of all the ways things could turn out badly, very badly. And knowing Raffi is soon to arrive has only made things worse. Still, he has yet to appear. Maybe he won't make it in time, just like last month.

Raffi never discussed his plans with her, but she isn't stupid. His endless questioning about the deliveries, and even more so regarding the final pick-ups, has left little to her imagination. There was a point she felt wrong about betraying the stranger in Marvin's room, but those feelings vanished earlier when he glared at her with such intensity, just for stepping outside of her room for a walk.

Carmela's thoughts are now on Raffi's safety. Maybe things will turn out all right and change things for the two of them, together. Maybe this will lead to her getting out of this life, working part-time jobs for the minimum wage, and living on assistance in a cheap motel.

Suddenly, she hears the whine of squealing tires and the roar of a car entering the courtyard. At she pushes a curtain aside, she's almost dizzy with excitement, but it's not hope she's feeling. She can hardly breathe, sick with fear and the realization that whatever is about to happen, she played a critical role in setting it in motion.

⚔

Minutes earlier, Tim lights a second cigarette after deciding it is definitely time to move on from Cyndi. As he continues to lean against his car, the door to the next room opens and a sharply dressed man emerges. When the guy notices him there, smoking and shoeless, his expression morphs almost instantly from one of surprise to anger.

In an attempt to keep things light, Tim puts on a leering smile as he says, "How's it going? Pretty thin walls, aren't they? I hope we weren't too noisy for you."

Eddie is totally pissed off finding this jerk outside. It's made worse by his sophomoric effort to make sure he knows what's been going on in their room. Sneering, he barks at Tim, "Fuck off. Matter of fact, you need to take a hike, buddy. Right now!"

He can hardly believe this moron is here at the very moment the pick-up car is arriving. Glaring at him over his shoulder, he steps into the parking area hoping to see the car. He's confident his tough-guy attitude and harsh words will have the necessary effect, chasing the guy back into his room.

Shocked by Eddie's words and tone, Tim quickly senses this guy is no one to mess with. Responding meekly, he says, "Sorry, man. No problem."

Starting toward his room, Tim literally jumps when he hears the sound of a loud car crash that can't be far away. The noise was even more startling due to the lack of warning sounds or skidding tires, just a sudden explosion of crushing metal. Instinctively turning in the direction of the sound, he takes several cautious strides before stopping and craning his neck as he tries to see what has happened.

When he hears the crash, Eddie fears the worst: a hit on the pick-up car. Then, he's able to relax as the Mercedes appears from behind the rise and turns into the motel's lot. In the relief of the moment, he forgets about Tim. His only desire is to finish this last part of the consolidation quickly. With the car circling into position, Eddie pivots back toward Marvin's room. Opening the door, he grabs the straps of the bags he left waiting there.

⅄

TD is watching Slick confront Tim when he hears the sound of the crash. Muffled by the noisy AC unit, the direction of the accident isn't clear to him until he sees both men turn towards the motel entrance. With the camera continuing to record, he stands up and carefully edges one side of the curtains back.

There's nothing to see related to a crash but another car is now arriving, a nicer more imposing vehicle. Initially, Slick stares intently at the car before turning toward his room. TD instantly realizes this isn't a delayed delivery. This is it, the pick-up.

He continues watching as Slick opens the door to the room. Instead of entering, he reaches down for something and then turns back towards the courtyard. Hanging by their straps, he now has a gym bag slung over each shoulder. Much larger than the bags used in the deliveries, TD assumes everything must now be inside these two.

The bags' straps pin Slick's sport coat to his shoulders, causing the jacket's side panels to flare open. Nestled against the guy's left side, TD can see a holstered gun. Though not alarmed by what he sees, it still ratchets the tension of the moment. Moving back behind the camera, he leans down and adjusts the zoom to capture a broader tableau, one that now fully includes the car and Slick, as well as Tim.

The driver of the Mercedes had heard the crash as well, but made no connection with it to the reason he is here. After opening the trunk remotely, he gets out of the car but stays next to it as he scouts the courtyard. To his surprise, Eddie is already out of the room with the bags, even before he has given him the signal to proceed.

Eddie stops cold when he notices Tim still standing there, staring in the direction of the crash. He spits out his words, yelling, "I thought I told you to take a hike, you fucking asshole! Move it now or you'll regret it!"

Again, Tim gets the message. Throwing Eddie a quick sneer, he moves toward his room.

Satisfied the idiot is finally leaving, Eddie shifts the weight of the bags on his shoulders. Then, giving the driver a thumbs-up, he heads for the rear of the car and the open trunk.

Suddenly, there's a new blast of sound. Coming in fast, a grey sedan is rocketing directly toward the pick-up car. Tim has again stopped and turned to see what is creating this new noise, but Eddie is focused on the arriving car. He can see there are two men in the front seats and it appears the passenger is raising a weapon.

In that split second, Eddie knows his apprehension all evening was warranted. These guys are here to take the money.

Relieved that Tim was finally getting out of Slick's way, TD now also sees the approach of the second car. He watches fascinated as it barrels toward the Mercedes. Looking more closely, he notes the stern look on the driver's face as well as the weapon the passenger is holding.

TD immediately realizes this evening isn't going to wrap up smoothly after all. Not for him and certainly not for anyone now out in that courtyard. With the camera still recording, he prepares for a quick exit. He wants to leave at the first opportunity and definitely before any police arrive. There's no way he wants to be involved as a witness to whatever is about to happen.

He needs to stay focused and rely on his ability to adapt to rapidly changing scenarios. He prides himself for staying at least a step ahead of the people he's investigating, intuitively knowing how individuals will react as events arise. Right now, it's easy to see that he needs to get out of here. Obviously, he'd prefer getting a few more pics of Tim and his date, particularly leaving the motel room, but that's unlikely to happen now.

He works rapidly, but deliberately, as he removes the camera from the tripod. Using one hand, he collapses the telescopic legs and shoves the aluminum stand into the bag already on his shoulder. He plans to continue recording as best he can until the last feasible moment. He's not sure why, but there's no reason to stop either. He also knows whatever is about to transpire won't take long.

He no longer worries about being detected as he slips the curtains aside a couple of inches to better record the action. No one will be looking in the direction of his room now, not with everything going on in the courtyard.

As he watches the scene in front of him unfold, TD notices his pulse quickening, something he never experiences in his reclusive lifestyle. If only for a few moments, at least this evening's work has provided him with a jolt of energy. He's also experiencing an unexpected and intense feeling of excitement. It's a feeling he definitely likes.

Raffi hasn't stopped yelling, even as Javier desperately prays for the brakes to stop them before they hit the car dead ahead of them. Moments earlier, Raffi was excited, whooping and yelling as they roared around the corner. Now he's screaming and cussing for them not to crash. Making things worse, he's swinging his gun around so wildly Javier is afraid it might go off.

Javier's greatest fear is that he has misjudged the distance across the lot. There's simply nowhere to fit another vehicle between the pool and the parked car, and the spots of loose gravel are only worsening his chances of avoiding a crash. At the last moment, the tires grab enough of the remaining asphalt as they skid to a halt, leaving a foot or less between the cars' front bumpers.

As he vaults from the car, Raffi is screaming in a mix of Spanish and English as he continues waving his gun in every direction like a maniac bandit. Javier quickly joins him outside the vehicle, pulling his own weapon. The extra show of force helps Raffi calm down some. Back on plan, he points his weapon at the driver of the pick-up car.

The driver, built like an offensive lineman, shifts his stare between the two assailants, seemingly unintimidated. Even though he's standing outside the car, the open door shields his body. With Raffi covering the driver, Javier points his weapon at Eddie, ten feet from the trunk of the car, the two bags still hanging from his shoulders. For a brief moment, there's an eerie quiet in the courtyard as they all rapidly assess the situation.

Raffi breaks the silence, yelling at the driver to move away from the car and waving his gun to indicate where he wants him to go. For some reason, the driver refuses to acknowledge the command, creating suspicion that he's considering making some kind of move. Despite that, Raffi is unworried; he knows the balance of power has shifted his way.

Marco and Nelson have appeared from behind the motel and taken up positions with their guns now leveled at the driver as well. Maintaining a stony stare, the driver slowly nods at Raffi. Then, raising his hands a little above his shoulders, he takes a couple of slow short steps away from the car

He hasn't moved completely clear of the vehicle, but Raffi settles for it, sensing he's finally gaining control. A broad smile appears as he shifts his eyes toward Eddie. Waving his gun in that direction, he shouts, "You can put the bags down, motherfucker. You don't need to carry them no more."

⚔

Tim is terrified and physically shaking. All he wanted tonight was a little hot action on the side. Now he's half-dressed and barefoot, caught in the madness of some kind of violent shakedown.

When he first saw the guy pop out of the car screaming and waving a gun, his first thought was to get back to his room. Unfortunately, he had come too far while trying to catch a glimpse of the accident they'd just heard. He'd never make it all the way back to his room and get the key in the door without drawing too much attention.

Instead, he scrambles part of the way before dropping to his knees and crawling between the Cadillac and his BMW. Cowering between the cars, he's terrified one of the gunmen will discover him. Afraid to move a muscle or even breathe, he doesn't know how long he can stay crouched and motionless.

⚔

Resigned to the fact that he has screwed up big time, Eddie knows he must keep his mind in the moment if he's going to figure a way out of this. The car crash he heard had to have involved his sentry; he would have received a warning signal otherwise. It must have been the first phase of the attack. That also means he can't count on any backup. Petey would have been here by now if he were unharmed.

Eddie decides his best bet is to try ratcheting down the tension while trying to gain an advantage. He has a gun inside his jacket and the driver is also carrying. And even though they're facing four gunmen, at least two appear quite raw and clearly nervous. He doubts they've ever used their weapons, considering how they're holding them.

The odds they're facing will only improve if he can just buy a little time. Based on the way the attackers have positioned themselves, he doubts they're aware there's an additional armed man on his side of the equation, someone yet to show himself.

Instead of dropping the bags as instructed, Eddie tries slowing things down. Ignoring Javier, whose gun is pointed right at him, he makes eye contact with Raffi, who is obviously in charge. Using a calming, supplicating tone, he says, "Hey man, let's be cool. Maybe we can work something out."

Raffi's look of contempt immediately tells Eddie he has misjudged the situation. His words may have actually had the opposite effect from what he had hoped they would. For the first time, he begins to taste real fear.

Raffi can't believe this guy with the designer clothes is still holding the bags and trying to talk to him. He's obviously pretending to cooperate. Worse, he's acting as if there's going to be a negotiation. Things are already starting to take too long.

Waving his gun at Eddie, he shouts, "Shut the fuck up, man. Don't say another fucking word unless I ask you a question, you understand? You understand me, man? Put the goddamn bags on the ground now, or you're fucking dead!"

With a quick look back to his right, Raffi yells at the driver, "And you. I know you got a gun. So take it out very slowly, from wherever you got it, and put it on the ground. You understand me? When you finish, I want you on the ground."

Catching his breath, Raffi adds, "And move more away from the goddamn car so I can see you good. You understand me? Do it wrong and you're also a dead man."

Between all the cussing, and repeatedly asking if they 'understand' him, the driver can see Raffi is struggling to control himself. And though he's reluctant to surrender his weapon to the kid without a fight, he decides he has little choice. Giving Raffi another nod, he slowly reaches inside his jacket and removes his gun. Placing it on the ground, he slowly takes two steps away and lies face down on the parking lot, still only a few feet from the vehicle.

The deliberate motions of the driver serve to steady Raffi. Turning back toward Eddie, he says, "It's time for you to get on the ground too, pretty boy."

Dropping the bags to either side, Eddie first kneels, and then slowly lies down, all the while fighting the urge to make a move for his gun. He can't believe this punk is trying to pull a job like this. He's so inexperienced, he hasn't even checked to see if he is armed.

It won't be easy getting to his weapon now that he's flat on the ground. He doesn't want to die today, but he's also not ready to give up the money without some form of resistance. Rapidly working through the possibilities, he carefully steals a glance upwards, towards the smoked glass of the pick-up car's right rear window.

With Raffi barking out orders, Javier carefully approaches Eddie, all the time pointing his gun at the prone man. Now only a few feet away, his nerves get the better of him and his hands begin to shake.

Raffi quickly scans the scene before making his next move. He can't help noticing how twitchy his crew appears. They need to finish this quickly before someone makes a stupid mistake. Overall, though, he's pleased. The job is going almost exactly as planned, if only a little slowly. It's clear the two 'businessmen' are a tougher pair than he expected, but they're becoming more docile and cooperative. They should be out of here with the money in just another minute, leaving these guys on the ground without weapons or a vehicle.

Suddenly, he glimpses a flicker of movement, or maybe it was a reflection in one of the windows. Was there someone moving near the guy with the bags? It appears Nelson is reacting to the same thing.

It's Tim. His nerves, along with a leg cramp, have betrayed him.

Pointing his gun at Tim now, Nelson yells frantically in Spanish that there's a man without shoes crouching between the cars. Fearing Nelson might shoot him, Raffi shouts for him to hold his fire.

Understanding no Spanish, and fearing for his life, Tim slowly stands. As he raises his hands, he blubbers, "Don't shoot. Please don't shoot me."

Surprised by the appearance of a trembling, half-dressed man, Raffi mutters "What the fuck?" He then yells at Tim to lie down next to the guy with the bags.

With the loose gravel grinding into his feet, Tim gingerly walks from between the cars. As he settles onto the warm pavement, he sees Eddie looking over the top of the gym bag separating them.

With a sneer, Eddie whispers, "You should have taken that hike, asshole."

As a wave of helplessness rolls over Tim, Raffi yells at Javier in Spanish to check them both for weapons. After that, he's to throw the bags into the still open trunk of the Mercedes.

Watching him, Raffi can tell Javier is extremely nervous. He's sliding his feet but barely moving forward. It's obvious he's going to need help. Before going over to him, he calls for Marco to move more toward the driver's side of the Mercedes and to keep his gun on the driver. He then re-positions Nelson more to the rear of the car. From there he can cover the driver as well as the two men on the ground.

With everyone in position, Raffi finally moves to help Javier. After first turning to go around the back of their car, he changes his mind. Instead, he begins to wriggle through the small gap between the front bumpers.

Javier has forgotten about checking for weapons. Having made it to a point just out of reach of the two men on the ground, he's trying to figure out how to keep his gun pointed at them while he reaches for the bags. To get to the farthest bag, he's either going to have to reach over the first guy, or walk around behind him. He decides to wait when he sees Raffi coming his way, squeezing between the cars.

Amid all the shouting of orders and repositioning, the motorized purr of the pick-up car's lowering rear window goes unnoticed by everyone but Eddie. A leather-gloved hand emerges above him, gripping a semi-automatic assault pistol with a large ammo clip. Unseen behind the smoked glass windows, the on-board guard in the back seat has decided the game is changing.

Opening fire, he cuts down Javier with a short, but lethal burst. His torso pummeled and shredded, Javier staggers backwards several steps before collapsing dead. Moving on to his next target, the guard sweeps his gun toward the front of the car, firing at Raffi, seemingly stuck between the cars.

Missing high with his first salvo, he pauses only long enough to lean further out the window for a better angle. Now gripping the weapon with both hands, his next burst of fire shatters the windshield of the assailants' car before ultimately reaching its intended target.

Amazingly, only one bullet strikes Raffi. It hits him high up the chest on his left side, exiting clean through and missing his heart by inches. The bullet's impact briefly bends him back over the hood of the car before he slides down the front between the vehicles, ending partially perched on the bumpers. Having dropped his gun, it has bounced away from him and now lies on the ground not far from Javier's body.

Any thoughts of finishing the robbery are erased from Raffi's mind by the shock of the sudden retaliation and the agonizing pain in his chest. From this point forward, there can only be surviving. Before he can think about how he'll do that, there's another barrage of gunfire.

When the guard in the back seat opened fire, the driver took that as his own cue to act. Hoping that whoever is guarding him is distracted, he makes his move. Quickly pushing up from the pavement, he lunges toward his weapon a few feet away. He comes nowhere close to making it. Marco, positioned perfectly by Raffi, kills him instantly with a quick volley of shots.

With shooting all around him, Eddie can wait no longer. Rolling onto his side, he pulls his gun free of its holster. He immediately finds an easy target no more than ten feet away. Nelson is standing dumbstruck, staring at Javier's lifeless body. Ignoring everything around him, his gun hangs at his side.

Eddie fires two shots from his spot on the ground. Both are direct hits, rocketing into the center of Nelson's chest and knocking him back before he falls in a dead heap.

Hearing his shots echo through the courtyard, Eddie realizes the shooting has stopped. That includes the gunfire blasting from the car window.

Then he sees the guard's gun on the ground just a few feet away. For some reason, despite still holding his own weapon, he begins crawling toward it.

After making easy work of the driver, Marco had released a hail of gunfire into the back seat of the car, instantly killing the guard. Then, remembering the two men on the ground, he worked his way to the back. When he comes from behind the car and sees Eddie, he opens fire.

Eddie looks up as the attacker's gun blasts directly at him from only a few feet away. Bullets fly all around him but somehow fail to hit. Finally, the shooter scores twice, knocking him back down flat. Once again, he's on the ground looking over at Tim. In the craziness of the pain, he finds himself thinking it's too bad the guy didn't heed his warning to get out of there. It looks like he's been hit by at least one of the stray rounds that missed Eddie.

For Marco, it feels like he's in a video game, with easy targets at every turn. He has taken down four men in less than a minute. Along with the driver and the guy in the back seat, the two on the ground at his feet are both hit and bleeding badly. Gaining confidence now that the shooting has ended, he quickly looks around to make sure there's no one else that might cause them trouble.

The first shot that hit Eddie blew into his left side shattering two ribs. The second tore a deep hole in his left shoulder. Somehow, he's still holding his gun. Barely able to think, he looks up, squinting through the massive pain.

Inexplicably, the shooter is standing there ignoring him. He's looking around in every direction except at the ground immediately in front of him. Just as before, Eddie fires off back-to-back shots. And just as before, both slam into the chest of his target, killing the second gunman foolish enough to stop and stand directly in front of him.

Again, there is silence. As the seconds pass without anyone shooting, Eddie wonders if the battle is over. Is it possible he'll survive? From where he lies, he's unable to see in front of the car, but three of the four attackers are dead around him. Maybe the lack of gunfire means their leader is also dead.

Eddie can tell his own wounds are bad, very bad, but a quick assessment determines his lower body is unharmed. Maybe he can still get himself out of there, though he has no idea how he'll carry the bags. As he attempts to rise, he hears a groan from somewhere near the front of the car.

Though he's shot through the chest and bleeding badly, Raffi thinks his wound might not be fatal if he can get medical attention; but that will require getting out of there. Not knowing or caring if anyone else remains alive to shoot at him, he uses the bumpers to push himself up. Finally, he makes it to the point where he can lean on the hood of the Mercedes. There he pauses, trying to muster more strength.

He can see Javier is dead, but can't get a good view of anything behind the car. Grunting as the pain shoots deep through his chest, he slides his way to the front corner of the car. From there he can see Eddie. Though he has been shot, he's still moving. Worse, he's armed.

He can see there are two guns near Javier's body just a few feet away. Seeing Eddie turning his head toward him, Raffi knows his life ends here and now if he doesn't get to one of them. Overcoming the pain, he lunges forward as the blood continues to flow from his wound. Feeling dizzy, he slumps toward the ground, kneeling close to Javier. Then he hears a shot.

Eddie is hurt much worse than he initially thought. When Raffi appeared at the front of the car he moved to shoot him, but he had almost no control of his right arm. In a spasm of pain, he accidentally pulled the trigger and the shot missed badly.

The effort is more than he can handle and he collapses to the pavement again. Knowing it may be the last act of his life, he inhales deeply as he rises again, for what will undoubtedly be his last attempt.

Raffi has made it. After grabbing one of the guns, he now only needs to steady himself. Kneeling on his right leg with his left foot planted on the ground, he aims and fires. The shot misses wide, ricocheting off the pavement before thudding into the side of the Cadillac. Squinting, he grips the gun more firmly and refocuses on his target. He can see the man is rising again and still has a gun. With no time left to aim, Raffi pulls the trigger.

Eddie also fires, but realizes he's too late when Raffi's second shot slams into his gut. He thinks he saw the kid react; maybe he also scored a hit. Losing consciousness, his last thought in life is how this attack will surely spoil his chances of moving up in the organization any time soon.

Knocked back by the impact of Eddie's final shot, Raffi doesn't even know if he got the guy. The bullet struck him just above his right knee, shattering his lower femur. The searing burn of the leg wound now rivals the pain in his chest. Altogether, it's more pain than he could have imagined was possible.

Though, he remains alive, he can hardly think. The one thing he knows is that he can't stay here, waiting to either die or face arrest. Drawing from strength rooted deep within his will to live, Raffi begins dragging himself back to his car.

⚓

TD feels a jumble of horror and amazement after watching the shooters cut each other down at near point blank range. His own proximity to the violence further magnified the ugly brutality of the killings.

With the battle apparently over, the only person moving is the young guy who led the attack. Though shot in both his chest and one leg, he's apparently tougher than he looks. TD can hardly believe he's alive, yet he's still moving, trying to get back to his car.

Unfortunately, it's not easy to be optimistic about Tim Crane's chances for survival. There hasn't been any movement from him since he was shot during the gunfight.

⚓

Cyndi had finished her shower. She was wrapped in a thin towel, taking a sip of wine when the gunfire first started. Realizing that Tim was outside smoking, she rushed to the window and watched the melee from there, mesmerized with fear.

Initially, she couldn't locate him and figured he was hiding somewhere. Then a man rushed around the back of the car and started shooting at the ground. There was Tim, on the ground alongside another man and some bags. She watched in stunned silence as he was hit once, and then again before the gunmen stopped. Unable to grasp what was really happening, she began to cry and scream wildly when the man on the ground next to Tim suddenly gunned down the attacker.

She regained some control when the shooting stopped and her crying slowly devolved into sporadic sobbing between deep breaths. It was then that she realized she was standing naked, having absentmindedly dropped the towel. Staggering backwards until she found the side of the bed, she grabbed for the sheet and pulled it around her.

Now, sitting there trembling, she has no idea what to do.

🜨

Carmela had also watched the raging battle from inside her room. Raffi was kneeling on the sidewalk only a few feet from her window when he was shot the second time.

When the gunfire first started, she had called out to him. Part of her had desperately wanted to rush outside to help but she knew it wasn't safe. She felt herself torn again when he began slowly crawling toward his car. Still, she knew she couldn't go to him.

Though his pain gripped her heart, a harsh realization had come over her. Even if he survives, she no longer wants to be with him. She can never be with someone so greedy, someone whose plans so carelessly and ruthlessly result in so much death.

Like Cyndi, she fell back on her bed crying, wondering what will happen now.

🜨

Mortally wounded, Tim is barely conscious. He knows he was hit at least once, but he's not feeling any pain. Nor is he aware of the growing pool of blood forming underneath his body. He tried to roll away when the gunfire started, but the shots hit him in the back. One bullet paralyzed him, lodging in his spine at the base of his neck. The other ripped through his liver.

Lying on his back and confused by the lack of pain, the possibility he's rapidly bleeding to death doesn't cross Tim's mind. Instead, his last thoughts are how embarrassing this will all appear. Being shot at a cheap motel while on a date won't fly well with his wife, or with his colleagues at work.

▲

TD glances around the room one last time to make sure he's leaving nothing behind. After replacing the phone book and moving the furniture back, there's nothing to indicate he was there. It's time to leave.

Checking the courtyard again, he's surprised to see the kid has somehow made it to his car. He wonders if it will even start, having taken a heavy spray of gunfire, but then he hears the engine turn over.

There's still no sign of movement from Tim or anyone else on the ground. TD debates if he should go out and check if anyone is alive and needs help before he leaves. Part of him says he should, another tells him to let the EMTs handle things.

Besides, now is probably the best time to get out of there unnoticed. It's only a few steps from his door to the corner of the building and he can be on his way.

▲

Bobby Tomlin had run out into the courtyard when the attackers' car had gone flying by. Yelling as he chased after it, he didn't get far before halting in shock. After somehow avoiding another crash, two men had then jumped out, waving guns as they screamed at Eddie.

Instinctively, Bobby knew he couldn't remain standing out in the open. He quickly retreated to the area around the vending machines, in the enclosed walkway running between the front office and the rooms. As he crouched, between a soda machine and the constantly broken icemaker, he remembered that he had never called 911. He had also left his cell phone back at the front desk.

He briefly considered working his way back to the office; he could keep going through the walkway and come around from the other side. Instead, with his fear prevailing, he stayed put. Then the gunfire had erupted in the courtyard.

Bobby instantly regretted ever taking Eddie's gratuities. Whatever was happening, the police would surely arrive any time now. And they will be asking questions. How can he explain to them, or his boss, that he regularly takes cash from Eddie? Or why he hasn't reported the suspicious activities taking place each month?

And there's more. Bobby thinks he recognizes one of the gunmen. If he's right, he has seen the guy visiting Carmela plenty of times the past few months. She even mentioned his name once, 'Raffi', or something like that. And now he's out there running around with a gun.

When the gunfire finally stops, Bobby is still cowering next to the soda machine. Its humming compressor is making it difficult for him to hear if anyone is moving in the courtyard. With overwhelming curiosity, he emerges from his hiding place and cautiously peers around the corner. So shaken by what he sees, his legs buckle. Whatever he had expected to discover, it didn't include a blood-soaked Raffi, struggling as he pulls himself up into his car amid the nightmarish carnage of bodies strewn everywhere.

Bobby watches as Raffi uses the car's door to pivot into the driver's seat. Blood covers his chest and he's hardly able to stand due to a terrible wound on his right leg. He can't believe Raffi thinks he can drive; he obviously needs urgent medical assistance. With compassion overcoming his fear, Bobby moves toward the car, hoping to stop him from trying to drive. Maybe he can provide some kind of first aid before the guy bleeds to death.

Raffi is completely unaware of Bobby's presence. Despite agonizing pain, he has made it behind the wheel. His next prayer is answered when the engine starts on the first attempt. He knows the crippled car won't make it far before overheating, but that's no worry; he's not going to make it very far either. Right now, he has only one goal: reaching Cesar near the Qwik Lube.

To exit the motel, he's going to have to first back up and then swing around to get moving in the opposite direction. As he sends the car in a reverse arc, the rear bumper slams into the low chain link fence surrounding the pool. Though he's driving like a drunk, the maneuver is effective. With waves of pain radiating through his body, Raffi floors the accelerator.

Barely holding his head up, he's stunned to see the motel clerk waving both arms, standing only a few feet ahead. Confused, as to why he's trying to make him stop, Raffi attempts to swerve around him but his reactions are slow. Between the pain and only one useable arm, he can hardly control the vehicle.

Bobby has no chance of getting out of the way. The impact from the front bumper shatters bones in both legs. As the car's fender slams into him, it propels his body back toward the building. Landing near the entrance to where he had just hidden, his head hits the sidewalk with a terrible smack.

His last thoughts as he loses consciousness are of his wife and kids smiling at him. Then, oddly, he thinks about the chemistry exam he was studying for just minutes earlier.

⅄

TD has stepped out of his room just in time to see the fleeing car ram the desk clerk. The ongoing spectacle of violence that has now engulfed another innocent bystander further disheartens him and leaves him motionless. At the same time, he realizes his idea of slipping around the corner and getting out of there is nothing but a delusion. There's no way he can leave without checking to see if anyone is alive and needs help.

Unfortunately, a quick scan of the bloodied bodies tells him the problem may not exist. Neither the driver of the Mercedes nor its passenger could have survived. The number of wounds and the amount of blood loss make that implausible. The two attackers who arrived on foot are both victims of massive, clearly fatal chest wounds. Rounding the rear of the car, he sees the other attacker, dead in a bloody heap on the sidewalk.

The only ones who appear to have any chance are Tim and Slick, and that's being really optimistic. Still, if there's a chance, he should help. Moving in closer, he uses his foot to edge aside one of the bags before squatting down next to them.

⋏

Cyndi has regained some composure, thanks to the lengthening silence in the courtyard. Wrapping the towel around her again, she moves to the window, hoping to see a sign that Tim has somehow survived.

As soon as she looks out, she nervously jumps to one side; there's a man coming from around the back of the car in her direction. He doesn't appear to have a gun, but the small bag over his shoulder seems out of place. Unexpectedly, he stops. After pausing and looking down, he lowers himself toward Tim.

⋏

Once he's close enough, TD presses two fingers firmly against Tim's neck. Sadly, there's no pulse. The large amount of blood pooling on the other side of his body is also telling. And now that he's closer to Slick, he can see there are just too many wounds and too much blood.

Sensing movement, TD notices the curtains swaying in Tim's room. There, peering from the side of the window, he sees the distraught, tear-streaked face of Tim's date. Making eye contact, he frowns as he slowly shakes his head.

Again, he feels the urge to flee. Anytime now, he'll be hearing the first of many sirens. Looking toward the desk clerk, lying limp and motionless on the sidewalk, he decides there's no reason to go over. He saw the car strike him as well as how his body was tossed aside. And that was before his head smacked the ground. Even if he has miraculously survived, TD doesn't know what he could do for him.

⋏

Raffi can go no further. Turning the car onto the main road is all he can manage before slumping over the wheel, causing the vehicle to veer sharply to the right. Even without his foot on the gas, there's enough momentum for the front wheels to hop the curb.

The car comes to a stop after a slow motion crash into the frame of a bus stop canopy. It's the best thing that could have happened for Raffi, possibly saving his life. Immediately past the bus stop is the parking lot exit where Cesar is waiting.

With the crash partially blocking traffic, Cesar is able to pull out into the right lane and then back up close to the bus stop. Jumping out and circling behind his car, he ignores the honking and cursing of the drivers now trapped in the lane behind him.

Cesar is horrified when he sees Raffi's condition. He can't believe his friend made it this far. Working quickly, he drags Raffi's bloody, semi-conscious body to the front seat of his car. When he's back behind the wheel he floors it, taking off into the late-evening traffic, headed anywhere he can find Raffi some help.

⅄

As he stands, TD is careful to avoid picking up any blood on his shoes or pants. It's then, looking at the pavement for a clean spot to step, that his attention is drawn one last time to the bags alongside the two dead men. Letting curiosity trump his need to leave, he decides he must learn what the target of tonight's mayhem was.

Lifting the closest bag by the strap, he pulls the zipper back several inches before quickly reclosing it. He isn't surprised; the bag appears to be loaded with cash. Without setting it back down, he stares over at the second bag, while appreciating the wholly unpredictable nature of the moment.

The only reason he's here at this random place and time is that Tim Crane felt like getting laid tonight and it's his pathetic job to take photos proving that. But instead of a routine surveillance, a set of completely unrelated events has dropped him into this violent, bizarre circumstance, standing next to two lifeless bodies, holding a bag packed with an untold amount of money.

With blood and death all around him, and the approaching sirens now in his ears, adrenaline has started racing through TD's system. Without warning, a wave of unbridled elation washes over him. It's as if he's a completely new and different person than he was just seconds ago. Suddenly, anything seems possible.

Shaking his head, TD reminds himself nothing has changed. He's obviously suffering some kind of psychological reaction to witnessing a violent death for the first time. He needs to simply calm himself, put the bag down, and get out of there.

Before he acts, the feelings of euphoria return. Without another thought, he decides he will take the money, all of it. It doesn't matter that he has no plan, or a single idea of what he will do next.

Stepping over Slick, TD shoulders the second bag and turns to leave. He almost loses his balance attempting to squeeze between the bodies and the rear of the Cadillac. To avoid falling, he braces himself on the car, triggering a flashback and another rush of excitement. He can vividly visualize Slick patting the trunk as the first delivery car pulled off.

Looking down, he nudges the dead man's jacket with his foot and hears the jingle of keys. Within seconds, he has the trunk open and is rewarded with a third bag. Throwing it over his shoulder with the others, he strides briskly from the courtyard. A final look back confirms he still got out of there before anyone else arrived or dared to come out of their room.

After rounding the corner of the building, he tries picking up his pace. Despite the effort, he begins moving increasingly slower. Carrying the three bags, along with his own, is proving awkward. The straps keep slipping from his shoulders and he's beginning to struggle under the weight. By the time he approaches his car, he's laboring to catch a breath.

A

Marvin Williams had been killing time since finishing his dinner earlier. Eddie had asked him to stay away for three hours tonight, but that's stretching it for someone with so little to do. Tired of receiving dirty looks from the restaurant manager, Marvin had finally started back to the motel using his usual shortcuts.

When he was about a block away, he heard gunfire. He could tell it was close by, but was unsure where the shots were coming from. Choosing to avoid whatever was going down, he had crouched behind a low hedge surrounding the bank parking lot. When the shooting finally stopped, he waited a little longer before finally continuing on to the motel.

About halfway across the small parking lot, he's surprised to see a man coming toward him carrying a heavy load of luggage. It's all a bit unusual, particularly since there's no sidewalk connecting the bank to the motel. Only a few locals like Marvin even know you can access the property from this side.

The man is really struggling as he continues forward. He's breathing heavily, with his head down, and looks as if he might tip over if he doesn't crash into Marvin first.

Speaking up to warn him, Marvin says, "Whoa there. You need some help, sir?"

Startled by the unexpected voice, TD jerks his head up. A slender, older man is standing between him and his car, staring at him with a confused look. TD had almost bumped into him. Embarrassed, he mutters an apology. After declining any help, he quickly maneuvers around the older man.

Taking no offense, Marvin shrugs his shoulders and wishes the man a good evening. He knows it's none of his business, but why had the guy parked way over here, instead of in front of his room? As odd as it seemed, including all those bags, he wonders if it had anything to do with the shooting he just heard.

A

After getting the bags stowed in the trunk of his car, TD sees that leaving quickly is going to be difficult. Traffic is bumper-to-bumper blocking the exit from the bank. Some kind of accident down to the right, past the motel, has slowed the vehicles in front of him to an almost imperceptible crawl. It's a huge problem; it can't be safe for him to continue sitting here for any amount of time.

Luckily, cars in both lanes are being forced to the curb as multiple first responders fight their way through the clogged traffic. He decides to dart into the first gap that opens and force his way across the two lanes in front of him. A left turn at the break in the median should soon put the gridlock in his rearview mirror.

With sirens growing louder and converging from multiple directions, TD finally sees the smallest of openings and propels his car into the street. Instantly, he's greeted by a blaring horn and a single whoop from a siren. As he slams on his brakes, he's nearly broadsided by a police cruiser squeezing through the center of the eastbound lanes.

Firing off another short blast of the siren, the young patrolman glares at TD. He then impatiently waves for him to continue though and move out of his way.

TD doesn't hesitate. Putting his foot on the gas, he finishes crossing to the westbound lanes. Moments later, he's rapidly moving away from the motel.

⅄

By the time he's several miles away, the ramifications of what he has done have started sinking in. With no forethought, on nothing but an impulse, he made a decision that instantly changed his life. Whatever happens going forward, he'll never be the same person again.

There's no time for considering why it happened; that can come later. Right now, he needs to figure out what he wants to do and the steps needed to achieve that. It's a topic he has given zero thought.

Later on, when he finds the time to reflect on these critical moments, he's sure he'll be disappointed with his decisions. He's already feeling a few regrets. He the hopes cash isn't drug money, or money gained by violence or exploitation. He tells himself it doesn't have that feel, but he knows he's really just guessing, with no basis in fact.

He's also aware that his emotions are affecting his thinking. He has already come up with several lame excuses for taking the money, like not wanting to leave it lying there on the ground for just anyone to grab. Another was not wanting to leave it there for some corrupt cop to take a piece.

The problem is none of the excuses makes much sense. And they have little to do with him, or why he took the bags. They're simply justifications he fabricated to overcome the objections his subconscious continues raising.

Deep inside his rational mind, he knows there's no logical way to defend the idea that the money should be his. But the reality of the situation is simple. At that deciding moment back at the motel, he wanted to take the money. And the current reality is that he wants to keep it.

Though it's not clear why, tonight's events have released him from the lethargy that's been strangling him since his wife left. From the moment he confirmed the bags were full of money, he has felt energized like never before. He can't remember having ever acted so boldly and decisively.

And the money, that's something too. Conveniently forgetting he already has plenty in the bank, TD begins thinking about the cash and the freedom it can bring. He wonders how much there is, and if it could be as much as he thinks.

He begins dreaming of what he might do with it, of where he might go, and how it will change his life. It's all quite exciting.

It's almost as if he has achieved some kind of victory this evening, some kind of personal triumph.

Monday Night

S hadows have begun to cloak the gruesome seen as darkness settles on the motel courtyard. The first law enforcement personnel to arrive are Fairfax City Police Officers Kenny Clarkson and Sean Landry. Both are young, African-American, and up-and-comers on the small town's police force. It's a police force with little experience handling violent crime. Over the coming hours they will both prove their value.

Clarkson is first on the scene, but he almost didn't make it in one piece. Less than a block from the motel, he had barely avoided ramming a car that suddenly pulled into traffic directly in front of him. Now, as he slowly rolls into the parking area, he brings his cruiser to a stop as its lights illuminate the carnage.

Surveying the motionless and bloodied bodies, his attention is suddenly drawn to an older man he hadn't noticed when he first pulled in. Head down, moving from Clarkson's right toward the rooms, he appears unfazed by the bodies he's walking past. Clarkson watches as the man finally stops and stares down at two of the victims lying to the rear of a bullet-riddled car.

Clarkson wants to determine quickly if any of the shooting victims require medical attention, but he needs to deal with this fellow first. He doesn't know whether he's a part of what just happened or a curious interloper. Whichever it is, the guy has ignored the presence of a police car with flashing lights while walking into the center of a bloody crime scene.

Jumping from his car, Clarkson draws his weapon and shouts, "Freeze! Get down on the ground!"

Marvin is confused by the contradiction of the commands. How can he 'freeze' and at the same time 'get down'? Having seen police in action too many times, he decides that lying on the ground is probably what the frantic young cop really wants him to do.

As he gets down, the officer begins to approach him from behind. Looking back toward him, Marvin pleads, "What did I do, officer? I didn't do anything. I just got here."

Clarkson responds by issuing more commands. "That's all fine, but I want you to stay on the ground. And put your arms behind your back."

As the man again complies, Clarkson reaches down and grabs his wrists. As he applies handcuffs, Marvin softly moans, "I don't know what I did. What did I do?"

Kenny feels badly about restraining the old man. His first instinct is that the guy is just a witness, maybe trying to help someone he knows. But Clarkson has never been confronted by such a massacre, and the grisly crime scene has put him on edge. Besides, there's no reason to take chances. What if the man is armed, or connected in some way to what happened?

With the cuffs secure, Clarkson frisks him while barking out questions. In rapid succession, he asks for his name, what he's doing there, and if he knows anything about the shootings.

Faced with another round of multiple requests, Marvin decides to keep it simple. "No sir, I don't know anything about this. It's like I told you, man; I just got here. Just like you."

Marvin's calm, pleading demeanor helps Kenny relax a bit. Seeing the flashing lights of additional police and emergency vehicles climbing the driveway also lets him know he won't be alone for much longer.

As he holsters his pistol, he says, "Alright sir. I'm going to help you stand up now. Unfortunately, this is a bad situation here and I found you standing in the middle of it. Hopefully we can get those cuffs off soon, but first I'm going to need some more information. Now, please tell me your name, and then exactly what you're doing here."

"My name is Marvin. Marvin Williams. And I live here." Nodding toward the open door of his room, he says, "I was just coming home after dinner. That room over there is mine."

"Which room?"

"Room 112, Sir."

Looking past the bodies, Clarkson can see the door to the room is open. At the same time, he notes what could possibly be two bullet holes in the wood siding adjacent to the door. The room may very well belong to Marvin, but with the open door and a potential connection to the shootings, no one is going in there for the moment. They'll have to wait for the detectives and further questioning.

Having finally concluded Marvin is not a safety risk, Kenny decides to un-cuff him. "Alright, Mister Williams, I'm sorry to have had to restrain you, but I'm just doing my job. I'm going to un-cuff you, but you may not leave here, at least for now. I'm pretty sure one of the detectives is going to want to question you. Unfortunately, you also won't be allowed back inside your room until someone from the police gives the okay."

Kenny decides the best place to have Marvin wait is the sidewalk area in front of the rooms at the end of the row. He tells Marvin that even though it may take a while, he's to wait there until someone from the police interviews him and clears him to leave.

Sean Landry is the second officer to arrive and there are two EMT's on his heels. After stopping his cruiser immediately behind Clarkson's, the first thing he observes is Kenny removing handcuffs from a man. As Sean moves towards them, Clarkson yells over, "I've got this. But I haven't had time to check if anyone is alive."

Landry begins taking in some of the details in the area illuminated by the cruisers' headlights. The number of victims and size of the crime scene stun him. He carefully works his way along the sidewalk in front of the rooms, encountering body after body. Each one appears lifeless. As the EMTs begin checking the victims more closely, he works his way over to Clarkson, who has left the guy he was with and is now standing by the driver's side of the Mercedes.

"Hey Kenny, can you believe this? I've never seen anything like it. I've got the count at seven. It looks bad. I'd be surprised if any are alive." Nodding toward Marvin, he asks, "Who's that over there? A witness?"

Clarkson is closely studying the Mercedes. As he bends over a little further, he begins peering inside as he tells Landry that Marvin claims to live at the motel. He's having him wait off to the side for further questioning. Looking up at his fellow patrolman, he says, "Hey Sean, did you count this guy in the backseat? If not, I think it's going to be eight. Eight victims."

Both men shake their heads. Neither has ever seen a shooting death since joining the force, nor for that matter any death other than in a car accident. Fairfax City has had a total of only four homicides for the past three years combined.

Clarkson says, "I'm calling Roberts. And we need to protect this crime scene. Why don't you start setting up a perimeter? As soon as I'm off the phone I'll come and help."

'Roberts' is Carl Roberts, Chief of Detectives on the small force and currently lead investigator for major crimes in Fairfax City. Clarkson leaves him a brief but urgent message when the detective's phone rolls over to voice mail.

The act of making the call focuses Kenny on the work that needs to be done. It also heightens his awareness of what's going on around him. He sees that the doors to several more rooms have opened, but at least for now the occupants are staying inside. Additionally, onlookers are gathering at the entrance to the motel, where Landry is running the first line of police tape.

Moving to help, Kenny begins to think about what may have happened here. He also notes that with such a large amount of work to do, maybe there will be a role for him. He'll find out soon enough. By the time they finish securing the crime scene, someone higher up the chain of command will have arrived.

⅄

Less than ten miles away, TD is nearing his condo apartment in Burke Centre. For the moment, he has stopped fantasizing about the future. More sobering thoughts have begun occupying his mind as the powerful emotional rush from taking the money begins to wane.

Obviously, police investigators will want to talk with anyone who was at the motel tonight. But that's not his real problem. There will soon be people out there trying to locate and retrieve their money.

As he pulls up in front of his building, he reminds himself to stay calm. Even with the police arriving as he departed the motel, it's too early for them to have developed any real understanding of what happened there this evening. It's also highly unlikely anyone at the scene can identify him. They might be able to provide a vague description, but certainly not his name.

Regardless, it's probably not a good idea to sit around his apartment tonight, waiting to find out if he's correct. Instead, he'll hide out somewhere close by while he figures out what he wants to do next.

⚐

With an assist from Clarkson, Landry has finished enclosing a large part of the courtyard with yellow police tape. Surveying the crime scene, he notices two of the EMTs on their knees. They appear to be administering to the victim most separated from the others, close to the alcove near the front office. There are also a handful of spectators hovering there, edging closer to the EMTs with curiosity.

The presence of the onlookers causes Landry to realize there are still 'civilians' inside the police tape. Stepping towards them, he calls for Clarkson to follow and help with crowd control. As they approach the alcove, one of the EMTs rises from his crouch. He tells them that though the victim is unconscious, he's alive. But he's the only survivor.

While Sean continues talking with the EMT, Clarkson quickly moves the spectators back into the alcove behind a new line of police tape. While doing this, he discovers they are all residents of the motel. Unfortunately, each has a room on the backside of the building and there's not a witness among them. He does learn the surviving victim works part-time at the front desk. His name is Bobby.

Moving back into the courtyard, Clarkson sees Landry is now taking notes as he huddles with two other EMTs. With several objectives in mind, Kenny begins knocking on the doors of the rooms facing the courtyard. He needs to confirm there's no one else hurt, or that someone involved in what happened isn't hiding inside one of the rooms. At the same time, he hopes to identify potential witnesses.

His quick survey finds no one injured, nor in any way suspicious. The occupants of Rooms 102 and 104 are unharmed and relatively calm, both claiming to have seen nothing. But two other individuals stood out. A young woman in Room 110 was noticeably distraught and had been crying heavily. Another in 114 had also been crying and was visibly shaken.

Kenny told each of them to stay put and to expect someone to come by with a more questions. He's fairly sure that the two who were crying witnessed some part of what happened. And he can't forget about Marvin Williams, now pacing in front of the rooms at the end of the row, looking increasingly nervous.

He then sees Detective Roberts, already firing off questions at Landry as he steps under the police tape. Clarkson walks over in time to hear Sean finish his debriefing on the casualties: seven dead from gunshot wounds, one critically injured survivor. A car leaving the scene apparently struck the young man. After waiting for Roberts to digests the news, Clarkson tells him about the potential witnesses he has lined up.

Roberts listens to the patrolman's report with raised eyebrows, finally saying, "Good job, Clarkson; you too, Landry. That's exactly what I need to know. Okay, listen up. Right now, we need to control this crime scene until the evidence techs arrive. It's also obvious we need more help. More patrolmen are on their way, but I think I'm going to call the County for some reinforcements."

Roberts looks intently at the two young officers assessing if they're up to the task. "Listen. We need to interview these witnesses before they start imagining things they never saw. Landry, for now, you control access to this crime scene. We have to keep everyone from tromping all over the evidence. They'll be moving that survivor out of here any minute. After that, no one gets in here who doesn't need to. And help get some lighting set up ASAP so we can see what we're doing."

Quickly glancing at the nameplate on the other patrolmen's chest, Roberts proceeds. "Alright, Clarkson, I need you to help with witness interviews. Start with the occupants of 102 and 104."

"Yes Sir."

"And Clarkson; think like a detective. I know they said they saw nothing, but we need to make sure. Think about what they're not saying almost as much as what they are. And ask every question twice. You'll do a good job. Yell if you find out something major. I'll check back with you in a couple of minutes after I call the Chief and we get all hands on deck."

Both patrolmen are flush with excitement as they move off to their assignments. Though disappointed at drawing the logistics role, Sean grins at Kenny and gives him a thumbs-up. Kenny is walking on air as he suppresses a smile, heading toward his first witness interview ever, for a major crime.

Carl Roberts looks around making sure he has a solid grasp on what he's facing before putting out requests for help. His working assumption is this was a matter of bad guys versus bad guys. Your average law-abiding citizen is simply not running around with either the armament or the attitude required to create the results in front of him.

The whole affair is quite possibly drug related. Often there's large-scale trafficking involved when you see this level of violence. For help on that angle, he'll rely on the City's lead narcotics investigator. He'll want some hard evidence before his theory is more than simple conjecture. Having learned from Landry that three of the dead are young Hispanics, he also makes a note to involve the County's Gang Taskforce at some point.

⋏

On the Beltway, already miles away, Raffi is still alive but bleeding badly as he lies back in the passenger seat. Next to him, Cesar is driving just over the speed limit, trembling as he grips the wheel with both hands.

Cesar had considered stopping at nearby Fairfax Hospital, but Raffi vetoed the idea. Even in his delirium, he knew that wouldn't work. Only five miles from the motel, if he had spent any time in the hospital's emergency room his arrest would be guaranteed. Emergency rooms always report gunshot victims to the police. Connecting him to the nearby shootings would be short work. Besides, they might be bringing in other survivors, if anyone else made it.

Raffi knows he needs help or he'll die. He just doesn't have the connections to find a private doctor quickly enough. Through the fog of pain, and Cesar's exhortations to keep his eyes open, he manages to tell his friend to head south. There aren't a lot of choices and he's going to have to gamble on using an emergency room. They'll drive to Woodbridge and he'll take his chances at Potomac Hospital. He'll work on some kind of a story for the gunshot wounds and hopefully he can be treated and get out of there before the police intervene.

Raffi had passed out before they finally approached the turn into the emergency room. He would be sharing Cesar's disappointment if he were awake. The place is swarming with people unloading two ambulances delivering victims of a recent traffic accident. There's even a State Police car parked in the driveway.

Briefly panicked, with no one to suggest options, Cesar drives past the hospital without entering. He then remembers there's a new medical center in Stafford, further south towards Fredericksburg. It's another twenty miles, and still not far enough to avoid the police forever, yet it may be the right balance of risk. There's also the fact that it hardly matters. It's the next closest hospital, and about as far as Raffi will be able to go and still survive.

Trying to remain optimistic, Cesar tells himself if his good friend can just make it to Stafford alive, he might have a chance at making it through this.

⟁

Inside his apartment, TD wrestles with a balky zipper on one of the two bags he brought in with him. Once the zipper finally relents, he can see the bag is filled with straps of cash. Disappointingly, it appears they're each made up of only twenty-dollar bills. It's a lot of money, but he expected more.

His reaction is quite different after opening the second bag. This time it's a mix of excitement and awe when he finds nothing but hundreds, wrapped in tight straps worth ten thousand dollars apiece. He won't count it now, but a quick guesstimate indicates a large sum. Depending on the contents of the third bag, still out in the trunk of his car, the total could approach seven figures.

Before closing the zippers, he quickly rifles through both bags to ensure money is all he has acquired. He can't risk having unwittingly gained possession of a stash of drugs, or some other surprise like a stolen weapon. Finding nothing, he makes a mental note to inspect the third bag later.

As he decides on what to do next, a thought strikes him. When he leaves this place to hide out somewhere, it's likely not going to be just for one night. It's quite possible that he's leaving for good, and that's no small thing. Is he really prepared to leave the area where he has lived his entire adult life?

There's certainly no attachment to this apartment; he only purchased it a little over a year ago. He once shared a nice home with his wife and even continued living there for some time after she was gone. Eventually, he sold it and moved here. The move was one of self-isolation. He has no connection to this neighborhood, either past or present. Since living here, he has had no more than a few thirty-second conversations with a single neighbor.

He remembers when the real estate agent showed him the odd, almost hidden residence. The builder had created separate, basement-level apartments beneath the rows of town homes; it was a way to cram a few extra units into the small development. With only a single window and sliding glass door on the rear side, the cave-like property was perfect for the way he felt at that time in his life.

Now, from the perspective of his imminent departure, TD can see he never truly lived here. Sure, there's ample evidence someone occupies the place. Along with the furniture, there are several shelving-units loaded with books. There's also food in the kitchen and clothes in the closets. But other than the reading material, there's nothing indicating any personal connection. There's not a potted plant, no knickknacks, nor a single picture or piece of artwork on any wall.

The austere living space makes it easy to refocus on getting out of there. As he does, a sense of the adventure ahead begins to lift his spirits. Moving to his bedroom, he begins packing his largest suitcase with a limited selection of clothes. In parallel, he works on a mental inventory of other items he should take. Logistically, he needs to travel lightly.

He can certainly afford to replace anything he leaves behind, but he hates the idea of abandoning his books. He considers packing several boxes and somehow arranging to get them later, but soon snaps out of the drifting thoughts. With the urgency of the situation reasserting itself, he decides the smart thing to do is get away from here fast, with no contingencies. Anything he's taking must fit in the suitcase, a carry-on bag, or his laptop briefcase.

As he leaves the bedroom, his eyes fall upon the only photo in the apartment, framed and sitting on the end of the dresser. The picture is of an attractive woman in her thirties, a 'glamour' shot, using professionally applied makeup and lighting. He remembers it fondly. He had arranged to have it taken several years ago as a present to his wife.

Picking it up, he hesitates. Glancing around, he looks for something to wrap the frame in to pack safely in the luggage. Then his eyes return to the photo. After a long, close study, he changes his mind and sets it back in place.

Quickening his pace, he moves to the apartment's second bedroom, which serves as his office. A large desk, along with more bookshelves lining every wall, covers nearly all of the floor space. Rummaging through the drawers, he searches for items that might prove important or useful. He pockets an old Swiss Army knife for no particular reason. Nearly every other item he rejects. He finally extracts two portable computer hard drives from a bottom drawer. The drives contain digitized versions of every photo he has taken on any case. They also contain information on the personal contacts he has accumulated over the years and scanned copies of his favorite case files.

Inside the room's closet, next to a four-drawer file cabinet, a small fire-proof safe is bolted to the floor. After keying in the digital combination, the first thing he removes is a handgun, along with a box of ammunition. Next, he grabs a clasped envelope containing his passport and birth certificate. This is followed by a second envelope containing a set of excellent fake IDs for several different names. He had acquired the forgeries several years ago as a tangent to a fraudulent claims investigation.

As he begins to close the safe, he realizes that taking the gun with him requires a decision. Does he intend to load it and keep it at the ready? Is he planning to pack it in his luggage?

Choosing a third option, he returns it to the safe. There has been enough killing over the money now in his possession. If a weapon is necessary to maintain that possession, then he doesn't want it.

⚊

On his way to the motel, Carl Roberts had listened to the radio as dispatch called for all on-duty officers and ambulances. Even before arriving, he had guessed the crime scene might be too large for the city's small force. His debrief with the patrolmen told him things were worse than anticipated. Since he took this job, Fairfax City has averaged just over a single killing per year. Now it looks like they've had more than five years' worth in just one night.

The work in front of them will easily overwhelm the manpower at his disposal. A recent spike in robberies has swamped his small team, leaving them tired and stretched thin from working overtime. Other than himself, he has only one free man to put on this. And there's no way they have enough evidence technicians.

His only option for getting the resources they need is going outside the department. He can call the Virginia State Police, but historically the city has chosen to liaison with Fairfax County. The county maintains a huge police department, scaled to serve a sprawling, wealthy, and heavily populated area. It has always been able to assist when asked.

Roberts calls the city's Chief of Police, Bill Simmons. Fielding the request, Simmons wastes no time phoning his counterpart with the county. Unfortunately, he's forced to leave a message. Out of professional courtesy, he waits several minutes before making a second call. Using an established procedure for situations exactly like this, he contacts the county's Deputy Chief of Operations.

After the briefest of niceties, Simmons gives him the headlines and communicates the need for two or three evidence technicians and at least one experienced homicide detective. The Deputy Chief tells him he'll they'll be happy to do what they can. His Chief of Detectives, Frank Aldretti, will be in contact soon.

$\blacktriangle$

TD is ready to hit the road. He also wants to call Phil Madrigal. It was Phil who had cajoled him into taking the job of tailing Tim Crane to begin with. He knows Phil's wife won't be thrilled with him calling at this hour, but he's convinced of the need to talk with his closest friend and at least let him know he's leaving

If it weren't for the odd hour, TD would look like any businessman leaving for a trip. As he moves out the front door with his first load, he's pulling the carry-on behind him, with one of the gym bags perched on top, and his laptop case over a shoulder. With his free hand, he calls Phil's cell phone.

He had hoped his buddy would answer quickly, but he never picks up. Leaving a voice message, TD tells him it's critical that they talk, preferably no later than first thing in the morning. He also asks Phil to meet him at Noon, at a bar called The End Zone.

With the first load stowed in the car, TD returns inside a final time to retrieve the second bag of cash and the remaining luggage. As he's locking the deadbolt on the front door, Phil returns his call.

Starting in immediately, Phil uses a loud whisper to complain about TD calling so late. Without pausing, he adds that he definitely can't make it for a meeting at Noon. "Maybe you forgot, but some of us still work for a living," he says sarcastically.

Failing to elicit a response, Phil senses he may have been too harsh on his friend. "Is everything okay, TD? If you really need to talk right now, let's do it. Or can it wait until tomorrow?"

"You won't believe what happened to me tonight, but that's okay, it'll hold. Though I'm telling you, it's big, really big."

"Thanks, man. I probably shouldn't talk now. Anne's giving me the evil eye. Look, let's do this; I should be able to get there by two at the latest. We'll talk then. I'll let you know if my schedule improves and I can make it earlier."

A car turns onto TD's street just as he ends the call. Watching it slow as it approaches his row of homes, its headlights fall directly on him. For a brief moment, he's brightly illuminated as he stands in front of his door.

When the car passes, he can see it's just one of his neighbors. Still, the incident is enough to spook him. Grabbing the luggage, he moves quickly for his car.

⋏

Kenny Clarkson's first interview is a total bust. Keen with enthusiasm to highlight his investigative skills, he ends up with little of value to the case.

A woman in the first room was watching television when she heard the shooting begin. She immediately ran to the bathroom and huddled in the tub. She claims to have had just left the bathroom and was preparing to look outside when he had knocked on her door a little earlier. Having seen nothing, she has no idea what happened.

Back in the courtyard, Clarkson sees things are much busier. Sean Landry is helping set up portable lighting with one of the evidence technicians that have arrived. Another tech has also started working. She's carefully moving around the bodies, leaving small weighted flags to mark various spots while circling other areas with chalk boundaries. At one point, Roberts calls to her, pointing at something he wants her to examine.

Clarkson also notices Marvin Williams, smoking a cigarette as he continues walking in front of the rooms at the far end. The man looks far more agitated than earlier. Clarkson considers questioning him next, but then remembers his orders. He decides to finish the second interview he was assigned, then he'll head over to talk with Marvin again.

⚔

Pacing, as he puffs on one Newport after another, Marvin is thinking about Eddie King. Earlier, he only got a quick look behind the Mercedes before the policeman detained him. Since then, he kept telling himself he couldn't be sure what he had seen.

Once they started turning on the additional lighting, he was able to get a clearer view of the bodies. Now, he has no doubt. Eddie is dead, lying in a wide pool of blood. Besides feeling deep sadness, Marvin is also becoming increasingly nervous.

He's well clear of the probation he served, but that doesn't mean he wants to start dealing with the police again. Just look at how the young cop had treated him, yelling all those confusing commands. And then he cuffed him, all for nothing more than walking home. Just a moment ago, he had caught the same damn cop staring at him from across the way.

Lighting another cigarette, he considers how rapidly this night has turned bad. His benefactor is dead and he's even forbidden from entering his own room. Worse, the police will soon want to question him.

⚔

Marty Carpentier is one of the youngest members of Eddie's team. He has worked for The Group for over a year, primarily as a driver. He was recently added as a courier for the consolidations and was second to make his drop tonight. Within minutes of leaving the motel, he was atop a stool at the Hooters, just down the block, across the street from the Qwik Lube.

Marty is a regular at the restaurant's bar and well liked. One of the barmaids gave him the nickname 'Frenchy', mostly because of his last name, but partly due to his ceaseless flirting with the buxom waitresses. He's finishing his second beer when another of tonight's couriers calls with an invitation. He's with a couple of girls looking to party. Marty flashes a broad smile as he agrees to meet up with them.

Outside the restaurant, he's shocked to see the mayhem that has descended on the area. It couldn't have been more than an hour since he made his drop and headed for the bar. Looking around, he can see clusters of people gathering across the street and traffic is badly snarled. Police and emergency vehicles are weaving their way in and out of the motel. Then it sinks in; he should get over there. Barring some kind of bizarre coincidence, Eddie might be in trouble.

As he crosses the four-lane boulevard, he sees a small crowd gathered near a car that has wrecked into the bus stop. That can't be what this is all about, there must be more. Before going to the motel, he decides to check in with Petey Bowman.

Behind the Qwik Lube, he encounters what used to be Petey's car, now a misshapen pile of metal with a second vehicle embedded in its side. A rescue team is working to get inside the vehicles, but with no real urgency. There's an EMT standing to one side, yet no one is attempting any emergency medical care. The meaning is clear.

Now even more worried about Eddie, Marty wastes no time. Circling back around the front of the building, he makes it to the motel driveway before a line of police tape blocks his progress. Frustrated, and becoming desperate to find out what has happened, he resorts to asking others in the growing group of onlookers standing along the tape.

With an air of excitement, one spectator tells him there's "a bloodbath" at the motel. A young man wearing a name badge from the mattress store in the shopping center turns to them both and says, "Yeah, I hear there are bodies everywhere. When they were shooting, it was like Call of Duty came to life over there for a couple of minutes."

Marty can't believe he was sitting in a bar across the street and missed whatever happened. With Petey dead, and reports of a gunfight, he knows what he's supposed to do.

Rushing back across the street, his cell phone in hand, he looks up a number he has never called before. Once inside his car he makes the call. He needs to stay calm and focus on what he's going to say to whoever answers.

⅄

Daniel Keach handles security matters for Wilkins Investment Group, a long-standing privately held firm specializing in real estate development across the region. Behind the public façade of its real estate business, Wilkins also operates the organization known as The Group.

Fit and handsome, in his late-forties, Dan Keach has already garnered over twenty years' experience in his field. His career started with an eight-year stint as an officer in the military, working in special-ops. He followed that with a series of overseas tours as a contractor for a global paramilitary security firm.

Motivated by a desire to settle down stateside, Dan reinvented himself. Supplementing his experience with a fresh Master's Degree, he tailored his skills to meet a growing demand in the field of corporate security and risk management. Though a lot less exciting then his prior endeavors, there were plenty of clients. He also avoided the considerable risks associated with working in some dusty overseas province.

Unfortunately, he soon found the work too mundane. And his earnings were nothing spectacular. His solution to the problem was to seek different clients with targeted service offerings. He began offering security and risk management consulting to organizations that pursue activities of questionable legality. Sometimes there was no question at all.

It took a while to learn the ropes of approaching such clients but he soon found plenty of work, always through referrals. A good portion of what he does would be termed corporate espionage. After helping companies counter such activities, he now advises how to launch them. Sometimes he handles the work personally.

Keach finds his new trade to be significantly more lucrative. And the nature of the some of the assignments, along with the elevated risk, provides much of the missing excitement he craves. On top of that, he'd be the first to tell you that he is good at what he does.

A few years ago, he received a referral to Richard Wilkins. In this case, there was no request for black ops. Wilkins needed help establishing security protocols and money-laundering schemes for less subtle endeavors.

Now the firm is Keach's primary client, providing him with eighty- to ninety-percent of his income. His written contract barely exceeds one page, and along with the invoices he submits, designates his work as 'Risk Management Consulting'. He reports directly to Richard Wilkins, as well as providing counsel to the firm's CFO, Robert Owen. His compensation is piecemeal, though quite generous. Each month he receives checks from Wilkins Investment Group, as well as several of its unofficial subsidiary companies. For certain services, he receives sizable off-the-books cash payments.

Keach manages personnel like Eddie King, overseeing the operation and security of The Group's cash handling processes. He also advises the CFO regarding the requisite and complex money-laundering regime. He's always scouting new opportunities for sanitizing the increasing amounts of cash.

He also manages issues related to the collection of outstanding customer loan balances. His personal approval is required before 'resources' are to be deployed for what he terms as 'remittance compliance'. Keach may manage the organization's muscle, but he loves using corporate speak.

Tonight, things are not going well for Keach. He has become increasingly alarmed as each minute passes without receiving the 'All Clear' call from the consolidation's pick-up driver. He's even tested both of the cell phones he carries to eliminate bad reception as the problem. That was after repeatedly failing to contact either the driver or the pick-up car's onboard guard. It's inconceivable that neither can take his call. After also failing to reach Eddie King, he knows he faces a huge problem.

Finally, one of his phones rings. Unfortunately, it's a number he doesn't recognize using the line dedicated for emergencies. It's their newest courier,

Marty Carpentier. Rapidly, but without panic, he describes for Keach what he saw, what is rumored, and the little he knows as fact. Only then does he speculate about what has happened. He thinks someone attempted a hit on the pick-up car and has possibly succeeded.

After listening without interruption, Keach instructs Carpentier to hover near the scene for another half hour. He's to seek concrete information, but under no circumstances is he to engage with the police. He's to call again if he learns anything else. After thirty minutes or so, he's to return to his home and stay in place until someone contacts him.

Though briefly rattled, Keach's rising anger begins taking over, along with his desire to rectify the situation quickly. Losing over a half a million dollars is a major disaster, but it could be far worse than that. In a conversation with Robert Owen just last week, he learned the firm is facing extraordinary liquidity problems that are threatening its solvency.

For many years, Wilkins Investment Group relied heavily on a strategy that leverages the firm's cash and other assets to the maximum level. Every asset is fully collateralized. Profits are used to service debt or are poured into the next round of investments. This worked well when the economy was booming, but the recent recession and massive correction in the valuation of commercial real estate have nearly sunk the company.

Many firms with similar portfolios have already failed or been acquired for pennies on the dollar. Lately, the only thing keeping the company afloat has been infusions of cash from its illicit operations. Owen had requested a meeting last week to discuss the projections for those proceeds. He also wanted to explore possibilities for increasing them in the short-term.

If there was a successful hit on the consolidation tonight, it is paramount Keach locate and recover the money. To achieve that, he needs to learn exactly what happened and who's behind the job. There will also need to be some level of retaliation. You don't just sit back and absorb a hit like this without responding. He'll need to work that track in parallel. Right now, his priority is information, factual information.

⅄

Detective James Richter has been with Fairfax County's police department for twenty-two years. A solid cop over his early career, his rise through the ranks leveled off when he made Detective. He's currently assigned to Major Crimes, after multiple stints with Homicide and Vice.

Richter should be a lead detective, based on his years of experience, but he's plagued by mediocre results and a lack of drive. He has almost no chance of further promotion. His boss, Frank Aldretti, considers Richter a utility player, using him to fill slots for colleagues on leave or to supplement overloaded areas.

A little over a year ago, Richter found himself in debt to the wrong people. He loves playing poker, particularly No-Limit Texas Hold-em. He believes his investigative skills provide a real advantage, helping him identify his opponents' tells, the subtle facial expressions and behavioral idiosyncrasies that unmask a player's cards or intentions. Richter is actually correct in his beliefs; he's quite adept at spotting tells. Unfortunately, he gives off so many of his own that they more than offset any advantage he gains.

After a sustained run of moderate success at low-stakes home games, Richter sought bigger action. Using a referral from another card player, he gained access to a local private game with higher stakes and deep-pocketed players. He didn't care that it was an illegal game and they didn't seem to mind his presence, despite knowing he was a cop. It was the most well run game he had ever played in; everyone was friendly and took the card playing seriously. He even made a connection there to a bookie who would take his sports bets.

The new game was tougher and he no longer won as easily, but he still had some profitable nights. Over time though, the amount he dropped during his losing sessions began overshadowing his wins. Despite that clear signal, he continued playing at the higher level, telling himself he could beat the game with just a little better luck.

Then the pattern changed for the worse; he became a steady loser. Blaming an "unbelievably bad run of cards", he lost over $25,000, blowing through his meagre savings. Convinced he could win it back, he started borrowing from the host of the game. The losing accelerated as he pressed the action, playing several nights a week. After dropping another $25,000, he was informed his line of credit was exhausted. Finally coming to the realization that he had a problem, Richter decided to quit playing.

Unfortunately, the situation was far more complex than simply recognizing he was a bad card player; he was flat broke and maxed out on his credit cards. After paying alimony, rent, and modest living expenses each month, he had nothing left over to repay the money he owed. He also didn't know that his private game was one of those operated by The Group, or that his debt had come to the attention of Dan Keach.

About two weeks after the last time he played, a man called wanting to meet him for an early lunch. The voice was firm, almost commanding. It was time to discuss settling his gambling account. They agreed to meet at a pizzeria just outside the Beltway.

No one else was in the restaurant when he arrived. After taking a seat in a booth, a tall casually dressed man came through a swinging door behind the counter and walked toward him. He looked to be in his early-thirties at most, with long blonde hair tied in a ponytail that reached his shoulders. Richter expected him to offer a menu or ask to take his order. Instead, without saying anything, the man sat down across from him.

Smiling pleasantly, he introduced himself as Samuel. Then, with no other preliminaries, he got down to business. Using a calm soft tone, he said, "I believe that there's a relatively painless way to eliminate your outstanding debt. Do you like painless solutions, Detective Richter?"

Richter didn't miss the man's subtle emphasis on the words 'painless' and 'detective'. Both confused and a little fearful, he said nothing. This was not the voice, or the manner, of the guy on the phone who had set up the meeting.

Refusing to wait for a reaction, Samuel continued, using the same understated tone. "You often work Vice and know the detectives there. We don't want much. Just let us know when there are any investigations into gambling in the county. Also, anything related to loan sharking. You know, just a simple heads up if anyone is getting too close, or something might be coming our way."

Richter clearly understood the opportunity presenting itself. It could very well be a way out from under his debt, for what was probably very little in exchange. The department cares little about local card games or bookies, unless they become notorious. Friendly home games, along with private high-stakes games like those that The Group operates, draw little attention. And he had heard nothing in quite a while about illegal street finance. But there was an issue

Looking across at the blond-haired man, Richter said, "I might be able to help you. We rarely look into that kind of stuff, but when we do, I could let you know. However, there's one problem. How would I determine if something we're investigating is yours?"

Samuel's response was immediate and terse, no longer delivered with the same measured tone. "Then you'd better just let us know about anything like that. I mean anything at all. Because if we end up being harmed, others will be harmed. I'm sure you can understand that, Detective."

They stared at each other for a few seconds before Richter slowly nodded. Samuel smiled as he stood. Looking down at Richter, he said, "Why don't you stay and enjoy lunch on me. The chicken parm sub is excellent here."

Staring intensely at Richter for several seconds, Samuel finally added a warning. "Oh yeah. You also need to quit playing cards, Jimmy."

The use of a name no one had called him since he was a little boy felt like a smack across the face. It was even worse coming from this disrespectful punk. But Richter could do or say nothing. He watched as Samuel turned and walked past the counter, leaving by the door he had come through earlier.

Almost immediately, a teenage employee appeared at his booth with a plate containing the aforementioned chicken parmesan sub, chips, and a pickle wedge. Richter quickly spotted the business card peeking out from under the napkin. It was almost blank. There were no names or company logo printed on it. There was nothing other than a phone number.

Since that lunch meeting, he has played cards a few times, but only at a friendly game with some other cops. He never heard a word from anyone about the money he owed.

He had called the phone number on the business card just once. An investigation was gearing up to look into an alleged multi-table poker game running out of a home near Reston Town Center. They were not only dealing poker, but also selling drinks from a cash bar. It was rumored women were available at a nearby townhouse if players sought a different form of recreation. Richter related everything he knew to the man who answered his call. He received only a one-word response, "Thanks".

⬥

Tonight, Richter has been off-duty for several hours. After getting off a little late, he met a colleague for dinner, followed by several rounds of beers at the Irish pub near the courthouse. He's just starting on his way home when his cell phone rings. Not recognizing the number, he scowls at his phone, tempted to ignore it. Right before it rolls to voice mail, he takes the call.

Dan Keach begins talking the moment Richter answers. "How fast can you get over to the Gateway Motor Inn in Fairfax?"

"Who is this?"

"It's unimportant who I am, other than I arranged your debt settlement a while back. I need your help with a situation. Now. Tonight. Do you understand?"

Sneering, Richter responds with attitude, "Look, I don't like this, buddy. And it's getting late. Why don't you call back tomorrow and I'll work on helping you out then."

Richter's retort is followed by an extended moment of silence, long enough that he thinks the call might have been dropped. Then the caller begins speaking again.

"Listen closely, asshole, because I'm not in the mood to repeat myself. If you help me out with this situation tonight, you might get to keep your job. I may even consider your debt fully paid. But if you choose to fuck around with me for even another minute, then you're going to be worse than ruined."

After another considerable pause, Keach adds, "Are you ready to listen closely?"

Knowing that he is screwed, Richter mumbles, "Yeah, go ahead."

"That's better, Detective. Again, how fast can you get over to the Gateway Motor Inn in Fairfax? There were some shootings there tonight and someone may have taken a large amount of money that doesn't belong to them. You need to get in on that investigation. I don't care as much about the shooters as the money, for starters. Later, I'll want them as well."

"The Gateway? Wait a minute; that's inside the city limits. Sorry man, that's out of my jurisdiction. No can do."

"Look, jurisdiction is your fucking problem to figure out. I don't care if you have to quit your job and volunteer for duty. Get your ass over there and get me some information; and get if fast. Use this number to call me back. I'm serious. Don't screw this up. There are no gray areas here Richter. Help get the money back and we're square. If you fail, consider yourself totally fucked."

Richter is stunned, but knows he must at least try to do something. Even though it's not his jurisdiction, he knows it's not necessarily impossible. County detectives have worked with the city before. "Okay. I can be there in a couple of minutes, but…"

Before he can say anything more, the line goes dead.

As he turns his car toward the motel, Richter ponders his situation. He knows he messed up getting into such a big hole with poker, but he's furious at himself for something worse. He should have never agreed to a deal that could so easily put his career in jeopardy.

Now, with no idea what he'll find when he gets there, he has to figure out how to gain access to the investigation.

Every day is a long day for Frank Aldretti; it's the nature of his job. And when the Deputy Chief called, he knew it was about to get even longer. There has been a multiple homicide shooting in Fairfax City and it's more than they can handle. He's to call Chief Simmons right away detailing how much help they're able to provide.

Evidence technicians won't be a problem tonight, he can send several right away. An investigator is another matter. After scrambling a few techs, he scans the duty roster looking for a detective he can spare.

⋏

Though he had been only two miles away, it took Richter almost ten minutes to plow through the traffic surrounding the motel. When he finally reached the entrance on the main road, a patrolman told him he would have to park at the small shopping center next door.

After passing not one, but two odd car accidents, and weaving his way through the growing clusters of spectators, he can tell the city boys have a huge mess on their hands. And that's when it hits him. If this thing is actually that big, they're going to need help from the county. It's possible they've already requested it. Richter chuckles, realizing his threatening caller might have gotten it right after all. Volunteering might just work.

Frank Aldretti has yet to call Chief Simmons when his Caller ID shows Jim Richter is on the line. Definitely not a fan, he wonders why the man is calling at this hour. To his surprise, Richter is at the scene of the shootings. He claims he was having a few beers down the street when it all happened. Since he's already there, he's wondering if the city force has asked for help and if Aldretti wants him to make contact with someone on their team.

The detective's offer presents a perfect solution for Aldretti. Richter is currently doing follow-up work on two unsolved bank robberies, both taking small amounts. The investigations are moving slowly, and obviously not as urgent as this. Sparing him will present no real hardship, and it helps Aldretti and his department look good for sending over an experienced investigator so quickly. After giving Richter the go ahead, he immediately calls Simmons with the details.

Richter is thrilled having been attached to the investigation without a hitch. Maybe it's a sign his luck is finally changing. Though optimistic, he reminds himself to stay levelheaded; he still has to come through with some information. And he knows that a guy like the one he's dealing with may never be completely off his back. Still, who knows? Maybe this one is honorable. When he calls him back with the news, Richter is pleased to hear the man's tone shows an improved level of respect from their prior conversation.

Keach quickly provides a small amount of background information, followed by a terse set of directives. "Focus on finding the money. And let me know if the investigation turns up anything that links to a legitimate business."

Richter asks for clarification of the oddly worded second request, but gets none. Instead, losing his patience, Keach barks, "Just find out who has the fucking money!"

⅄

After hanging up on Richter, Dan Keach immediately calls the company's CFO. "Robert, we have a problem. It looks like someone hit the consolidation tonight. It's possible they got everything. I'm mobilizing for a recovery, but you need to understand there's a real possibility we could fail."

Keach can hear the fear and confusion in Owen's voice.

"What do you mean hit the consolidation? Someone stole our money?"

"Yeah, that's what I said."

Instantly, Owen becomes hysterical, "If that's true, then we're fucked. I'm telling you, Dan, WE ARE FUCKED. We need that cash right away or we're going to flat line."

"Robert, you need to calm down. You told me about the cash flow problems. I know this is serious. I'm going to work this hard, but I need you to settle yourself. I'm going to call Richard..."

"No, don't do that. I haven't told him yet how bad things are."

"Look, he needs to know. I'm setting up a meeting for nine tomorrow morning. Be prepared to talk frankly with him at that time. We can't solve this if we don't know the facts. You need to provide a snapshot of where we're at financially and what we need to do to address any problems that may arise. Until then, talk with no one about this."

Having calmed himself, Owen says, "The situation is bleak, Dan. There's not much we can do if you don't get that money back."

After a brief silence, Keach says, "Then I assume I have your permission to use whatever means are necessary to recover the cash?"

"Sure. Sure. Of course. Whatever you need to do."

It takes Robert Owen several seconds to realize the call had ended.

⚊

Keach braces himself for his next call. He knows Richard Wilkins's reaction won't be one of panic, as Owen's was. Still, it could be just as volatile; Wilkins is renowned for his bad temper.

Even though he's likely to be at home at this hour, Keach decides to call Richard's cell phone, actually hoping he doesn't answer. The man has a right to know what's going on, but he would be of little help with matters tonight. If he's lucky, he can leave a message setting up the morning meeting and break the news then, possibly with a more promising outlook.

When the call rolls to voice mail, he leaves a short message. After asking Wilkins to meet him at the office at nine, he says, "A serious security issue has arisen. It's critically important that we meet."

Keach is pleased he doesn't have to get into it with Wilkins now. Not only will he have more time to gather information, it also leaves his reins as loose as possible for whatever methods or 'resources' he may need to employ to fix the problem.

⚊

TD is back on the road, although his mood has changed considerably. There was something about the sweep of the headlights illuminating him as he left his apartment. It put him on the defensive, feeling hunted. It has also tempered his excitement about taking off with the money and starting a new life, though that's not a bad thing. He needs to focus on his current situation.

Obviously, the police will be seeking anyone involved. And whoever lost their cash will want it back. But it just doesn't seem possible that anyone could be looking for him; at least not specifically searching for 'TD Adkins'. The police will be focused on the shootings, with nothing that could link him to the assailants, the men they battled, or the money.

He tells himself there's no reason to continue going over this. He reaches the same conclusion each time he completes the exercise. Admittedly, he's a little less convinced than the first time he worked through it, but he remains confident enough. It's time to move on to other concerns.

Shifting his attention to his imminent departure, TD begins to realize the complexity of the task confronting him. He also understands that it would be a bad idea to attempt his disappearance ad hoc, in some kind of freewheeling maneuver. Before he makes too many moves, at a minimum he should come up with a solid idea of where he's heading and how he'll cover his trail.

The issue is where to do that planning. He knows he should already be on the highway, fleeing the area. If he drives through the night, he could easily be five hundred miles from here by mid-morning. With plenty of adrenalin still running through his system, he feels like he can drive forever. Right now though, he's on a side road heading toward the US Route 1 corridor, hardly ten miles from the motel.

TD also knows that the sooner he leaves the area and begins masking his trail, the better his chances for success. Within five days he can be almost anywhere in the country. But that's not the plan he's following, at least not yet. For now, he's staying in the immediate area, and will remain here well into tomorrow.

The good news is he's not lying to himself. He's fully cognizant of the reason he hasn't left yet. He doesn't want another personal relationship to end abruptly, without an explanation.

For the past two years, TD has spent much of his time in solitude. There have been times when a week or more might pass with his only human contact being with a random store clerk or restaurant server. Somehow, tonight's events have dramatically changed him, feeding a latent desire to end his self-imposed isolation and start his life anew.

Even before tonight, there have been signs his emotional isolation was ending. For several months now, he has frequently visited the same bar. The trips were always during the day, practically following a schedule. Right now, he's driving toward that same bar, located on Route 1.

The reason he hasn't yet left the area is so he can see a young woman who works there. That will have to wait until tomorrow. He needs to tell her he's leaving. It's even possible she'll consider coming along with him, though he understands the concept is probably silly.

Instead of dwelling on the idea, he shifts his thoughts back to the logistics of his departure. Finishing a quick mental inventory of everything he had packed, one item he left behind stands out: the framed photo of his wife. Maybe that's a sign he views tonight as a breaking point from the past.

For longer than a year, he had brooded constantly over her departure. Then he took to blocking out any thoughts of her, or their marriage's abrupt end. It allowed him to find brief moments of happiness, after a long period of when there was none; yet even that came with an emotional toll.

He only recently put the picture back out. He had placed it on one end of his bedroom dresser, hoping to find a balance between remembering her, and moving forward with his life.

⋏

TD's marriage had never been great, but it was by no means a bad one. Having no children was the only ongoing source of pain and disagreement. Over time, he had idealized the idea of becoming a father, while at the same time anxiously hoping he would be good at it.

His wife did not harbor the same desires for a family. She gained tremendous satisfaction from her work, fiercely pursuing career success. TD respected her ambition, but they both paid a price during the early years of their marriage. Their arguments over raising a family left emotional scars. Eventually they avoided the topic, neither of them left with a taste for the fighting. At a certain point, he surrendered to the idea of being childless.

TD carries only a few memories of his father despite a unique early childhood. He was born in the late Sixties to parents who lived in a group home with three other families. Their situation wasn't due to poverty; it was by choice. TDs parents embraced an alternative lifestyle. Known at that time as hippies, they reacted to the revolutionary social confusion of the Sixties by 'dropping out' of normal society.

His parents were part of a group of close friends who met while attending college in DC. A few graduated, the rest left school early. Together, they acquired a badly run-down farm in the Shenandoah Valley for a bargain. Starting a commune, they began the slow process of rehabilitating and expanding the seventy-five year old house and farm buildings.

TD was born there; his odd name an artifact of his parent's life view. Always seeking opportunities to ignore society's conventions, they named him using the first letters of their own names, Tom and Deborah. His legal first name is TD; just the two letters, both capitals, no space, no periods. He has suffered endless questions about it his entire life.

His parents never considered the impacts of imparting their counter-culture thinking to their son. His mother spoke mystically of Karma and emphasized the goal of achieving balance in life. His father was only slightly more grounded and often absent. He provided TD with scant real world guidance, preferring to speak using hollow aphorisms. His favorite was, "You only need to be true to yourself and the society of man."

They were the most impractical parents a kid could have. Into his early teens, there were no newspapers or a television at home. There were a few books, but no magazines, and no one even mentioned current events. At times, TD appeared odd or disconnected to those outside the family. He regularly missed the meaning of popular cultural references. He only gained knowledge of major news events when he heard about them at school. Classmates looking for fun sometimes tricked him with fake stories or false information.

TD quickly developed an inquisitive, but skeptical nature. Early on, he understood that he couldn't rely on what he was taught at home. He learned society's norms by watching closely how others behaved in given situations.

Undeniably, it was the origin of his skill for reading people and their intentions. It's the only practical legacy he received from his parents.

Their commune had struggled from the start and failed after just a couple of years. A spiritual worldview can't change basic truths. Governments levy taxes on property. Businesses require payment for goods. The group possessed few liquid assets after acquiring the farm. The cash generated from their modest agricultural surplus was insufficient to pay their taxes. Attempts to sell handcrafted products, or barter labor for essentials, fared little better.

Weary of the hardship and the threat of foreclosure, they sold the farm and shared the meager proceeds. TD's family moved to Northern Virginia, where Tom Adkins hoped to tap into the boom that was fueling Fairfax County's growth to an eventual population of over a million.

Even a booming economy has trouble accommodating thirty-year-old hippies. A good job is hard to find with no work history and few skills other than farming and leatherwork. Tom Adkins became a real-life caricature of the forlorn hippie, forced to conform to society's demands. He worked a variety of retail jobs on and off, drove a taxi part-time, and dealt pot on the side. The family barely managed to get by, relying heavily on the small amount Deborah earned working at a day care center. Tom's jobs kept him out of the house most nights and weekends. He spent little time with his son, never establishing any real connection.

When TD was twelve, his mother explained that his father had left and wouldn't be returning. There was little notable change to his life. He had already learned to make up for his father's constant absence by developing a few close friendships. In high school, those relationships eventually narrowed to just one, with Phil Madrigal. They were the closest of friends. TD drank his first beer with Phil. He had quickly agreed when Phil suggested they attend the local university together. In their junior year there, Phil introduced him to Elizabeth Parker.

A tall lanky brunette with deep brown eyes, Elizabeth was a year ahead of them. She was close friends with Phil's new fiancée, Anne. TD hit it off well with Elizabeth and they began dating, continuing into his senior year, even after she had graduated.

Elizabeth had majored in Political Science and dreamt of working in government. TD had no idea what he wanted to do, but he wasn't worried. He was never short of cash. In addition to classes, he worked full-time waiting tables or bartending at a high-end steakhouse.

They married two months after TD graduated. It was then that Elizabeth, never Liz or Betty, made it clear that she expected him to find a "real job", pointing to Phil as an example. After graduating, Phil had jumped right into selling insurance for a large national carrier. Always conscious of her image, Elizabeth wanted to be able to mention TD's job around her friends. Bartending certainly didn't qualify.

Having not yet found her own ideal position, Elizabeth worked for one of the city's upscale temp agencies. She regularly landed short-term administrative assistant positions, often at large law firms. After a series of temporary stints, she gained a full-time job at one of DC's most prestigious practices specializing in lobbying on Capitol Hill. She loved her job and the law firm and soon found herself singularly focused on a new career.

At the same time, she ratcheted up her demands on TD. He needed to find a full-time white-collar job. It needed to be a position befitting of the lifestyle she envisioned for them. There were several reasons TD was attracted to Elizabeth. For starters, she loved him. She was bright, ambitious, and beautiful. And though she could be a little domineering, having come from a completely unstructured childhood, he sometimes welcomed her controlling ways.

As with many other times in TD's life, Phil was there to help. He could get TD an interview for a position as an entry-level claims examiner with his company. TD was interested, even after being warned the job was neither glamorous, nor paid particularly well.

From the moment he started, TD genuinely enjoyed the work. And the company loved the results he produced. He was unsurpassed in his department for sniffing out fraudulent claims. It was only a few years before he was considered the company's top investigator.

Elizabeth's career was also taking off. She was an alert politically savvy employee who endeared herself to the top attorneys in the practice with her ideas and hard work. She got her first big break when the lawyer she was working for left the firm. Her search for a new assignment landed her a position supporting one of the senior partners. His long-time assistant had grown weary of the long hours and intensity the job demanded.

A couple of years later, another opportunity arose when the firm acquired a smaller practice. Elizabeth's boss was chosen to oversee the merger. While he managed the financial and legal aspects, he put her in charge of the small working group handling the operational issues of the merging the two firms. She shined in the role.

Elizabeth's consummate organizational skills were highly prized. Within eight years, she was the business operations manager for the entire firm, a position that came with its own assistant. She was compensated well, and earned significantly more than TD. They moved from their apartment in Alexandria, taking out a huge mortgage on a home in McLean with a sleek contemporary design. It was a stretch for them, even with two solid incomes, but Elizabeth made it work, carefully managing their finances.

She was also keen on them utilizing one of TD's company benefits. She wanted them to take advantage of the discounted employee premiums for purchasing life insurance policies underwritten by the company. The firm encourages its employees to use the benefit to insure themselves at well below-market rates.

TD felt it was a lot when she had them each purchase a policy with a $500,000 benefit. Later, with her income increasing, they added a $250,000 investment policy for Elizabeth. TD had little interest in the concept, but Phil was enthusiastic about the idea and he trusted his friend's judgment.

All of the policies contained a double indemnity benefit for accidental death.

⋏

A glance at the speedometer tells TD he's driving more than twenty mph over the limit. Over the past several minutes, both his tension and the car's speed have been increasing. He needs to get off the road and out of sight.

Right now though, he needs to slow down. He doesn't need to be pulled over for any reason.

Adding to his nervousness is that he simply doesn't like to drive much anymore. He drives quite cautiously these days, usually just over the speed limit. If he passes by a car accident, or simply observes a close call between two other vehicles, it almost always triggers thoughts of his wife.

A car accident had changed everything. It happened just over two years ago. Elizabeth had attended a business lunch, listening to a pitch from a temp agency offering contract paralegals. Knowing she had nothing on her schedule for the remainder of her day, she allowed herself two drinks. An hour later, she headed over to the JW Marriott Hotel for the firm's annual employee recognition event.

It was not the first time Elizabeth received an award for her dedication and service to the firm. At the reception that followed, she received a champagne toast from the senior partners and had one other glass of wine. She felt a little buzzed when she was leaving at four-thirty, but was in no sense feeling intoxicated. After briefly considering taking a taxi, she chose to drive home.

Forty minutes later, she stopped for a traffic signal at an intersection not far from her own neighborhood. While waiting for the light to change, she watched a young mother on the opposite corner shepherding her little daughter while also pushing an infant in a stroller. They were out for a walk, waiting for the light to change before crossing. Soon, the little girl began walking heel to toe along the curb, back and forth, as if she were a gymnast on a balance beam. It didn't take long for her mother to grab her firmly by the arm and pull her close to her side.

The classic family scene entranced Elizabeth. Thinking about her decision to forego children, she reassured herself that she and TD were both okay with that. After the light turned green, it took a short honk from the car behind her to break her train of thought. She stepped on the accelerator and took off without looking.

Already approaching from the crossing street was a car being driven by a young man. He was once again running late for his part-time job and in a hurry. Fiddling with his phone, he glanced up and saw the traffic signal was yellow. Determined to get to work on time, he accelerated to beat the light. Distracted by a new text message, he failed to notice the signal had turned to red well before he sped into the intersection.

He made it nearly half way across before Elizabeth slammed into the rear side of his car, launching his vehicle into an uncontrollable spin. The front of Elizabeth's car was crushed, but the airbag spared her major injury. She suffered nothing worse than some nasty facial abrasions and oddly, a broken ankle.

Careening out of its spin, the other car had flipped into the air and finally landed on its side at the spot where the mother stood with her children. No one understood how the infant in the stroller survived. The mother, and her daughter who was pirouetting only seconds earlier, were killed. Though they had to cut him out of his crumpled car, the young man came through it all relatively unhurt.

Elizabeth learned of the deaths while at the hospital. She had admitted to the patrolman that she consumed alcohol earlier and blood tests were performed. Luckily, her blood alcohol came in below citable levels. No mention of it was made in the officer's final report, which was unequivocal. Two eyewitness statements and the video from the red light camera were in total agreement. The accident was solely the fault of the young man.

Elizabeth was morose, blaming herself for what had occurred. Counseling sessions failed to help her address her feelings of guilt. She took an extended leave of absence from work.

At one level, she knew it wasn't her fault. If he had stopped for the red light, there would have been no accident. But she knew she had been drinking that day. She also blamed herself for not taking a taxi, and then for being so preoccupied that she had entered the intersection without as much as a glance. She reasoned that if she had been clearheaded and paying full attention it would have all been different. No one would be dead.

And that's how things remained. Even after months of counseling, and regardless of what others argued, she had convinced herself she was to blame for the accident. Nothing could change her mind.

⚑

Having run out of side roads, TD has arrived at Route 1. He promised himself when he reached this point he would revisit his decision to stay in the area. If he turns right, he can hop on I-95 southbound in just a few miles. It's the smart way to go and it leaves behind anyone looking for him.

Turning left puts him at exponentially greater risk. But he drove in this direction for a reason and he wants to see that through. He'll stay in Northern Virginia one final night. Once he's through the stretch of highway running through Fort Belvoir, he can choose from several cheap motels straddling the roadway north of the base.

⚑

After announcing himself to a patrolman, Richter crosses under the police tape that now surrounds the entire motel. Instead of immediately checking in with Roberts, he quickly begins poking around the edges of the crime scene. His immediate goal is to position himself for a closer look at the pick-up car. It's unlikely the money is still here, but if it is, that presents an entirely different set of problems.

Sean Landry had been watching Richter since he ducked under the tape. Finding Kenny Clarkson close by, he moves next to him and silently nods toward the man who is now circling the Mercedes. As they watch, Richter pauses and leans closer to the car, peering through a blown out window.

The guy has the look and feel of a cop, but they know each of the city's detectives and this guy isn't one of them. They also assume Roberts would announce the presence of any non-departmental resources, particularly to facilitate cooperation. Clarkson looks around and sees Roberts is preparing to knock on the door of another room. Calling out for him to hold up for a moment, Kenny shrugs his shoulders as he points toward the unknown man seemingly working the crime scene.

Clarkson and Landry became friends after going through training together. The experience bonded them and they've maintained a close friendship outside of their jobs. Sean's given name is DeSean, but he prefers the shorter version, and introduces himself to others omitting the prefix. Kenny still uses it on occasion, but has learned to drop it when they're around others.

Sean is quite proud of the nickname he came up with for Kenny. Annoyed by his friend's constant singing along with any music he hears, he started calling him 'Kelly Clarkson', after the American Idol recording star. Later he changed it up, calling him simply 'Idol'. The nickname works beautifully, silencing Kenny any time he starts to warble. As a bonus, several other officers got wind of the moniker and started using it. Sean still gets a kick watching Kenny bristle whenever he hears the nickname.

Now, as they watch Roberts move toward the unidentified plainclothes cop, Landry asks, "Hey Idol, you think he's a county detective?"

Refusing to acknowledge his friends poke, Kenny responds, "Yeah, probably. We'll know soon enough. You know, this could be a big night for us Sean. There's lots of work to do and opportunities to look good. Who knows, it might help position us for some better assignments."

Feeling a little sorry for himself, Landry says, "Yeah, sure. But, you got the good stuff, witness interviews. I got crowd control and logistics crap."

"Well, don't sweat it. Just keep your eyes open. Maybe you'll see something that helps with the case. I have to get going with this interview. Let's catch breakfast tomorrow and compare notes."

Smiling at his friend, Landry laughs as he replies, "I doubt I'll have any notes, Idol. But I'll keep my eyes open. Later, man."

Carl Roberts was preparing to knock on the door of Room 110 when Clarkson had alerted him. He was initially unsure what the patrolman was trying to tell him before he finally noticed the man standing near the car. Something is definitely familiar about the guy, but he can't put his finger on it. Postponing the interview, Carl strides purposefully towards him. Calling out, he asks, "Can I help you?"

Along with a nod and a slight smile, the man extends his hand. "Detective Jim Richter, Fairfax County Police. You must be Roberts. Lieutenant Aldretti sent me over to help you guys any way I can. A couple of evidence techs are also on the way. Should be here shortly."

Despite the man's affability, Roberts is miffed by the detective's freelancing at his crime scene. "I don't know how you guys do it, but we usually check in when we come into someone else's jurisdiction."

As Richter begins to respond, Roberts cuts him off; they don't need to start things off on a bad foot. "I'm glad you're here to help, though. We're swamped. I'm Chief of Detectives Carl Roberts."

"Nice to meet you, Sir. I'm sorry if I overstepped. I was just surprised by the number of bodies and the level of violence. You sure don't see this kind of thing much. So, what's happened, and what do you need me to do?"

Roberts provides a quick recap of what they know. So far, that's not much. It looks like there was a hit on the Mercedes, but they don't know why it was at the motel. There are seven dead and one bystander in bad condition on his way to the hospital. At least one assailant fled in a single car.

He then asks Richter to coordinate the work of the evidence technicians and integrate the county techs when they arrive. Additionally, Roberts would like him to focus on quickly identifying any of the bodies they can, while he continues interviewing witnesses. In a while, they'll huddle up and share what everyone has learned.

The prospect of access to eyewitnesses tantalizes Richter, but it would be pressing things to ask for a different assignment right out of the gate. Besides, the activities Roberts has tasked him with should provide some leeway for working on his own priorities. Before moving on, he says, "I noticed several of these guys look Hispanic. Do you think this is gang related? I can possibly get one of our gang taskforce experts to swing by."

Happy to get any assistance available, Roberts accepts the offer. Richter makes the call on the spot, and Aldretti gives the green flag without hesitation. The Lieutenant knows that gangs pay little attention to jurisdictional niceties unless they've laid them down themselves. And he's always interested in getting violent offenders off the street.

Finally starting to work, Richter spends only a few minutes talking with the evidence techs before he leaves them on their own. He tells them he wants identification of each body as soon as possible, with the Hispanics a priority. Having fobbed his assignment off on the techs, he shifts his attention to developing leads that could help locate the money. His first focus is getting a closer look at the getaway car.

After finding no sign of the money in the Mercedes, Richter remembers Roberts mentioning only a single car being involved in the attack, and that one having gotten away. Roberts had made no reference to the car that crashed into the bus stop. Despite only minor body damage, Richter had noticed much of its windshield was missing or shattered. And the front of the car was peppered with bullet holes. It's simply too much of a coincidence. It has to have been involved, but it appears Roberts has yet to make the connection.

A surge of energy bolts through Richter as he realizes the money might remain close by. If not, at least the car should provide a few leads. As he turns to head to the bus stop, he sees the two county evidence techs have arrived. It takes him several minutes to give them instructions and get them hooked up with their counterpart.

Finally able to break away, Richter sees Roberts is entering another room for an interview. The timing is perfect. Telling no one where he's going, he makes his move. Unfortunately, as he's approaching the perimeter tape, someone shouts his name. It's the gang expert from the County coming up the driveway; he also happened to have been close by tonight.

Frustrated, Richter realizes inspecting the crashed car is going to have to wait.

⚔

Roberts had come away from his initial conversation with the county detective a little concerned, but not completely put off. Even though he had appeared to be paying attention while they talked, there was something about the man that seemed a bit unfocused, almost distracted. And the way he had walked onto the crime scene and begun poking around before checking in was wrong on several levels. Still, the offer of a gang expert was perfect. And he certainly can't expect the County to send over their best and brightest.

Putting those thoughts aside, he returns to interview the potential witness in Room 110. Clarkson had reported finding a distraught young woman there. She had claimed to see nothing, despite being in one of the rooms with the closest proximity to the action. If that's so, Carl wonders why she's so upset.

From the moment she opened her door, the young woman named Carmela was trembling, seemingly scared of something. She had clearly been crying and was struggling to restrain more tears. She had trouble looking at him. And despite his pressing her with questions, she stayed consistent with her initial position. She knows nothing of what occurred in plain view of her window.

The problem is there's no way he's buying it. It doesn't add up that she's so resolutely unknowledgeable, yet so deeply distressed. Her story that she saw nothing while hiding behind the bed isn't the problem; it just doesn't jibe with her obvious nervousness during his questioning, and the same with the crying. Both belie her proclaimed lack of knowledge about what happened. Trying a different approach, he asks her directly why she's so upset.

Looking up at him, she says, "Because of all the senseless death."

Roberts waits to respond, letting her think he has accepted her answer. Then, making eye contact again, he says, "How do you know there has been so much senseless death if you didn't see anything?"

Carmela is briefly stymied by his question. For a long moment, she has no answer while he continues staring at her. Then, with renewed confidence, she says, "I just looked out a minute ago and saw all the bodies."

Despite limited experience dealing with witnesses of violent crimes, Roberts is not naïve. Even if her claim was true, her visible, and deeply emotional, reaction is unlikely that of someone who simply looked out the window and saw a few bodies. Though he doesn't have a strong feeling that she's central to what occurred tonight, he believes she's somehow connected to events, possibly through one of the victims.

Right now though, he needs to gather as information as rapidly as he can. And without knowing the value of what she did or didn't see, he decides to come back to this witness later. Giving her his business card, he tells her not to leave the area without calling him. "I'm sure I'm going to have more questions for you."

As he says this, he senses her relax a bit, possibly believing that she has gone through the worst. He finishes by saying, "Look, there's something you should understand. We're definitely going to talk again. And when we do, you need to be ready to tell me everything you know about what happened here tonight."

He watched her closely as he spoke this last piece. It was easy to notice the flash of fear in her eyes. He has no doubt that she's lying.

Coming out of the room, Roberts sees the courtyard is morphing into a well-managed crime scene. Since arriving, his phone has been buzzing non-stop with messages. Checking the growing list, the only one requiring immediate response is from the Chief, seeking an update. After filling him in, he decides to leave the rest of the messages for later.

There were two there from his ex-wife. The first asked him to call to discuss a last-minute decision to send their seven-year old daughter to a music-themed summer camp. Immediately following was a reminder not to call too late. Both are matters that can wait until tomorrow.

His divorce three years ago was amicable and the best outcome for all involved. Roberts is from Richmond, Virginia, his wife from a small town in South Carolina. They'd met as freshmen in college where they were both on scholarship. They married after dating for over two years. Their marriage came under stress when he started in law-enforcement, but they managed. It was when he got the opportunity with Fairfax City and then moved to Northern Virginia that the problems worsened.

The hectic pace of living was too much for his southern-raised wife. Carl thrived in the environment, but despite some of the best public schools in the nation, his wife had no desire to raise their daughter in the sprawling suburbs. Roberts knew his conservative, deeply religious wife was uncomfortable with the increasing diversity and liberal tone of the area. After their divorce, she and their daughter moved to be near her family outside of Charleston. He threw himself into his increasingly successful career.

His hard work has paid off and his Chief trusts and relies upon him. Roberts gets the most out of his small contingent of detectives and there are few unsolved cases. His men consider him firm but fair, and they reward his fairness with hard work and loyalty. Carl knows he's on track for a command role if he stays with the city's small force. He very much likes the idea of that.

He also knows that tonight's events and how he handles this case will have a significant impact on his career. This is a multiple-homicide event and people don't fight to the death over small matters. There's no doubt that large amounts of money, drugs, or both were involved. But before letting the scope of the investigation grow out of control, he reminds himself his job is to deal with the crimes at hand.

His job is to find out who was killed and who did the killing. That's his sole focus for now. He'll collect all the evidence, but it will be up to the chief and the city attorney to decide how they want to handle the other issues. Issues like the use of assault weapons, possible gang involvement, and the presence of organized crime in their suburban community.

Sean Landry has completed his initial assignments. Aided by the arrival of additional officers, he completed establishing a perimeter around the entire motel. The portable lighting had also arrived and been set up to help the evidence techs do their job. Since then, he has pretty much been a traffic cop, helping deal with the congestion caused by the increasing number of vehicles now parked along the narrow entrance driveway.

With so little room to maneuver, it was difficult getting the last of the ambulances and a fire engine out of there. As the vehicles passed the front office, Sean directed them to turn right, and proceed up the short rise to the top of the driveway. There was a well-lit area there in front of the self-storage facility with enough room to turn around. From there they could head down the hill and exit.

In contrast to the shabby motel, the self-storage property is clean, and well lit. Sean had noted the multiple security cameras along the roofline, situated to capture images of any activity at the business. Watching the last ambulance complete its turn, he sees that one of the cameras is locked in on the card-key operated security gate. Another is focused on the uphill drive-way approach. The camera setup starts him wondering. Is it possible there are recorded images of vehicles using the driveway and entering the motel?

Hurrying back into the courtyard, he finds Kenny Clarkson and tells him about the cameras. With Kenny agreeing it's worth a shot, he seeks out the lead detective. Roberts is thrilled with the discovery and makes a note to contact the company's security offices.

"That's solid work, Officer Landry. I'd like you to continue inspecting the areas immediately around the motel. Maybe you can find something more."

Shouting out, "Will do, Detective", Landry turns away so rapidly that Roberts is unable to see the wide grin on his face as he hustles off.

After striking out on both of his initial interviews, Kenny Clarkson is desperate to show Detective Roberts he can contribute to the investigation. There's even more pressure after watching his buddy Sean discover the security cameras. Then he remembers Marvin Williams. As he makes his way across the courtyard to where the man is standing, Kenny hopes this won't be another waste of time.

"Alright, Mister Williams, I know you claim you don't know anything, but I've got a few more questions before you can go. Also, there's a small problem. It's going to be awhile before you can get back in your room. Is there someplace else you can stay tonight?"

Marvin's look of surprise quickly changes to a scowl. "Are you kidding me, man? You think I live here AND I got some place else I can stay?" Shaking his head as he looks down, he mumbles, "Man, I should've never let him use my room."

The importance of Marvin's last words hit Clarkson, "I'm sorry, Mister Williams, what did you say? Who did you let use your room?"

With his shoulders drooping even further, Marvin begins talking about Eddie King. Kenny listens closely, taking notes as fast as he can write. Though what he hears might not break open the case, it's a major piece of information. It looks like tonight was one of many when Room 112 was used for something out of the ordinary. And whatever that was, it was probably why there was an attack.

After Marvin has apparently related all he knows, Clarkson politely says, "I'm sorry you got wrapped up in all this, Mister Williams, but thank you. What you've told me is very helpful. If you think of anything else, anything at all, please let us know."

"Well, I'll tell you Officer. While I've been waiting here, I've been thinking about one other strange thing." Marvin then proceeds to tell him about cutting through the bank parking lot on his way back from dinner. And how a man almost stumbled into him rushing away from the motel, "….carrying more bags than one person needs."

Marvin tells Kenny it seemed like the guy was sneaking away from the motel. And now he thinks he might have been part of what happened tonight. "I think he took those bags from Eddie."

Kenny is ecstatic. This is huge. In addition to information about the room, a potential assailant was seen fleeing the scene immediately after the shooting, carrying multiple bags. Roberts is going to love this.

Again apologizing to Marvin, Kenny tells him he's going to have to hang around a little while longer. They'll see if they can find an empty room where he can wait more comfortably.

Then he moves off quickly to find Roberts.

Right from the beginning, Roberts finds his interview with Cyndi moving in the opposite direction from the one with Carmela. Cyndi has also been crying but has regained her composure. And she's a font of information.

She tells him all about Tim Crane, their brief affair, and that this was not their first time coming to this motel. Tim must have gone out for a smoke while she was in the shower. She heard the gunfire while she was drying off. When she looked out the window, she was just in time to see Tim shot as he lay on the ground.

Though this makes identifying one of the victims a lot easier, it's not likely to help them understand what occurred. As Roberts speculates on that aspect, he realizes Cyndi has continued talking, describing events after the shootings. He interrupts when he hears her say, "… then he stood up and took off around the front of the building with the bags."

Carl politely asks her to repeat the last part and Cyndi tells him again about the man who suddenly appeared, bent down, and then checked Tim for a pulse. Then, after a brief pause, he grabbed the bags and fled on foot.

Containing his excitement, Roberts pummels Cyndi with questions, asking her to repeat step-by-step exactly what the man did. As for a description, she remembers little, nothing more than white, middle aged, average height, and average weight. A little embarrassed, she draws a complete blank as to what he was wearing.

After several additional, but fruitless queries, Roberts thanks her profusely. He ends with the standard spiel about remaining in the area. He also tells her she can leave the motel as soon as an officer comes to escort her past the crime scene.

Leaving the room, he's thrilled to have gained such a significant lead so quickly. This is just the kind of break they need.

⊼

Kenny is having trouble holding in the news he learned from Marvin. With Roberts inside talking with Cyndi, he decides to find Sean and tell him. He locates his friend near the motel's entrance, where they watch an arriving police car barely avoid colliding with another trying to depart. The scene triggers a flashback to his own near miss when he was arriving earlier. Then he makes the connection.

With a quick, "I'll be right back", Kenny heads off toward the other end of the motel. On the way, he tries to recollect the details. Unfortunately, he has only a hazy memory of the man's face, and remembers nothing of the car.

When he reaches the area around the small bank, he's sure the car he almost struck was leaving this lot. Disappointed he can't recall anything specific about the vehicle, he remembers the security cameras at the storage company. A glance at the bank building confirms they also have cameras. It looks like they cover the drive-thru, ATM, and parking lot. Bingo!

⊼

With Kenny suddenly running off, Sean decides to continue using his mandate to explore the area around the motel. The next thing to draw his attention is the car wreck at the bus stop. Another officer had already been sent to investigate and help get the wreck cleared, but there has been little progress. The tow truck had only recently arrived after fighting though the snarled traffic.

Sean finds the patrolman on the scene and the tow truck operator discussing how to disengage the car from the bus stop canopy without dragging the whole assembly with it. Meanwhile, the rear of the car continues jutting out into the road. Then he notices something odd. The damage to the front of the car and the amount of blood in the front seat seem out of proportion to what appears to have been a low-speed crash.

As he prepares to ask the patrolman about the status of the driver, Sean takes a second look at the vehicle's shattered windshield. He can see that some of the damage is clearly from a bullet passing through it, not from a low-speed crash into the bus stop. A closer examination of the front of the car reveals additional bullet holes. Could this be the getaway vehicle, abandoned after the crash?

Sean immediately tells the other officer to stop the plan to move the car. Instead, he's to tape off the area around the vehicle and touch nothing else until an evidence technician returns.

Sprinting back to the motel to alert Roberts, Landry passes Richter, who is headed in the opposite direction. Slowing as they pass, he tells him, "You might want to hear about this before you leave."

Together, they quickly find Roberts, who is just finishing a conversation with Kenny Clarkson. Full of enthusiasm, Landry shares his latest discovery.

Before Roberts can say anything, Richter blurts out, "Why don't I go over and check it out?"

Without hesitating, Carl says, "Thanks Detective, but I want to keep an experienced investigator here with the evidence techs. Landry, why don't you and Clarkson take this together? Run the plates and find us a witness. I want that car secured and taken over to our garage."

Sean and Kenny have soon interviewed several witnesses. One is a cop's dream come true. Having just arrived to catch a bus, he was lucky to avoid the initial crash. Then, using his smartphone, he started snapping photos. Almost immediately, a second car had arrived. Along with photos of the license plate and the driver, the witness took video of the young man pulling a near lifeless body from the wreck. Though the images are not sharp enough to determine if his wounds were from gunshots, it's obvious they're greatly out of proportion to the car crash.

At that point, Clarkson hears two spectators talking about a crash behind the Qwik Lube and another person killed. Somehow, even though EMTs made it quickly to that wreck, it has gone unattended by law enforcement so far. Leaving Sean at the bus stop, Clarkson heads to the second crash. There, he encounters the strange pileup, with one car nearly rammed through the garage door.

Getting closer, he sees there's a body wedged in the driver's seat. One of the EMTs informs him it's likely the driver was dead upon impact. Earlier, he had crawled across the hood to reach the trapped driver, but the damage from the impact was massive. Along with whatever internal wounds there may be, the odd angle of the victim's head suggests his neck was broken. They're now waiting for heavier equipment to separate the cars before removing the body.

Clarkson considers the role the crashes play in the story that's emerging. They have two car wrecks occurring within minutes of each other. Both are within a one-block radius of the motel and both involve an abandoned vehicle. Though it's unclear how it all fits together, he knows it's unlikely to be a coincidence.

⋏

Richter's performance is looking a little better in Carl Roberts's eyes. All night, it has felt like the man has reluctantly accepted his assignments. However, he coordinated the evidence techs effectively and they're making solid progress. He also produced additional help from the County as advertised, introducing Roberts to one of their Gang Task Force specialists, Sargent Hector Cruz.

After a few minutes talking with the detectives, and making a few laps around the motel property, Cruz has seen enough. He tells the detectives there's no evidence of gang-related colors, tattoos, or territorial markings. Nor are any of the men a readily known gang member.

Also of importance to Cruz is the nature of the crime and the group that was attacked. None of it fits the profile of any gangs operating in the region. Despite the ethnicity of the attackers, he's confident tonight's events are not gang related.

After thanking Cruz, and taking an inventory of where the investigation stands, Roberts checks his watch; it's well past midnight. Before they call it a night, he wants a recap with his team. He tasks Clarkson with getting a key from the office for a vacant room near the end of the row. They can hold a debriefing there.

⁂

At nearby Fairfax INOVA Hospital, Bobby Tomlin has been prepped for surgery. In addition to both legs being shattered and six broken ribs, he has suffered a heavy concussion. Luckily, the x-rays show no skull fractures. His head injury will require little treatment other than stitches and many days of rest.

Bobby regained consciousness not long after arriving in the emergency room. He currently remembers little of what happened and lacks the energy to think about it. At one point, he asked if a car had hit him. That was the only time he spoke, other than an occasional yes or no in response to medical inquiries.

The on-call Orthopedic Trauma Surgeon will be in the lead tonight, focusing on stabilizing the multiple fractures of Bobby's legs. They also need to map out a long-term course of action to address the extensive damage. This will not be Bobby's only surgery, but if they're going to save his legs, it will be the most important.

⁂

Sixty miles away, Raffi Flores is also in surgery. Unlike the procedures Bobby will undergo to allow him to walk again, Raffi's surgery is to save his life. Due to the damage from the gunshot wounds, the amount of blood loss, and the time elapsed since incurring the injuries, it's not clear he will survive.

When they had initially reached the emergency room, Cesar drove past the entrance as he scouted the situation. There was little activity and just one ambulance parked near the front door. Still, getting Raffi inside and receiving medical care would be problematic. He couldn't just throw him out of the car, but he also couldn't check him in at admissions. Remembering that he was driving a stolen car, one not easily traced to him, Cesar made a decision.

As he steered them into the circular drive, Caesar looked over at Raffi, hoping he would make it until the ambulance driver returned. Cesar drove the car just past the parked ambulance. He then backed up until he was flush with its front bumper where they would have to notice it. Holding his good friend's hand, he wished him luck. Then, he calmly pulled his baseball cap farther down over his forehead, stepped out of the car, and walked away.

It was the best thing Cesar could have done. Only two minutes passed before Raffi was discovered and they rushed him into the emergency room. Identified only as a John Doe for the moment, the hospital staff began working to save his life.

⚓

Having committed to staying in the area one last night, TD's thoughts drift back to his wife. Sometimes he forgets how far things had deteriorated during their final year of marriage. There were plenty of irritants. Elizabeth's job was increasingly stressful, consuming all of her energy. And despite his success, it was apparent she looked down on his career. Once, during an argument, she referred to his occupation as being "a snoop". They didn't speak for a full week after that.

Still, there were long stretches when they found contentment together. They had built a partnership in life, even if they weren't as emotionally attached as either would have preferred. Elizabeth worked endlessly, including many Saturdays. His was a more ad hoc schedule, often determined by the cases he was working on. With constant scheduling conflicts over that final year, they had done very little together, including taking separate vacations.

The car accident worsened everything. Elizabeth was sullen and uncommunicative well past her physical recovery. She didn't return to work for two months, susceptible to deeply dark periods lasting days at a time. There was a noticeable increase in her drinking. On occasion, she openly mixed prescription pain pills with alcohol. TD had no idea how to react. Instead of confronting her, he hid from it, burying himself in his work. It left their relationship resembling that of two casual housemates.

When things reached a nadir, she suddenly snapped out of it. More cheerful and engaged, she announced she was ending her leave of absence from the law firm. Though outwardly happier, she remained somewhat distant, rarely talking about things that had mattered to her before. Looking back, TD realized he had ignored the signs of bigger problems. She was maintaining an odd schedule, but he wrote it off to her being behind after her extended absence. Only much later did he learn that she had never returned to her job, not even for a single day.

Two weeks after her apparent return to normalcy, TD came home to find she had prepared dinner, something quite rare those days. It was one of his all-time favorites, pot roast with roasted carrots and mashed potatoes, all to be drowned in homemade gravy. After dinner, she came into the family room with an old photo album and curled up on the couch next to him. Together they paged through the pictures, many of them fifteen years old.

He recalls that night vividly, with all the laughter and warm feelings as they reminisced. Elizabeth seemed genuinely happy. At the end of the evening, she told him about a three-day business conference she was attending in Annapolis, Maryland. She would be leaving early the next morning. He immediately knew that she was lying.

Even if his built-in lie detector wasn't on full tilt, there were plenty of other reasons not to believer her. Besides her having never mentioned it before that night, Elizabeth had never before attended such an event without rigorous planning. There would be shopping for at least one new outfit and plenty of pre-packing. In anticipation, she would frequently mention some interesting side trip in route, or a sight to see at the destination that she had added to her itinerary. This time there had been none of that.

He chose not to question her that night, determined not to spoil her best mood in months. It did worry him that she would so brazenly lie as she left home for several days. He doubted she was having an affair. With her recent mood swings, it could be almost anything. Maybe she was taking some form of therapy she was unwilling to discuss.

The next morning she was up quite early and in the shower by four-thirty. After drifting off, it was about an hour later when he heard her leaving. She left without saying anything, but called him just after seven-thirty when she knew he'd be awake.

Out of the blue, she told him she loved him. He couldn't remember the last time she said those words. She told him she had been thinking about her life recently. She was sorry to have been so depressing and such a burden on him. At some point, she made a statement that she had "…figured out a way to fix all of my problems."

He said little during the call. At times, he was only half-listening, while wondering where she was really going. He fought the urge to confront her. Ultimately, he told her that he was glad for her. She sounded very believable, but he was sure she was lying about the trip. At a certain point, he realized there had been a pause in the conversation.

Elizabeth broke the silence, saying, "Goodbye TD." He wondered if he had missed her saying something important while he was fretting about her lying.

Later, he thought about the pause, followed by the 'goodbye'. He can still recall exactly how he felt right then. It seemed like such an odd, uncomfortable way to end the call.

It was their last conversation. He never spoke with her again.

⅄

Spotting a motel on his side of the road, TD pulls into the lot, but chooses to park away from the front office. Both physically and emotionally exhausted, he lingers in the car. Despite his earlier excitement, all the reminiscing about Elizabeth has saddened him.

Her leaving changed his life forever.

⅄

He was surprised and worried when he didn't hear from her for the rest of that day. He tried reaching her several times but she never answered. With his feelings about the situation whipsawing, he left a 'good night' message on her phone as he turned in. Despite the odd feeling at the end of their call that morning, he remained encouraged by her seeming happiness the evening before. It had been a long time since seeing her that way. Even though he was sure she was lying in some significant way about her trip, he hoped her more buoyant sprit indicated a new phase in her recovery.

He resumed trying to reach her the next morning, but his calls went immediately to voice mail. It appeared her phone was turned off. On his way out of the house, he noticed her phone charger plugged in over the kitchen counter. On one hand, that would explain her phone being off, maybe she was conserving the battery. On the other, it raised more questions. The fact that she had left her charger behind spoke volumes about her lack of preparation. And she still should have called. She could borrow someone else's phone or charge the call to her room. Something wasn't right. Against his intuition, he found himself hoping it was simply that she was feeling depressed and wanting to hide from the world. Admittedly, he was beginning to feel a little scared.

At work, TD was between major investigations. Recently, he had been tasked with creating a revamped training course for new claims adjusters. He hated the whole exercise. He found it difficult expressing concepts that for him constituted informed intuition. He would struggle for hours trying to capture the essence of years of experience in bullet-pointed phrases.

He was delivering part of the course for the first time that day. It was nowhere near his best effort. He had become increasingly distracted by his wife's absence and total silence, now well into its second day. Finishing early, he left for home. To cheer himself up, he planned to head back out later for dinner at his favorite Chinese buffet. It was a restaurant Elizabeth would never agree to visit. He had only ever eaten there alone.

There was a message on their answering machine when he arrived home that afternoon. It was from the Virginia State Police requesting that he call a given number. He instantly knew it concerned Elizabeth, even though she had claimed to be travelling to Maryland. An administrative assistant took his call and informed him a state trooper would call him back soon. Despite repeated queries, he was unable to learn anything about the reason the police wanted to speak with him.

Ten incredibly tense minutes later, his phone finally rang. After an extremely brief preamble, the trooper informed him of Elizabeth's death in a single-car accident on Skyline Drive, high above Virginia's Shenandoah Valley. Her car was discovered forty yards down a steep rocky incline, below one of the scenic overlooks. She had apparently lost control of her vehicle and crashed through a low stone retaining wall. Though confident it was his wife, they still wanted him to come to the morgue to verify her identity.

In total shock, he managed to depart within minutes. To this day, he can't remember any of the long, rush-hour drive out I-66 to Front Royal. After TD identified Elizabeth, the trooper began asking questions. TD was a bit perturbed with the timing, but the officer was polite and earnest. His inquiries were routine, asking where Elizabeth was going and if TD knew why she was traveling on Skyline Drive. TD had few answers and told the truth. Elizabeth had said she was going to Annapolis, over a hundred miles to the east.

He was stunned to learn the coroner's preliminary report placed the time of death early the prior morning. TD had mistakenly assumed the accident had occurred that morning, not the day before. If the coroner was correct, it must have happened not long after she called him. Deep in his mind, dark inklings about the manner of her death began to stir. He considered commenting about her recent state of mind, but in the end, he stayed silent.

The police investigation of the incident concluded the following week. The crash was determined to be an accident. Given the additional time to consider the matter, TD felt there were certainly a few reasons one might think otherwise. Still, whatever suspicions he had about how his wife had died, he said nothing about them to anyone.

He hated dwelling on the matter, but he often replayed the last two days of her life. The cell phone records showed her last call to him was three minutes long, at seven thirty-four AM. The accident occurred sometime soon afterward. He was saddest when he thought about their last evening at home together, or that final phone conversation. At other times, he was able to put it all aside and remind himself no one really knew what happened.

It was a fairly straightforward investigation for the police. Based on the phone records and witnesses, they knew TD had been nowhere near the scene. Her car had also checked out to be free of any defects that could cause such an accident. He was never suspected of being involved.

Elizabeth had been travelling at a high rate of speed. The most probable scenario was that she had lost control trying to avoid a deer or some other animal. Such accidents occur frequently enough along Skyline Drive, though rarely resulting in fatalities. There was no motivation for the police to conclude the crash was anything but an accident. There were some troubling aspects to the toxicology report, but that was the only thing much out of the ordinary. And it was of no real concern to them why she had lied to her husband, or was driving along the mountainside road at that early hour.

For the insurance company it would be a completely different matter.

After Elizabeth's death, TD transferred his one open case file to another investigator and took a paid leave of absence. Even if he had stayed out for a couple of months, it wouldn't drain his rarely used leave balance. By the time four weeks had passed, he was ready to resume work. One of the last personal matters he addressed before returning to work was getting the required documentation in order and filing the life insurance claims.

He had no specific need for the money, nor a plan for using it, but he couldn't see a reason not to file the claim. It was very large. With her death determined to be accidental, double indemnity kicked in. Adding the accumulated value of the investment policy, the total benefit would be nearly $1.6 million. The amount dismayed TD, but he rationalized that his discomfort was because the large payout was coming from his own company. At his core, he knew the real reason it felt wrong; his internal lie detector works just as well on him as it does on others.

On TD's second day back to work, a senior claims investigator from a different regional office contacted him about the claim. He was in town seeking time to meet, hoping to gather a few final pieces of information regarding Elizabeth. Unsurprised by the call, TD agreed to talk that afternoon. It wasn't necessarily a red flag that a senior investigator had been assigned. The size of the payout, combined with it being an employee claim, meant that its processing would be circumspect.

Not long into their meeting, TD found himself on the defensive, almost offended by the nature of some of the questions. Part of him respected his counterpart's skill, subtly mixing innocuous requests for routine information with more pointed queries. Sometimes it was not so subtle. There were questions about Elizabeth's use of prescription pain medications since her first accident, as well as about her state of mind in the weeks before her death

TD responded honestly to the questions, but at times with key omissions that some might consider evasive. Considering the range of questions being asked, as well as the depth of information the investigator already possessed, it was clear a significant amount of work had already been completed in the limited time since he had filed the claim.

During a short break, TD called Phil Madrigal to vent about what was happening. He was surprised to learn the investigator had talked with Phil the day before, asking many of the same tough questions. Phil had agonized all night over letting TD know. He had finally decided to violate the investigator's instructions not to alert TD; he just hadn't gotten around to making the call yet. TD wasn't angry and told his best friend not to sweat it.

When he returned to the conference room, TD asked to see the case file. Out of professional courtesy, his colleague agreed to let him read an overview he had prepared for just this contingency. What TD saw wasn't pretty. He read things he didn't know about his wife or the accident.

He was shocked to learn Elizabeth had never returned to her job. She had actually tendered her resignation weeks before the accident. He also didn't know she was still seeing a psychiatrist and on medication, despite telling him that her sessions had ended. There was no evidence of alcohol involved with the accident, but the toxicology report indicated she was loaded with painkillers and anti-depressants at the time of her fatal crash.

TD had always had his doubts about the accident. Now, here was a detailed review of the whole event. He was also shown a separate file including the police report and photos taken at the scene. The car was estimated to be travelling nearly eighty miles per hour when it hit the low stone wall, a terribly reckless speed for the scenic serpentine section of mountainside parkway.

And then there was the problem of the skid marks. The police concluded they were the result of her braking and swerving to avoid one of the many animals traversing the road in the morning hours. But in the insurance company's file, attached to photos of the skid marks, was a one-page summary of their internal expert's analysis.

That report agreed that the skid marks were due to a rapid steering adjustment, such as a sudden sharp turn at high speed. But unlike the police, the expert believed they were not consistent with the applying of the car's brakes. The report also noted the total absence of any skid marks, or other signs of braking, over the last few yards of pavement before the car breached the low retaining wall. The car had never slowed before launching itself off the edge of the overlook.

Coupling the information in the files and the questions being asked, it was easy for TD to grasp where the investigation was heading. The company believed it was examining a possible suicide, masquerading as a car accident.

TD knows there are insurance companies out there that are ruthlessly profit-oriented, with corporate practices that initially deny, or delay the payment of all claims above a given threshold. He also knows his firm has never countenanced such practices. On the contrary, they can be quite tenacious if they believe there's a legitimate reason for denying a payout.

Even though the man in front of him was doing his job, and his questions and theories were credible, it didn't mean TD wasn't upset about it. He was hurt partially because they had focused so quickly on the possibility of suicide. If that theory was true, what did it mean about what Elizabeth was going through at the end of her life? And what about his own lack of awareness and failure to help her? Had he passively ignored this possible scenario?

There was also a troubling contradiction at the root of why he was rapidly growing angry at the situation. As both an employee and a top investigator, the fact that he had filed the claim implied his belief in the accidental nature of his wife's death. If it was otherwise, if he believed her death was at her own hands, then he had filed a fraudulent claim.

As he stared again at the photo of the skid marks arcing toward the breach in the low wall, he realized the claims investigator had resumed talking. He had heard enough to understand he was asking additional questions regarding TD's awareness of Elizabeth's mental state. Then, quite bluntly, he was asked if he thought she was capable of harming herself. At that point, he lost any remaining self-control he possessed.

Half kicking his chair away as he stood, he shoved the files back across the table. With a simple, almost whispered, "fuck you", he walked out of the conference room, never breaking stride until he reached the elevators. He left the building without talking to anyone.

From his car, TD called his boss's office extension. He knew his boss was out of the office and the call would reach his voice mail. He didn't really want to talk to him. He left an erratic message, mumbling something about having mistakenly returned to work before he was ready. Once he was back at home, he battled a flurry of conflicting emotions including rage, sorrow, and embarrassment. An hour later his boss called, but TD refused to answer. The terse message asked him to not to return to the office until they had a chance to talk.

Hoping to repair the damage, TD called his boss in the morning, intent on apologizing profusely. Almost immediately, he was told that he needed "…to shut up and listen." His boss held TD in great esteem personally, as did the company as a whole; and they were all sympathetic to his situation. To avoid further problems, they wanted him to remain on paid leave while they finished reviewing the claim, another week at the most. He was reminded that he should know well enough how these things progressed. The investigator was obligated to follow-up on the evidence that was in front of him.

As his boss talked, TD was aware of his pulse starting to race. Trying to maintain his composure, he began mumbling out another apology. Again, his boss interrupted him.

"Apology accepted, TD. I'm sorry it came down to this, but I'm sure we'll get past it. You're a good man. Besides, you know we're just doing our job. I need you to try to stay calm and step back. It might help you gain a little perspective. Surely you knew things could go in this direction?"

Deep down, TD had always understood suicide was a possibility, and thus a reasonable investigative route. He had simply refused to spend any serious thought on it before ultimately suppressing any thought of it. He had settled on a rationalization that the police had deemed the event an accident, and anyone who thought otherwise was dealing with the matter emotionally, ignoring the facts.

Now, he found the implications of his boss's last question to be both damming and repulsive. It drove a stake into the heart of his personal and professional pride. His response was to yell into the phone, "Look, if I thought it was a suicide, I wouldn't have filed the fucking claim."

He still isn't sure what was said during the brief remainder of the call. He does remember ending with, "… and you can go fuck yourself." That had come after resigning his job on the spot. He talked twice more with the claims investigator, but refused contact with anyone else from the company.

Over lunch one day, Phil let him know that almost everyone at the firm he had talked with understood TD's reaction. Also, the company had not formally terminated his employment and still wanted to explore the possibility of him returning. Unfortunately, TD was too resentful, and too embarrassed to consider that at all. He soon discovered he was still receiving paychecks, auto-deposited into his bank account. After finally submitting a terse, dispassionate resignation letter, the deposits stopped.

Ultimately, the firm paid out the claim, including the double indemnity. During the long wait, TD had never followed up, not once. It took almost three months for them to issue the benefit check. TD swore he would never speak to anyone from the claims group again. He put the money into low-yielding CDs. Since then, he hasn't touched a penny, living off the excess proceeds of selling their home and drawing a little from his savings as needed.

⋏

Snapping out of his reminiscences, TD realizes he has been parked in front of the motel for over thirty minutes. He's lucky someone hasn't noticed and called the police.

Thinking about Elizabeth was cathartic. Though he has worked through most of the same thoughts before, it has been many months since he went through it all. At least this time, he feels like it might be a final rehashing.

Though thinking about it has brought him down from the rush of tonight's events, it has also reminded him of a cold reality. He has been living with his life on pause since Elizabeth's death. As he finally exits his car, he makes a silent declaration. That chapter of his life is closed. Tonight marks a fresh start.

Entering a motel office for the second time in a matter of hours, this time he doesn't care about the room's location or view. All he's interested in is getting some sleep. He suddenly feels so completely exhausted, that he may just wait until later to find out how exactly much money is in those bags.

⅄

Carl Roberts is optimistic as his team wraps up their work for the night. Having generated some potentially significant leads, he hopes that at least one of them will result in a break for the investigation. Without that happening, a case like this is capable of consuming endless hours of resources; resources that he doesn't have, or are already stretched too thin.

After putting Marvin Williams through a third round of questioning, they arranged for him to sleep in a vacant room. Yellow police tape seals off his original room, along with the one Tim Crane used. Based on Cyndi's interview, and an examination of the check-in records, they've also sealed one other. They think the man she saw taking the bags might have checked into the room at end of the row. It's possible he coordinated the attacks from there.

Despite getting Richter on loan from the county, Carl knows he remains shorthanded, particularly with the growing list of follow-up work. Impressed with results achieved by the two patrolmen, Clarkson and Landry, he has decided to use one of them full-time on the investigation. It was a close call, but he chose to go with Clarkson.

It's a huge break for Kenny, but the news leaves Sean Landry facing warring emotions. It was great seeing his friend snag an awesome assignment, one far better than the patrol work he'll resume tomorrow. And he doesn't begrudge Kenny his success. It's just that he wishes he could have been included.

Inside the motel's last vacant room, Roberts has gathered his small team for a recap. Though cramped, it provides a quiet spot where everyone can sit while getting up to speed on the case. Along with Richter and Clarkson, Steve Czarniak is there. Czarniak is his most senior detective, and the only other investigator from the city's force available for deployment tonight.

Together as a group for the first time, Roberts explains that the four of them will constitute the team handling the investigation. The scope of their inquiry will include not only the shootings, but also the two unusual car crashes that occurred during roughly the same timeframe, both within a block of the motel. He believes the wrecks will prove to be parts of a single unified event.

Having talked with each of the men as their work progressed tonight, Roberts is the only one with an overview of what they have collectively learned. Standing before them, with the two detectives sitting on opposite sides of the bed, and Clarkson straddling the wobbly desk chair, he begins a summary.

"Okay, let me take a stab at putting this all together. We have a group of at least six men executing a coordinated attack against another group working something out of this motel. It appears most of the attackers came rolling in by car, probably the one wrecked at the bus stop. From that point, things got nasty fast. We still don't know what was going down here. It may be drugs, but as of yet we have no evidence supporting that."

"One of the victims was using Room 112 as his point of operations. That room's current resident is Marvin Williams. Williams has had some legal problems in the past, but he doesn't look like a suspect. Interestingly, this isn't the first time they operated out of 112. According to Williams, the same man has been using that specific room for a while now, a few hours at a time, pretty much monthly."

This last piece of information clearly registers with the group. All react in small ways, nodding as they add this tidbit to their notes, quickly grasping how it adds additional flavor to the narrative they're creating.

"One assailant was seen leaving the motel on foot. He carried away a number of large gym bags, contents unknown. Apparently, the bags were the target of the attack. Now, he didn't have to hoof it far. He had parked his car at the bank next door. He was observed leaving, heading west, in a dark colored late-model sedan, possibly a Honda or a Toyota."

While Roberts was providing this last bit of information, Kenny Clarkson looked down, blushing with embarrassment. At least he didn't tell everyone that Kenny had failed to notice either the model, or even the color, of the car he almost ran into. Glancing up as Roberts briefly pauses, Kenny sees the senior detective wink at him with a slight smirk on his face.

Continuing, Roberts tells them, "This suspect is a middle-aged Caucasian. Unfortunately, that's all we have for the moment. None of our witnesses remembers any details of his description. The good news is we may have video of both him and the car from the bank's surveillance system. Consider him armed and dangerous. Finding him is one of our two top priorities. It's possible he organized the attack. It's unclear if he was a shooter, but we believe he checked in to the room right next door to where we're sitting. A witness spotted him in the courtyard immediately after the shooting stopped. She watched him take the bags and flee."

"We also know at least one assailant left by car, a silver, older model Ford Taurus. He didn't get far before crashing into a bus stop. The car's plates don't match the registration and both are stolen. Unlike our man with the bags, this guy was badly wounded in the gunfight. We have an eyewitness to the crash who took video while another man pulled him from the wreck. This second guy drove up, and after stopping in the middle of the road, dragged the wounded man over to his car and drove away."

While relating this information, Roberts notices Richter looking up, seemingly paying more attention than before. "Do you have a question or something to add, Detective Richter?"

For a moment, it seems Richter will remain silent, but then he speaks. "It all seems so odd and ad hoc. We have one guy leaving by foot and parking at the bank, while another guy flees the scene by car. And then he's picked up by another guy with a car, and it's not even the man who left with the bags of money."

As soon as the last three words are out of his mouth, Richter regrets it. Saying no more, he hunches his shoulders while giving a look of confusion.

"Yeah, I agree, it does seem odd," Roberts responds. "The whole damn thing is pretty odd if you ask me. As for bags full of money, well, I'm not sure we can draw that conclusion yet, but I certainly lean your way. It could be some kind of drug deal gone south, but it doesn't have that feel, does it? Not with the monthly use of the room."

Roberts leans back until he's sitting on the edge of the room's small desk. "The problem is we have no evidence of any kind of deal occurring. We found nothing left behind in any of the rooms or the car, and no one saw anything being removed from either of the wrecks. We've found no drugs, or any trace evidence of drugs. So, if there are no drugs, and there are no goods, like maybe guns, then it's hard to see it as a deal gone bad. The more I think about it, it looks like a straight rip off. Maybe the guys were getting ready to pay for a delivery, a regular delivery, and they got hit. I have to admit, this is an area where we really have nothing so far."

Richter wants to shut down this whole line of thinking. Sensing a small opening as Roberts pauses, he jumps in quickly. "Yeah, I think you're right. Nothing makes too much sense. But we do have at least three guys on the run."

Giving Richter's remarks scant thought, Roberts continues, "Yeah, okay, where was I? Right. The men at the bus stop wreck were both Hispanic, mid-twenties. The car they departed in is a ten year-old Dodge, with stolen plates. It was last seen heading east on Fairfax Boulevard. Finding these men is our other top priority. Obviously, they should also be considered armed and extremely dangerous."

Roberts pauses to let his team digest what they're learning, or to chime in if they have something to add. Hearing nothing, he continues. "To top it all off, we have this bizarre wreck at the Qwik Lube next door, opposite side of the motel from the bank. Some of this just doesn't fit, but what we have is a man sitting in a car, parked right up next to the building, well after business hours. Another stolen car with bad plates rams him at speed, killing him. Those who have seen the wreck agree that there's no way a driver was inside the ramming vehicle at impact. We assume he jumped out, but we have little else so far. There were no witnesses, no indication of who was driving, or why they rammed the other car. We have a few people who remember hearing this wreck and they place it immediately before all the shooting started."

Looking at each of them, he says, "So, I'm not buying that we had another accident, with another stolen car ramming someone at the same moment this other crap is going down, and it not being related. I consider this part of the whole show. Anyone disagree?"

Hearing no objections, Roberts continues, "Okay, that's what we have so far and here's what we're left with. By my count, we have a total of eight individuals shot, plus the guy killed in the crash behind the Qwik Lube. That makes eight dead and one seriously wounded. He's on the run, along with at least two others. We also have one critically injured bystander. He was alive when he left here in the ambulance, but with multiple injuries. His name is Bobby Tomlin. He was working the front desk. He apparently came out into the courtyard after the shooting stopped, only to be struck by the vehicle of the fleeing assailant. Oh yeah, I almost forgot. One of the fatalities appears to be another bystander, though maybe no so innocent; his name is Timothy Crane."

With raised eyebrows, Roberts tells them, "Mister Crane is married. He was at the motel on a date with a woman who is not his wife."

During the course of his recap, Roberts has noticed all three men nodding regularly as they listen with interest and take notes. This is the first time they're hearing everything presented in a coherent narrative, even if it is incomplete and evolving.

"Now, Besides Tomlin and Crane, everyone else here was ready to rock and roll. It looks like we have three dead shooters, plus three more dead from the home team. They were well armed, and clearly determined to defend whatever was in those bags. As for the deceased, three of them have no identification. Those three appear to all be Hispanic and in their twenties. Considering a variety of factors, particularly the positioning of the bodies, it's likely they were all part of the attacking group."

"Additionally, based on their style of clothing, the lack of gang tattoos, and even the nature of the attack, I agree with the county's expert that this does not look gang related. Thanks again to Detective Richter for getting that help so quickly."

After acknowledging Richter's contribution, Roberts continues. "On the identification front, we believe the victim in the vehicle parked behind the Qwik Lube is one Peter Bowman. We have no priors on him. How he and the car crash are related to this mess at the motel is unclear, though Officer Clarkson brought up one possibility that works."

Smiling, Roberts nods toward Clarkson. After an awkward pause, Kenny realizes he should speak. "Yes, well, I think maybe he was a sentry, or back-up for the guys at the motel."

Roberts jumps back in, "That makes sense, but if it's true, it also means that he was targeted. And that indicates exceptional advance scouting and planning by the attackers. The three other victims of the attack have also been identified as Edward King, Frank Tomasso, and John Wells. King and Tomasso both have multiple priors for weapons and gambling, but nothing recent. King's body was on the ground next to Crane in front of the rooms. Based on what I saw, and the techs will help us with this, it appears he took down at least two of the attackers. Tomasso was the driver of the Mercedes, and Wells was the passenger in the back seat. And, just so you know how ready for action Mister Wells was, he came to the party armed with a state of the art SIG Sauer machine pistol."

After one last glance at his notes, Roberts finishes, "Lastly, the Mercedes is owned by a company called Construction & Corporate Vehicle Services. We have nothing on that firm at this point."

For the second time, Roberts notices Richter visibly react to a specific piece of information. This time it was a subtle jerk of his head, but there was no eye contact or comments. Roberts wonders, is the guy just twitchy, or does he know something he's not saying?

Ready to wrap things up, Roberts remembers Landry's discovery. "Oh yeah, another thing. We may also have video of vehicles entering the motel. Just up the driveway behind this place, there's a self-storage company with a solid security system. Overall, I think we're damn lucky with all the video we have."

Roberts adds that the wounded man should be the easiest to locate since he's clearly in desperate need of medical care. The emergency rooms in the immediate area have been put on notice. Roberts had a specific alert issued, even though the hospitals are required to contact the police about any patients with gunshot wounds. He wants to heighten awareness and create a sense of urgency for the ERs to call in at first contact.

He then asks Richter to focus on this aspect of the investigation. He also tells him to extend the alert to hospitals in the next ring of jurisdictions if they don't hear something. Carl again notices a visible reaction from the man as he receives the assignment. Richter seems visibly disappointed and ready to say something, but in the end, he simply nods his assent.

Roberts assigns Clarkson the duty of notifying Tim Crane's wife of his death. It needs to be taken care of tonight. It's doubtful there's any connection between Crane and the attack, but they need to be sure. He reminds Clarkson to be respectful as he delivers the news, but to remember he's also there to gain information. He's to ask Crane's wife if she has any idea why her husband was at that motel on this specific night. Also, Kenny should avoid mentioning Crane was at the motel with another woman.

Like Richter, Kenny isn't thrilled with his assignment. As he tries keeping any reaction from his face, Roberts reads his mind.

"Look, Clarkson, I know this one stinks, but it needs to be done. In the morning, I want you to team up with Czarniak."

Turning to Czarniak, he says, "Steve, first thing tomorrow I want you two to meet with the both the bank and the storage company's security people. See what images they have that can help find these guys."

Roberts announces he'll take on the task of contacting the company that owns the Mercedes. The car represents one of their most solid leads. He'd definitely like to learn why their vehicle was at the motel tonight. And more importantly, why there were two heavily armed men onboard.

Again, Roberts could swear Richter has something to say. Then, just as before, the moment passes. He wonders what's behind all that. Maybe it's simply being on loan and a little uncomfortable. Maybe it's taking orders from a younger man that's bothering him. Or getting what he perceives as a less than a choice assignment. Maybe it's some part of all those reasons. Whatever, it's making it hard to like the man.

After a brief round of follow-on questions, Roberts schedules their next meeting for two in the afternoon at the city's headquarters. Each of them will provide updates on any progress they've made. His final instruction is for them to get some sleep.

As they move back outside, he pats Clarkson on the shoulder, telling him he did an excellent job tonight. Overall, Roberts is in a great mood. When you get past all the tragedy, it's an intriguing case. And they really do have some quality leads to work. By tomorrow, they should know a lot more.

⋏

After the recap meeting, Richter calls Dan Keach from his car. As the detective begins to get deeper into the details of his report, Keach interrupts, telling him he needs to ignore anything that doesn't help him find the money. When Richter tries explaining that Roberts's orders point him in another direction, Keach explodes.

"Look, I don't give a shit about your orders. You need to find that money. That's your priority. You should be working on that twenty-four hours a day. I want to know who this guy is who took the cash, and I want to know in the morning. And I want the wounded guy as well. I want them both."

Keach pauses long enough to calm himself. "Look, just relay the leads to me as you get them. And share as little as you have to with anyone else. If you give me enough, I'll find the guy. And that's how I want it to go down.

I need to reach him before you and your cop buddies, that way I'm the one who gets the money back. After that, you can have him. As for the wounded shooter, he's a dead man. Just let me know who he is and where he's at."

Acknowledging Keach, Richter remembers to tell him about the Mercedes. "Look, Roberts will probably call the owners first thing in the morning. He may even stop by their offices. The best way to slow him down is to shutter the place for a couple of days. At the same time, you need to make sure any documents on file relating to that car point away from whoever you're protecting."

Keach thanks Richter for the suggestions, satisfied the cop is beginning to see the larger picture. Adding a stern reminder to get him some information fast, Keach ends the call.

⅄

Kenny Clarkson slowly rolls his police cruiser into the circular driveway fronting the Crane's residence in Great Falls. The home is beautiful and huge. Kenny knows he'll never live in a home like this. He hopes to save enough to purchase his own place one day, and wonders how much you have to earn to afford a place like this.

Kenny has never performed a death notification. Nervous, he's somewhat reassured when he sees multiple lights are on inside the home. He has been dreading having to wake the victim's wife with such terrible news. Soon after he rings the bell, the door opens. Standing in front of him is an attractive woman, wearing a modest, but luxurious robe.

After identifying himself and confirming that he's speaking with Tim Crane's wife, Kenny asks if he can come inside. Without inquiring why he is there, Julia Crane nods and steps aside as he enters. Once he's past her, she closes the door but goes no further. It's clear she intends for them to remain standing in the spacious two-story foyer.

Kenny solemnly delivers the news, finding himself a little surprised by Julia's muted response. Though clearly surprised by Tim's unexpected death, she displays little emotional reaction. There's no sign of shock, nor any overt display of grief. He wonders what kind of marriage they had that would leave her so unaffected. Maybe she knew all about her husband's sketchy behavior.

Nearly finished with his task, he writes the phone number and address for the Coroner's office on a fresh page he tears from his small notebook. Before handing it to her, he adds his own name and the headquarters' phone number if she has any questions. As she takes the slip of paper from his hand, he remembers the information Detective Roberts wants. Knowing that he's heading onto thin ice, he asks if she's able to answer a few questions.

Julia agrees, but tells him to keep it brief. Responding to his questions, she makes it clear she was aware of Tim's constant affairs. Full of contempt, she tells him she has no idea why he chose the Gateway and that she has never heard of the motel. When he attempts another question, she stops him. "I think that's enough for now Officer."

Turning toward the open staircase, she pauses, appearing to have something else to say. Now wearing a slightly sadder expression, she speaks, "If you want any more information about my late husband's disgusting habits, I suggest you speak with TD Adkins. I'll call him in the morning and instruct him to cooperate with you."

"I'm sorry, ma'am. Can you please repeat that name?"

"TD Adkins. He's the private investigator I hired to follow Tim. If he was doing his job, he would have been there tonight."

With that, she said goodnight, turned her back on him, and proceeded up the stairs.

Once outside, Kenny checks his notebook. Seeing the badly scribbled name, he takes a moment to re-write it more neatly. This is big news.

It's been a long night and he's anxious to get some sleep, but this is exciting. He can't wait to team up with Czarniak in the morning. He'll also be giving this Adkins fellow a call. If he's lucky, they just may have another witness, and another opportunity for him to impress Roberts.

Immediately after hearing from Richter, Keach calls the manager of Construction & Corporate Vehicle Services. He knows exactly who to call because the firm is wholly owned by Wilkins Investment Group. It's just another of the many front companies used to avoid taxes and muddle the flow of cash.

Once the man is awake and paying attention, Keach reels off his instructions. First, all staff are to stay away from the office until further notice. Secondly, the manager is not to answer his phone unless he's sure who is calling. The company's voice mail greeting should be changed to state the office is closed for the day and to leave a message. Keach then asks if he knows who authorized the lease for the Mercedes. The manager isn't sure, but says it was probably handled the same as all the others.

Keach knows notionally who that should be and hopes they followed the procedures he established. Such leases are assigned to staff who are several layers removed from Richard Wilkins or Robert Owen. The cost of the Mercedes should be rolled up into a monthly invoice for all vehicles the firm procures, including construction equipment. The accounting department processes the invoices. Keach tells the manager to get over to the office now, confirm the status of the lease documents, and then call him back.

As long as things have been handled as planned, Keach believes they can deal with the consequences. Without a massive document switch, that could itself leave a trail, the police will inevitably trace the car to Wilkins Investment Group. They will also ultimately learn that the car was often used to chauffer Richard Wilkins, and that his personal driver, Frank Tomasso, was driving it tonight.

His short-term goal is simply to slow law enforcement down while making sure everyone has their story straight. Anyone the police talks to will adamantly assert that the driver was using the vehicle for his own purposes that night. Additionally, his use of the car was unauthorized, prohibited by company policy, and done without the knowledge of Richard Wilkins or anyone else at the firm.

When he registered at the motel on Route 1, TD paid with cash and presented one of the fake IDs he brought along with him. He used a Maryland driver's license bearing his picture, but with a different name. The name and the license number are both valid, only for a different individual. The age, height, and weight listed on the card all match TD's.

As an additional precaution, he has decided to park his car somewhere close by tonight, but away from the motel. Before he can do that, he needs to move his luggage and the cash into the room. As he puts the gym bags on the bed, he makes a bet with himself. From what he saw with the one peek earlier, there could be as much as a half a million dollars inside the bags. That will be his over/under. Like most people, he has never seen or handled that much cash. The mystery of how much there is will have to wait though; he needs to move his car.

A quarter of a mile up the road he spots an older gas station, now operating as a repair shop. Pulling in, he's able to slide into a tight spot between two cars parked off to the side of the building. He'll need to get back early in the morning, but he's more comfortable with it parked there, than having it sitting nakedly in front of the motel room where he's staying.

During the quick walk back to his room, TD considers his latest actions. In the past hour, he has abandoned his home, gotten a motel room using a bogus ID, and hidden his car. They're all necessary acts if he's being hunted, but is he being paranoid? It's really hard to conceive anyone could already be on his tail.

Still, by the time he gets back to his room, he has convinced himself; it's a smart thing to take precautions, right from the start. If he's to vanish successfully, free and clear, he can't leave footprints. Letting someone know where he has been, leads them part of the way to where he is going, wherever that may be.

It's also time to stop playing mind games and get a full understanding of his situation; it's time to count the money. As he leans over the bed and reaches for one of the bags, he suddenly feels lightheaded, almost losing his balance. It almost feels as if he's going to faint.

Pulling the room's only chair out from under the desk, he turns it around and quickly sits. He needs to calm down. It's then he remembers having eaten nothing since lunch. And he's been going non-stop, under pressure, for several hours. Slowly tilting the chair back, he props his feet on the edge of the bed. Counting the money can wait. As he slows his breathing, he closes his eyes. Trying to relax, he reflects on how he came to this point on this wholly unpredictable night.

Up until now, there have been two primary arcs to his life. The first was a disjointed progression, almost of happenstance. After growing up with little adult guidance, he now lived a life deeply influenced by others. Sure, he had found his career enjoyable and intellectually rewarding, but it was not a vocation he had aspired to. It was born of an unglamorous job offer arranged by his best friend, simply to help relieve pressure from Elizabeth.

Then, after her passing, he travelled along a second sharply downward arc. His life devolved into that of a careless recluse, wallowing in his perceived misfortune. Since then, he has lived with little purpose, full of doubts. Dark doubts about how and why Elizabeth's life had ended. Deep troubling doubts about whether he would ever regain any motivation. Lately, he has had a few glimpses of better times, but it's been a long while since he gave any thought to the future.

Tonight, that second arc ended the moment he walked among the dead bodies at the motel and picked up those bags of cash. Now, it feels as if there's a new TD Adkins. A man triumphant over the hang-about he had become, and on the verge of a new arc; an arc not yet defined, though still enticing.

But TD also senses a faint unease, a distant sensation that not all is right. As excited as he is about new possibilities, he senses a concern. After a few minutes, he understands the problem. It's the cash. He must answer whether he's willing to set off on this fresh journey in life with someone else's money, while knowing they had died battling to keep it.

He ponders the question for several minutes before deciding to continue down the path he has already taken. Yes, he took the money, but those he took it from are gone. And he was in no way involved in their killing, nor could've done anything to prevent it. Besides, if he hadn't taken the money, someone else would have. He may have to live with a few regrets, but that's something he believes he can learn to ignore.

His choice is clear. There will be no more looking back.

Having absentmindedly risen from the chair, TD finds himself pacing the confines of the small room, his mind swirling with critical questions and shifting emotions. If he's definitely moving forward, then what's next? Where's the best place to relocate? How much money does he have to work with?

He has been toying with counting the cash but repeatedly putting it off. Maybe he doesn't really want to know how much there is. Maybe he should just stop this whole damn thing right now. He can turn himself in and give the money to the police. Call it no harm, no foul.

Stopping his pacing in front of the dressing mirror, he stares back at a man looking edgy and tired, almost frantic. Talking aloud to his reflection, he says, "Enough, you fool."

Turning around, he slides one of the bags to the edge of the bed and pulls back the zipper. As he does so, he notices a faint smear of blood on one side of the bag. About an inch long and almost dry, it unsettles him. Hesitating, he senses that counting the money represents a point of no return. Then he realizes there's no logic to that at all.

The bag contains only twenty-dollar bills. When he finishes removing the straps and stacking them on the bed, he finds a piece of paper pressed along the inner side of the bag. In a neat, legible handwriting is written, 61 x 20 = $122,000. The last number is underlined twice.

The tally matches the straps of cash that he has piled on the bed, but the overall amount seems rather low to him. Flashing back to Slick and his colleagues, defending the money with their lives, TD knows the other bags must contain much more than this.

The second bag is heavier, increasing his anticipation that its value is much greater. He sees he was right as soon as it's open. Not only is it packed more densely, there's nothing but straps of one hundreds. He finds the inventory sheet tucked in the same place. It states the bag contains seventy-three straps of hundreds: $730,000. That's even more than he had estimated, and well on the way to a million with one bag remaining. He isn't greatly surprised though. Slick and his men demonstrated considerable professionalism. This was no small-time operation.

The final bag, the one he removed from the trunk of the Cadillac, contains a mix of denominations. When he locates the inventory sheet, his eye for detail notices a few small differences. The most obvious is the handwriting. It isn't the same, and a different color pen was used. This bag contains $236,000. Doing the math in his head, the total comes to $1,088,000. It's more than a million dollars. That's why Slick and his crew fought for it. And that's why someone out there will be looking to get it back.

Feeling the fatigue that's rapidly increasing its grip on him, TD knows he must get some sleep. Planning what comes next will require a fresher mind than he currently possesses. Tomorrow he'll confer with Phil Madrigal and say goodbye. Then he'll take the first step of a plan he has yet to conceive; a step he won't let himself think about tonight.

After repacking the bags, he stretches out on the bed fully clothed. Almost immediately, his thoughts return to money. For the first time tonight, he remembers the large amount of funds he already has from the insurance settlement. He has never spent a dollar of it, yet maybe even that will change. Combined with what he has acquired, he has a small fortune. He may very well need one if he wants to disappear in comfort. For the first time he begins thinking about logistics. How is he going to deal with all this currency? How can he access any of his current assets without leaving a trail?

Deciding to shift his thoughts to a more pleasant thread, he considers where he might live. As he continues to unwind, he finally begins feeling drowsy. Only half-awake, he ponders a life of leisure on a tropical island. Then, the imaginary venue changes to a nicely appointed mountain cabin, somewhere far from the East Coast, maybe Oregon.

His reverie is suddenly shattered by the thump of two car doors slamming shut in rapid succession, the sound coming from directly in front of his room. Leaping from the bed with rising fear, he reaches the window with one long stride and edges the curtains back. What he sees triggers a nervous laugh as he watches a young couple moving away from their car, walking toward a room a couple of doors down.

The tension of the moment puts him on edge again. How much time these past few hours has he spent peering out windows or checking his rearview mirror? Unfortunately, this is his current reality. It'll be quite some time before he's no longer on the run and able to relax. And clearly, some part of his mind believes he's in danger. Otherwise, he wouldn't be jumping to the window upon simply hearing a car door slam, something that's a perfectly routine sound in a motel parking lot.

As he continues standing by the window, he begins the questioning again. Did he really get away tonight unseen? Could someone already be hunting for him specifically?

Thinking back to the chaos at the motel, and even before that, he makes another inventory of anyone who could possibly identify him. The desk clerk might provide a good description, but wasn't he killed when the car hit him? Even if he survived, TD paid with cash and used a fake name.

The only others to get a decent look at him are Tim Crane's girlfriend and the man he encountered in the bank parking lot. Neither has any idea who he is, and they could only provide a general description. The girl was clearly in shock. The man at the bank could conceivably recall his car, but he would've had no reason to remember it, or take note of the license plate. He feels confident that the only way any witness could point to him, is if the police nab him using some other method and then stand him in front of them for identification.

Realizing that he's winding himself up again, TD stops his fear based thinking. He can't continue constantly replaying this. From this point forward, he's sticking with a basic assumption: it will take considerable time and investigation before anyone can identify him as either being at the motel or taking the money. If that ever happens, by then he will be gone. And to cover the small possibility that he's wrong, he has done the right thing leaving his home. It doesn't matter if he's being overly cautious. Many of the people he investigated over the years thought they were being careful enough, yet they still fell prey to top investigators.

It's time to sleep. Checking the bedside clock, he's surprised how much time has slipped by; it's almost three AM. He sets the alarm for nine. He's not optimistic he can sleep that late, though it would be great for both his body and mind. Tomorrow he'll start formulating concrete plans for the next phase of his life, but only after he talks with the young woman he has come here to see.

At least one decision is final. He's leaving the area. He'll lay low for a day or two at the most, build a solid plan for his getaway, and then execute it.

As he attempts to fall asleep a second time, his feelings of satisfaction, and even a sense of victory, are ascendant again. He's confident he can change his identity and make TD Adkins disappear. He knows the tricks of the trade and the many methods people use to hide. He also knows which of those methods fail and he won't make the same mistakes. He simply needs to stay relaxed, and plan his next moves without putting himself under too much pressure.

Ready to take on a new life, he's finally able to block out tonight's events and sleep. As he drifts off, his thoughts linger on the woman he will see tomorrow.

TUESDAY

Richard Wilkins's morning ritual includes fresh brewed coffee and a bagel, along with a leisurely read of the Washington Post. His mornings are almost never rushed and he rarely arrives at his office before ten.

This morning he has a voicemail; the call must have come after he turned in last night. After listening to the short message twice, he calls Dan Keach. As the call connects, Wilkins considers their relationship. Though cordial, they are definitely not close. He finds himself particularly turned off by Keach's brusque, often condescending demeanor.

Despite that, the man has earned his respect. He appreciates the efficient manner Keach employs addressing the security concerns the firm faces. There have also been occasions when his CFO referred to a problem that Keach had 'managed'. Problems Richard had known nothing about. Problems Keach handled without any need to consult or involve him. He enjoys that aspect of Keach's management style most of all.

Still, he's definitely not thrilled with the voice message. What could be so urgent that Keach needs an appointment so early in the day? When he answers, Richard skips any greeting, "What's this meeting about, Dan?"

"I apologize for starting your day with a problem, sir, but it's critically urgent I meet with you and Robert Owen this morning. It's not something we should discuss over the phone. I'm positive you'll understand after we've talked."

Digesting both the content and the tenor of Keach's message, Wilkins responds, "Alright Daniel, say nothing more. I understand, and I trust your judgment. I'll see you at nine sharp in my office. Thanks."

Wilkins knows he doesn't understand anything. He also knows he doesn't need to. That Keach has politely demanded a meeting and termed the matter urgent is all he needs to know. Leaving his coffee and the newspaper unfinished on the kitchen counter, he quickly heads upstairs to shower. He's soon on his way to his Tysons Corner office, much earlier than normal.

⚓

Richard Wilkins's success as a real estate developer is due far more to market conditions than from any skill on his part. And even that success came only after inheriting a thriving business his father had built over many decades.

The only person Richard has ever worked for was his father, a man who came to the region in the late-Sixties with a plan. His goal was to buy as much property as he could in the scenic, rolling countryside of western Fairfax County, an area that was mostly farmland.

When his father retired, it was after more than a quarter of a century of steady expansion for the DC metro area. The wealth he accumulated was befitting of his vision and hard work. He turned his company over to Richard with one condition: he must personally manage the firm and continue building the family business.

Initially, Richard was successful and continued growing the firm's assets and reputation. He was also impatient, always on the lookout for opportunities to convert his generous inheritance into even more wealth. Seeing many less-experienced competitors generate instant fortunes with highly leveraged deals, he desperately wanted into the game.

Wilkins decided to first increase the firm's scope of operations by expanding into the construction side of the business. His father advised against it, but Richard plunged ahead. To jump-start the new business model, he orchestrated the buyout of one of the region's largest commercial builders. As a consequence of the deal, Wilkins Investment Group, along with its new subsidiary, was now anchored in debt. At the same time, the firm would now be financing and managing projects of a scope and complexity it had never handled before.

Suddenly, his father was dead of a stroke. His passing robbed Richard of both his mentor and his most savvy deal reviewer. Deal selection is critical, and Richard's eye for an opportunity was less keen than his father's. Acting as both the developer and builder, Wilkins failed to break even on consecutive large projects. The losses weren't too heavy, but the firm no longer had the cash reserves able to absorb further defeats, nor the profits to leverage into new deals.

Richard began making mistakes on the real estate side as well. The most damaging, a series of ill-conceived investments in large tracts of land purchased prior to a soft period in the real estate market. With his capital locked up in projects that would take several years just to break even, he had rapidly driven the firm to the doorstep of insolvency.

⅄

Richard's true passions in life are gambling and nightlife. He regularly plays in local high stakes poker games and takes frequent trips to Atlantic City or Las Vegas, sometimes just for the weekend. On his trips, if he isn't gambling, he's living large, running up staggering tabs at bars and strip clubs.

On one of his early visits to Vegas, massive gambling losses left him out of cash on just his second day in town. With his credit cards nearly maxed to the limit, but unwilling to call it quits and fly home, he needed to get his hands on some money. After two different casinos he regularly played at refused to extend his line of credit, he sought advice from the VIP host at one his favorite strip clubs. Using a referral from the host, he had access to a cash loan within hours. Richard borrowed plenty.

Surprisingly, luck was on his side. He managed a huge comeback over the next two days playing blackjack and craps. Happy to be paying off his debt before leaving town, he was both shocked and impressed with the fee for the loan, the 'vig' that the loan shark charged. Even though he paid everything back in just two days, the amount of interest was no small amount. It wasn't lost on Richard that it represented an enormous return on investment for the lender.

It was during that flight back from Vegas fifteen years ago that he decided to get into illegal financing. He coveted the huge profits you can generate from charging sky-high interest rates and paying no taxes. He even had a ready batch of clients within the real estate development business, a sector crowded with independent sub-contractors. Cash flow for these small businesses is always a problem, and many are tapped out with conventional sources of credit.

Most importantly, the idea offered the ability to generate significant cash flow using the limited funds he still had available to him. Ultimately, it could provide the seed money he needed for new development deals. Taking the leap, he poured every remaining dollar the firm had into the new line of business, as well as all it could borrow. He had a young accountant, Robert Owen, set up shadow firms to shield Wilkins Investment Group from both image and tax problems. Owen soon learned to move funds adeptly between the various entities.

Wilkins had discovered a natural and somewhat untapped market. He was also lucky when none of the initial loans defaulted. Within a year, both the size and the number of loans had increased considerably. They also began acquiring customers in different business sectors, some legal, others not so much. The Group, the name Richard like to use to refer to all his businesses, now had a growing and exorbitantly profitable new revenue stream.

It was another personal experience that gave Richard Wilkins the idea to establish his second illicit cash cow. While playing poker, one of his wealthy playmates kept complaining that he couldn't get a hold of his bookie to bet on a college football game. Wilkins offered to take the bet for him personally, on the condition he could charge the same vig as the guy was already going to pay.

He ended up taking two bets at the poker table that day. One paid off, the other lost. Because of the vig, he still showed a profit. Sensing another opportunity, Richard had The Group launch a bookmaking operation targeting high-end customers. It wasn't long before business was booming.

Over the next several years, The Group experienced outstanding success with its new trade. It also faced little organized competition. Due to the long-standing success of the FBI, and the presence of so many other Federal law enforcement personnel, no major crime syndicate has ever established a territorial, monopoly style presence in the DC area. The region is ripe for small, independent operators, and The Group filled the niche nicely with its low profile, professionally run ventures.

Wilkins drew great enjoyment from building a thriving, profitable business from scratch. He decided to expand The Group's geography, targeting Richmond and Baltimore. As they began establishing a presence further north of DC, Richard was contacted by representatives of organized crime. They were out of Philadelphia, but also operated in Baltimore. He was informed, "Interested parties feel it's time for a little talk."

Wilkins feared he had stepped on the wrong toes, possibly a huge mistake. A dinner meeting was set up in a restaurant's private dining room. He felt some relief as the meal progressed cordially with little more than pleasant conversation. After the main course, the discussion shifted. He was lectured that he needed, "…to show some respect for the way business is done." And that it was, "…time to develop a mutual understanding."

The understanding was quite straightforward. It was explained that when one becomes involved in certain lines of business there is no free lunch. Gambling and loan sharking are businesses on that list. If he would like to operate in certain geographies, then there are costs. For example, his dinner hosts informed him, he had neglected to consider whether he had any competitors, as well as the cost of protecting himself from them.

It quickly became evident that his counterparts had a surprisingly detailed knowledge of The Group's operations. As they finished with coffee, they told him they didn't mind Wilkins working in a given area, as long as he didn't overstep boundaries. His geography, along with protection from competitors, could be guaranteed for the right price.

Along with a real sense of relief, several thoughts crossed Richard's mind. They didn't want to hurt him or put him out of business. Quite the contrary, it was a classic shakedown. And as for his earlier belief there were no taxes on his profits, well that was certainly naïve. Going forward, he would clearly be paying taxes, just not to the government.

He found it easy to reach a comprehensive arrangement. In addition to paying a small percentage of his gross revenues, he agreed to a few restrictions on his new businesses and any he may think to expand into later. He was not to deal in drugs or prostitution, nor could he be involved in any manner with the horse racing industry. All other betting on sports was acceptable.

The agreement with his new friends allowed The Group to finance illegal loans, operate illegal gambling venues, and run a sports book in the region starting just south of Baltimore and throughout Virginia and West Virginia. The possibility of future joint real estate development deals was discussed. They also suggested he consider setting up fences to traffic in stolen property; it was lucrative business and helped with processing illicit cash. He was welcome to enter that line of business as long as he interlinked with their existing fences and help circulate the goods they acquired.

Wilkins assembled a dedicated team that was quite successful at expanding The Group's illicit businesses. Within just three years, the profits being generated rivaled those of the sickly real estate development side. Slowly, the firm began curing its financial ills as Wilkins used the fresh earnings to pay down the company's enormous debt.

Though the illegal operations started modestly, that would not remain the case. Whether by serendipity or foresight, Richard Wilkins had perfectly positioned The Group to exploit two emerging mega-trends.

⅄

In 2003, a Texas Hold-em Poker craze began sweeping the nation. Interest in the game skyrocketed after amateur Chris Moneymaker's victory in the

2003 World Series of Poker Main Event. Richard Wilkins quickly grasped the explosive potential of the market for live poker. Building on his own experience, he had The Group rapidly establish dozens of illegal poker games at secure, discreet locations across the DC region.

The games catered to mid-level and high stakes players with neither the time nor desire to trek to Atlantic City, the closest venue for legal gaming. Under the guidance of Dan Keach, they avoided the traps leading to the downfall of many illegal games. They shunned publicity, screened new players, and limited the number of tables at each location. Weapons and any use of drugs were strictly prohibited. Within a year, they had games running in every decent-sized town from Baltimore to Norfolk.

Richard also understood that providing access to the sports book dove-tailed nicely with the card games, magnifying the amount of revenue each site generated. Within five years, The Group coordinated its growing businesses through multiple regional hubs. Each hub operated dozens of poker games and sports books, along with fences, pawnshops, and loan sharking. They all generated a river of cash.

Initially, finding the right people to operate the growing businesses was a constant problem. The small group of employees working for Wilkins Investment Group only focused on real estate development deals. They were ill equipped to manage or staff the new operations. A variety of unique skillsets were needed, including poker dealers, bookmakers, street lenders, collectors, security staff, and the leadership to manage them all. There were several missteps finding the right individuals.

Early on, a referral from Richard's contacts in Philadelphia led to the hiring of Dan Keach. Keach provided much needed help identifying and recruiting key staff. Once guys like Eddie King were on board, they performed most of the ongoing recruiting. Everyone was paid in cash. They had no idea who they ultimately worked for, nor did they really care.

The legalization of casino gambling in West Virginia and Maryland presented a serious challenge to The Group. Revenues took a serious hit, but finally steadied at a lower, entirely acceptable level. Wilkins had known the casinos were ultimately coming. For several years, he had focused all of his expansion plans on Virginia. Thanks to the continuing growth there, and the ongoing diversification of their operations, revenues eventually rebounded to the level of prior years.

By their very nature, the illegal operations generate large amounts of currency. To help with the problem, Wilkins Investment Group began legally acquiring a variety of small businesses. Restaurants, leasing firms, used car lots, dry cleaners, and ironically, even laundromats were added to the firm's portfolio. They weren't acquired for their modest profitability. What they provided was another channel for laundering and legitimizing all of the cash being generated by the illicit businesses.

In parallel, Wilkins had carefully hand-selected a small team of in-house accountants to deal with the financial intricacies. Anyone working those spreadsheets would have no question as to the nature of their job. Their mission was to account for the cash generated by the diverse illegal operations and run it through multiple layers of the small businesses. Ultimately, the profits all landed in the coffers of Wilkins Investment Group.

Utilizing the fresh funds now available, Richard was well positioned to take advantage of a second mega-trend, one of the largest real estate bubbles in US history. It's difficult to lose money during the upswing of such a market and Wilkins Investment Group began hitting home runs again.

With renewed confidence in his business skills, Richard led the firm into increasingly larger development deals, leveraging the profits gained from the illegal operations. It was a great marriage of business concepts. By his side was Robert Owen, his Chief Financial Officer. One of the first accountants hired for the secretive work, Owen had quickly risen to the top of the organization, doing the heavy lifting in the financial management area.

Working with Daniel Keach, Owen keeps Richard Wilkins relatively insulated from the illegal businesses. This allows Wilkins to play the role of a successful, second-generation real estate mogul, enriching himself and those around him with his demonstrable talent to spot and engineer development deals. Of course, it's much easier to gain an edge in business when your firm is self-financing, using a torrent of illegal cash, and carrying none of the costs of credit that his competitors face.

Yet even that advantage has withered in the face of the recent recession and collapse of the real estate market. Not naïve about the marketplace, Richard is aware that things on the legal side of his businesses have turned bleak once again.

▲

As he pulls into his office's parking garage, Richard notices Robert Owen's high-end Lexus sedan is already in its space. His appreciation for his CFO's skills has deteriorated rapidly the past year. The firm's recovery from the correction in the commercial real estate market has been excruciatingly slow. Recently, he was forced to sit through several dire presentations by Owen regarding the critical cash flow problems they face.

Too much of the firm's limited store of cash is tied up in outstanding loans, either legitimate and not. The firm possesses considerable assets in land, buildings, and equipment, but there is little to no equity. The level of debt incurred against the firm's revenue projections is beyond any level of prudence.

Owen had recently warned that certain aspects of the firm's bookkeeping were nothing more than a Ponzi scheme. During their last meeting on the topic, Wilkins realized that for some time now, his handpicked CFO had been less than honest with him about how badly stretched the firm's finances were becoming.

Richard had also learned that for most of the past year, the legitimate side of the business would not have remained afloat without the constant infusion of profits from the illegal operations. After digesting the news, he rationalized it wasn't that big a deal. He didn't care where the money came from, as long as the public entity of Wilkins Investment Group didn't appear to be failing. That could result in a loss of faith from their bankers and the onset of grave legal problems.

With it being more critical than ever for the illicit operations to generate significant profits, Wilkins was greatly disappointed to learn there were problems in that area as well. Gambling revenues had increased the past year, but less than costs had risen. At the same time, profits from their loan business were tanking.

The value of non-performing loans on their books represented a significant and rapidly increasing amount. None of the firm's legitimate loans were being paid and forcing collection would likely lead to default. On the street side of the business, threats of harsh treatment from Keach's enforcers could not change the fact that many of their customers were totally broke.

Despite the problems, there's still plenty of positive cash flow. The issue is getting the funds to Wilkins Investment Group quickly enough to help. Unfortunately, laundering money requires time. Pumping through too much cash, too quickly, creates serious risks. If the firm is suddenly flush with money that hasn't been cycled through the proper accounting processes, it will eventually set off alarms with the IRS. Based on what he has learned, Richard fears they're already running dangerously close to that situation.

And now, this morning, something else is seriously wrong. And there's more to this than just financial or accounting problems. Otherwise, Dan Keach wouldn't have been the one to request the meeting.

λ

Raffi Flores has no memory of his arrival at Stafford Hospital Center. Following a series of emergency surgeries lasting several hours, he has finally regained consciousness and a slow awareness of his circumstances.

He's in better shape than he could have imagined considering the trauma his body suffered. Few people survive two close-range gunshot wounds and a car accident, all in a matter of minutes. He doesn't know if he's capable of getting out of bed yet, but it doesn't matter; he's alive. Now he needs to start figuring a way out of here.

Roughly fifty miles from where he was shot, the hospital and surrounding county were not included in the area receiving Carl Robert's initial alert for a shooting victim. Despite that, established protocols require the hospital to report gunshot victims. After Raffi was admitted and sent off for surgery, an ER staffer called it in.

The information was immediately entered into the local police department's incident management system. Based on pre-defined rules, the system generated a departmental alert with a link to the report. The alert for Raffi was given a case number and assigned to the investigative division for follow-up. Based on its prioritization, the case was slotted near the top of the work queue.

At another time of day, or just a different night, a detective would have been available almost immediately. That was not the situation last night in Stafford County. Every on-duty investigator was on a high-priority case, and it is that way again this morning. It will be many hours before anyone starts working the case.

As Raffi's head continues to clear, it doesn't appear to him that he is under guard. His range of view is limited, but the door to his hospital room remains open and he hasn't seen anyone that looks like security or the police. Also, a nurse has been in to check on him twice. Neither time did she pause upon at entering, as if there was someone guarding his room.

Slowly, Raffi begins edging towards the side of the bed, fighting the urge to cry out over the agonizing pain in both his shoulder and leg. His goal is to reach the bedside phone without drawing the attention of a nurse. If he's successful, he'll call Cesar to come and take him out of there as soon as he can.

⋏

The offices of Wilkins Investment Group occupy the top floor of a sixteen-story office tower in Tysons Corner. On a clear day, you can easily see the Washington Monument, a little more than ten miles to the east. Richard Wilkins prefers the west side of the building, giving his personal office a view of the distant Blue Ridge Mountains.

At precisely Nine AM, Robert Owen enters Richard's office with a firm rap on the open door. Head down as he comes in, he's ostensibly studying the printout of a spreadsheet. He needn't have bothered with appearances;

Wilkins has his back turned, peering out at the series of ridges to the west. Before either man has said a word, Daniel Keach follows Owen through the door, closing it behind himself.

Having turned from the window, Wilkins gestures the men toward two leather sofas sitting astride a broad smoked-glass coffee table. The furniture sits in a large open area, well away from his desk. Greeting them with a brusque tone, Richard says, "Good morning, gentlemen. Daniel, I believe you called this meeting, so let's not waste time. What problem brings us together so urgently?"

Keach walks them through what he knows. With a surprising level of detail, he tells them the cash consolidation operation was hit last night. A number of their men were killed and the cash taken. The raid appears to have been well planned. Though all of their men at the scene died, they took down most of the assailants during the attack. Based on that and other information, he does not believe this was an inside job, though he won't rule that out completely.

After a period of silence approaching nearly a minute, Richard speaks. "Based on your knowledge of events, is it correct to assume that we, or I should say you, have the ability to stay on top of what the police know?"

"Yes. That is correct."

"I also assume you would have already told us if the police understand the nature of the operation that was hit. Or that it is easily traceable to us."

Keach shakes his head, "That is generally true. But unfortunately, the police currently have at least one lead that will ultimately connect to this firm. When our team was wiped out, their car remained at the scene, the Mercedes. Still, I don't anticipate any problems handling that aspect."

As Keach continues, both men listen intently

"Obviously, from law enforcement's point of view, this was more than just some argument, or random violence. They also have eyewitness reports of a man leaving the scene with several gym bags. Still, they can only speculate as to what was going on at this location, or as to the contents of the bags. And at least for now, their focus will be on capturing the assailants. Investigating whatever else was going on will be a priority only as it assists them in that task. Of course, depending on how things unfold, they might develop a greater interest in what was happening before the attack."

Pausing only long enough to allow them to digest what they were hearing, Keach looks directly at Richard Wilkins as he resumes. "Sir, with your approval, I plan to continue targeting all of my energies on asset recovery. That means we have to find out who did this, track them, and get to them before the police do. Remember, if the police pick them up first, any cash they recover will be impossible for us to claim."

Keach again pauses. During this last bit, both men have been nodding vigorously in assent. Now he intends to complicate things.

"Look, I have every confidence we will eventually find out who did this. But this next point is important. Even if the police don't get to them first, we only have a couple of days to pull this off; after that, the chances of recovering the cash diminish drastically. Frankly, I think that would become quite unlikely."

With his audience no longer nodding, Keach hits them with the crux of the problem. "Before I move forward, I want to make sure we understand something. Executing a successful recovery will require a small team of professionals, the cost of which will not be minimal and could easily exceed six figures."

Looking back and forth between the two men, Keach finishes his thoughts. "Gentlemen, based on the amount of money at risk, versus both the cost of a recovery and the chances of its success, well, I believe we need to at least discuss the cost/benefit ratio of pursuing a full bore recovery attempt."

Robert Owen had been perched on the front edge of the sofa anxiously leaning forward while he listened. As Keach was finishing, he had hopped up and begun pacing around the outside of the sofas. When he finally speaks, it's with considerable emotion. "I don't need to tell either of you that this is a *real* problem. We have a *severe*, I must reiterate, *severe* cash flow problem. Wilkins Investment Group itself has nothing coming in. I had planned...I mean..."

Briefly losing his train of thought, Owen stops his pacing and continues. "What's important to understand, is that the firm will go under if we don't continue bringing funds over from the subsidiary companies to the Wilkins side to meet our obligations. I've been over this with both of you. I'm not exaggerating; we were standing on the brink even before this incident. Some portion of the funds we need for the short-term are available. But without the cash from this month's consolidation, we're going to have difficulty making payroll at many, if not all of our subsidiaries. We might make it through this week, but next week we're going to start having problems. Big problems."

Owen stares at the coffee table as his remarks draws a derisive snort from Wilkins. At some point, Richard had gotten up and walked over to his desk. Keach looks away as he also rises. The three men, all now standing, have spread themselves apart across the large office.

Looking at Keach, Wilkins breaks the silence, "This whole thing really pisses me off. And there's more to it than just cost/benefit to consider. I will not just sit here and tolerate someone ripping me off. Go ahead. Put together a small team and run these fuckers down. Get it done. But do me a favor Daniel. If this reaches a point where you honestly believe we're really wasting money, then let me know. We can always decide to shut it down."

Turning to look out the window again, Wilkins continues. "Robert, please make sure payroll is met. The truth is I don't give a shit if these people are paid. Hell, they've been paid damn well for a long time. I just can't have it hitting the news that any of our companies are having trouble meeting payroll, or any other basic business needs. That means you need to figure out how to keep the trains running around here a few more days. At least until we know whether we're getting this cash back, or if I need to raise a loan from somewhere. I can make a call to get the cash we need if I have to. It'll just cost dearly. Fucking dearly."

Richard is seething as he continues staring at the horizon. Both men have let him down. Keach failed to provide adequate security for their operations and Owen allowed the firm's finances to sink to their current dire condition.

Only partially masking his disgust, he ends the meeting, "I've heard enough for now. You know what you need to do, so take care of it. Use any means necessary, just maintain the level of discretion that I've always taken for granted from both of you. Thanks Daniel. Robert, can you hold back for a moment please? I need to understand a little more about the financial impact of this shit."

◣

After the meeting, Keach retreats to his office and calls Richter for an update. They still haven't received a hospital report matching their gunshot victim and there's no other fresh news. Richter reiterates that when he finds the gunman, he'll call Keach before sharing the news with the other investigators.

Frustrated, Keach asks, "Why aren't I hearing anything about the money? I need you to help find the fucking money. Then you can work on delivering the shooter."

"Look," Richter pushes back. "I heard you last night and I haven't forgotten. The leads are being run down as we speak, only by other guys on the team. We have a status meeting early this afternoon. I'll know everything we've got then, as well as what direction to move in."

Preparing for additional threats, Richter hears only a dead connection. At some point, Keach had hung up on him.

◣

TD wakes a few minutes before his alarm was set to go off at nine. Considering everything that occurred last night, he slept surprisingly well and he feels somewhat recharged. After confirming his decision to keep the money, he focuses on preparing to leave the area. Though he must act quickly, there's also a need for balance. He knows running off willy-nilly without a plan will only increase the odds of his being found.

An inventory of the tasks in front of him underscores what he needs to accomplish. Seeing that it's probably more than he can complete in a single day, he stops by the motel's office on his way out to breakfast. Paying with cash, he books an additional night.

As he hands TD his change, the clerk smiles and says, "Thanks, Mister Wilson, it's all taken care of. Have a nice day."

Leaving the office, TD reminds himself of his current identity, Roger Wilson, the name on the fake ID he's using. For the short-term, it's who he is.

With his accommodations settled, TD's first priority is eating; he has had nothing since lunch yesterday. Across the highway, a conveniently located Denny's beckons to satisfy his need for food and caffeine. While he waits for a break in traffic to cross the road on foot, he thinks about the money sitting in the motel room unattended. Deciding that it's all right to leave it there for the short time while he eats, he suddenly remembers his car. He can't believe he forgot it. How stupid can he be? Auto repair shops open early and someone is bound to have seen it and wondered why it's there.

Quickly jogging the short distance to the shop, he sees the doors on both service bays are now open with mechanics busy at their job. An older Asian man is standing in the doorway of the shop's small office, watching as he approaches his car. Once alongside the vehicle, TD opens the car door and looks back over his shoulder. With a smile, he shouts towards the man, "If this damn thing has trouble starting again, I'm going to need you to take look at it."

Within a second of turning the ignition, TD shifts the car into gear. Waving at the man who's still watching him, he backs out of the space and swings the car into traffic. Moments later, he's back at the motel. Having changed his mind about leaving the money in his room, he loads the bags into the trunk of his car. This time he chooses to drive across the road and park behind the restaurant.

TD is soon devouring his meal along with a large Diet Coke instead of coffee. He should be planning his disappearance while he eats, ensuring he doesn't miss a critical step. Instead, he finds himself reminiscing over how he obtained the fake IDs. He acquired them about three years ago as the indirect result of an investigation involving a complex insurance fraud.

The investigation ultimately exposed a multi-state scam underpinned by high-quality fake IDs. Over a two-year period, there had been a significant spike in the number of questionable injury and disability claims against his firm's policyholders, as well as those of other insurance providers. The policyholders were all retail businesses. Though claims from such firms often include customer injuries involving slips and falls, what triggered a deeper investigation was a completely anomalous number of cases involving soft-tissue back and neck injuries. Oddly, all were the result of store inventory falling from shelves onto customers.

When the fraud was finally unraveled, one aspect of the case particularly intrigued TD. A small group of individuals had incurred all of the 'injuries', hundreds and hundreds of claims. They did so by repeatedly posing as different claimants. They used the personas of others, employing excellently fabricated IDs and supporting documents. It wasn't the first time TD had encountered professional forgery in an insurance fraud and he wanted to learn more. Unfortunately, once arrested, the scammers were uninterested in exposing trade secrets to an insurance investigator who had nothing to offer toward solving their legal problems.

TD immersed himself in researching identity theft and the fake documents industry. He was particularly interested in understanding the accessibility and cost of high-quality products. Law enforcement agencies provided helpful information, but he wanted to know more than they were willing to share. A large portion of his investigative work was performed on the company nickel, completed in parallel with other cases. Some of the work came out of his personal time.

TD learned there are plenty of easily accessible sources for fake identity documents. Some were quite affordable. He also learned that only a few sources generate high-quality pieces along with supporting documents, all capable of withstanding a detailed inspection. Some of the documents he encountered during his investigation were excellent, reflecting the work of a highly skilled technical artist. The price for such work was not inexpensive.

After more than a year of part-time research, he believed he had located one of these master forgers. It appeared he was working out of the Baltimore area. TD considered involving law enforcement, but he sought knowledge not arrests. For the time being, he chose to keep his findings to himself and continue working solo.

Carrying the investigation to its logical conclusion, he attempted to arrange a discreet meeting with the forger, posing as someone in desperate
need of a completely new identity. After several unsuccessful attempts, he
tried one last approach. If he failed again, he promised himself to stop the
work and turn over what he already had to the police.

TD was thrilled when he finally made contact and a meeting was set.
At the initial encounter, it didn't take long to realize he was talking with an
intermediary, sent there to determine his legitimacy. Somehow, he passed
muster. A second meeting was set to discuss cost and logistics. From that
point, things headed south.

The second meeting was held in a restaurant near the Maryland State
Fair Grounds in Timonium, north of Baltimore. This time there was a
different man sitting across from him. Despite perceptible tension, TD
pressed forward and requested a variety-pack of identity documents. He
was informed that no work would begin until he produced a cash deposit;
one representing a considerable percentage of the full tab. TD hesitated,
asking for twenty-four hours to gather the funds. He then hurriedly left
the meeting.

He had always intended to walk away if things became uncomfortable,
and that's how he felt now. He was disappointed that he hadn't thought
through the logical consequences of such an encounter. It should have been
obvious they would expect some kind of payment guarantee and he wasn't
prepared. Another aspect of the meeting increased his discomfort. Though
nothing said came off as a lie or deception, something about the overall
vibe felt inauthentic to him.

TD realized he had allowed his investigative zeal to take things a little
too far. At least he had gotten away from the situation without any harm.
And due to his research, he and his company had gained valuable insights
into the state of the art in forged identify documents. After thinking it
over for several days, he concluded there was little upside to taking things
further, and certainly too many risks. He also decided there would be no
unmasking the forger to the police. Instead, he would wrap up his research

and produce an internal company paper addressing his findings. He may even publish an article in an industry journal.

As for any risk to himself, he felt comfortable that he had made it through the second meeting without exposing his true identity. He knew men in such a business would have layers of security and he had planned accordingly. He used a rental car for both meetings. He was particularly vigilant during the trip to Timonium. He was sure he wasn't followed either to or from the restaurant.

Confident in his own skills, TD forgot that there are others just as adept at finding and following people. The man he met at the second meeting was also not the forger. Almost from the moment of his first contact, TD had been made. They had quickly come to know who he was and that he was sniffing around their business.

When the forger determined that TD wasn't in law enforcement, he was initially confused. He was tempted to have him threatened, or worse. Instead, his own intense curiosity and need for security came in to play. He settled on a different approach. It would be useful to understand how TD had managed to identify and locate him.

About a month after that second meeting, TD was shocked to encounter the man he had met and presumed was the forger. He was sitting at the bar in a restaurant where TD was dining with Elizabeth. Several times during the meal, TD had felt an odd sensation. Looking around, he finally noticed the man staring at him intently, wearing a wry smile.

TD knew it was no coincidence. He was scared, but there was no need to overreact. There was also no reason to attempt to flee. The man already knew who he was and had obviously followed him. At the end of the meal, TD went to the men's room. The man entered moments later, telling him they needed to talk, that night. They agreed to meet in an hour at a nearby restaurant.

Near the end of the drive home with Elizabeth, TD pretended to discover he had left his wallet behind. He even confirmed it with a bogus call to the restaurant. After dropping Elizabeth at home, he headed back out.

He met the forger that night, introduced to him by the man he had now seen twice. The forger explained he knew all about TD. He made it clear that if TD ever exposed him to anyone, he should consider his life forfeit. Finished with threatening him, the forger offered to buy a round of drinks.

Under questioning, TD openly described his motives and actions. He was simply an insurance claims investigator doing research. At a certain point, the forger became satisfied with his responses and made him an offer. First, TD would provide more information about his investigation. He would also relate in detail the steps he took to locate the forger. In exchange, he would be left unharmed and receive a gratuity for his cooperation. They would then go their separate ways.

Sensing he had no real choice, it was easy enough to agree. Over a few more drinks, they went over everything he had learned. In the end, they shook hands amicably, with the forger expressing his respect for TD's skills and tenacity. As he stood to leave, his expression turned serious. Locking TD's attention with his stare, he looked down at the table where a letter-sized portfolio lay to one side. It was dark enough in the bar that TD hadn't noticed if it had been there all along, or if he had just placed it there.

TD waited a few minutes after the forger departed before taking the leather folder and leaving the bar. Once inside his car, he opened it and found a set of IDs for several different identities, each with matching related documents. All were top-shelf forgeries, including licenses from several states. The IDs each had a different name, but all had his picture; it was the exact photo from his own current license.

Prior to last night, the IDs had sat untouched in his safe. Now, finishing his breakfast, he considers how valuable they've become. As part of his disappearing act, he might also have to reach out to the forger again.

In the meantime, he's Roger Wilson.

ᛉ

Kenny Clarkson is excited about the opportunity Detective Roberts is giving him. Determined to make the most of the assignment, he knows that working well together with Detective Czarniak is essential. He's also intrigued by the lead he picked up last night from Julia Crane, though it's potential remains unclear. If this Adkins fellow had been at the motel tailing Tim Crane, then they should have come across him during the witness interviews. Regardless, it's a lead he unearthed on his own and he's determined to run it down.

Anxious to get started, he arrived at headquarters a little early and headed for the detectives' work area. Then, using the computer on an unoccupied desk, he pulled up all of the readily available information on TD Adkins. While doing so, he noticed the phone numbers for the man's home and business are the same.

Kenny's not surprised when a call to that number rolls to voice mail. While listening to Adkins's recorded voice, he sees Czarniak has arrived and is coming his way; then he hears the beep. Saying nothing about the purpose of the call, Kenny leaves his number along with a request for Adkins to get back with him as soon as possible. He'll do the same for the cellphone number next.

By the time Kenny hangs up from his first call, Czarniak is now towering over him, standing just inches from his chair. Grinning at the young officer, he uses a mocking tone, saying, "Hey Idol. I'm sure it's a real blast playing detective, but that doesn't mean you should make yourself at home."

A little intimidated, Kenny is unsure how to respond. Experience tells him anything he says will likely turn out to be a mistake. Quickly standing, seemingly at attention, he replies, "I'm just here to help out anyway I can, Sir."

Still smiling, Czarniak says, "Okay, Clarkson. You can cut the crap calling me Sir; I'm just busting your chops. Now listen up. I already put a call in to the bank's security officer and we have an appointment for eleven-thirty. Meanwhile, we're heading over to the security firm used by the storage company. We'll take my car. Traffic's clogged everywhere so you're driving. Let's roll."

The security firm's offices and monitoring center are located in an industrial park in West Springfield, one of many regional centers operated by the nationwide firm. During the drive there, the veteran detective shares a tip with Kenny: using a friendly, respectful attitude goes a long way when dealing with security outfits.

Czarniak tells him the firms employ many individuals who at some point pursued a career in law enforcement. Whether they failed to achieve that goal, or had left the field, it means the companies are staffed with plenty of good people looking to help. They also have some first-rate technology at their disposal. As they pull into the parking lot, he tells Clarkson to pay attention, take good notes, and let him do the talking.

Within minutes of Czarniak describing what happened, and what they're seeking, the center's supervisor, Greg Tolman, leads them over to a large video monitor. As the three of them look on, one of his technicians brings up the prior day's recording from the storage company. Unfortunately, the camera's focus is on the facility's entrance gate. Still, down the hill at the edge of the screen, they can occasionally glimpse a car arriving at or departing the motel.

Czarniak then asks to fast forward to the period just prior to the shootings. As they watch the images flash by, one thing is clear. There was a considerable amount of traffic at the motel last evening, far more than the small property warrants. Over a very short period, numerous cars turned into the lot. With the exception of Tim Crane's BMW, they all appear to exit almost immediately. At the jerky, accelerated pace of the video, it's as if they arrived with no other purpose than to drive through and quickly leave.

Replaying the same period again, this time only slightly sped up, they confirm that the Mercedes was next to last in the procession of vehicles to arrive. The car carrying the attackers then quickly followed. When they finish reviewing it, Czarniak asks Tolman to ensure preservation of the original on his system and to provide a copy for the police as soon as possible. After Tolman tells him that he's glad to help, the technician chimes in. He can have a copy ready for them in a matter of minutes.

Accepting a proffered cup of coffee, they return to Tolman's office. There, Kenny earns a nod from Czarniak, when he comments that it would be helpful to know if there's that much traffic at the motel every night.

Tolman quickly volunteers to review several similar periods and let them know, obviously happy to do a favor.

It's not much longer before the technician reappears, "Here's your copy, detective. I also created a bunch of single image files. They include a freeze frame of each car entering the motel from Noon until the shootings. I bumped them up as much as I could. There are a few clearly readable plates and several more with close to the whole number. I hope that helps."

Smiling broadly, Czarniak thanks them both. As he's standing to leave, an idea comes to mind. He asks Tolman if by any chance he knows who handles security for Commonwealth Dominion Bank, the small bank next to the motel. The supervisor's quick smile and rapid nod tells Czarniak he scored a hit.

"That's also us. I need to call the bank and get their permission to show you the video, but I'm sure it won't be a problem. I had already called ahead and cleared it with Castle Guard."

Pleased with their good fortune, Czarniak and Clarkson watch as Tolman punches in a number on his speakerphone and the call goes straight through to the bank's security chief. After introducing the officers, Tolman explains the scenario. With no hesitation, they receive permission to proceed.

Though it takes a little longer for the technician to bring up the video from the bank, it ends up being well worth the wait. It's all there and it couldn't be clearer. Clarkson inhales sharply as he sees the lone car parked in the lot, its license plate easily discernible. As he quickly makes a note of the make, model, and plates, he tells Czarniak that he's positive it's the car he nearly struck.

With no action, the image on the monitor appears to be a still shot. The only thing moving is the rapidly changing timestamp in the corner of the frame. When Marvin Williams walks into view, the technician slows the playback to real time. Marvin soon stops to look at something off camera. Almost immediately, a harried-looking man appears and barely avoids colliding with Marvin. After clumsily loading several heavy gym bags into the trunk of the car, he drives off.

After they finish viewing it, the technician provides a copy of that recording as well. Czarniak then thanks them both, also complimenting them on the professionalism of their company. On the way out to their car, the two policemen share knowing smiles.

⋏

Besides Czarniak and Clarkson, the other members of the investigative team aren't making much progress. A zero response to the gunshot victim alert has Carl Roberts particularly frustrated.

Along with instructing Richter to extend the area, Roberts tasks him with making a phone canvass of emergency rooms immediately outside the perimeter of the initial alert. He tells him, "Those wounds were bad, and it's been over twelve hours now. If he survived, someone has to have helped him."

Richter hates the mundane work he's being assigned. As the morning progresses, his anger is slowly rising. Each call he makes to learn if there was a matching gunshot emergency room admittance is an exercise in mind numbing tedium. He spends seemingly endless periods waiting on hold after working his way through hospital switchboards and phone tree menus. It's not only maddening, but it robs him of critical time to pursue the stolen cash.

After grinding his way through over a dozen calls, it's clear that the system isn't designed for this; hospitals aren't set up to quickly respond to phone inquiries. Even worse, he has come up empty. At this pace, it could take several days to finish. After wasting an entire morning, he decides to break for lunch.

On the way out, he touches base with Roberts. Bemoaning his difficulties contacting the hospitals and the lack of results, he suggests being shifted to help search for the guy who fled on foot. Roberts isn't interested in the idea, but he sees some validity to Richter's complaints.

"You know, I think I made a mistake. If he ended up in a hospital, I'm sure they'd call it in, even without seeing our alert. But if that were the case, they wouldn't know to call us. They'd call their local jurisdiction. That's who we need to be calling."

"But they have the alert as well."

"Not if he made it outside the initial coverage area. Even though that's been extended, it can take a couple of hours for these things to percolate through the system and be noticed. And if some hospital has already called it in, they're not going to do it twice. Yep, we need to be calling local law enforcement in a circle around the initial alert area. I don't want to rely on someone else putting the pieces together. They're busy and they're not focused on this. The last thing we need to do is give this guy enough time to be treated and get away again."

As Richter starts to protest, Roberts, cuts him off. "I know this is boring and tedious, but it may just be the key to finding this guy. And it'll be a lot fewer calls than to hospitals. I promise to try and get you some help."

The new assignment does nothing for Richter's worsening mood. Dispirited, he leaves Roberts's office, vowing to himself to do nothing more before the afternoon briefing. He hopes someone else on the team is making some progress.

Roberts isn't surprised with Richter's frustration, but there's little he can do. They're going to solve this case with teamwork, assembling the pieces of the puzzle that they each produce. He also knows Richter's assignment is grunt work. As soon as he can afford to, he plans to release him back to the county. Hopefully, that will be sooner than later.

Carl is becoming exasperated as well; his own efforts this morning have been fruitless. He had gone to the hospital to interview the motel clerk, but found himself completely stymied. He should have called ahead. The young man was heavily sedated and unavailable for questions until at least tomorrow. He also whiffed working a different lead, failing to make contact with anyone at the company that owns the Mercedes.

⋏

With Clarkson again behind the wheel, Czarniak tilts the onboard computer toward him and enters the license plate number Kenny had scrawled in his notebook. Once he has the owner's information, it's just another click to pull up the matching driver's license data. Within moments, a photo of TD Adkins is staring back at him.

Speaking to the monitor, Czarniak says, "Well, well, Mister Adkins. I must say I'm looking forward to talking with you."

Clarkson echoes, "Yes indeed!" Then after a second, it hits him. "Wait a minute. Did you just say Adkins? Is that TD Adkins?"

"Your damn right it is. You know this guy?"

They can hardly control their excitement as the young patrolman tells the detective what he learned last night. At the next intersection, Clarkson turns the car toward Burke and the home address on record for TD Adkins.

⋏

Sleep and a meal were just what TD needed. By the time he leaves the restaurant, he has a renewed confidence that he can pull this off. Some of that comes from remembering the considerable knowledge he already possesses; knowledge he can put to use planning his disappearance.

Over the years, several questionable death benefit claims had landed on his desk. They were cases with no corpse, along with a suspicion that the person might have faked their death and changed identities. Most of the frauds weren't too difficult to track down, but there were a few that were never found. From those and other cases, he learned many of the tricks people use to disappear, including those by individuals who had invested great effort and expense into not being discovered.

Now he simply needs to reverse the polarity of his thinking; no longer in the role of a hunter, he has become the prey. His first priority is avoiding the common mistakes that light a path for those searching for you, particularly mistakes caused by excessive haste. At least with it still unlikely anyone is looking for him, he should have the time to plan his exit carefully.

He decides a public library will be his first stop today. He can hang out there until his meeting with Phil. Most importantly, he can do research on the internet without leaving a digital footprint that reveals his identity and location. His first task is coming up with a short list of places he'd like to live. Then he needs the outlines of a plan for arriving there without leaving a trail. He also wants to check the news for anything about last night. He doubts the morning papers will have much, but there might be something on one of the local news stations' websites.

The library should also provide a relatively quiet, distraction free place to think. He has several key decisions to make. Once he chooses a destination, how should he make his way to his new home? Should there be any intermediate stops? Would that help shake someone who has picked up his trail later? Or should he proceed directly to his destination and quickly burrow into the landscape with a new identity? He could even choose to stay on the move before settling down, maybe for as long as a year.

One thing is already decided. There are no questions about his mode of transportation. With all the cash he's carrying, neither flying, nor any other type of public transportation is really an option. Travelling by automobile is his only practical choice. And since he can't continue using a vehicle registered in his name, he'll need to acquire one that isn't.

Arriving at the library, TD is glad he didn't start in on all of this last night. Now that he feels somewhat refreshed, he has a more upbeat sense about the future. If he can successfully plan his escape, then this new phase of his life could not only be financially rewarding, but emotionally as well.

▲

Raffi's struggle to reach the phone by his bed and call Cesar had ended in defeat. Besides the agonizing pain the effort generated, he had realized he couldn't remember a single number other than his own. Without his phone, he's unable to call anyone. Though he would never know it, his phone is in the room's small closet, just across from the foot of his bed. Out of battery power, it's there inside a plastic bag, along with what's left of his bloodied clothing.

A couple of doctors had checked in on him, hardly listening to his claim of being the victim of a drive-by shooting. They were far more interested in telling him how lucky he was to be alive. He learned that the first bullet had passed close to his heart, but had exited his body without causing critical damage. It would take some time for the wound to heal, but the prognosis was good.

His leg is a much bigger problem and he faces a long difficult recovery from the extensive bone and tissue damage. The second bullet shattered his femur not far above the knee. He's lucky it missed the femoral artery or he would have bled out before he made it back to his car. He also asked about the large metal apparatus attached to his leg; his nurse had called it an 'ex-fix'. It looked as if it was constructed using an erector set.

That was when the doctors explained there was more work to be done. The ex-fix will keep his leg and its shattered thighbone straight until they can operate again. For the fracture to heal properly, he'll need several metal plates inserted and screwed into place to hold the pieces of bone together. It's a lengthy surgical procedure, and more than he could have withstood considering the condition he was in when he arrived. They believe he will be strong enough to handle the next surgery in a few more days.

The news hit Raffi hard. Still, he has no intention of laying here waiting for more surgery and whoever might show up looking for him. Despite the difficulties presented by the contraption attached to his leg, he must leave the hospital if he hopes to avoid arrest, or worse.

Soon after the doctors left, an administrator came in requesting his personal information. Along with the police, Raffi expected someone like her would visit him sooner than later. He had considered pretending he couldn't speak English, but figured they'd easily produce a translator. Giving an unverifiable fake name wouldn't work either and would only cause more problems. What he needs is to create as little suspicion as possible.

Prepared for this eventuality, Raffi smoothly lied. As she wrote everything down, he gave the name and address of a slightly younger cousin who lives in Annandale. It wasn't much, but it should buy him a little more time. He also told her he had no medical insurance, which was true for both him and his cousin.

Raffi is thrilled when Cesar shows up only a few minutes later. Concerned about his friend's life, he had stayed in the immediate area through the night. He had actually arrived a few minutes earlier when the administrator was still with Raffi. After walking past the room, he waited in a restroom down the hall.

After Cesar closes the door almost all the way, the two begin speaking softly in Spanish. Their voices soon return to normal as Raffi describes his wounds and they marvel at his survival. Cesar is happy his friend is alive, but his smile suddenly disappears when Raffi asks him to bring him some clothes so he can get out of there.

Vehemently protesting, Cesar says, "You're not well enough, my friend. And what about that thing on your leg?"

"I don't care. I have to get out of here," Raffi cries out.

Now sitting up fully, he instructs Cesar to purchase some double extra-large sweat pants to fit over the ex-fix. When Cesar again objects, Raffi cuts him off. He's adamant. It's going to be tough, but he'll find the strength to leave.

Despite his words, at the moment Raffi lacks the strength needed just to continue talking. The short debate with Cesar has left him utterly spent. Struggling to take a full breath, he falls back on his pillow, his head reeling with thoughts. Maybe his friend is right and he needs more time. The police haven't shown up yet. Maybe they aren't coming. In great pain and hardly able to move, Raffi decides he must take the risk, but only for one more day.

Grabbing Cesar's hand, he thanks him again for saving his life. Then he tells him to come back with the clothes, but not until the next morning. Cesar finally agrees. He also needs to get rid of the car he's driving; the police could easily be looking for it. In the meantime, they can both think about how they're actually going to get Raffi out of the hospital.

Lurking just outside the door, a young Latina nurse's aide has been listening to their conversation. She was coming to check Raffi's vital signs and change the dressing on his chest wound. Upon hearing their intense exchange in Spanish, she had stopped short of entering.

When she hears one of them mention the police, she decides to interrupt. Knocking sharply on the door, she enters with a bright smile acting surprised to see Cesar. She tells Raffi that she's glad he has a visitor and if he'd like, she can come back later.

"Thanks," Raffi tells her. "But my friend is just leaving."

After she finishes attending to Raffi, the aide rushes to the nurse's station and tells her supervisor what she overheard. The staff had been briefed at the start of their shift about the John Doe gunshot victim on the floor. They had instructions to report anything of note.

Thanking her, the supervisor lifts the phone to call the police but finds herself interrupted. A little later, she's forced to put it off a second time. She won't get around to making the call until just before the afternoon shift change at four o'clock.

⋏

The Stafford County detective assigned to investigate the John Doe gunshot victim had been forced to put the case on hold before even getting started. Two armed robberies had been called in from different gas station convenience marts less than a mile apart. The second hold-up went down just ten minutes after the first. He was quickly assigned to the robbery investigation with instructions to give it his highest priority.

By late morning, he found the time to contact the hospital. After gathering the pertinent information, he gave them his number and told them it was unlikely he would make it by for a visit that day. He wasn't concerned about the delay. Considering the patient's condition, it was obvious he wasn't going anywhere soon.

It won't be until after seven this evening before he reads the message from the nursing supervisor about the overheard conversation. Tired and hungry, he will again decide that it can wait, at least until after he's picked up some fast food on his way home.

⋏

The area around Route 1 south of the Beltway is one of many contrasts. A scenic riverside parkway runs roughly parallel to the aged highway, passing through long established upscale neighborhoods. The parkway ends at Mount Vernon, George Washington's classic colonial home with its vistas of the Potomac and the Maryland shore.

The parallel section of Route 1 is neither scenic nor historic. An endless commercial strip runs south from Alexandria to Fort Belvoir. Shopping centers, gas stations, fast food restaurants and a grab bag of motels line the roadside for miles. Included in that hodgepodge of businesses is The End Zone Gentlemen's Club.

By the time he leaves the library at Noon, TD's upbeat mood has faded, reflecting the unproductive time he spent there. At least he had a plan for dealing with the car. Having settled on a couple different models of SUVs, he still must purchase the vehicle without leaving a trail. He decided his best bet is to cut a deal at a used car lot not connected with a big dealership. One who'll take no issue with a quick, all cash transaction of the size he'll be making. He should have plenty of lots to choose from right on this stretch of Route 1.

He's also down on himself for being sloppy again. After forgetting to retrieve his car earlier this morning, he left the library without checking for news stories about the shootings. He'll have to wait until later to somehow check the internet or catch a local news broadcast.

He did make some progress on selecting his destination, compiling a list of a half-dozen remote locales that he'd surely enjoy. Places where he'd comfortably blend into the local fabric of life. But a half-dozen isn't one and he knows he must whittle the list to a single location. He also needs a solid plan for arriving there without a whirlwind on his tail. He did none of the planning for that.

Everything is taking longer than he anticipated. He has started thinking it might be better to select an intermediate location where he can hide out for a short period. From there he can select his ultimate destination and carefully plan his final moves. That also fits better with his other problem. How do you choose where to live without the input of someone you hope will join you there? He spent over an hour in the library thinking about nothing but that someone.

Her name is Les. Leslie Allison Stevens. TD has grown quite fond of Les recently. For some reason, last night's events have accentuated his desire to see her again.

TD's first visit to The End Zone was about a year ago. For several weeks, he had been mired in another stretch of inertia, accentuated by an unhealthy dose of self-pity. Midway through another day cloistered in his apartment, he felt the urge to get out.

After a period of aimless driving, he found himself on Route 1 when something triggered the desire for a cold beer. While searching for a place with a bar, he passed The End Zone. He continued on, but after seeing no better choices, he turned around and headed back. There were only a few cars parked in front when he entered the club.

⬥

The End Zone is laid out in the classic pattern of such establishments and is not particularly spacious. Surrounding a stage with two stripper poles, a long oval bar with stools for about twenty occupies one side of the main room. A good number of small tables take up most of the remaining space, along with a dartboard and a coin-operated pool table in the corner opposite the bar.

The club is poorly lit and sparsely decorated in a football motif. There are a few autographed pictures on the walls interspersed with an assortment of fading team pennants and memorabilia. The mediocre sound system blasts out strip club classics, predominately hard rock. Nudity is illegal, so the dancers opt for either a string a bikini, or a revealing cut-off tee shirt along with a thong. They earn the vast percentage of their tips from the patrons sitting around the outside of the bar while dancing on stage.

Across the spectrum of such clubs, The End Zone is quite tame. There's no 'VIP Lounge' and personal dances are prohibited in the main room. Two rooms tiny enough to be closets are furnished for private dances, but they're rarely used; any physical contact between the dancers and a customer is against the law and enforced at the club. In between shifts on stage, many of the girls spend their time in conversation with customers at the tables, often garnering a free drink or something to eat.

The dancers at The End Zone earn nothing like their counterparts at luxury clubs, but they still do all right. Most importantly, the club is safe;

something that is of great value to them. The management isn't predatory and makes sure they have no problems with the customers, employing bouncers to provide the security such a place needs.

As a business, The End Zone turns a solid profit. It charges the girls a small fee for each shift they dance, offers a typical menu of bar food priced at a premium, and sells single draft beers at roughly the cost of a six-pack from a convenience store. There's a cover charge after seven each night when there's an average of twenty-five to thirty customers, more on weekends.

⚓

After climbing on a stool and ordering a beer, TD let his eyes adjust to the relative darkness. He hadn't realized it was a strip club when he first drove by, but it doesn't matter to him. After a few sips, he grabbed his glass and moved to a table. From there he could better watch one of the two big screen televisions hanging from the walls.

Only one dancer at a time was on stage in the middle of the afternoon and TD counted just four other customers. Soon after moving to the table, the bartender came over. She appeared to be in her mid-thirties, wearing only a leather vest for a top and a pair of painted on blue jeans. After apologizing for there being no waitress that day, she asked, "You want something to eat, honey? The burgers are *real* good here."

Having noticed that several of the customers had ordered food, TD decided to have a bacon cheeseburger. He was surprised at how good it was. The juicy burger had been cooked to order and was topped with crispy bacon. Along with a side of fresh hot fries, it really hit the spot. As he enjoyed the food, TD doubted he would ever return to watch the laconic dancers, but he'd certainly consider coming back for another burger, particularly if they were always this delicious.

Several weeks later, he did return, during another period of wallowing and laziness. Forcing himself to get out of the house, he decided to drive to the club for a burger despite the fifteen-mile trip. This time he sat at a table to begin with. Before long, a waitress came to take his order. It was Les.

He was expecting the barmaid in her skimpy leather vest, or a similarly attired former dancer-now-waitress. Instead, here was a young woman in her early-twenties, with an indescribably all-American, girl-next-door appearance. Along with her blue eyes and slightly curly sandy-blonde hair, she had one of the greatest smiles TD had ever seen.

Her outfit consisted of a simple sleeveless blouse tucked in to snug every day jeans, with a pair of white athletic shoes. Showing only a modest amount of cleavage, there was little overtly sexual about her clothing or the way she carried herself. It was completely out of context with the outfits and manner of the other women at the club.

TD had no idea how long he had been looking at her, smiling wistfully. He was a little embarrassed when she broke the silence.

"That's a wonderful smile you have, darling. Can I get you something?"

She showed no impatience waiting for him to speak as he continued staring. Casually bending one knee, she leaned a hand on her hip and returned his smile. Finally, he came to his senses and ordered a bacon cheeseburger and a beer. She returned quickly with his drink and gave him a cute little wink before heading to the kitchen to place his order.

TD was ashamed for behaving like some kind of leering pervert. At least he had himself under control by the time she returned with his food. Thanking her, he tried not to smile too much as he ordered a second beer.

There was something about her modest clothing and fresh relaxed manner that unsettled him. He felt like a schoolboy with a crush. Oddly, he wanted her to notice he wasn't paying any attention to the dancers on stage. Staring intently at one of the televisions, he rapidly ate his food. After leaving an overly generous tip, he departed the bar less than an hour after arriving.

That was a Friday. He found himself thinking about visiting the bar on more than one occasion that weekend. He knew it was because he wanted to see her again, he just couldn't figure out why. She had to be nearly twenty years his junior and had done nothing to indicate she was interested in him. Why would she be?

He returned on Monday. Thrilled to she was working, he was also nervous. He wondered if she would remember him as he took a seat at the same table as before. He got his answer immediately.

As she approached his table, she flashed her beautiful smile and said, "Well, if you're going to be a regular here, you might as well tell me your name. That way I don't have to keep calling you honey or darling."

Her light banter helped TD relax; this time he responded immediately. "TD. My name is TD. It's just two letters together, T and D."

"Well, it's nice to see you again TD. My name is Leslie, but my friends call me Les. What can I get you today?"

He ordered the same as before. While waiting for his food, he noticed the bar was practically empty. There were only three other customers. One was at a different table and two were sitting together at the bar. They were wearing matching shirts that appeared to be from the service department of a nearby auto dealership.

When Les brought his food, she gave him another of her cute little winks, just as before. Feeling himself blush, he was glad she turned away before seeing his red face. He watched as she sat at a table in the corner where there was a little light from the passage to the kitchen. She was reading some kind of large book or manual while sipping a soft drink and nibbling at a sandwich.

She broke off to take care of another customer that had come in and then stopped by to see if he wanted another beer. After ordering one, he asked her what she was reading.

"Oh, that? It's a user's guide for some really powerful graphics design software. I graduated recently and I'm trying to stay sharp in case I get a job interview. Like *that's* going to happen."

He observed her closely as she talked, noticing her openness as her emotions played across her face. It was all there to see, from the pride of graduating, to a determination to do well, along with the frustration of job hunting. She was so cute and bright, and so unexpected in this place. He knew no one like her and he wanted to prevent the conversation from ending.

"So you're a computer programmer?"

"Not really. I just use the software for graphic design. But studying the user's guide helps me stay fresh and understand how to get the most out of the software. If I could get my hands on a programmer's guide, well, that would really be cool. I guess you could say there's some part of me that's a bit of a geek."

TD could see the self-assurance shining from her bright blue eyes. "Well, you're the cutest geek I've ever met."

They both blushed when he said that. And though he had embarrassed himself in front of her again, she broke the awkwardness of the moment with another smile. "Thanks, TD, that's very nice."

With another wink, she spun on her heels. Calling back over her shoulder, she said, "Let me get you that beer."

Since then, he has become a regular at The End Zone. He stops in a couple of days a week, never more, always for lunch. He has a bacon cheeseburger and a couple of beers, along with lots of chitchat and gossip with Les. They've become good friends.

Though he hates to admit it, he has quite a crush. Most importantly, seeing her is pretty much the only aspect of his life that he has places any value in these days.

⋏

For the past six years, Les Stevens has been in hard pursuit of the American dream. Along with every ounce of her energy, she has invested every spare dollar she could earn into a college education. It was a real grind working full-time while taking classes, but she finally has a degree. Now her goal is landing a job that not only pays well, but also offers work that she can enjoy and be proud of doing.

In high school, Les did quite well in both art and mathematics, a relatively unique combination. She never shunned her schoolwork, but also devoted ample time indulging her mischievous side. With a small cadre of friends, she helped orchestrate several elaborate pranks at school. She found enjoyment in the planning and anticipation of the grand schemes as much as the execution. Despite her good looks, she rarely went out on dates, preferring the comfort of the close friendships she forged within her small group.

Les faced a battle royal with her mother when she announced plans that didn't include going directly on to college. Her mother had saved diligently for many years and put great hope in her only child being the first in the family to earn a degree. She couldn't understand Les's adamant desire to 'take a break' and was skeptical of her promise to continue her education afterwards. Les soon refused to participate in the increasingly heated arguments. Facing the difficult choice of fracturing their relationship or trusting her daughter to find the right path, her mother became silent on the topic.

Les had saved a surprising amount of money from several part-time jobs in high school. She spent a year after graduation hanging out and travelling with friends. Her first big trip was to Costa Rica. Later she toured Italy for a month. Between her excursions, she would find more part-time work to replenish her funds. It also helped that she always had a free place to live with her ever-patient mother.

Les enrolled the next school year, pursuing a major in graphic design. She not only found the classes challenging, but the cost of tuition was far more expensive than either of them had anticipated. Les was determined not to drain her mother's savings, nor graduate with a mountain of debt from student loans. She also felt it was time to move out of the house and live more independently. Added all together, it meant she would need to work full-time while attending school, even if that delayed her receiving a degree for several years.

The best paying job she could get was waitressing. She worked at two different restaurants, six nights a week to maximize her earnings. There was no other way to pay the bills. She attended school during the day, but had to limit her class load each semester to make decent grades. After starting at the local community college, she transferred to George Mason University in Fairfax. It took a little over six years to complete her degree.

Exhausted from the grind, she quit one of her jobs after graduation. Unfortunately, she soon lost the other due to cutbacks. Shrugging it off, she devoted full time to searching for a position in graphic design. Unfortunately, she had started job hunting during a major economic recession. Companies weren't hiring; they were cutting jobs. She didn't receive a single offer. Even waitressing positions had become difficult to find before she finally caught a break. Using a referral from a friend, she landed the weekday waitress slot at The End Zone.

Trying to start a career in a tough economy can be emotionally grueling, but at least she is getting by financially. She earns about the same from working at the club as she would in an entry-level position in graphics. Plus, there's hope for a change; as the economy slowly improves, she's starting to see job openings in her chosen field appear again.

She also found a new place to live. Though it's seen better years, she loves the cute stone-clad bungalow she rents in the Groveton area, not far from her job. And though it was unplanned, she recently added a roommate. Sure, she's working in a bar and not remotely using her degree, but life could be a lot worse.

It was not quite a year ago when she met TD. His crush on her is obvious, but it doesn't bother her. He's a great person, and she genuinely cares for him. He's kind, smart, and always calm, a quality she greatly admires. And though he can be moody and a little secretive, she gets a big kick out of how intuitive he his.

Les is glad that TD has never tried moving their relationship outside the context of his visits to the bar. She would definitely be interested in exploring a deeper connection if they were closer in age, but she's twenty-six and figures he's in his mid-forties. Though he has become a great friend, it's just too many years difference. There's also another issue, if you could even call it that. She has been secretive herself, and needs to level with him about something. Despite his intuitiveness, he's totally clueless about an idea she has been considering that will completely alter their relationship.

Recently, she has been gently probing him about his past. She has also asked about the kinds of things that bring him happiness. Initially, he was extremely reluctant to respond. Depending on his mood, he sometimes refused to talk about such things at all.

Slowly, she has learned more. She's now aware that he's a widower, but there are wide boundaries around that topic and she knows none of the details. On a different occasion, he revealed that a couple of years ago he came into some money and quit his regular job. Uncomfortable about how to react to that information, she chose to wait before asking him about the how and why. It was a good choice. She could sense that he was relieved when she showed little interest in that aspect of who he is.

Over the past several months, she has watched with great satisfaction as his state of mind steadily improved. It hasn't been linear, and there've been a couple of difficult periods, but lately he has been much sunnier. With him clearly feeling better about himself, she has come to believe that he's ready for what she has been brewing.

⚔

By the time he arrives at The End Zone, TD has made up his mind. Despite the risk of embarrassment, he's going to ask Les to join him. He can't remain in the area, so what does he have to lose. By not asking, he'd be guaranteed to leave alone. And even if she were to respond negatively, isn't the upside worth the risk?

His plan is to cast last night's events as a windfall, and his imminent relocation as the ultimate adventure. Maybe she'll find it all intriguing and join him. That's the real upside: the possibility of complementing this exciting re-start of his life with someone to share it all.

Thinking about how she will react to the news, TD believes there's one large hurdle to overcome. Having come to know Les, he believes it's going to be a real challenge for her to get past how he acquired the money. He must approach that topic carefully. The problem is he doesn't have a lot of time, or a single idea for how to go about it.

There's also a possibility he won't have to. Les has been noticeably friendlier and more caring toward him lately, almost affectionate. One of the club's regulars has begun jokingly referring to TD as Les's 'boyfriend', though TD is sure he has never dared say that in front of Les.

Yes, there has clearly been a shift in the nature of their relationship. Whenever business has been slow, Les has spent her spare time sitting with him. Lately, she has taken to grilling him about his life and interests. Other questions have been more philosophic in nature. It has become common for them to have long running conversations, only interrupted by the need for her to take care of other customers. Occasionally, she has casually touched him, gently laying her hand on his arm or shoulder, often while laughing together at some inside joke.

Reflecting on it all, TD believes there are plenty of signs that Les is developing more than a casual interest in him. He understands there's no smoldering romance, just waiting for a catalyst to unleash it, but he trusts his instincts. And those instincts tell him Les genuinely cares for him. Who knows, she might just say yes to his proposed adventure. Regardless of the risk to his emotional psyche, he's ready to do give it a try.

As he pushes through the bar's front door, he's quickly engulfed in the familiar feel of cool air and subdued lighting. Almost immediately, he senses something isn't right. Taking a seat at his regular table, he sees Karen the bartender coming toward him with a beer, not Les.

When he asks where Les is, Karen reminds him that she has a big job interview and won't be in at all today. TD had completely forgotten with everything going on. Now he remembers how excited she was over the opportunity. Les had taken the whole day off to make sure she would arrive downtown with no problems, ahead of schedule for her early afternoon appointment.

Though disappointed, TD feels a sense of relief. As he sips his beer, he realizes how unprepared he is for talking with Les about leaving. How will he even broach the subject with her? Boiled down to its core, his message is basically, 'Hey, I just found a shitload of money and I'm leaving town for good. Do you want to come along?'

To say that he needs to improve on that is an understatement. If he hopes to minimize the shock effect, he needs to come up with a reasonable narrative and then deliver it in pieces. He won't succeed if he hits her with it all at once. And he needs to give her enough time to digest the news before asking her to come along. Hopefully, his skill at reading people will help him quickly gauge her reactions and manage the conversation.

Surprised that he finished his beer so quickly, TD signals Karen for another. He needs to stay sharp, but two beers aren't going to trip him up. Even without being able to see Les today, he remains optimistic. With a little more time, he just might find the right words to convince her to come along. Besides, given all the other tasks he faces, waiting until tomorrow to see her won't materially postpone his departure.

Shifting his thoughts, TD once again considers the risks associated with delay. He knows there's only a slim chance someone can identify him, but if that has already happened, then every hour he remains in the area increases the chances he'll be found. Weighing it all, his gut tells him it's safe to stay a little longer. Hopefully his gut is right; his life may depend on it.

As he waits for Phil, he sets a hard deadline for leaving the area. It has to be tomorrow afternoon at the latest. In the meantime, he needs to stop making mistakes. He also needs to avoid leaving any footprints.

Returning from a long lunch, Richter still arrives a little early for the status meeting. To avoid looking lazy, he goes through the motions and makes a few calls to outlying police departments. He had been calling hospitals in suburban Maryland earlier, so this time he'll target the region to the south.

On each call, he repeats what they're looking for and leaves his contact information in case something turns up. It's not a whole lot easier than dealing with the hospitals. After calls to Quantico, Stafford, and Fredericksburg, he abandons the tedious work. Edgy, and feeling the pressure from Keach, he decides to wait in the conference room for the meeting to start.

Carl Roberts soon appears, moving quickly through the mazelike grid of desks and cubicles toward his office. As he passes the conference room, he sees Richter staring out the window with his back to the door. Steve Czarniak is also there, looking over Kenny Clarkson's shoulder at something he's typing on a laptop. Roberts has already heard the headlines of the progress they made earlier and he's quite pleased. After filling his coffee mug, he returns to kick off the meeting.

They spend the first few minutes recapping what each has learned since last night. Roberts relates his fruitless efforts to contact Construction & Corporate Vehicle Services, the owner of the car attacked at the motel. No one is answering his calls, nor was anyone at their small office when he stopped by. Roberts asks Czarniak to take over that lead, knowing he'll probably pawn the task off on Clarkson.

Continuing, Roberts says, "So let's summarize. We have zero on the wounded assailant and his partner who fled the scene. To me, that's a big problem. The good news is that some solid police work and a few breaks have given us the identity of our other prime suspect."

After a brief pause and a barely noticeable grimace, Roberts continues, "I have to say, there are aspects of this that don't fit snugly enough for me, but other parts are undeniable."

Looking at his notes, he says. "Okay, here's what we know. We have a recently licensed PI none of us has ever heard of, with the weird name of TD Adkins. Based on eyewitness testimony, he checked the pulse of two of the victims, Timothy Crane and Edward King. Then he fled the scene on foot with several bags full of what, we still don't know. We also have video of him putting the bags in a car registered to him that he had parked at the bank next door. His work and home address are the same and not too far from here in Burke. The county has been sending a cruiser by intermittently for us, in hopes of picking him up for questioning. So far, there's no sign of him. Frankly, I don't expect him to show."

Richter, who Roberts notices is now more focused than at any time since coming on board, interrupts. "Sorry, Sir, I'm a little confused. You mentioned picking him up for questioning. Do we have a warrant for him yet? What are the charges?"

"We don't, but we're working on it. I wasn't positive I could get a warrant on the homicides, so I ended up going with conspiracy to commit armed robbery. I expect to have it within an hour."

"But there are some issues related to this Adkins fellow," Roberts continues. "We have no witnesses or evidence tying him to the attacks. Only that he clearly takes what it appears the shooters were after. And thanks to Idol's work...uh, sorry Kenny. Thanks to Clarkson's work, we now understand he had a legitimate and seemingly unrelated reason for being at the motel last night."

Smiling, Clarkson says, "Thanks, Sir. No problem."

"And when I said some things don't fit snugly enough for me, this is what I'm talking about," Roberts continues. "We know that Adkins appeared in the courtyard and took the bags, there's no disputing that. But how could all of this possibly come together?"

With a skeptical look, he says, "First, Adkins gets hired to follow this guy Tim Crane, who has used this motel before to cheat on his wife. Now, for this to make sense, our trusty investigator also needs to be involved with an otherwise all-Hispanic crew in parallel; a bunch of wise guys who have planned an intricate attack to take down a wholly unrelated target. And it all goes down the same night Crane's poking some waitress there. Finally, to top it all off, unlike everyone else involved, Adkins uses his own damn car."

Roberts has noticed Richter nodding several times during his summation. Richter remains silent, until saying, "That does have a really strange feel. And while I was listening, I was thinking that somehow maybe Crane was in on it too. But that doesn't make any sense."

"Right. A whole lot of this doesn't make sense," Roberts responds, accompanied by vigorous nodding by Czarniak and Clarkson.

Not wanting his team to think they shouldn't remain focused on Adkins, he adds a final remark. "Still, no matter whether it fits or not, there's no denying this guy fled the scene with the victims' property and has now gone missing. We absolutely need to bring him in."

He then tells them about his plans to interview Bobby Tomlin, the injured desk clerk. He hopes to learn more about the motel's residential guests and see if coming at the problem from that angle helps. "Unfortunately, he has a bad concussion along with other serious injuries. I'm going to give it a shot again tomorrow morning."

Wrapping things up, Roberts quickly reviews a list of follow-up assignments. When the meeting ends, he asks Richter to hang back for a minute. He tells him that one of his other detectives is going to be able to help, easing the workload, and freeing up Richter. "After today, I think we can let you return." As he says this, he notices a look of concern briefly flash on Richter's face. Then it's gone.

Now wearing a slight smile, Richter says, "I understand. I'm glad to have been able to help, though I'm sorry I didn't come up with very much."

"No worries, it's a team effort. And we got a lot done last night. If you can finish making the calls to the outlying areas that would be great. And let me know if you hear anything back from that. Oh yeah, and please thank Frank Aldretti for me. Tell him I really appreciate you guys helping us out."

"I'll do that. And you know, if things heat back up or you get stretched too thin, then just holler."

"Okay. And thanks again, Jim."

At the door, Richter pauses, "Listen, I'm actually intrigued by this one. It's as you said, this Adkins fellow doesn't quite fit. Can you let me know if you find him and bring him in?"

Roberts smiles, "Sure, absolutely. And if you don't hear back from me after a while, give me a shout. You know how busy it can be."

As they part, Roberts makes a mental note to call Aldretti. Richter was definitely helpful at the scene last night. And though he hasn't produced much more, he was professional and pleasant enough; that's not always the case with inter-department loans. Because he's so busy, Roberts won't get around to making the call to Aldretti either that day or the next.

On his way out, Richter decides to work out of his car for the rest of the afternoon. He can't risk the kind of calls he needs to make from the city's offices, and if he returns to county, he'll have to check in for assignment. If he works this right, he'll buy himself the rest of today and maybe even a good part of tomorrow to focus on finding Adkins and the money.

His first call is to Keach. After a quick summation of where the investigation stands, Richter gets little response. Wrapping up the call he says,

"I know I'm racing against the city investigators to find Adkins, but at least for now I have as much info as they do. And I won't be hung up getting warrants or shit like that."

Expecting some kind of response, Richter realizes the line is dead. He's slowly getting used to the lack of feedback from Keach, and it isn't as if he needs supervision. Still, the silent hang-ups are a little unnerving.

⏶

By two o'clock, the number of patrons in the bar is slowly growing. TD is now one of eight customers, most sitting separately in the club's semi-darkness.

His emotions have seesawed while waiting for Phil to arrive. At one point, he reached the conclusion that taking the money was a colossal mistake. The thought was devastating. Then he reminded himself of the flip side: it also has the potential to be a life-liberating event. If he keeps the money, he can be sure his life will be nothing like the last couple of years, whatever the future brings. For that reason alone, he owes it to himself to go forward.

A few minutes after two, his cell phone rings with a call from Phil. He had already called earlier to warn TD that he might be running late. Now, before he can needle his friend for his tardiness, Phil starts in on an apology. Unfortunately, it's not for being behind schedule, he has to cancel altogether. A business lunch that he thought would be only an introductory meeting has turned into a probable sale. He's taking a quick break from his client, and after they finish he has another appointment.

"I'm really sorry man. But hey, I bet I know what you want to talk about." Lowering his voice, Phil asks, "Were you at that motel where they had those shootings last night?"

"Yes, I was. But how did you know that?"

"I knew it! Anne called me this morning. She heard about Tim's death from one of Julia Crane's friends. Based on your calls and knowing you were working for her, I put the two together."

With a disappointed tone, TD says, "Well there's more to it. And I had really hoped we could talk today. I wanted to run an important decision by you. I also need your help with something."

"I'm really sorry, TD, but I'm booked solid. And I have important dinner plans tonight. There's no way I can break them. Believe me; I really look forward to hearing all about it."

Not wanting to get into things over the phone, TD changes his tone, "This is bigger than you think Phil, much bigger, but I can wait until tomorrow to talk. Just please don't say anything about this to anyone, not even Anne. There is a small favor I need though; maybe you can get to it this afternoon."

Earlier, in a secluded corner cubicle at the library, TD had reviewed the video he took at the motel. From that, he wrote down the license plate numbers of the cars making the drop offs, as well as of the pick-up car.

"I know you're busy, but I need the ownership information on a short list of vehicles? I have the models and license plates, but no VINs?"

"I don't want to be rude, buddy, but I'm slammed. Can't you do that yourself?"

Patiently, TD says, "I know you're busy but I'm not being lazy. Look, it's all tied together with what I want to talk with you about. And I really need this information. You just have to trust me when I tell you I can't be the one inquiring about it."

Sounding exasperated, Phil responds, "Alright TD, don't go all cloak and dagger on me. It's just that I can't deal with it right at this moment. Like I said, I'm with a client and I need to get back with them."

Feeling a little sorry for his friend, Phil has an idea. "Look, just e-mail or text me the plates. I'll call in a favor from one of the guys in claims. I should have it by tomorrow. I sure hope the story behind this is damned good."

Before hanging up, the two friends agree to meet at one the next afternoon, once again at The End Zone.

⚔

Jim Richter knows one of the fastest ways to locate someone is by tracking their cell phone. Hopefully Adkins has been using his. To get the data he needs quickly, Richter calls a confidential source who works at one of the area's leading wireless carriers. Though it is plainly illegal, the source provides information that normally requires a warrant, without the hassle and delay for the police of actually having to obtain one.

A few years ago, a guy was busted for possession of several ounces of marijuana in his car, along with a scale and other paraphernalia. He was facing multiple charges, including intent to distribute. A colleague of Richter's was involved with interrogating him about the source of the pot. During the questioning, they learned the accused worked for the phone company in the IT department. As part of his job, he had access to the company's billing systems and call record databases. Sensing an excellent opportunity, the detective decided it might be better to let the guy off with a deal.

They offered to let him walk, with a promise that he would occasionally provide the police with someone's cellular call data. The number of requests would be limited, but when called upon, he would produce the data without letting anyone else know. Most importantly, there would be no warrant. The guy jumped at the deal. He didn't care about the legal niceties. He knew his company was already providing warrantless data to the government. Why couldn't he do the same to save his ass from an arrest that would cost him plenty, including possibly his job?

To get the most value out of the situation, his colleague shared the confidential source with a few other detectives. Richter had used the guy twice with excellent results, once saving considerable time locating a suspect. Whenever the police found the data of value, they'd quickly seek a warrant in parallel, in case one was needed later to justify in court how they had obtained the evidence.

Richter catches a nice break when the source confirms Adkins is a customer of his company. He requests a report of all calls and texts Adkins has made or received in the past two weeks. If they are also customers, the report will include the names and addresses associated with any of the numbers Adkins contacted. Most importantly, the report will provide Adkins's approximate location at the time of each event. Though it doesn't indicate his exact position, it will have the location of the closest cell tower.

His source has no problem with the request, telling Richter he should have the data for him in a couple of hours. Always willing to help, he offers to run a fresh scan at least once a day or provide updates as needed, whichever Richter prefers.

▲

The call from Phil leaves TD reeling. Until now, his comfort level has been grounded on the premise that there was no easy way to link him directly to the events at the motel. He now realizes the lamentably poor job he has done thinking through this exceedingly important aspect of his situation. If he has missed such an apparent connection, what else has he missed?

TD also understands that this failure of critical thinking could be a case of self-deception, particularly by someone with his experience. It's a type of lying he often unmasks in others. Is that what's going on here? Does he want to disappear and change his life so badly that he's not being rational? Or did he simply miss the obvious connection with Tim Crane because it was just that? Regardless, this is exactly the kind of mistake that could sabotage all his efforts.

One thing that doesn't cross his mind is any consideration of abandoning to decision to keep the money and leave. Instead, he simply resolves to be more thorough and move more quickly with his preparations. Then he'll hit the road as soon as he has talked with Les tomorrow.

Determined to be more careful, he decides to return to the library where he can get online and send Phil the license plate information. Fifteen minutes later, after finding his way to the same corner cubicle, he quickly sets up a new e-mail account using a fake name he's sure Phil will recognize. After listing the plates, he blathers on about the importance of discretion and confidentiality before finally deleting everything except the numbers. In place of the deleted commentary, he instructs Phil not to reply to the e-mail. He should print the results and bring them to their meeting tomorrow.

So as not to bother Phil with a call during his meetings, TD sends him a rare text message: 'I sent you the numbers.'

⚔

While waiting for the cell phone data, Richter remembers that when he was calling around requesting information on gunshot victims, he had left his personal contact info instead of that of Carl Roberts or the Fairfax City Police. He did it out of habit, but now he realizes it will actually work to his benefit. Any alerts that come in will be filtered through him.

Over two hours pass before he receives the records from Adkins's phone. It had taken awhile for his source to be able to run the query, but at least the report is fresh; it was produced just thirty minutes earlier. Disappointingly, there's not much to work with, hardly more than a dozen calls and a single text. A more detailed scan reveals the list of numbers involved is even shorter. Besides a single call with the cell phone of Julia Crane, the rest involve only two numbers: the home and mobile lines of someone named Phillip Madrigal.

Then, as he slowly begins to grasp the significance of the information in front of him, Richter understands that things are finally starting to look better.

⚔

Before getting some dinner and holing up for the night, TD commits to making some tangible progress on his preparations for leaving. There are items on his task list that he can complete which are independent of his ultimate destination, or whether Les comes with him.

Atop that list is getting a different car. Normally a meticulous shopper when it comes to vehicle purchases, he understands that he's probably not going to get a great deal today. What does matters is getting it done quickly, without leaving a trail.

Finding a used car dealership on Route 1 is easy and he turns into one of the first lots he encounters. It contains about forty vehicles of fairly recent vintage, surrounding a mobile home serving as the sales office. Out of a group of SUVs clustered in one corner of the lot, he quickly identifies four that should meet his needs.

Within moments of getting out of his car, a salesman has left the trailer and is rapidly approaching him. Upon being greeted by a man roughly his age bearing an eastern-European accent, TD's first request is that they move inside to talk. In keeping with his need to be more cautious, he wants to avoid spending too much time standing in the open, in plain view of the road.

Once inside, he peppers the salesman with a short set of questions about each of the four SUVs. Despite the salesman's efforts to tout various features, TD is focused almost exclusively on two criteria: the amount of mileage on each vehicle and if there have been any major repairs. Along with providing the requested information, the salesman promises that each of the vehicles is in perfect condition.

TD gets a strong feeling that one of the cars might be trouble. Conversely, the salesman's assurances about the others feel truthful. Making a choice, he selects the newer and more expensive of the group, a three-year old Nissan Pathfinder, already bearing high mileage. The asking price is $23,999, which is probably about right if it came with about thirty thousand miles less than it has.

After taking a brief test ride, they return to the office. With no preamble, TD offers $20,000 all-in, taxes and fees included. With poorly masked contempt, the salesman scoffs that it had cost them more than that to acquire the car.

TD smiles and says, "That may very well be the case, but that's my offer. That's twenty thousand, cash. You can close the deal right now."

The salesman hesitates for a moment as he looks TD in the eye. After standing, he says, "If you can please be so kind as to give me one minute, Sir."

TD watches as he retreats to consult with a man sitting behind a desk at the far end of the office. Two minutes later, they have a deal. Shaking his hand, the salesman asks TD for some form of identification so they can begin the paperwork.

"My name is Tom Taylor. I'll give you my ID and the money when I return. I should be back in about a half an hour."

As he arrives back at the motel, TD calls for a taxi. He arranges for a pick-up in twenty minutes, to take place down the road at the repair shop where he had parked overnight. It's a simple precaution and leaves no record of a fare at the motel where he's staying. He then takes one of the bags of cash back into the room. Once inside, he counts out the money he needs and stuffs it in an unmarked plastic laundry bag he removed from a hangar in the closet. Then he grabs the spare ID with the name Thomas Taylor from his luggage.

At the door of his room, he faces a decision. He has been carrying the money around with him in the car all day; now he has to decide what to do with it. Schlepping the bags along with him in the taxi and on into the dealership won't work, so he'll have to leave them unattended in either the room or his car. After choosing the car, he parks it behind the motel, out of sight from the road.

Overall, he's away from the car dealership almost forty-five minutes. Relieved to see his customer return, the salesman's broad smile disappears when TD hands him the plastic bag stuffed with money. Looking inside, he mumbles, "I don't know about this. I didn't realize you actually meant cash."

By this point, the man working the desk in back has gotten up and is quickly approaching with his hand out. Introducing himself as the owner, he shakes TD's hand and thanks him for making the purchase.

The owner had been watching and listening and now wants to take control of the deal; he quite likes the idea of a large cash payment. Meanwhile, the salesman has begun searching through the drawer of a file cabinet after saying something about the need to complete a currency transaction report.

Gesturing TD towards his desk, the manager says, "Thank you, Vassily. I think we have all the information from Mister Taylor we're going to need. Don't worry about a thing; I'll finish this transaction for you."

From there, it's only a few more minutes before TD has the keys in hand.

On the ride back to the motel, he considers the currency transaction report the salesman mentioned; a report required by the IRS for any cash transaction of ten thousand dollars or more. It's another damn oversight on his part, though he's sure the owner isn't going to fill one out. TD could tell he was happy to take the cash. Still, it's another issue he failed to anticipate.

He really has to do a better job of thinking ahead. He has to start considering the possible impacts of every action he takes, especially when there's the possibility of a paper trail. Just because his real name wouldn't have been in the report, there's no need to start leaving a trail for Tom Taylor. He may need to reuse that ID.

⚔

Richter had continued poring over the limited amount of call data before calling Keach with his analysis. It was easy enough to see that the calls were primarily with just one person, but there were additional nuggets to be gleaned. Before the ambush at the motel, Adkins's location during the calls had always been in Burke or the nearby Fairfax area. Last night his location shifted to the southeast part of Fairfax County, along Route 1.

The timing of the calls was also interesting. Before this, Adkins and Madrigal talked once every couple of days, never more than once a day. That frequency skyrocketed starting last night. Adkins had called Madrigal at his home number and on his cell, indicating a possible urgency to talk. The two had communicated multiple times again today. That includes a call just after two this afternoon as well as a recent text message.

Richter is enthusiastic when he finally calls Dan Keach and shares his insights.

For the first time, Keach's tone is pleasant from the start. He even throws in a compliment. "Good job, Jim, this is excellent. I want to make sure I understand what you're telling me. One, you believe Adkins is currently hanging out along Route 1, just north of Fort Belvoir. And two, you believe he's somehow involved with, or possibly trying to meet up with this guy Madrigal."

"That's where I'd put my chips."

"Yes, well, why don't we dispense with the gambling metaphors since that's how we got to know each other? But I think I agree. Also, this name, Phil Madrigal, it sounds familiar to me. I just can't think why. See what you can find out about him. And do it quickly now."

Richter volunteers, "Do you want me to head over there and look for Adkins tonight?"

"No. I'll cover that. Just let me know what you come up with on Madrigal. I'd like to get someone on his ass as well."

Proud of himself, and caught up in the chase, Richter says, "Will do. That's all I have for now. I've requested regular updates on Adkins's phone usage and I'll keep you posted. Is there something else you'd like me to focus on?"

Richter's words trail off in volume as he finishes the question. Again, he finds he's speaking to no one.

⅄

Dan Keach is quite happy with the results Richter is producing. A lot of guys put under this kind of pressure don't step up, but Richter has surprised him. If things continue to work out, he may have to let the guy off the hook for his debt. The idea doesn't give him any pleasure, but at least he will have earned it.

Now it's time to go after Adkins. His first call is to one of Eddie King's couriers. After providing him with a description of Adkins and his car, Keach instructs him to assemble a team of three and immediately start scouting the Route 1 area. If they spot either the man or his vehicle, they're to call Keach immediately. They should not approach him, but are to keep him under surveillance.

About an hour after his last call, Richter is back on the line with an update on Adkins's phone traffic. He has made another call, this time to a taxi service. The call was from the same general area and an indication that he might have ditched his car. Richter also provides Keach with addresses for Madrigal's home and place of work. He lives in Oakton, and works for an insurance company. His office is in Old Town Alexandria. Richter points out that Old Town isn't very far from where it appears Adkins is located.

Keach is rapidly gaining confidence that they just may get their hands on Adkins. It will be a miracle if it happens this easily. His next call is to another of the couriers. He's to enlist another man, locate Madrigal, and put a tail on him. In addition to regular updates on Madrigal's activities, they're to call Keach immediately if he leads them to Adkins.

His final move is to call in a specialist. He's not directly associated with The Group, but Keach knows him to be discreet and highly effective. They originally met years ago while working together for an elite private security firm and they've stayed in touch. At times, they throw some work each other's way. Keach uses him sparingly, and only for more challenging assignments.

The man he calls goes by the name Jonathan Stark these days, though Keach knows he was born as Ezra Welker. Keach isn't sure of the rationale behind the artifice, though in his chosen line of work it doesn't hurt to have an alias. He has always thought it might be because Welker was self-conscious of his given name. Possibly, he perceives his adopted name connotes more strength. Regardless of what he wants to call himself, Keach knows that Stark is a top professional. If Adkins is to be found and the money recovered, Stark is the man to get the job done. The price tag for his services won't be cheap, but it should be the only external cost they incur; everyone else he's deploying is already on the payroll.

After a quick review of Keach's needs, Stark has only a few questions. He should be able to have someone in the Route 1 area tonight. Keach knows the man is too professional to mention fees, and sees no need to broach the topic of costs himself. They each have a good understanding of the going rate for such services.

After the call, Keach reviews his cost estimate for the recovery. The price tag for Stark's team may reach fifty thousand dollars, even more, but they need to recover the money quickly. He also needs to include a reserve for when they finally locate the shooter. Dealing with that scumbag will be another assignment for Stark. Despite the growing price tag, his stance on the cost/benefit of the pursuit has definitely shifted.

Wilkins and Owen had initially balked this afternoon when they heard his preliminary estimate. He had to remind them that unforeseen costs occasionally arise in this trade. He also told them they should re-think their chosen business if they're going to allow someone to hit them like this without hitting back. Every single guy involved in the attack needs to pay. And that payment needs to be public enough that word gets around that nobody should fuck with them. Wilkins had loved the last part of his speech.

Keach is starting to feel a lot better than he did when he first received the news last night. For the first time, he thinks there's a decent chance that he can clean up this mess. And with Stark in play, Adkins and his guys are going to get what they deserve.

He knows that will involve a world of pain. If they're lucky, they'll die quickly.

⚓

With the car purchase taken care of, TD is ready to move on to the next item. So many issues require a resolution if he's going to convince Les to leave with him. How can he ask her to join him when he doesn't even know where he's going? He has yet to identify a first stop, let alone where he'd like to settle. And even if she surprises him and agrees to come along, he can't expect her to run out the door with him the moment he asks.

Before he does anything else, he needs to get some food. He stops at a Chinese buffet, The Lucky Star. He has never been to this one, though he has passed it often enough on his way to The End Zone. TD is a connoisseur of Chinese buffets, pretty much the only style of restaurant he frequents for dinner these days. He chuckles as he spoons some Kung Pao Chicken onto his plate; he could write a restaurant guide for Chinese buffets in Northern Virginia. After sampling a few of the dishes, he knows this restaurant wouldn't rate well. The sauces are either too sweet or too fiery, with no subtly in the preparation.

His thoughts are on Les as he eats. He thinks about how steady and mature she is, but also lighthearted. There are times she reminds him of Elizabeth, with her work ethic and practicality, but Elizabeth was single-mindedly focused on advancing her career. Les also has plans and goals, but she's willing to roll with life's punches, smiling the whole time she seeks a way forward.

The depth of his feelings for Les surprises TD. Despite having only been around her at the bar, he feels closer with her than he does with anyone besides Phil. And there's no denying she has showed an increased interest in him the past couple of months. His instincts tell him that her increasing attention is completely genuine and part of a growing bond between them.

But he must be careful; the tumultuous events of the past twenty-four hours have certainly heightened his emotions. And despite his vaunted intuition, he needs to remember he isn't working some insurance fraud investigation. This isn't some case to be resolved by simply laying out the facts and logically drawing a conclusion. After his long period of self-imposed isolation, it's completely possible he's misreading nothing more than gestures of friendship on her part.

On the short drive back to the motel, he has an idea regarding his approach with Les tomorrow. He'll start by telling her he's moving away. He's leaving the area and unlikely to return any time soon. Opening with such an unexpected declaration should allow him to read her reaction. If she's genuinely disappointed, he'll tell her he'd love to have her visit once he settles in.

If she shows enthusiasm for that concept, he'll take the next step. He'll confess his budding affection, but couching it within the context of how much he's going to miss her. If he then reads that she shares the same feelings, he'll make the final leap. He'll suggest she stay with him when she visits. He can even joke that she might like it so much she'll want to move in.

With a sigh of relief, he commends himself for taking the time to think things through. This is a much better plan. He might have really blown it if he had talked with her today before knowing what he wanted to say. This approach provides a chance to observe her reactions to the news and pull up before making a huge mistake. It should also help dampen any embarrassment either has if he has guessed wrong about her feelings. Still, he believes there's a good chance things could work out.

Back in his room, he reminds himself to watch the local news at ten o'clock to see if there's anything on the shootings. While he waits, he tries watching ESPN but is too distracted. Instead, he starts reviewing the items on his list. One priority is determining the personas he wants to use for the short- and long-term. Like his plans to travel first to an intermediate destination, he has decided to wait before settling on a permanent identity.

The use of short-term identities will also come into play as he attempts to salvage his liquid assets. He needs to move the funds away from his personal accounts immediately. His experience tracking the movement of assets between camouflaged identities should help with the execution. He has learned methods of financial subterfuge that are so effective, they're nearly impossible to unravel. The only problem is they require careful planning and execution. Luckily, with plenty of cash on hand, he won't need the funds right away. With a little help from Phil, he should have the time to do this right.

With the local news show about to start he tries calling Phil but it goes unanswered. Remembering his dinner engagement, TD waits to leave a brief voicemail as the broadcast begins. It starts with a female news anchor, breathlessly working her way through the teasers for the lead stories. One of them is riveting: "A bloody shootout at a Fairfax motel leaves police with more questions than answers."

Hanging up without leaving a message, TD sits on the edge of the bed with his pulse racing. No more than three feet from the screen, he nervously waits through a flurry of advertising. To his agony, the first item covered is about a fatality on the city's metro system. Another cluster of commercials follows.

When the show resumes, it's his story. He notices they've already given the event a catchy tag. Along the bottom of the screen, a red banner with white characters reads, 'Fairfax Motel Massacre'. After a quick introduction from the anchor, they play a pre-recorded piece. It's the voice of a field reporter talking over scenes taped from last night. Other than a lot of flashing lights and people milling about, there's little for the viewer to see. The reporter seems almost enthusiastic to be covering such a dramatic story, though she has few details to relate.

A video clip of a police spokesperson's statement follows. At the end of the report, the anchor comments on the severity of the gun battle and the historic number of homicides for the generally peaceful town. She closes with the remark, "According to the police, the investigation remains in its early stages."

TD never hears her final words. His mind is locked on a sentence near the end of the police spokesperson's statement: "Our investigation is focused on locating two suspects who were observed leaving the scene separately, immediately after the shootings."

The words hit him like a thunderclap. He had expected to hear they had captured the wounded gunman who fled in his car. It couldn't be that difficult considering how badly he was wounded, yet he must have gotten away. But they had said 'two'. Does that mean he's one of the suspects they seek?

The only person that could have gotten a good look at him would have been Tim Crane's girlfriend. He has always believed she would be too terrified from witnessing Tim's death to give the police a usable description. Maybe there was another witness? Or just maybe they're talking about someone else leaving the scene that he failed to observe?

Thinking of Tim's date staring at him from the motel window triggered something else in his memory. He forgot to call Julia Crane this morning. She's the only person besides Phil and Anne who can tie him to one of the victims at the motel. It's too late to call her now, but he still needs to do it in the morning as a preventive measure. He'll offer his condolences as if he heard indirectly about Tim's death, implying he wasn't present last night. He will also try to determine if she informed the police that she had hired him to follow her husband.

Still frozen in place on the edge of the bed, TD can feel his heartbeat thumping in his chest and neck. He needs to calm down and once again replay his every move last night. He'll examine each of his actions individually, but this time only from the perspective of the police.

When his phone rings, it startles him badly. As he stands, he checks the Caller ID and sees that it's Phil. Without a greeting, he blurts out, "Man, am I glad you called. We really need to talk. You got a minute?"

"Hey buddy, I saw you called. I just finished dinner with Anne and some friends and we're on our way home. Anne's right next to me. She says hi."

With it clear their conversation will have to wait, TD tries to formulate a response. Before he can say anything, Phil is talking again.

"I got your earlier message. Lunch sounds great."

With a hint of desperation, TD responds, "Good, that's all I need. It's just really critical that we talk. And hopefully you'll have that info for me."

"That sounds great, buddy. My morning is jammed, but I promise I won't bail on you like I did today."

Hearing more deflection, TD knows assurances are all Phil can give him tonight. Quickly ending the call, he takes a few deep breaths. Then he reaches for his laptop.

⅄

While he's waiting for another update from his phone company source, Richter's cellphone rings with a number he doesn't recognize. On the other end is a detective from Stafford County.

"I apologize for not calling you sooner, but I had a non-stop day. We're understaffed and I'm juggling a number of major cases. Well, anyway, I was waiting in line for the drive-thru at the Chick-Fil-A, when for some reason I started remembering something about an alert you called in. Later, after I got some food in my belly, I finally put two and two together. I'm sorry it took me so long. You see, one of the cases I haven't been able work on much is a John Doe gunshot victim over at the hospital. Now, I had already called over there earlier, but I decided…"

Unable to control his impatience any longer, Richter interrupts the garrulous detective. "I get it. Thanks. Can you give me a general description and the time he came in?"

The detective's description of the victim, wounds, and arrival time the night before is a perfect match for Richter's suspect. But instead of confirming that he's the man they're seeking, he remembers Keach's instructions. "Well, I sure appreciate the call sir, and don't worry about the delay. What a coincidence. Unfortunately, it's not our guy."

"What? Really? It's a damn near perfect match with both the timing and the description you sent on your alert."

"Yeah, I know. Sorry, but we received some new information since I called. And we just heard that they've picked up some guy in a Maryland hospital not more than an hour ago. It looks like he's our guy. I really appreciate you calling though."

Sounding a little dejected, the Stafford detective says, "No problem. You gotta admit it's one helluva coincidence. Guess I'll get over there tomorrow and see what's up. He's not going anywhere."

Richter immediately calls Keach and breaks the news.

After praising him warmly, Keach reminds Richter that no further follow-up on the shooter is needed. And he's not to share his discovery with anyone else. "I want you to forget about him now. He'll soon be getting what he has earned from this misguided attack. You're only focus now should be on finding Adkins. I really appreciate the good work you're doing Jim. Call me with news anytime. Don't worry about the hour."

Richter smiles as he ends the call. He likes the way Keach is showing him some respect now. Soon, he just may be free and clear of this guy and can relax a little. Who knows, with his luck changing, he might even start playing some poker again.

λ

TD had re-watched the video of the shootout to place himself in the moment. Now, experiencing some of the same emotions, he begins walking through everything he did from the time he stopped recording. He starts by rifling through his bag to confirm he left nothing behind in the room. Then he moves on to the issue of witnesses, including anyone who might have seen him before or after the event.

Once again, he reaches the same conclusion: nobody at the motel can identify him by name. He never showed any identification to the desk clerk, and neither Tim's girlfriend nor anyone else peering out from a motel room could know who he was. The only other person he encountered was the older man in the bank parking lot, and he had nothing to do with this. Even on the small chance the police have talked to him, like the others, he could only give a description.

Yet despite all that, TD knows there is an easy way to link him to the motel last night, at least indirectly. Having never called Julia Crane, he doesn't know if she mentioned him in any way to the police. That in itself is not a critical problem. It wouldn't be an obvious thing to connect that information with the attacks. But a zealous detective might find some interest in it, particularly if he has nothing else to go on. Simply looking up TD's driver's license information will display a photo that could match the description of the man seen fleeing the scene.

It's all a little farfetched, but he won't completely discount it. Hopefully, he can learn when he calls her in the morning if she gave them his name. For now though, he needs to avoid dwelling on what is simply an additional hurdle to overcome if he's to succeed.

As TD puts the problem of Julia Crane aside, there's a sudden change in his thinking. Maybe this latest issue was simply one too many to worry over, tipping the scales. Maybe it was twenty-four hours of accumulating stress and the unknown path forward. Whatever the cause, as if experiencing an awakening, his thoughts reverse course.

Instead of planning for a new identity, he spends the next several minutes considering a completely different proposition. If he wants to, he can stop running before he really starts. He can simply blow the whistle and signal the end of the match. Tomorrow, he'll contact the police and let them know he's not involved with the shootings. He'll arrange his surrender, tell them everything he knows, and clear his name.

He knows the police have one true interest: arresting the surviving perpetrators of the attack. They're after killers, not someone who scurried off with some gym bags. In a way, he'd be helping them out with their investigation and they would learn exactly what happened. Even in the worst case, where they try to charge him with something, he has two huge things going for him. He has the video recordings and he has a contract with Julia Crane. That kind of hard evidence ensures he'll be able to absolve himself of any involvement in the violence that occurred.

Working through the whole concept in more detail, he begins envisioning how the process of turning himself in would go. And then the questions start coming. What if it the whole thing backfires and he ends up being arrested? What if he has to go on trial and it somehow turns out terribly wrong?

As his thoughts rapidly darken and spiral downward, he grabs onto remnants of the optimism and anticipation he has been experiencing since taking the money. Stopping his descent, his newfound enthusiasm for surrender quickly wanes. He's soon laughing aloud, slowly shaking his head in derision at the ill-conceived concept. Turning himself in would be a horrible idea. Not only would he have to return the money, the whole thing is a proposition loaded with downside and risk.

With renewed determination to move forward, he considers the risks that direction holds for him, along with potential consequences that cannot be ignored. Seeing the video again has reinforced his thinking on a different aspect of his situation. Far more problematic than being hunted by the police is being hunting by a different group: the people whose money he took. This is an adversary that demands his focus.

Reminded of their staunch defense at the motel, and considering the amount of cash involved, he's convinced that whomever he took the money from will be highly motivated to recover it. And though they may not have the same resources as the police, they'll be much less constrained in the methods they use to locate him. Most importantly, if they were to succeed, the consequences will be immeasurably worse than being arrested. Reading him his rights, or allowing a lawyer to be present during his interrogation will not be on their agenda.

Sobered by the challenges he faces, TD recommits to leaving the area tomorrow. Regardless of the outcome with Les, he needs to be on the road by mid-afternoon. As he ticks off a list of things he must complete so he can leave on time, he remembers he still has to transfer his possessions to the new car and do something about the old one.

The thought of his car sends a sudden shock through him. Unlike last night, it's parked here at the motel. At least it's in back, not right in front of his room; but if someone is looking for him, he has effectively hung out a sign saying, 'TD Akins can be found close by'.

Out of the room in a flash, he quickly transfers everything to the new car. Less than a mile down the road, he pulls into another motel where he sees a decent number of cars in the lot. Choosing a row in back, he slides into a space and quickly leaves on foot, relieved to have discovered another omission before it has cost him badly.

On the short hike back to his room, he maneuvers behind buildings and stays in the shadows as much as he can. Along the way, he formulates a plan for disposing of his old car. He'll move it during the morning rush hour and park it somewhere even less noticeable. Knowing he can't involve Phil in everything he has to do, TD thinks of Pen, an aspiring private investigator he has been mentoring the past few years. He'll call him tomorrow for help moving the car out of the area altogether.

Back in his motel room, TD begins to relax. There's no doubt he needs to be more focused on security concerns. At least he'll be out of here with the money tomorrow. Once he's on the move, driving a car that can't be associated with him, he feels confident he can stay off the radar of whoever might be looking for him.

Exhausted, TD finally settles into bed and soon starts drifting off. For some reason he thinks of Phil Madrigal. Maybe it's because he might not see Phil much after this. Their friendship has endured for over twenty-five years. Phil has often played the role of an older brother, prodding him to set goals and look to the future. There were times he really needed that, having no close relationships other than with Elizabeth.

He has never been able to rely on his parents for advice. His mother passed away from breast cancer fifteen years back and they had never been close. His relationship with his father is non-existent. TD had learned that his father lived quite modestly on a ranch in northern California. Approaching the age of seventy, he earns his room and board doing light chores. To generate extra cash he produces handcrafted leather pieces. Evidently, he has a great reputation, specializing in items such as finely tooled belts and guitar straps. He also has a small following with west coast bikers. They covet the heavy portfolio wallets with a short chain that he custom designs for them.

TD smiles at the thoughts of his father, someone who has always lived off the grid. Hopefully that won't be who he becomes? If he can successfully change his identity, he should be able to resume a relatively normal life, living in some pleasant town far from here.

As he drifts off, he wonders what the coming day has waiting for him. Playing with the possibilities in his mind, he again spends his last waking moments thinking of Les, and if she will choose to join him on his new adventure.

WEDNESDAY

He had hoped to start the day feeling rested and recharged, but from the moment he was awake, TD knew that wouldn't be the case. He had slept fitfully, in short bursts, never much more than an hour at a time. Twice, he had jerked upright in bed, suddenly awake and aware of his circumstances.

As he showers and packs the few items he brought into the room, he considers which direction to head when he leaves the area this afternoon. He remains unsure of his ultimate destination, but he has a sense it will be somewhere out west. After he moves his old car, he'll do some serious thinking about where he wants to end up living. It's a decision that will guide many of his actions and he should at least narrow it down to a particular region.

He also needs to watch the clock as he works his way through the morning. He wants to get to The End Zone early enough to have time to talk with Les before Phil arrives.

Just thinking about seeing her sends TD's spirits rising. Still, the good feelings can't overcome his underlying tension. Nor can they be allowed to distract him from the serious job ahead, that of thoroughly discarding the identity of TD Adkins. He also reminds himself of the refocused mindset under which he must operate. He needs to be ever cognizant that there are people looking for him and for what he took.

ᐞ

In the earliest hours of the morning, Jon Stark and two of his men had begun operating in the Route 1 area. Like TD, Stark had taken a room at a motel to act as a base of operations. It was hardly more than a mile north of where TD was struggling to get a few hours' sleep.

On their way there, Stark and one of his men had broken into TD's apartment, quietly cutting out a small section of glass and easily breaching the patio door. To Stark, the place reminded him of corporate rental housing, with a barely lived in feel to it. It took them almost no time at all to determine Adkins had packed and left.

Throughout the predawn hours, Stark and his men had rotated through a series of shifts cruising Route 1, looking for Adkins or his car. Based on information from Dan Keach, they knew he had placed multiple calls from a relatively small area along the highway. Keach also believes that Adkins remains close by.

At some point during their searches, each man drove by the motel where TD was staying, checking the cars that were parked there. Stark had nearly hit the jackpot when he drove through the motel lot where TD had stashed his old car. Inexplicably, he failed to spot it, despite driving directly by the vehicle, its plates in clear view no more than ten feet away.

The team split up at six o'clock, with one man making the trip to Phil Madrigal's neighborhood. Once there, he relieved the men Dan Keach had deployed and put himself in position to tail Madrigal wherever he went. Stark's most lethal operative, Samuel, had also departed. He was heading south for Stafford Hospital Center. Per Keach's request, Stark's team would deal with the injured shooter.

With his men assigned to Madrigal and the shooter, Stark will coordinate several of The Group's men as they continue trawling the area for Adkins or his car. Keach has sent him Marty Carpentier, along with two others who were also couriers for Eddie King. Stark instructs them to focus on motel and restaurant parking lots, as well as side streets within a block or two of Route 1. He makes it clear that their protocol is to call him the moment they spot either the man or his vehicle. They're to maintain surveillance, but under no circumstances are they to take any action toward Adkins themselves.

Stark speaks slowly, locking eyes with each man, one after the other, "I understand you harbor a strong desire to avenge your friends' deaths. The best way for you to do that is to locate this son-of-a-bitch and call me the moment you spot him. Let me coordinate how we proceed from there."

Each man nods. As they hit the long Route 1 strip, they're determined and confident they'll find Adkins if he has made the mistake of remaining in the area.

⚔

Just down the road, TD has checked out of his room and gone in search of a place to park his old car where it won't be so easily noticed. During the walk to the other motel, he began feeling pangs of insecurity over leaving the money unattended back in the SUV. It bothered him enough that he had to remind himself of the utter unlikelihood of someone choosing his vehicle to break into, and then to do so in a public area in broad daylight, all during the short time he'd be away.

He had briefly considered leaving his old car parked where it was; sort of hiding in plain sight, at a place he isn't staying. And now, after retrieving it, he's starting to regret not doing that. The search for a decent spot has taken longer than planned and he's growing increasingly uncomfortable. He has been out driving his old car for far too long, and the search has led him to an area too distant from the motel to walk back.

He finally finds the type of place he has been seeking, a sprawling garden apartment complex adjacent to Route 1. Initially, it appears to be another waste of time. There are plenty of open parking spaces, but each one he tries is marked 'Reserved'. Then he catches a break, spotting a commercial van leaving an unreserved spot. Comfortable with leaving the car there until he can arrange to have it moved again, he calls for a taxi. As a simple precaution, he gives the address of a building one street over for the pickup location.

Though the cabbie scowled when he learned his passenger's destination was a motel only a couple of miles away, he was satisfied with the five-dollar tip TD gave him on top of the small fare. When they reach the motel, TD has the cabbie drop him at the front office instead of where he is parked in back.

As soon as the taxi pulls off, TD heads for his SUV to confirm the bags of money are untouched. He doesn't remember feeling such anxiety yesterday, despite the cash sitting unattended for extended periods while he was in the library and the bar. He didn't think about it or check on it once. Whatever has changed, he had better learn to get past it if he wants to avoid driving himself crazy with worry. The problem is going to arise repeatedly until he settles down in one place.

As he pulls into traffic, he commits to keeping the issue from his mind, though he also suspects that telling yourself not to worry about driving around with a million bucks is easier said than done.

He starts out by heading north on Route 1 and doesn't go far before he stops for breakfast, intentionally choosing a different restaurant than the day before. He had no way of knowing that Jon Stark had chosen the same place to meet with Eddie's couriers.

Luckily, they had finished their briefing and set out in pursuit of him, not long before he arrived.

⅄

When they looked in on Raffi during their early morning rounds, the doctors explained their plan to operate again in two days. Raffi had few questions, knowing he must get out of there well before that. It can't be much longer before the police show up.

After the doctors move on, Raffi begins slowly testing his range of motion, trying to gauge the amount of pain he'll have to endure to leave the hospital. It's almost manageable with the drugs he's being given, but his lack of strength is another issue. As he's pondering how he will make it, his bedside phone rings. It's Cesar, calling to tell him he just pulled into the parking garage. He has the clothes Raffi requested and will be up to the room soon.

When he gets there, Cesar sees how difficult it's going to be to move his friend. Once again, he pleads with him to change his mind, but Raffi is having none of it. He's already pulling off strips of medical tape and tubing with one hand while reaching with the other for the clothing Cesar brought.

Cesar helps with each piece as Raffi groans with pain from the simple effort required to dress. When they're finished, Raffi falls back onto the bed. Taking a moment to regain his strength, he tells Cesar to go find a wheelchair to help get him to the car.

Hurriedly leaving the room, Cesar nearly collides with Samuel, the operative Stark has sent to deal with Raffi. Wearing a white doctor's coat, he was standing just outside the door, pretending to read Raffi's chart. Excusing himself, Cesar heads down the hall but stops after a few steps and glances back over his shoulder. Watching the blonde-haired doctor enter Raffi's room, he waits to hear if the man reacts to Raffi's state of dress.

Almost immediately, he hears the doctor say, "Well, it looks like someone is in a hurry to leave."

Having heard enough, Cesar begins looking for a wheel chair. He understands Raffi's desire to leave, but a part of him secretly hopes the doctor will somehow put a halt to the plans of his badly wounded friend.

In the room, Raffi has been wrestling with adjusting the leg of the sweat pants that cover the awkward metal apparatus. Looking up, he responds to the doctor's comment with a grimace on his face. "Doc, I'm sorry, but I'm afraid I gotta get out of here."

"I understand, let me help you."

Raffi's disappointment with being caught off guard is replaced with total surprise at the doctor's cooperative response. He quickly scans the man's face to see if he's joking with him for some reason.

It's only then that he catches a glimpse of the hypodermic needle in the man's hand, now plunging toward his neck. Raffi attempts to shout, but gets out nothing more than a brief muffled sound as the man covers his mouth with his free hand.

As he feels the pressure building in his chest, Raffi wonders how this whole job ended being so messed up. It's turned out worse than anything he could have anticipated. Then he thinks of Cesar, and the loyalty his friend has always showed him. Those are his last thoughts before it's finished. It has taken only seconds for the cocktail of heart stopping drugs to surge through his system and end his life.

Cesar was able to find an unattended wheel chair in the visitors waiting area. Rolling it back to Raffi's room, he moves steadily but not too quickly, hoping to avoid drawing the notice of anyone on the hospital staff. Approaching Raffi's room, he sees the doctor has left and is now walking briskly away.

Given a second chance to observe the man, Cesar senses something odd about the way he carries himself. And he's certainly moving faster than one would expect. Shrugging it off, he quickly maneuvers the wheelchair into Raffi's room. As he does so, he fails to see the doctor stop at the end of the hall and look back at him.

Once he sees his friend, Cesar immediately understands what has happened. Raffi is sprawled awkwardly across the bed. Though his eyes are wide open, he's clearly dead. It takes Cesar only a moment to recover from the shock and sadness before he realizes the need to get out of there. Pausing only long enough to touch Raffi's hand, he says, "Goodbye, my friend."

Instead of using the elevators across from the nursing station, Cesar exits by the stairs at the end of the hall. In his rush to leave the hospital, he fails to notice that Samuel has followed him from the building. When he reaches the parking garage, he becomes flustered. For a moment, he can't remember where he parked Raffi's Monte Carlo. He had driven the car today hoping to cheer his buddy up by driving him out of there in style.

Finally locating the car, Cesar digs in his pocket for the keys, oblivious to all else. As he opens the car's door, Samuel closes the final distance between them. No longer dressed as a doctor, he reaches around Cesar from behind with a knife in his hand. Using one long ripping motion, he slices Cesar's throat from ear to ear.

⋏

TD returned to the library after breakfast and again failed to accomplish much while there. He spent some time researching destinations and winnowing choices, but his mind constantly wandered in anticipation of seeing Les. Making any decisions before talking with her is just not going to happen. When he remembers to call Julia Crane, he leaves to make the call from his car.

When she answers, TD begins by apologizing for bothering her and offers his condolences over her husband's death.

With a terse, relatively formal tone, she says, "Thank you, Mister Adkins. It is unfortunate. I expect you would still like to be paid for your services."

"No, ma'am. The retainer you paid is all I can accept. Again, it's sad how this turned out. If you'll forgive me, there is one item of concern. I know this may seem indelicate, but since you contracted and paid for my services, I wanted to know if you would like a report and a copy of the information I gathered."

After a noticeable pause, Julia responds, "Well, I hadn't thought of that. Let's see. Why don't you put it in an envelope and mail it to me. And please make sure it's easy to see it's from you. I don't want to throw it away by accident. I'll probably just set it aside and decide later if I care enough to open it."

After another short pause, she adds, "Unless there's something in particular you think I really need to know, I mean considering that he's gone?"

"I don't think that's the case, ma'am."

"Okay, then just mail it to me."

Disappointed he hasn't found an unobtrusive way to work in a question about the police, TD waits before saying anything else. It's important enough for him to know that he decides to ask her directly. Before he can phrase the question, Julia is talking again.

"You know, I was thinking. Maybe you should share your information with the police. That is if you think it could help with their investigation. I'll leave it up to you. I told them the other night that I'd hired you to follow my husband, so they'll know who you are."

Though these are exactly the words he had hoped not to hear, at least now he knows. With no further need to dance around the topic, he asks, "Do you happen to remember who it was with the police you talked with? That way I could contact them directly."

"I have his information right here, just give me a moment. Yes, Officer Clarkson. Kenneth Clarkson. Is there anything else, Mister Adkins? I need to go now."

Sitting in his car, holding his phone well past the end of the call, TD ponders the ramifications of this news. It couldn't be worse. The police have his name along with a direct connection to one of the shooting victims. At least he can stop deluding himself with the idea that the police aren't looking for him specifically.

The most important fact is that regardless of whether the police think he's a suspect, they're going to want to talk to him; any decent investigator would. But from TD's point of view, there's only one way that talking with the police makes any sense. And that would be as part of turning himself in.

As he starts his car, he reminds himself that is simply not an option. He has already rejected heading down that road.

入

Carl Roberts had waited patiently for a seemingly endless parade of doctors, nurses, and assorted caregivers to minister to Bobby Tomlin. When the last doctor finishes checking on Bobby's condition, Roberts is given clearance to talk with the badly injured motel clerk. There are caveats. The detective's time will be limited and the interview must end if Bobby displays any reluctance or fatigue.

The doctor's last words are, "He's receiving drugs that are masking a considerable amount of his pain, though certainly not all of it. We have to be careful because of the concussion. To some extent, the drugs may distort his perceptions of both the past and present. And because of the concussion, he may remember nothing. I wouldn't expect too much. Please limit your time detective. Let's say ten minutes."

After a quick introduction, Roberts asks Bobby what he remembers about Monday night. Bobby tells him he remembers a lot, though sometimes he gets the order of things jumbled. "Maybe it would work better if you ask me questions."

Roberts would prefer to have Bobby simply relate what he saw, but he understands this interview may have to go differently. Trying a different tack, he tells him they're trying to learn as much as they can about the paying guests who were present at the time of the shootings. "Do you recognize this man, and if so, can you tell me anything about him?"

In his hand is a picture of TD Adkins, taken from his driver's license. When Bobby fails to react, Roberts suggests the man might have been a recent guest at the motel. When Bobby again says nothing, Carl remembers the doctor's warning. Then he sees Bobby smiling broadly.

With a more engaged demeanor, Bobby says, "Now I remember. I think that's the man who wanted to stay on the end. It just took me a moment to find the memory. Yeah, he didn't want any noise. Can I see the picture again?"

Roberts quickly follows with more questions. Unfortunately, there's little more that Bobby knows. The man paid with cash when he checked in earlier and Bobby didn't ask for identification, nor does he know the man's name. There was the request for a room at the end, but that's all he can remember. Questions about whether he came and went, what kind of car he drove, and other things all draw blanks.

Bobby doesn't understand the detective's focus; particularly having no idea that the man is considered a suspect. Tilting his head to one side, he scrunches up his face, expressing his confusion. Unfortunately, Roberts assumes he's just suffering a moment of increased pain.

After telling Bobby that the man's name is TD Adkins, Roberts asks a similar series of questions about Eddie King and Tim Crane. Bobby cooperates with enthusiasm, telling him everything he knows. Roberts isn't surprised to hear Tim Crane had been there at least once before. For a second, he reconsiders whether Crane could have somehow been involved as Richter suggested. Believing it highly unlikely, he sets the concept aside for now.

Of great interest was what Bobby had to say about Eddie King; and that it corroborated what they had learned from Marvin Williams. At one point, Bobby had sheepishly admitted to taking a tip from Eddie every month. Roberts told him not to worry about it.

Sensing that Bobby may be tiring, Roberts decides to wrap things up. He can always follow-up later, particularly since the young man is so cooperative. Going for one last question, he asks if Bobby knows of any personal relationship or other connection between Eddie King and Tim Crane, or Eddie and TD Adkins; and if he has ever seen any of them talking together.

Bobby answers no, displaying the same look of confusion.

Unfortunately, Roberts again assumes the kid is suffering from pain. "Is there anything I can do for you? Should I call a nurse?"

"No, I'm ok. I mean considering everything. I'm just a little confused. Can I ask you a question?"

With a nod from Roberts, Bobby continues. "Why are you so interested in the man in the photo? The man named Adkins. Did he do something?"

"All I can tell you is that our investigation has led us to believe Mister Adkins was involved with the attack at the motel Monday night."

Bobby had spent plenty of time thinking about what had happened, repeatedly turning it over in his mind as he had lain there yesterday. The drugs and the pain made it tough, but there was enough he remembered. He had gone over what he knew from before Monday, and put it together with what he could remember from the terrible shootout.

Bobby remembered seeing Raffi yelling at everyone during the holdup. It was at that moment he realized what was happening was in some way connected with Raffi's frequent visits to Carmela. He has now concluded that Raffi somehow exploited Carmela, though it's possible the two of them working together had planned the attack on Eddie King.

Regardless, it has never crossed his mind that the man the detective is talking about was involved, or any other guest for that matter. Even with the police implying that is the case, it makes little sense to him.

Using both his facial expression and the tone of his voice, Bobby displays his skepticism. "So you think this man Adkins is somehow involved with Raffi and Carmela in planning the attack on Eddie King?"

Roberts was stunned, having in no way anticipated Bobby's question. Here was someone else who clearly felt Adkins didn't fit into the puzzle. Just as surprising was Bobby's casual manner as he invoked the names of the two people whom he presumed had planned the attack. And it had all been expressed with an innocence that rang completely true to the detective.

Roberts tries to slow his thought processes, trying not to let his mind run too fast in this new direction. He's also aware of his witness's physical and mental condition.

Looking down at the injured man in the bed, Roberts asks, "Mister Tomlin, do you feel strong enough to answer a few more questions?"

When Bobby agrees with a smile, Roberts says, "Okay, let's back up just a little."

⋏

Earlier, upon leaving home, Phil Madrigal had driven directly to his office in Old Town Alexandria and parked his car in a reserved space next to the building where he works. It couldn't have been easier to follow him.

Stark's man parked in a municipal lot half a block further down the one-way street. From there he has an unobstructed view of Madrigal's car and the entrance to the building. If Madrigal leaves, he has to drive right past him.

Stark has already checked in twice to confirm Madrigal hasn't moved. The second time he reminded his man to keep a lookout for Adkins as well.

⋏

Carl Roberts continued interviewing Bobby until a doctor returned and put a halt to it. The session had lasted almost a half an hour. Despite his injuries and the drugs, Bobby was sufficiently alert and amenable to talking. A key takeaway for Roberts was learning of the relationship between Raffi and Carmela. The young woman's behavior during her interview makes a lot more sense now.

Outside the hospital, Roberts spends a few minutes reviewing everything he just learned. He then calls Steve Czarniak with an update. He also lets him know he's returning to the motel to re-interview Carmela. With what he knows now, his next conversation with her should go much differently.

With the investigation gaining momentum, Roberts's main source of frustration is continuing to draw a blank on finding the surviving shooter. Even if Carmella can provide some help, he doubts she knows where he is right now. And it may end up that she knows very little about him at all.

Unwilling to wait, Roberts tells Czarniak, "Our number one priority is finding this shooter. I need you to make a round of calls to every law enforcement agency in the region, have Clarkson assist you. We need to shake the tree and find this guy named Raffi. If he survived his wounds, he had to have some help. When I get back to the office, I want to hear something positive."

The two detectives have worked together long enough that Czarniak knows he can challenge his boss's thinking without coming off as insubordinate. Still, he watches his tone as he objects. "I appreciate you want this guy, but let's be realistic. Even if that was a good use of our time, we can't just make him appear before you return, simply because you want us to. Besides, I thought you already had Richter working on that?"

"Yeah, you're right, I forgot. It's the last thing I gave him to handle. All right, forget the calls. Just reissue the alert to an expanded area. I know it's not likely to yield anything, but maybe someone missed it the first time. And do me a favor. Call Richter and see if he has ever heard anything back from his calls. I just can't believe we've come up with absolutely nothing on this. And tell him we know the shooter's first name."

Before ending the call, Carl decides to revisit a concept that's been on his mind since early in the investigation. He had set it aside earlier, deciding it was something he had contrived from the facts. But after talking with Bobby Tomlin, he's becoming more confident of his theory's validity.

"There's something I'm sensing on this case and I want your take on it, Steve. Maybe I'm just imagining things that aren't there, but I think this guy Adkins might be nothing more than an opportunist."

"A what?"

"An opportunist, you know, like in the movie *No Country for Old Men*. You saw it, didn't you? It's the one where the guy stumbles onto the scene of a drug deal gone sour and ends up walking away with a briefcase full of money he finds. Only later, both he and his girl end up being killed for it. I think it's possible we have something similar here."

Czarniak chuckles as he responds, "Yeah, I loved that movie. Typical Coen brothers. Dark as hell, but a great flick."

"Yeah, well, I wasn't looking for a film critique, but I do respect your opinion. Chew on it for a bit and let me know what you think. It makes some sense. And for me, it fits a lot better than him working with that gang of shooters. Who knows though? We've definitely seen stranger stuff."

Roberts continues to sit in his car and think after the call. He likes to develop an overarching story line for the investigations he works; an interpretation of the events he can present in a unified narrative that accounts for all of the evidence. The story line for this case still has gaping holes and contradictions that must be reconciled before he can relate such a tale. And if his theory about Adkins is correct, then his narrative requires two entirely separate story lines to intersect randomly, resulting in an outcome no one would have predicted.

If you asked Roberts to tell his story now, it would start with Eddie King. For some time King has had something going on at the motel. Whatever it was, on a periodic basis he had something there worth taking. At some point, King was either sloppy or unlucky. Raffi learned about what he was doing and decided to take it down. Monday night he attempted to do that. He came close, but in this scenario, he appears to have failed badly.

Then, for this all to work, there is second, separate story line involving Crane and Adkins. Crane frequented the motel on his own business, cheating on his wife. Adkins was hired to follow him and was at motel Monday night watching Crane. Crane goes out for a smoke at the wrong moment and is swept up into the action and killed. When the shooting is over, Adkins comes out, checks on Crane, and impulsively takes the money, or drugs, or whatever. The sticking point for this construct is Adkins's behavior; taking those bags would have to be one hell of an impulse.

Whether he planned it or did it on a whim, it doesn't really matter. Roberts believes things are going to start getting pretty hot for Adkins. The owners will certainly want the contents of those bags back, and the more valuable they are, the more heat Adkins will feel.

As he heads toward his second interview with Carmela, Roberts thinks about the movie again. He hopes Adkins saw it. If so, he might realize the nature of the problem he has created for himself.

⚔

When TD pulls into the parking lot at The End Zone a little before Noon, there's nowhere for him to go. A small crew of workers appears to be finishing a repaving job, having covered the lot with a smooth, black, unmarked coat of fresh asphalt.

The small lot has never been large enough for the number of cars trying to park there on weekends. When it fills, overflow parking is directed to a small shopping center a half a block away. The parking surface has been deteriorating for some time. Over the past winter, a large pothole developed near the entrance causing even more problems, and refusing to stay fixed with a temporary patch. Bruce, the club's owner, has finally ponied up for the cost of resurfacing. TD has met Bruce a few times. He's a nice enough guy and not cheap, he has just been reluctant to pull the trigger on the costly project.

A few spaces near the club's front door are already occupied with cars, but the rest of the lot remains roped off or blocked by a paving roller. As TD maneuvers his car to back out, one of the workers signals for him to roll down his window. He yells that it will only be about ten minutes before they reopen the lot.

Preferring not to wait, TD makes the short drive down the block. After locking and relocking his car, he circles the vehicle once, examining it from a distance of a several feet. Deciding there's nothing about it that screams 'steal this one, there's a million bucks inside', he begins the short walk to The End Zone.

⋏

Phil's morning at the office is finished, though he still has to drop a package at the post office for Anne before meeting with TD. Phil knows his friend needs to talk about something that happened at the motel the other night; he's just not sure what it is. He sensed TD's intensity and urgency during the few calls they've had and he doesn't want to let him down today. He's almost out his office door before he remembers to grab the large business envelope from his desk. Enclosed is the vehicle ownership data TD requested.

Outside, Stark's man watches as Phil comes out of his office and walks directly to his car. He reports in that they're on the move as he follows Phil for several blocks north, watching him slow and turn into the post office. The many one-way streets in this part of Alexandria make it easier to follow someone, but this situation presents a small challenge. Luckily, he's able to avoid circling the block, sliding into a street-side parking space with a view of the post office lot.

Phil is back in his car in a matter of minutes. As he resumes driving north, there are no indications that he's aware of being followed. He soon makes a left-hand turn, followed by another at the next street. The turns put him on Route 1, heading south out of Old Town.

As he follows Phil from two cars behind, Stark's man calls in a brief alert. "We're headed in your direction."

⋏

TD pauses as he enters The End Zone, letting his eyes adjust to the darkened room. He has been here enough to navigate his way through the bar blindfolded, but today is different. On what is likely to be his last visit, he has the urge to take a mental snapshot of the place for his memory. His eyes linger at various spots as they move across the tableaux in front him, from the oval bar with its stripper poles and the tacky sports décor, to the table where he usually camps. There's no denying he has a fondness for the place, even above coming to see Les. In its own way, the club has served as a halfway house on his journey back to a more social existence.

As usual for this hour, it is sparsely populated. So far, there are only three other customers, one at the bar and two sharing a table. Karen gives TD a nod from behind the bar as she continues talking with Derek, the dayshift bouncer. Also known as Big D, he spends most of his time occupying a padded leather barstool he keeps positioned by the red curtained doorway that leads to the dancers' cramped dressing room. His perch affords him a good view of the entire main room along with a direct line of sight to the front entrance.

With no dancers on stage yet, the music is throttled back enough that you don't have to raise your voice to converse. It's another reason TD wanted to arrive early. At first, he doesn't see Les, but then he spots her coming out of the kitchen. After stopping at the bar, she finally sees him as well, waving enthusiastically as she ferries a couple of beers to the other table.

Les has some great personal news she wants to share with TD and has been looking forward to his arrival all morning. Karen also told her that he had come in looking for her yesterday, which has her curious. After reassuring the customers at the other table that a dancer will be on stage soon, she makes a beeline for TD wearing a big smile.

As she approaches, TD realizes the conversation he has been fretting over is about to occur. Anxious with anticipation, he holds his hands together on the table to keep from shaking. It's like he's back in high school, ginning up the courage to ask a girl out on a first date.

Before he can say anything, Les is talking. She's speaking so excitedly, he can hardly keep up with what she's telling him. He finally puts it all together; she's talking about yesterday's interview. And they called her this morning with a job offer. Suddenly she's finished; her serving tray tucked under one arm, a hand on her hip, standing proudly before him with that beaming smile of hers.

TD knows he needs to snap out of his shock and at least feign happiness for her. Instead, he mutters a lame response. "Well, congratulations. I guess that means I'll be seeing you around sometime then."

"C'mon TD," she says, playfully punching him on the shoulder. "I thought I could count on you for some enthusiasm and a little support. What's the problem? Besides, I'm not going anywhere, 'cause I'm not taking it."

"Why not? Isn't this the goal of all your studying and hard work? You've talked about it all the time lately."

"Well, sort of, but not exactly. The offer is from a company that does a lot of different things in my area, but they don't have any design positions open. I had a great interview and they liked me. Unfortunately, they only offered a tech support position until something opens up. And they were clear that there are no promises with that. But they really liked me, TD, and that's the most important thing. And maybe this is a sign the job market is beginning to loosen up."

Instead of recognizing and echoing the obvious pride and sense of accomplishment Les is sharing with him, TD filters out everything except what he wants to hear. Somehow, his takeaway is that the door remains open for what he wants to ask. Tossing his planned, step-by-step script overboard, he impulsively blurts out, "I have some pretty big news too. I'm leaving. I'm leaving the area for good. And pretty much right away. Maybe, you should come along."

Watching her smile vanish, TD realizes his sudden declarations have come off sounding like just what they are, a childish response, topping her news with some of his own. With his hopes foundering, and his thoughtless words hanging between them, he can think of nothing to say.

Les has looked away several times trying to mask the feelings of hurt on her face. While they've been talking, two more customers have come in and taken seats at separate tables instead of the bar. First one, then the other signals Les for assistance. Acknowledging them, she then turns back to TD.

Clearly disappointed, she says, "Wow, I don't know what to say. But I'm sure glad you're here today. It's obvious we have some things to talk about, but I need to take care of these guys first."

"I know, go ahead."

Before she leaves, Les leans in closely, gently laying her hand on his shoulder. Speaking with a friendly but confidential air, she says, "I really wasn't planning on taking that job, TD. Seriously, are you really leaving? I don't believe it."

As she steps back a little, she continues. "I'll come back over later, but you can see we're getting some early business. You have time to stay and talk, don't you?"

"Yeah, fine, absolutely. We need to talk; but it can wait. I'm also here to meet with Phil. Let's talk after you take care of your lunch customers. Promise?"

"Yeah, I promise. I want to also." Smiling again, but in a different way than before, she asks, "You getting something to eat? Your regular?"

With another promise to talk later, Les leaves to attend to her other customers. As she replays their conversation in her head, she wonders what is happening with TD. Her relaxed and caring, mildly flirty friend is missing, replaced by this edgy, uncomfortable version. She's also going to have to wait to find out what's really going on. Between taking care of the lunch customers and TD's meeting with Phil, it's going to be awhile before they'll have more than a moment to talk privately.

She can't believe TD is really leaving. Hopefully, it's not true. If it is, it pretty much scuttles his involvement in something she had been optimistically planning for some time now.

Within a few minutes, she sees Phil Madrigal arrive and wonders if he is the cause of TD's odd manner. She doesn't care that much for Phil, but she knows he and TD are very close. Sometimes when he comes in he drinks a little too much and focuses on the dancers more than she cares for.

Today, along with TD, Phil's behavior is markedly different. Almost from the moment he sat down, he and TD were engrossed in conversation. And one that was clearly not for her ears. They had stopped talking in mid-sentence when she dropped off a beer for Phil along with TD's burger. Since then, TD has continued to act jumpy and distracted. He even missed a smile and a little wink she gave him when she passed their table a few minutes later.

⅄

Stark is glad to have Samuel back in the area. Having returned from his trip to the hospital in Stafford, he's taking a short break before rejoining the search team. If they need to apply any pressure on Adkins after they locate him, Samuel is the man for the job.

Right now, Stark's hopes are running high. There's even a chance they might have Adkins in hand within the next hour. Stark is less than a mile away from a bar called The End Zone, where one of his men, Drew Waters, has followed Phil Madrigal.

Marty Carpentier is also on the scene. Per Stark's instructions, he has just checked the immediate area around the bar in hopes of spotting Adkins car. Unsuccessful, he and Waters are now parked across the road from the club with a clear view of the entrance, awaiting Stark's arrival on the scene.

⅄

TD is surprised when Phil shows up early. As soon as his friend is in his chair, TD jumps right into it, walking him through the events at the motel.

Phil had already guessed TD was there Monday night, but he's still shocked hearing about what he witnessed. And that was before TD dropped the bomb, telling him that he took the bags.

"Are you fucking with me, TD? I don't believe it. You really took their money? You're going to turn it in, right?"

Phil pauses, anticipating TD's answers, but there's no response. Frustrated, he says, "I think you've freaking flipped. I don't believe this.

237

Besides, if you were planning to keep the money, why in the hell would you still be here?"

Again, Phil hears nothing. Instead, he watches as TD slowly turns his head until he's looking at Les, the cute waitress. Phil knows TD has a soft spot for her. Then it hits him.

"No way. There's no goddamn way TD. Please don't tell her about this. And please don't ask her to help you somehow. You can't involve her in this."

Seeing the odd expression on TD's face, the other shoe drops for Phil. "Oh man, you're going to ask her to leave with you. Aren't you?"

Though it all seems totally crazy, Phil knows the past few years have been pretty tough emotionally for TD. Maybe the stress and trauma of a front row seat for the killings has finally put him on tilt. That would explain a lot. Regardless of the cause, this isn't the time or place to try to diagnose what is wrong or change his mind. He can talk some sense into him later, as soon as he's somewhere safe.

Grabbing TD's arm above the wrist, Phil leans over and stares at his friend until their eyes lock. "Listen, man, I've really gotta hit the men's room. But I'm telling you, when I get back to the table, if I find out you're playing with me I'm going to kick your butt."

Still looking at him intently, he continues. "But if you took that money and you're not turning it in, then you have to get out of here now; without her. And just in case you think I'm good with all this, you'd be wrong. I plan to convince you to turn yourself in, but that's for a little later. Right now, I only want to hear about when you're leaving town, and what I can do to help you make that happen as soon as possible."

Calming himself as he pushes back his chair, Phil remembers the envelope he brought along with him. As he stands, he says, "Oh yeah. Here's the information you requested. You know, there's something really interesting about it."

After a brief pause, he says, "Wait a minute; is this also about the other night? Because all of those cars, except for one, are the property of the same company. It's a leasing firm called CCVS. That stands for Construction &

Corporate Vehicle Services. A company called Wilkins Investment Group owns the other car. And it's not just interesting. It's an amazing damn co-incidence if you ask me."

TD looks up skeptically. "Sorry Phil. I'm not following you on the coincidence part."

"The coincidence is that I wrote the original policies. I wrote the car insurance policies that cover all of them!"

Tossing the envelope on the table, Phil turns toward the men's room.

As he passes by Derek, he gives him a smile and a nod. Phil has seen the guy before when he has met TD here for lunch. He probably played college football somewhere before ending up on that stool. Phil figures him for a linebacker. And he still looks fit, certainly not much overweight.

As he enters the men's room, Phil wonders how often there's really any need for Derek's services during the dayshift. It must be a terribly boring job.

⟁

The paving crew has cleared out by the time Stark arrives. He takes a spot on the back row opposite the front door, with a full view of the nearly empty lot. As soon as Waters and Carpentier join him, they review the plan of action.

Stark will remain outside as a sentinel while Waters and Carpentier enter the club. They're to sit well apart from Madrigal, but maintain a clear view of him and the entrance. There's a chance Madrigal is simply killing time before meeting Adkins elsewhere, but Stark thinks it's too much of a coincidence that Adkins has been making calls from this area and now Madrigal is here. His bet is that they're meeting here soon.

When Adkins shows, Stark will allow him to enter the bar unimpeded. Then he'll give him a few minutes to get comfortable before following him inside. That should increase their chances of surprise, as well as cutting the two of them off from their cars.

Interrupting, Waters asks, "Why even let him inside the place and get involved with whoever's in there? Let's just grab him when he pulls in."

"I thought about that. But right now, there are too few cars in the lot. We'd be completely out in the open, in full view of twenty-five cars streaming by every damn minute only fifty feet away. And there's a traffic signal just past here. Maybe you didn't notice, but when it turns red, those southbound lanes easily back up to this point."

Stark explains that he sees the bar as a manageable environment with several key advantages. Since the lot is practically empty, there can't be many customers inside. And by the very nature of the place, they're likely to be focused on the dancers, not each other.

"When I come in, I'll sit close to Adkins. Then I'll signal for you two to approach. When you're by my side, I'll introduce myself. I'll let him see that I'm carrying, and quickly explain that we're going to leave the bar for a discussion in my car."

Stark believes that being suddenly confronted by three armed men will be all it takes to convince Adkins to leave peacefully. If they execute this correctly, they should have him and Madrigal out of the bar in a matter of minutes, with hardly anyone noticing. Carpentier will take Madrigal to his car and Waters will bring Adkins to Stark's.

⚔

Les is concerned with TD's odd behavior. He's so nervous and twitchy, even while he talks with Phil he's constantly glancing around the bar. She'd like to talk with him again, but definitely alone. When she sees Phil stand and put an envelope on the table, she thinks he might be leaving. Instead, he heads towards the men's room.

Maybe this is the moment to steal a little time with TD. She won't have more than a minute or two, but at least she can reassure him a little, maybe help him to relax. She'll tell him she wants to hear all about his unexpected departure, even if she doesn't really believe that it's happening.

Les finally makes it over to TD's table after checking with her other customers, but only in time to see Phil emerging from the men's room. She decides to wait until they can speak privately before she says anything to

TD. Instead, she simply asks if he needs another beer. At least he looks a little a little less jumpy and even has a little smile for her.

Suddenly, TD is looking right past her wearing a look of concern. Something or someone behind her has drawn his attention. Turning to follow his stare, she sees his focus is on two men who have just entered.

▲

Before choosing where to sit, Waters and Carpentier quickly scan the darkened room to locate Phil Madrigal. At first, they don't see him. Then, nudging his partner, Marty Carpentier alerts Waters, softly, but with urgency.

"Heads up. Back wall, coming from the restrooms."

As they watch Phil move toward a seat, Waters motions them toward a table along the opposite wall from where Madrigal is heading. Once there, he points out that he has chosen a position that allows them to not only watch Madrigal, but the entrance as well. Marty doesn't appreciate having to listen to the tutorial, but he isn't about to say anything. It was his crew's sloppiness and overconfidence that cost several lives, a ton of cash, and is the reason he finds himself here right now.

Unbeknownst to either Waters or Carpentier, when they entered The End Zone, they had passed through a metal detector installed in a decorative archway immediately inside the club's entrance. At night, a bouncer works the front door, observing everyone who enters.

Even though the entrance is unmanned during the dayshift, the metal detector remains in operation. It's set at a high enough level to indicate objects only containing a considerable amount of metal, such as a weapon. Tripping the threshold illuminates three small LED lights above the archway. There's another set of lights installed behind the bar. Once triggered, the lights flash slowly and silently until someone hits the reset.

Having had her attention drawn to the two men, Les sees the flashing lights above the entrance. Checking to see if anyone else has noticed, she's relieved to see the bartender is already waving at Derek. So far, she has failed to gain his attention.

TD has been looking over everyone who has come in since he arrived. In this case, he had not only noticed that they set off the metal detector, but something else caught his eye. He's pretty sure he recognizes one of the men.

Then, as he watches them scan the bar, something odd happens. Right after Phil emerges from the men's room, one of them says something to the other, and they immediately lock their eyes on Phil. When they finally break their gaze, they move toward a table on the far side of the room.

Keeping his head low, TD gets a better look at them as they take their seats. Now he's sure. The younger of the two is definitely one of the couriers he saw at the motel Monday night. Refusing to believe the unlikely coincidence of the man's presence here at this time and place, TD knows he needs to act immediately.

With Les standing next to him, and Phil now only a step away from the table, TD barks out a command, "Quick, Phil, sit down. Not next to me, across from me."

Confronted with TD's urgency, Phil drops into the chair, unaware of the two men sitting across the room directly behind him.

Les is surprised by TD's harsh tone and again wonders what has him so irritated. After another quick glance at the two new customers, she turns back to TD and lays her hand on his shoulder. "You need to relax, TD. You've been wound up since you got here. Can you hang in there until we get a chance to talk?"

After getting a nod from TD and leaving the table, Les pauses to look back over her shoulder and give him a smile. Strangely, she can hardly see him. With another display of totally odd behavior, he has hunched over so far, it's as if he's now using Phil to hide from her view.

Giving up on TD for the moment, Les looks to see if Derek has noticed the flashing light. He has gotten off his stool, but as she walks across the bar, she can tell that he's unaware which customer has set off the alarm. Catching his attention, she tilts her head toward where the two men are now sitting. That's when she notices there's something unusual about that as well.

It's not that odd that they're sitting next to each other, instead of across the table. It's that they're not watching the dancer, or any of the televisions, or even conversing. They appear to be interested in doing only one thing: staring directly at Phil and TD.

For no conscious reason, Les decides to obstruct their view. Maybe it's because she doesn't like their look, or it's simply knowing that they're armed. Maybe it's the way they're eyeing TD, or how he reacted to their arrival. Whatever the reason, with a quick little zigzag she aligns her approach to their table, putting herself between them and TD.

Drew Waters is unhappy. Just as they were taking their seats, Phil Madrigal sat down at a table across from someone and they didn't see who it was. Madrigal now has his back to them and the person he's sitting with is hunched over behind him. Neither he nor Marty has yet to catch a glimpse of who it is, and now their view is blocked due to the approaching waitress.

Waters sends the girl on her way after snapping off an order for a couple of Cokes, but his frustration only grows; his view of Madrigal's table remains obstructed. A large man Waters figures to be the bouncer is purposefully heading across the bar, obstructing his view of Madrigal as he follows the same path the waitress just took.

As the man nears their table, Waters realizes he intends to speak with them. Nudging Marty, he says, "Let me handle this flunky. You keep a close tab on Madrigal. As soon I deal with this guy, I'm gonna get a better look at who our friend is with."

Leaning over to one side to peer around Derek, Marty sees Madrigal is now sitting alone. What happened to the other person?

Looking around, a hint of movement along the back wall attracts his eye. It appears someone just passed through a set of red velvet curtains hanging in a doorway that likely leads to the dancer's dressing room. Other than the dancer on stage, Marty doesn't remember seeing any other girls walking around, but he isn't sure. Maybe Madrigal was sitting with a dancer. Before he can say anything about it to Waters, the bouncer is at their table.

"I'm sorry to bother you, gentlemen, but I believe at least one of you set off the metal detector when you entered."

Waters spits back, "So what?"

Unruffled by surly customers, Derek responds using a well-practiced, pleasant tone. "I'm sure there's no big problem. It's just that something set off the metal detector and we don't allow any kind of weapons in the club. If you'd like to stay, I'm going to need to do a quick pat down. I promise to keep it light and brief."

Waters has barely controlled himself listening to the bouncer. "Look, big boy, there's not going to be any pat downs. Besides, I have a legal permit to carry. It's time for you to move on and hassle someone else."

"That may be the case, sir, but this is a private business. That means we have the right to forbid any weapons on the premises. There's a sign posted at the entrance."

While Derek and Waters have been talking, Phil has left his table and walked over to the bar. Eyeing him closely the whole time, Marty watches as he hands a folded up napkin to the waitress, as if it's a message.

Tapping his partner's shoulder, he says, "Hey Waters. Something's going on. You need to see this."

Les is a little confused when Phil hands her one of the small bar napkins and tells her to "read this". She's also wondering where TD has gone, as she watches Phil return to a now empty table. Assuming there's some connection to the napkin, she looks down and reads the note scrawled across the back.

URGENT!! MEET ME IN THE DRESSING ROOM WITH YOUR CAR KEYS. NOW!! TD

Her first thought is why is TD in the dressing room? And why does he urgently need her keys? Before she pieces things together, she's distracted by what's happening with Derek, now involved in some kind of confrontation with the men who set off the metal detector. One of the men is standing, and though she can't really hear what's being said, both his facial expression and body language signal trouble is looming.

Waters is now standing face-to-face with Derek, with no more than two feet between them. After Marty's warning, he's anxious to finish dealing with this guy and get back to the job they came in here to do. He's not looking for a fight, but he's also not ready to back down to some low-rent strip club bouncer.

"Look, buddy. We're not causing any trouble here. We're just here to have a couple of soft drinks, watch the girls, and relax. Then we'll be on our way. Why don't you go back to your comfortable little stool and leave us alone."

While Waters has been verbally sparring with the bouncer, Marty watched as Madrigal returned to his table, this time taking a seat facing in their direction. He also observed Phil glance toward the curtains Marty thought someone had just passed through. A few moments later, he does it again.

Marty is starting to think the person Madrigal was sitting with was TD Adkins. Maybe he was already in the bar before they arrived. With Waters and the bouncer hooked up in each other's face, Marty is tempted to go over and take a look behind the curtains to see who is back there.

Derek has run out of patience. Besides the fact that he doesn't like this guy, he has the feeling there's something more to this than these two just wanting to sip some Cokes and watch the dancers. He has also been keeping an eye on the younger guy, and though he hasn't said a word, he's now starting to get twitchy as well.

Using a different, far sterner tone, Derek speaks to both of them. "Gentlemen, the fact is you have a choice. You can either leave the premises immediately, or submit to a…"

Suddenly, the younger of the two guys is up and past him, moving toward the back of the club and the dancers' dressing room. Faced with a choice of his own, Derek opts for dealing with what he believes is the greater threat. With surprising agility, he spins and weaves through several tables, slamming Marty to the floor with a broadside tackle that crushes the wind out of the smaller man.

Before Derek can get up, Drew Waters crosses to where the two men are sprawled. With no hesitation, he smashes the heel of his foot onto the back of the bouncer's head. Out of the corner of his eye, he sees Madrigal is now standing. Satisfied they haven't lost the man they're following, Waters heaves the nearly unconscious bouncer off his partner.

Gasping as he struggles for a full breath, Marty points and manages to say, "I think Adkins is here. Behind those curtains."

Les watches in shock as the brawl breaks out, all the time clutching the napkin in her hand. For a brief moment, she completely forgets about TD's strange request. Then, she hears him shouting at her, his voice rising over the music. Partially hidden by the curtains, he's frantically waving for her. Sensing the rising danger inside the club, she grabs her purse from behind the bar, and runs the short distance to where TD was standing just a moment before.

After dealing with the bouncer, Waters also steers himself toward the curtained doorway. He never sees Phil coming. Trying to emulate Derek's tackle, Phil fails to make solid contact; still, it's enough. Staggered by the impact, Waters is unable to stay on his feet, keeling heavily to one side as he loses his balance.

Waters is able to protect himself as he tumbles to the floor, slowly crashing through several chairs and a table. Clearheaded, he reacts instantly when Madrigal lands on his back in an effort to keep him down. Disentangling an arm, Waters violently slams his elbow into Phil's chest. Then, using the separation gained by the blow, he quickly follows with another elbow to Phil's face, flattening his nose.

After shrugging Phil off his back, Waters begins to stand. He sees Marty is also up. As he passes Waters and moves towards the curtained doorway, he's clearly worse off from his encounter with the bouncer. His left arm is wrapped across his chest, reaching toward the pain generated by two freshly broken ribs.

The last thing Les sees before plunging through the curtains is a barely conscious Phil Madrigal slumping to the floor, blood gushing from his face. Suddenly TD is there, grabbing her by the wrist and yelling at her.

"Those men are here to kill me, Les. I have to go and I don't have my car. You gotta give me your keys or drive me out of here."

Les freezes. She's hearing and seeing, but barely processing what is happening. She has witnessed Derek and Phil Madrigal be beaten badly, and now TD is yelling something about men wanting to kill him.

"Les! I need to go now!"

Refocused, Les jerks free of TD's grasp, but instead of pulling away from him, she reverses the hold. Grabbing his hand, she quickly leads him toward the club's back exit. Once outside, they run the short distance to her bright yellow VW Beetle parked behind the club.

Back inside, Derek has recovered enough from the blow to his head to reenter the game, and just in time to deliver another blindside tackle. This time his target is the man who nearly knocked him cold with the cheap shot to his head. He's now standing a few feet away with his back to Derek, with a bloodied and barely conscious Phil Madrigal lying at his feet.

Still groggy, his vision slightly blurred, Derek launches himself at Waters. Again, he finds his mark, crashing into his assailant and taking them both to the floor. Unfortunately, this time his tackle lacks the ferocity he mustered taking down the other guy.

Enraged that he is under attack again, Waters quickly responds to Derek's assault. Rolling onto his side, he delivers three quick, devastating jabs to the bouncer's face. The last punch breaks Derek's jaw, rendering him unconscious and deepening the concussion he had already incurred.

Tired of the amateur hour, Waters pulls his gun and fires a round into the ceiling. The gunshot provides precisely the effect he intended, with everyone hitting the floor or scurrying for a hiding place. He's also sure it will deter any other heroes from coming forward.

The bad news is the second scuffle has cost him invaluable time. Once he's through the curtains, he finds an empty hallway leading past a dressing room to a now open back door. When he gets outside, he's barely in time to see a VW Beetle turn the corner of the building with Marty Carpentier lurching after it.

Jon Stark has remained in the front parking lot waiting for Adkins to show, unaware of the events inside. When he hears the gunshot, he knows something has gone wrong. Hesitating briefly, he finally leaves his car. As he approaches the entrance, he's nearly overrun by several customers running out of the bar.

At the same time, accompanied by a squeal of tires, a car appears from behind the building, accelerating towards the parking lot exit. As it passes immediately in front of him, Stark can see the driver is a young woman. There's also a passenger, but his attention is drawn to the look of terror on the driver's face.

Stark makes a mental note of the license plate as the car slows only enough to turn into traffic on Route 1. As it pulls away, he has a strong urge to return to his car and follow it, but he decides to continue inside. Before he can act, Marty Carpentier comes around the outside of the building from the same direction as the car that had just appeared.

Seeing the car is gone, Carpentier stops and stoops over, holding his body as if he's wounded. A moment later, Waters appears, his gun out, but down at his side. Raising the weapon, he aims as if to fire off a round toward the VW, but there's nothing to shoot at.

Now bent over almost in half, Marty struggles for a breath as he continues holding his ribs. Grimacing, he says, "Sorry. We fucked up. I finally got a good look him. That was Adkins riding off in the yellow car."

Stark realizes his instincts were correct. His hesitation has cost them. Sprinting back to his car, he yells for his men to follow. As he turns into traffic, he calculates they can't have much more than a two- to three-minute lead. It's not much. If they choose to stay on Route 1, the endless traffic signals may slow them down enough for him to catch up.

⚔

The third traffic light they encountered had turned red at least a full second before Les drove straight through it. TD was shouting the whole time, "Don't stop. Don't stop."

Once though the intersection, he continued shouting out instructions, first telling Les that they needed to get off Route 1, then yelling for her to turn left up ahead onto the Mount Vernon Parkway.

Les hasn't spoken since they left The End Zone, muted by a combination of fear and concentration. For some reason, the act of running the red light is the trigger for breaking her silence. "Stop yelling and tell me what in the hell is going on TD. I swear I heard a gunshot when we were running from the bar. Is someone really trying to kill you?"

Formulating a response helps TD regain some composure. He has been frantic from the moment they jumped in the car, his thoughts racing as he absorbs the realization of how foolish he has been. When he finally answers, he uses a tone that he hopes will help Les cope with the situation they're in, even as he delivers news that can only increase her fearfulness.

"I can't explain it all right now, but I won't lie to you; it's not a good situation. I honestly believe those men will hurt me badly if they get their hands on me. They may even kill me."

"Why? Who would want to kill you?"

"They believe I took something valuable of theirs."

As he says this, TD watches Les closely, gauging how she's handling his answer. She had cut their speed after turning off Route 1, and now the car is slowing even more.

After a brief glance over at him, Les returns her eyes to the road. Then a few seconds go by before she asks, "Well, did you?"

Just barely, but noticeably enough, TD nods.

Slowly shaking her head, Les checks the rear view mirror as she begins braking the car, pulling to a stop on the side of the road.

TD can't help from raising his voice again, "What in the hell are you doing, Les? Please, we need to be driving away from here. Fast!"

"I don't like this, TD. And before I forget it, this is the last time I'm going to tell you to stop yelling at me. Those guys beat up Derek and your friend Phil pretty badly. And I'm sure I heard gunfire. Worst of all, you tell me you took something from these thugs, and now you want me to drive you around with them chasing after you?"

Les's anger and fear are on full display, her trembling hands as she releases her grip on the steering wheel. Seeing that she's on the verge of tears, TD can't believe how the reality of what is happening is so completely unlike how he imagined the day would go.

"I'm so sorry this is happening, Les. Really. You can't know how terribly I feel. But please keep driving. I don't think it's safe for us sitting here in plain view. I promise I'll explain everything, but for now, for both our sakes, we need to get out of here. It's much too dangerous like this."

"Why don't we go to the police?"

"I can't, for a lot of reasons. Let's just say that I screwed up big time. I acted on an impulse and got into something way over my head. And now the police think I'm involved in an armed robbery that resulted in some people getting killed."

"Armed robbery? People killed?"

TD is becoming increasingly nervous. Instead of putting distance between them and his hunters, they're sitting in a parked car on the shoulder of a road only a few blocks from Route 1. And Les isn't helping. Instead, she's staring at him with an expression he can only describe as an amalgam of shock, fear, and disdain.

"Les, I swear to you I wasn't involved with any part of it. I was just in the wrong place at the wrong time; and then I did something that was probably stupid. You know me well enough to know I wouldn't be involved with anything that would hurt anyone."

He pauses briefly to let his words sink in. "But I can't go to the police, not yet at least. And please don't ask me when, because I don't know. I need some time to figure out where I'm going and how to handle the police. First, I need to deal with the men who are chasing me. For that I also need some time."

TD pauses again, as much for a breath as to measure the effect of his words. He can tell she remains skeptical. "There is one thing I can promise. I swear that I can prove to you and to the police, even to the men chasing me that I wasn't involved with killing anyone. I have proof beyond any doubt. But we need to get out of here, out of the open. Please, before it's too late."

"We? The only place I'm going is either home or back to work. I might be willing to let you borrow my car for a day, but I'm definitely not going anywhere with you."

TD knows Les is wrong. She has to come with him, and not because of some quixotic vision that they'll settle down together. For now at least, she has to leave because she's in danger. Those men saw her leaving the bar with him. If they can track him to The End Zone, they can certainly find her.

Reaching over to comfort her, TD puts his hand on Les's arm and says, "Please listen to me, Les. You need to let me help you. I know you don't like it, but you have to come with me."

Les immediately pulls away from him and crosses her arms. "What in the world are you talking about? There's no way I'm coming with you."

To his great relief, she starts to drive again. Unfortunately, she hasn't steered them fully back onto the pavement and they're moving very slowly; then he sees the turn signal and he understands. She's waiting for a car to pass so she can swing out and turn around. It's clearly time for him to change tactics.

"Les, you need to stop digging your heels in. Take a second to think about what's really happening. Whether you forgive me for getting you involved in all this doesn't matter. But refusing to acknowledge the reality of the situation could be fatal."

Having gotten her attention, he continues. "Those men saw your car and I have no doubt they got your license plate number. It won't be long before they're also looking for you. Please trust me. You've already seen these aren't nice men."

With her lips pursed tightly together, Les aborts the U-turn and puts them back on the road. She then makes a quick left onto a neighborhood street. It's clear that she's not headed anywhere in particular. For now, they're simply drifting along as she mulls her options. Every few seconds she glances at the rearview mirror and then over at TD, measuring what he said as she tries to cope with her sudden, real-life nightmare.

When they reach the next intersection, she stops the car with an exasperated sigh. "Okay, but this really stinks, TD. And you owe me big time. I'll help you get out of here, but that's it. And you have to figure out how to get me uninvolved as soon as possible, because I'm not coming with you. And don't forget you have a lot more explaining to do."

Suppressing a smile of relief, and knowing it would be risky for him to say anything at this moment, TD settles for the simplest response. "Thanks, Les."

After allowing a little time for the tension to subside, he suggests that they need to hide out somewhere close by for a day or two. He needs to figure out exactly what he's going to do, while keeping her out of sight until they're confident she'll be safe.

Knowing that Les lives close by, TD suggests they stop by her place so she can pack a couple of days' worth of clothes and anything else she needs. It should still be safe enough if she can do it quickly, in like ten minutes. As he's saying this, Les shoots him a glare. Despite the sour looks, he's pleased that at least for now she's willing to go with the flow, letting him lead them away from immediate danger.

Within minutes, they're at her place, a small stone bungalow set back in a stand of mature trees at the end of a gravel driveway. Once they're inside, TD glances around the front rooms while Les packs.

He quickly notices several indications that she shares the place with someone. Besides the two pairs of running shoes positioned by the kitchen door, there's the presence of small clusters of personal items and natural clutter in the main room that suggest two females live there. In a small way, the news surprises him. He's sure Les has never mentioned having a roommate before.

Calling towards the back of the house, he asks her if that is the case.

"Yes, I have a roommate, if you want to call her that," she replies. "But she must be out. Her car's not here."

TD had not inquired out of simple curiosity. "You know, I'm thinking she may want to stay away from here as well for a few days. It couldn't hurt, at least for tonight. Can you get a hold of her? I'll gladly pay so it doesn't cost her anything."

At first, Les doesn't answer him as she emerges from her bedroom with a small suitcase and a backpack slung over her shoulder. Visibly, her attitude appears to have softened a little, but when she speaks, her words and tone betray her continued contempt for the situation.

"Yeah, that's a great idea. I'll call and give her the wonderful news: You've just won a three-day vacation."

Failing to get a reaction with her sarcasm, Les pokes at him again. "Hey, I'd love to stand here yacking, but shouldn't we get out of here before the *BAD* guys arrive?"

TD ignores her insolence. Locking eyes with her, he uses a stern tone, saying, "Just so we're clear, it is exactly like you say. These men are bad guys. And I doubt they'll stop until they get their possessions back. I sure don't want to be here if they show up, so yes, we should go."

As she follows him outside, her silence and worried expression let him know that his words have hit home. He hates having to scare her, but taking things too lightly can carry its own risks. When they reach the car, he sees the large envelope Phil gave him back at the bar. He has no memory of taking it with him when he fled, but there it is on the floor in front of the passenger seat. Scooping it up, he lays it in back for now.

After agreeing that it's best for him to drive, TD begins steering them north towards Alexandria. His plan is to cross the Potomac River into Maryland using the Woodrow Wilson Bridge and then figure out the rest on the fly. Back on the road, with the risk of their being caught rapidly diminishing, he once again feels invigorated.

His reactions to the dangerous events of the past few days have not gone unnoticed. Clearly, a part of him relishes the risks he continues to take. Instead of rationally processing the choices he faces, he has remained determined to leave the area and start a new life, regardless of the perilous situation he's creating.

He's fixated on the idea that he can use what has happened to begin an entirely new life, walking away from the person he had become. The concept is simply too intoxicating, particularly with the added spice of starting over with the ill-gotten gains of someone else. And there's another dynamic. Even though it's not under ideal circumstances, at least for now, Les is with him.

Catching a glimpse of the bridge up ahead, he ponders his options. Wherever he goes, he needs to quickly figure out how he was tracked to The End Zone and make sure it doesn't happen again. As he considers that important question, it suddenly hits him that he has a much bigger problem. He no longer has the money with him. The bags of cash are in the back of his car, just down the street from the bar.

The shopping center where he parked will provide excellent cover for now, but that won't remain the case. By midnight, his vehicle could easily be the only one in the lot, drawing unwanted attention. He needs to get the car and the money out of there before that happens. Unfortunately, with the ruckus at the club, the whole area will be buzzing with police, and likely the men pursuing him as well. Trying not to panic, he tells himself this is just one more thing he needs a plan to deal with.

⅄

When Carl Roberts arrives at the Gateway to interview Carmela a second time, he notices the motel doesn't appear quite as run-down as he had remembered it from Monday night. Though the building itself is aged, the public areas are clean and free of trash. And other than the derelict pool, there's nothing in obvious disrepair. Of course, the absence of a crime scene with bodies strewn across the courtyard helps with appearances.

As he looks around at the patches of blood stained asphalt, he considers where the case stands. There are still a lot of pieces that don't seem to fit, and that makes him uncomfortable. His thoughts are interrupted when someone speaks his name from just a few steps away. So deep in concentration, he hadn't seen Carmela come out of her room.

He decides to begin the interview standing right there, starting with telling her he knows Raffi's name. As he watches her react to the news, he adds that he has witnesses who have seen her with Raffi multiple times prior to the shootings. It's a small lie, he only has the one witness, but he's sure he can find more.

Then he applies the real pressure. "Whatever you tell me from here on out had better be the truth. And you need to understand something. If you fail to tell me what you know, or you lie to me, I'll consider it an indication that you were involved with the attacks."

The warning works like magic. Within minutes, Carmela tells him all she knows. After describing how they met and started dating, she talked about Raffi's growing obsession with the man who regularly came to the motel and used Marvin's room to receive deliveries. She claims to know nothing about what Raffi had planned. He had never once talked about it with her, except to ask her to call him whenever the man showed up.

Her story rings true for Roberts. Not only does it fit with the events, and what Bobby Tomlin had told him, but it also explains her nervousness the first time they talked.

When he shows her a picture of TD Adkins she denies knowing him, and again Carl senses it's the truth. Telling her the man's name, he asks her if she has ever heard it before, or if it's possible that Raffi was involved with him in some way.

Again, she claims no knowledge. "Raffi had younger guys working for him. Like I said, I've never seen that man."

When he finishes the interview, Roberts makes the short drive to one of his regular lunch spots where he has arranged to meet Czarniak and Clarkson. Feeling much better about the case after what he has learned from Bobby and Carmela, he's anxious to share his thoughts with his senior detective.

As soon as the waitress arrives at their table, Roberts and Czarniak waste no time placing their orders. That leaves Clarkson self-consciously scanning the menu for something a little healthier than what they chose. With the waitress hovering and Czarniak glowering at him, he surrenders. Like his colleagues, he'll have the ten-inch steak and cheese sub with fries.

While they wait for the food, Roberts brings them up to speed on everything he learned this morning. It's now clear that Rafael Flores, if that's his real name, is their primary suspect. Roberts wants both Czarniak and Clarkson to focus on finding him. While they're on that, he'll handle the search for Adkins, along with the various threads of the case related to the victims. If the two of them need his help, they should just shout. Until they locate Raffi, he considers everything else to be of secondary importance; that includes finding Adkins.

Steve Czarniak begins protesting the concept of Adkins being considered secondary, reminding them that they have a witness and video of the man hustling away from the motel with the bags he took. As Roberts prepares to respond to his concern, their food arrives and they all dig in.

Czarniak has hardly made it through the first bite of his sandwich when his phone rings. He swears he's not going to answer it, but a quick check of the Caller ID indicates that it's from the main switchboard. It ends up being one of the administrative support staff relaying a message from the Stafford County Police; they have an update on a John Doe shooting victim. With Roberts and Clarkson looking on with anticipation, Czarniak wolfs down two more bites of his sub before making the call to Stafford.

The detective on the other end starts off sounding apologetic, "I know you guys don't think our John Doe is your suspect, but I decided to call again when you reissued the alert. There's also been a major change in his situation. A few hours ago, a man posing as a doctor entered his hospital room and killed him."

It takes Czarniak a number of questions to work through his confusion. Once he has the answers, it's obvious that the John Doe in Stafford is their guy, though it remains a mystery of why they wouldn't have thought so to begin with. That aspect of the news is particularly troubling, leading him to seek additional details. After another round of queries, he thanks his counterpart, ends the call, and resumes the attack on his lunch.

Carl Roberts is ripe with curiosity. Despite having heard only one side of the call, it still sounds like a major development in the case. Expecting his colleague to fill them in, he watches as Czarniak sits silently, slowly drizzling more ketchup onto his fries before taking another bite. Unwilling to wait any longer, Roberts demands an update.

With a heavy sigh, Czarniak sets down his fork and takes a long slug of iced tea. As he dabs his mouth with a napkin, he mutters something ending with, "... can't even enjoy a single damn bite."

Then, after another pause for affect, he looks up with a broad smile. "Gentlemen, thanks to that call, we are now in receipt of several fascinating pieces of news. First, let me give you the headlines. It looks like we have our shooter, though not in custody. He's in the Stafford County morgue. And I think you'll get a kick out of this, he did not die of the wounds he received in the gunfight."

No one is eating now, with all three men leaning in a little more closely as Czarniak continues.

"It looks like Flores actually made it to a hospital and had surgery. Then, this morning, someone entered his room and murdered him. Lethal injection. And it looks like they may also have the getaway driver. There was a second killing at the hospital and the victim matches his description. Someone sliced open his throat in the parking garage."

Czarniak pauses again, this time nodding at the looks of surprise from his colleagues.

No longer able to contain himself, Roberts starts firing off questions. "Why haven't we heard about this sooner? And how long have they had him? Are you sure he's ours?"

"Slow down Carl, and listen up, because it gets even better. First, I'm positive it's our guy. The timing of his arrival Monday night, the location of the gunshot wounds, and his physical description all match up. But part of the confusion on both ends of that call was because of this little gem. According to the detective I talked to, he had already informed us about the John Doe."

"Really? When?"

"You ready for this? Yesterday. And we told them it wasn't our guy".

"What?" both Roberts and Clarkson exclaim, nearly shouting.

"Yep. It appears our good friend Richter learned about it yesterday evening. And he told them it sounded wrong for our guy. Luckily, when you had me re-issue the alert this morning, the Stafford detective believed we were missing the boat and decided to give us a second call. This time, instead of contacting Richter, he used the number on the alert and the message was routed to me."

"That's great, Steve, just awesome," Roberts declares. "Okay, forget everything I said a few minutes ago. Get photos of these guys from Stafford so there's no doubt on this. If you need to go down there, then do it. We need to be sure. Then I want to know everything we can about these two."

After pausing briefly, he adds, "Wow, both of them killed. You know, it looks to me like whoever they hit at the motel has some friends out there settling the score."

As they resume eating, Carl continues, "Going forward, I'll focus on Adkins. I expect he's going to be feeling the heat real soon if he's stupid enough to have hung around. I wonder if he's aware of how rough the other team is playing. We still need to bring him in for questioning. And not just to confirm he wasn't involved with the attack. I have two really big questions for him. Why did he take those bags, and what's in them."

Kenny Clarkson hasn't said a word since ordering his meal. Sensing the inevitable, he has been hesitant to speak. He finally manages to ask, "What about me, sir? Do you still need my help on the case?"

Roberts smiles as he answers. "Based on this new information, we can probably handle things from here. I'll let you know if things heat up again. I really appreciate your help though, and the fine work you put in. We certainly know where to look the next time we have an opening for a new detective."

Beaming with pride, Clarkson looks down at his plate, barely suppressing a smile. He can't wait to tell Sean Landry what Roberts said. Feeling more relaxed, and with the case looking a little differently, he decides to add his own take. "You know, listening to all this, I've been wondering about something. If we don't think Adkins was involved with the attacks, has he actually committed a chargeable offense?"

The two detectives stare at him for a moment and then start nodding and laughing. As they discuss Clarkson's question, they come to the realization there's little the police can do about the situation. They can bring him in for questioning, but if it ends up he's clearly not involved with the shootings, then that's probably where it ends. Unless someone comes forward to press charges against him for taking the bags, it's unlikely a prosecutor would have enough to make a case for charging Adkins with theft.

As the lunch ends, Roberts reminds himself to call Richter. It makes no sense whatsoever that he would think the John Doe in Stafford wasn't theirs. It's either incompetence, laziness, or some combination of both. There's also one other possibility. It could be intentional. To be fair, he doesn't want to consider that dark prospect until he talks with the man. After that, he'll know better if he should call Aldretti over at County to let him know what has occurred.

⅄

Boxed in by heavy traffic and forced to stop for another red light, Jon Stark slams his fist against the steering wheel. He didn't even have the option of gunning it through the last intersection. Worse, it hardly really matters; he's sure he's too far back now. Adkins has had plenty of time to head off in any direction.

As a professional, Stark understands that not every job will go off as planned, but this one has unraveled spectacularly. Tailing Madrigal with the idea he would lead them to Adkins worked perfectly. Somehow, they turned that into a total failure. A trained professional, with an extra man alongside, allowed a strip bar bouncer and an insurance salesman to slow him down enough for their quarry to escape. His own performance in the fiasco was little better.

Despite his anger, Stark remains focused. The fact that Adkins brazenly remains in the area makes it clear the man is no pro. And they're nowhere near back to square one. He has already called Waters with instructions to trace the plates for the VW and learn the address of the owner. It might be where Adkins has been hanging out. And if that happens to be nearby, they can get a man there soon.

As he drives, Stark makes a few calls to redeploy his men. Samuel is already south of them on Route 1, in the direction Adkins was heading. Putting him on alert, Stark makes sure he's ready to join the pursuit from the southbound side of the busy road. If Adkins tries breaking out in that direction, Samuel will have an excellent chance of spotting him.

At the same time, he instructs the men Dan Keach loaned him to begin trawling the shopping center parking lots and close-in side streets along each side of the highway. They're to start from the bar and work their way south. Adkins and the girl might have pulled off somewhere and hunkered down, hoping to ride out the storm.

Within a few minutes, Waters calls back with an update. The car belongs to a woman named Leslie Stevens. She lives only a few miles from their current location. Sending Waters to that address, Stark remains on Route 1. He has finally gotten in cycle with the signals and is moving more steadily, weaving through traffic and passing other cars. Unfortunately, there's no sign of the VW. After a few more miles, he finally decides to break off pursuit and join Waters.

Not long after Stark turns back, Marty Carpentier calls in with major news. He has spotted Adkins's car, not the VW. It's parked at an apartment complex a block off Route 1, less than a mile from where Stark is now. With Waters already in route to the woman's home, he decides to check out the car, telling Carpentier to watch it from a distance until he arrives.

Stark isn't optimistic when he pulls into the complex. It's a relatively low-income neighborhood and he doesn't get the feeling this is where Adkins is hiding. With Carpentier on sentry a half a block away, he parks nearby and strolls over to examine the car.

He's both surprised and disappointed to find the vehicle unlocked. That means there's no way the money is still here. A quick check inside also provides nothing to indicate the man's whereabouts. Still, they need to keep it under surveillance; Adkins may have planned to have the woman drop him off here. For now, he'll leave Carpentier in place watching the car.

On the drive over to see what Waters has turned up, Stark calls Dan Keach. It isn't an upbeat report. Neither man is happy with the current state of events, but at least Adkins remains near at hand. Hopefully he will continue making amateur moves. As for his car, they agree that Adkins has probably ditched it for good. Keeping it under surveillance will become a real time sink, and expensive, but it needs to be done for at least a little longer. Keach suggests that they use only The Group's men to cover that surveillance.

Trying to find something to be positive about, Stark comments, "On the plus side, I think Adkins has done us a real favor by teaming up with this young woman. I hope it continues. It'll be a lot easier tracking two people on the run together than if he stayed solo."

With that thought in mind, he asks Keach about getting the woman's recent cell phone history included in the updates they've been receiving on Adkins. Keach agrees to check his source. If she uses the same carrier as Adkins, they should have the data in a couple of hours. Otherwise, it may not be possible.

After finishing his call with Keach, Stark reminds himself to be patient. If they can get just one more lead, or Adkins makes another mistake, he's confident they can nab him. There's no way he'll let this guy slip out of his grasp twice.

As he pulls into the driveway of Les's house, he sees Water's car is already there. Maybe this is where they'll get their break, right here and now.

⋏

TD can hardly believe it. Traffic has come to a halt just as they started onto one of the long approaches to the bridge. The Wilson Bridge is one of several drawbridges on the interstate highway system, and though it rarely opens in the daytime, it's happening now. At least for a while, they're effectively parked on the curving elevated ramp, unable to turn around.

He soon sees the reason for the delay and realizes the wait won't be too long. Off to the right, a towering three-masted ship is moving upriver, its sails capturing a light breeze. It appears to be one of the historic tall ships, likely heading for the Washington Navy Yard. With the drawbridge already open, they watch as the ship approaches the breach in the span.

Other than crossing into Maryland, TD has yet to decide where they're going. Wherever he chooses, it can't be far, not with the bags of money back there. As he considers how he might safely return to his car, he's also mindful of his visibly unhappy passenger. Since getting back on the road, Les has been repeatedly trying to phone someone and sending text messages in between the calls. When he asks if she's trying to reach her roommate, her response is a massive sigh, followed by turning and facing away from him.

Looking out at the river, she finally speaks. "Yes, I'm trying to call my roommate. I'm trying to warn her to stay away from the house, like you suggested."

"Good," he says. "If she has to go there at all, it should only be to pack a bag and leave immediately."

Before he can say more, Les interrupts, trembling and on the verge of tears. "And go where? I'm scared, TD, for her and for me. You had no right to bring this terrible mess into our lives. This is so wrong. I'm really pissed at you right now."

Seeing her so upset, a wave of sadness and shame rushes over him. He had never imagined fleeing from armed men, let alone with a terrified and angry Les at his side. He wishes there was something he could say that would make her feel better, but he decides not to attempt to console her right now. Instead, he'll use the remainder of the delay to work on the increasing number of problems he faces.

His first effort fails. At least for now, coming up with a solution to retrieve the bags of money eludes him. As for solving the matter of how he's being tracked, he's immediately distracted by a deeply troubling aspect of the problem. It wasn't the police who followed him to The End Zone; the men who showed up today were definitely after the money.

With the descent of the bridge's towering iron gates complete, the traffic slowly begins moving again. TD decides his first priority is finding a short-term hiding place. They'll leave the highway at one of the first exits and find another cheap motel. Then maybe Les will feel a little safer and he can start coming up with some answers.

Hopefully, the number of problems he must solve will stop growing larger. As it is, he has to figure out a way to retrieve the money and get out of the area without leaving a trail. He also has to make sure that not only

Phil, but also Les and her roommate can feel safe from any ongoing threat. And of course, he must change his identity and build a new life.

Silently laughing at the enormity of it all, he wonders why he's even attempting this. Nothing that has happened so far suggests this little adventure is going to turn out well, and so far, his situation has only worsened. Every move he makes seems to expose someone else to the danger he faces and it certainly doesn't appear his hunters are planning to leave the field.

As they finally move onto the bridge and begin crossing the river, TD senses the coincidental metaphor of the moment and reminds himself that he still has a choice. There's an exit at the end of the bridge he can use to loop around and come right back across. He could admit the stupidity of everything he has done, turn himself into the police, and rely on their protection.

Or, he can simply say to hell with it, cross the river, and just go forward. He knows his chances of success are extremely slim but it would be an awesome accomplishment. He could begin the next iteration of his life on the heels of an enormous personal victory and there might even be a bonus. If he could really make it all happen, then just maybe there'd be a chance for him and Les at some point in the future.

Once again, he chooses to press ahead, purposefully optimistic. Besides, he'd much rather think positively about the future. It's much easier than considering all the dark things that will certainly happen if he fails to find his way through this.

⋏

While in route to interviewing the manager of the vehicle-leasing firm, Carl Roberts receives a call from the county police. Earlier this morning, one of their officers had responded to a report of a break-in at Adkins's residence. A neighbor had noticed the damaged sliding glass door while walking his dog and had called it in. Roberts isn't really surprised at the news. It only confirms the danger the man is in.

He has been calling the leasing company for two days now, trying to determine who contracted for the Mercedes sedan. He had finally heard back from the manager, who claimed to have been out sick. After apologizing for not responding sooner, he had agreed to pull the records and meet with Roberts this afternoon.

The leasing manager wouldn't have responded if he hadn't received the green light from Dan Keach. Along with giving his approval to contact Roberts, Keach had coached the manager on precisely what he should tell the detective.

Initially, Roberts learns very little during the brief meeting. The Mercedes is leased to Wilkins Investment Group, a real estate development firm. The leasing manager knows nothing about who regularly drives the car or the purposes for which it is used. Though obviously nervous, the man is friendly and cooperative. Carl sees nothing to question the legitimacy of the leasing firm, or the information he has received. He also doesn't ascribe any suspicion to the man's uneasiness; plenty of people are anxious while talking with the police.

Just as he's leaving, his take on the meeting changes significantly. Without any prompting from Carl, the manager volunteers the name and phone number of someone named Daniel Keach. He refers to him as 'the head of security' at Wilkins. The manager says he talked with him earlier, and Keach told him that he would be glad to answer any questions the police might have.

Back in his car, Roberts immediately heads to Tysons Corner and Wilkins's offices. He has a general awareness of Wilkins Investment Group and its property development business, but no knowledge of the firm's background. He was always going to have an interest in whichever company was leasing the Mercedes, for no other reason than to learn why their car was involved in such suspicious circumstances. But after hearing the manager's last comments, there are now a few things he finds to be quite odd.

One of his first reactions was to question why such a company would need a head of security. And if this Keach fellow is actually interested in helping the police, why has he passively voiced his desire to do so via a message from the manager of the leasing company? With the number of questions growing, he looks forward to talking with Daniel Keach. It's a conversation he hopes will lead him closer to uncovering what was happening at the motel Monday night, as well as what was inside those bags.

As he arrives, Carl reflects on his choice not to call ahead and warn Keach of his pending arrival. It could end up being a wasted half-hour if the man isn't there, but if he's in, it will be difficult for him to refuse to talk. As it goes, his plan works well. After only a short wait at reception, he's informed that Keach is in the office and available to talk.

Roberts introduces himself as Chief of Detectives for Fairfax City. He finds Keach relaxed, with a friendly, but professional manner. His first questions are intentionally broad, delivered with the hope they might be answered in an open manner. He wants to know if Keach can provide any insight as to what their company-leased vehicle was doing at the Gateway Motor Inn Monday night, or why it would be attacked in a bloody assault.

Keach displays a combination of genuine concern and confusion. He explains the firm uses the car to ferry Richard Wilkins, or other executives, between meetings and the various properties the firm is developing. With the heavy traffic in the area, it allows them the convenience of relaxing as well as remaining productive while in transit.

It's a total mystery to Keach as to why the driver and the vehicle were at the motel. The driver was off duty and no one at the company had reserved the car for Monday evening. He also states that any use of the car by the driver for his own purposes was definitely without the knowledge or permission of the firm.

Keach provides very little in response to Roberts questions about the deceased driver; only that he had worked for the firm for several years without incident. He also has no idea why the driver was armed or why there would be another armed man onboard. The company never requested that the driver carry a weapon. Keach also professes no personal knowledge of Eddie King, nor is there any company association with King or any of the men killed at the motel.

Throughout the questioning, Roberts closely monitors Keach's manner. To his credit, the man stays on a perfectly even keel, never showing the slightest emotion, or any impatience with the interview. As he asks his next question, he focuses on Keach's face to spot any reaction.

"Has the company or any of the executives who have used the car recently lost anything of value?"

Keach responds without hesitating. "I'm not aware of any losses. Is this also part of your investigation?"

"I'm just trying to determine if there's any connection between the shootings and your firm, other than the driver being an employee and the vehicle being leased by you."

"Well, again, as I said, I am not aware of any."

"Alright, sir, I won't take up any more of your time past one last question. I understand you're the head of security here at Wilkins Investment Group. Can you describe that role for me as it fits within a real estate development firm?"

This time Keach pauses before answering. As he waits for his response, Carl notices the first traces of impatience in the man's countenance. When he finally begins speaking, his friendly manner has clearly shifted to one of condescension.

"Well, first, I think the title head of security is a misnomer. And to be clear, I'm a consultant to the firm; technically, I'm not a company employee. I prefer to describe my purview as risk management, not security. Some of the tasks I handle for Wilkins are straightforward security, such as contracting for the protection of properties we're developing. You'd be surprised how expensive some of the equipment and materials are. And of course, you're probably aware of the amount of theft that goes on at such sites."

Continuing his lecture, Keach says, "So, I guess it would be easy for someone to misinterpret my job if they viewed it only from that aspect, but there are many others. I oversee the security of our computer and communication networks and company data. Additionally, I analyze a variety of financial and security oriented risks a firm like ours faces. Real estate development is a volatile industry. For example, I evaluate the background and credit checks we run on every one of the business partners we deal with. But maybe I'm boring you with this primer on corporate risk. Have I answered your question officer?"

"Detective."

"Pardon me?"

"Detective. I'm Chief of Detectives for Fairfax City."

"Well, congratulations, Detective. Or should I say Chief Detective? I'm sure you're very proud of such an accomplishment."

Roberts refuses to reward Keach's rudeness with a verbal reaction. Instead, he stares blankly at the man, knowing he'll eventually become uncomfortable and speak.

Finally breaking the silence, Keach is noticeably terser. "I'm afraid I have no more time for you today, Detective. If you have any follow-up questions, please don't hesitate to call. Or stop by again, even without an appointment, like you did today."

Roberts had started not liking Keach before he was halfway through his little lecture on corporate risk management. With the contempt the man has now displayed, he sees no reason to offer his hand when he ends the interview and departs the man's office.

During the elevator ride down to the garage, Roberts replays the meeting in his mind, taking care to separate his distaste for the man from any unwarranted suspicion. Keach's bearing was obviously that of a veteran and Roberts knows there are plenty of ex-military types who gravitate to this type of work. He makes a note to check on his background, as well as to see if he has a prior record of any involvement with this type of thing.

The scenario Keach presented, in which the driver of the Mercedes was acting without either the consent or knowledge of the firm, is not at all farfetched. Carl thinks it may even be the most likely. And he has to admit that Keach showed little dismay at the events, nor any significant interest in the status of the investigation. Despite his misgivings before he talked with the man, Roberts feels like he would have noticed something if there was a relationship between the company and whatever was happening at the motel. Though he still needs to do a little follow-up, it looks like his interview with Keach may end up being a dead end.

Once he's back in his office, Roberts reviews the caseload facing his small team. With no spare capacity, he ponders how much longer he should keep this case open, particularly if Czarniak confirms their last shooter was the one found murdered in Stafford. As for what was going on at the motel, he makes a note to discuss the matter with one of the Commonwealth Attorneys. It will be up to that office to decide if there will be an ongoing investigation.

Of course, they'll devote more time to looking for Adkins, but the case will have to move to the back burner if they don't find him soon. As Kenny Clarkson pointed out, since no one knows what the charges would be, it's unclear they can even hold him. That will be another decision to be made by the prosecutors. If they show no interest in the purloined gym bags, it's going to be hard to justify assigning any of his limited resources to an on-going search for Adkins.

Jon Stark had circled around to the rear of Les's house and entered where Waters had already gained access by breaking in through the kitchen door. Stark notices the kitchen is small and neatly maintained, but it's the last room that looks like way. Waters has angrily ripped through the rest of the place like a tornado, searching for evidence of the money or any clue as to where Adkins may be heading. The house is a wreck and several pieces of furniture will need repairing.

Stark locates his man in one of the bedrooms, sitting at a small desk and staring at a computer monitor. After watching him for a moment, he asks, "Find anything?"

"Not a fucking thing. I'm downloading her address book in case there's something there, but otherwise nothing."

"Did you enjoy ripping her place apart?"

Waters looks up with a sneer before remembering that it's Stark across from him. Ignoring his boss's question, he replies, "I'm almost done. Give me thirty seconds."

Knowing that he needs Waters to remain effective and motivated, Stark allows the brief moment of tension to pass. "Okay. Then let's get out of here and go find Adkins. He'll use that phone again or she'll use hers. Then we'll have a fresh bead on where he is."

⚐

Not long after the detective left his office, Dan Keach slammed his fist on his desk in a rare display of anger. His day had already been going badly and the strain of maintaining his composure while patiently enduring the cop's questions had finally caused him to snap.

He had ended a call with Robert Owen only minutes before Roberts had showed up unexpectedly. The CFO reported that their short-term liquidity was rapidly deteriorating and would reach a critical state sooner than anticipated. The company was in need of an immediate and significant infusion of cash. Owen had speculated that their banks would probably decline them and suggested it may not be wise to go through the process of requesting the funds. If the answer was sure to be no, there was no upside in exposing the glaring weakness of their current financial position to their bankers. In the end, he felt that Richard Wilkins would soon need to resort to borrowing from less orthodox sources.

Keach had asked his most important question first, "Can we make payroll?"

"I'm not sure we can," Owen had responded timidly.

"You're fucking kidding me. We're running things that tightly?"

"We'll be fine in a week or two, but right now, we're busted flat. I've got to tell you, for me personally, life's going be a shit storm without a paycheck."

Keach remembers the disgust he felt hearing Owen's last remark; the man's whining sickens him. Once they get clear of this mess, he plans to talk with Richard Wilkins about starting the process of replacing their CFO.

"Alright, I get it", he had told him. "And I don't need to hear about your personal finances. I'll let Richard know we're probably going to need a spot loan."

Now, with Owen's update and the interview with the detective behind him, Keach returns his focus to retrieving the money. His next call is to Jim

Richter, who unfortunately has nothing but disappointing results. Adkins hasn't used his phone for several hours. Worse, the woman's cell service is with a different company. He's not going to be able to provide any call data for her.

Hoping to catch a break, but anticipating more bad news, Keach makes his next call.

⟁

Standing next to his car in the driveway of Les's house, Stark takes the call he has been dreading. He had postponed providing Keach with an update, hoping to have better news, but now his employer is on the phone. Despite the recent catastrophe, Stark appreciates the respect Keach shows him. Dan lets him do his job, and when they talk, he speaks to him differently, not with the impatience he shows for nearly everyone else.

After they've updated each other, Keach reiterates the need for urgency in locating Adkins. Stark responds with a reminder that his team is dead in the water without fresh leads. Frustrated, both men know that with every passing hour, the odds of finding Adkins and the money turn heavily against them.

While Stark paces the driveway talking with Keach, Waters joins him in front of the house, using the time take a physical inventory. Several parts of his body have begun to ache fiercely, a fresh reminder of the struggle and failure at the bar.

When his call with Keach ends, Stark turns to Waters. "Let's take a break and grab something to eat. We need an update on Adkins's location before we go flying around again. I'm pretty damn sure he's not going to be parading up and down Route One."

⟁

A half a block away, Les's roommate Laura sits in her car trembling as she watches two men talking in front of her home. Returning from a short trip to the grocery store, she had spotted their cars before she turned in. She was poised enough to continue driving past without slowing and had pulled over and parked in front of another house about a hundred yards up the street. After sinking down in her seat, she had angled the car's mirrors so she could stay out of sight but continue watching.

For a short while, one of the men had talked on his phone while the other walked aimlessly in the yard. She definitely doesn't get the feeling they're the police, which only increases her apprehension. A part of her wants to confront them and find out what they want, but her fears quash the thought. She would have already called the police if she had her cell phone with her. Unfortunately, she left it at home; something she does on a regular basis.

When they finally get in their vehicles, Laura re-starts her own car and slowly pulls away. A quick glance in the mirror confirms they're leaving as well, following in her direction. Instead of circling back and returning to the house, Laura decides to drive directly to The End Zone where she can tell Les what she has seen. Unless Les was expecting visitors, Laura thinks they should call the police.

The good news is she'll be at the bar in just minutes and Les will know exactly what they should do. She's so bright and always has a plan.

Laura Stevens has always had a lot of confidence in her daughter.

▲

Laura Stevens's youthful appearance causes people to guess her age to be much younger than it is. In her mid-forties, people sometimes mistake her for Les's older sister when they're together. Along with many other features, they share the same great smile. Les had mentioned to TD that she had found a new housemate when Laura moved in six months ago. For some reason she had chosen not to say anything about it being her mother. In fact, the only person she has told was Karen, the dayshift bartender. And that was only after learning Karen's mom had done the same thing.

Les felt a little uncomfortable with the reversal of dependency in their relationship, but it was nothing that would stop her from helping. Her mother had encountered some misfortune and she was glad to be there for her. At work, she joked with Karen that they were starting a new trend.

Later, she read an online article highlighting that very topic. The number of parents moving in with their adult children is on the rise, one of the many impacts of the recent economic recession.

Laura was quite young when her daughter was born. Les was conceived the night of her senior prom; by August, she knew she was pregnant. She had already been worrying about their relationship. Her boyfriend would soon be leaving for college on a football scholarship at a school nearly a thousand miles away. There had never been any plans for her to go along.

Knowing that they needed to talk, she asked him to take her for a late-evening walk. Though still warm at that hour, there was a light breeze as they strolled along their favorite lakeside path. Almost from the time he picked her up, throughout their walk, he spent nearly every moment talking about college. He was brimming with excitement. With early football practices slated to start the following week, he could hardly wait to leave.

When they returned to the car, he paused before taking her home. He told Laura that he had come to the decision that it was best for both of them to take a break. With football games, he would have only one free weekend before December. He didn't think he could handle a long distance relationship. Most of all, he claimed, he wanted to be fair to her.

Laura had almost nothing to say and agreed with him without argument. They barely spoke on the ride home, both pretending to listen to the radio. She never saw him again after that night. Despite the opportunity, his college career was finished in two semesters. An off campus arrest for underage drinking, a serious knee injury in spring football, and a nearly perfect record of failed coursework cost him his scholarship. She never told him he was a father.

Les was born two months past Laura's nineteenth birthday. Laura worked hard, holding down multiple jobs, all the time maintaining a single-minded focus on doing the best she could raising Les. She wanted to make sure that her daughter had the opportunities that Laura felt she had missed out on. Like so many of her generation, she put great stock in the importance of a college education. Her primary goal in life was making sure Les would earn a degree.

Laura eventually settled into a full-time job at a women's health clinic, working there for over a decade as one of the administrative staff, slowly moving up through the office hierarchy. She secretly admired one of the young doctors working at the clinic, developing a deep crush. She had wrestled for some time with the idea of making him aware of her feelings after she heard he and his wife had finalized their long anticipated divorced. Before she could summon the courage to act, he surprised her with an invitation to dinner. She was thrilled to find he was interested.

It was definitely more than that. Their relationship took off, with him proposing after only a half a dozen dates. They were married within another three months and she quit her job. Sadly, her dream come true evaporated when her husband died of a heart attack just a year later. He had never experienced any health issues. Laura was devastated. Worse, she soon found out she was broke.

As part of the divorce settlement, her husband had agreed that his ex-wife would remain the beneficiary of his life insurance until his two children were adults. His share of the medical practice was also deeply leveraged in debt. Drained by substantial alimony and child support payments, his finances were a wreck. Any wealth he had accumulated over the years was nearly gone. There was next to nothing left for Laura.

The partners offered to buy out her husband's share of the practice. Her lawyer recommended Laura accept what he termed 'a very generous offer'. Whether generous or not, at least it provided enough to pay off their personal debts. With everything settled, she was left with a huge mortgage, and no equity, in a large home she could no longer afford nor wanted. Devastated with grief, and without a job or any source of income, she didn't know what to do.

She finally sold the home, moved in with Les, and began nursing her shattered heart. Her short-lived relationship was the first time she had shared her life with anyone. After years of raising Les alone, giving everything she had for her child, she had finally found the happiness that comes with being loved.

Out of it all, she has learned that she no longer has a taste for living life alone. Ready to move on, her first priority after landing a new job is getting out there and finding the right man. She wants to feel the same way she did for that year of marriage. She wants to enjoy her life and share it with someone again.

∆

Waiting to turn into The End Zone's parking lot, Laura's anxiety is sky-rocketing. There's a police cruiser sitting in front of the entrance, with an ambulance parked behind it and another cruiser parked in the lot. She hopes she wasn't mistaken about the two men at her home. Could they have been the police trying to contact her? Had they come to tell her some terrible news about Les?

In a full panic, Laura rushes inside but is unable to see Les anywhere. On the far side of the room, a policeman is talking with two men who are being treated by paramedics. Both show signs of having been in a brawl. In a way, the scene provides her with some relief, hinting at nothing worse than a bar fight; still, she needs to find Les. When she introduces herself at the bar, the immediate look of concern on the bartender's face does nothing to help her relax.

Karen quickly explains that there was a fight in the bar and Les ran out as it was happening. Seeing the fear on Laura's face, she tells her not to worry. Les called a little while ago to say she's fine; she just got a little scared. She also said she wouldn't be returning to work today. Unsure about everything that's happening, Karen decides not to tell Laura anymore. Hearing the details of her daughter's departure is not going to help.

Laura is happy to hear Les isn't hurt, but remains confused as to why she left the bar and isn't coming back. And what does any of this have to do with two men at their home? Desperate to talk with her daughter, she borrows Karen's phone and moves to an empty corner of the bar to make the call.

∆

It was easy for TD to learn her roommate's name as Les grew increasingly frustrated with her failure to make contact. She was soon accompanying almost every attempt with a demanding, 'Answer the phone Laura', or 'Turn on your damn cell phone Laura'.

At one point, he watched as she lowered her head. No longer fiddling with the phone laying unattended in her lap, he thought she had finally given up. Instead, she soon regained her purpose and resumed the cycle of calls and texts. When he tried asking if there was something he could do to help, her withering glance silenced his query before he could mumble more than a few words.

After the bridge re-opened, he spent the first couple of miles confirming they weren't being followed. To his relief, no cars broke from the pack behind them to keep up with his increased speed or lane changes. Still, an expert could be back there. The point became moot when he suddenly swerved to the right, slicing through two lanes of traffic to hop onto an exit ramp at the last moment. Watching his mirrors the whole time, he was finally convinced; if anyone had been on his tail, they weren't any longer.

The quick exit from the highway left them heading south on Branch Avenue, near Camp Springs and Andrews Air Force Base. It was a random choice and TD decides it will do fine. They'll continue toward Clinton, Maryland and go to ground in another cheap motel. As he's driving, he resumes work on the question of how he was tracked to The End Zone.

He's positive he wasn't followed to the club. He had been driving his new car and had carefully watched for a tail. There was absolutely nothing suspicious, yet there's no denying that they found him. The big question is how, particularly if he wasn't followed. How did they know he would be there? Other than the staff, Phil and Les are the only people who know that he frequents The End Zone, or that he would be there today.

He soon shifts his thinking to a different possibility. A few minutes back, while waiting for the drawbridge, he found himself speculating on the number of people simultaneously using their phones within the small radius around the bridge. He thought about how many cars were occupied with someone like Les, sending text after text or making call after call. Others would be surfing the web or retrieving data from the cloud, all interacting with the cellular network.

Now he's thinking about his own phone. Just because he hasn't been using it doesn't mean it can't be found. Has he been that stupid? Is he simply holding a beacon to his location in his pocket?

TD knows that a phone will identify itself to the closest cell point on the network as long as it has power and is turned on. But it takes sophisticated equipment to locate and track a cell phone real time, especially one that's not in use. It would also require a warrant and the time to set it up. That's why he hasn't been worried about it yet. It just seems unlikely that he's being tracked in this manner, and certainly not by someone who isn't in law enforcement.

It also doesn't make much sense if they were tracking him by the calls he has made. The only people he has called since Monday are Phil and Julia Crane. And he didn't use his phone at The End Zone today, or anywhere near to it. He did call a taxi, but that was several miles away and hours before going to the bar.

Having already done so several times, TD replays the scene at the club. He remembers that it was not until after Phil arrived that the two men entered the bar. Is it possible they were following him instead? Were they hoping Phil would lead them to him?

TD used the tactic himself on an investigation ten years ago; putting someone's family or close friends under surveillance is a tried and true practice. Sometimes they'll lead you straight to your target. But if they followed Phil, how had they have discovered the connection between them so quickly? The only plausible answers keep coming back to his phone.

TD feels he's approaching a kernel of truth. Despite his earlier stance, he has to concede the possibility he was identified at the motel. If that were the case, then the police would already have his address and phone numbers. Someone tracking his phone, or even just the data for his calls, would have two vital pieces of information. They would know where he has been and with who he has been talking. That would be all they needed. Seeing the number of calls between him and Phil since Monday night, they might consider him a suspect as well.

He doesn't have time to flesh out every nuance but it's a good working theory, albeit one with a significant problem. It remains difficult for him to believe that someone outside of law enforcement pulled this all together so quickly, monitoring his phone traffic and following Phil. Yet he's certain it wasn't the police who showed up looking for him at the bar. Regardless of who is tracking him, he has to accept what now seems obvious. He can take no more chances with his phone.

Pulling into the parking lot of a roadside convenience mart, TD quickly scans the storefront. Luckily, he finds exactly what he's looking for. Mounted on the front corner of the building is and aging payphone. After jotting down a few phone numbers in his notepad, he switches his phone off and removes the battery. Turning to Les, he says, "I'm sorry, but I really think we need to turn off our phones."

"Well you can forget that. I won't turn it off until I talk to my roommate."

"Okay. But after that will you please agree to…?"

It badly startles them both when her phone rings mid-sentence. Fumbling for it in her lap, Les checks the Caller ID before saying, "It's Karen, from the club."

TD is a little confused listening to Les's side of the conversation. She had told him it was Karen calling, but it appears that's not the case. It seems she's talking with her mother. He wonders how it came to be that her mom is using the bartender's phone. As the call goes on, Les seems to become even more upset. Finally, after multiple assurances that she's safe and unharmed, Les tells her mom she'll call her right back.

Immediately the story spills out. Failing to fight back tears, Les tells him that her mother came upon two strange men and their cars in the driveway of Les's house. She didn't stop, and immediately drove to the club to tell Les about it. When she didn't find her daughter there, she borrowed Karen's phone.

Hurting and angry, Les grabs TD's arm as she cries out, "What am I going to do now, TD? What's *SHE* going to do? Those men are at my house!"

TD senses Les is spinning out of control. Trying his best to sound reassuring, he says, "I know this is bad, but from what you told me, your mother didn't stop. And it doesn't sound like they saw her or followed her. If that's true, then she should be safe."

"Yeah, sure, she's safe for now. But where's she gonna go?"

TD is trying to empathize with Les's concern about her mother, but he feels like she needs to maintain some perspective. Les and her roommate are certainly at risk, but all this worrying about her mother is starting to be a little irrational. This time when he speaks, he uses a much firmer tone.

"Listen Les, I'm sure your mother is capable of taking care of herself. I really think she should just return home for now and try to forget about it. I know it's going to be hard not to worry about you, but I think that's her best bet. Don't you?"

Les had been looking out the side window while he spoke, preventing TD from seeing her expression morphing into a mask of horror. As she responds, there's no missing the contempt in her voice.

"How could you possibly suggest that? She can't go back there. Those men could still be there, or they could be watching the place."

TD finally gets it; Les's mother is Laura. Her mother is her roommate. Now that he understands the situation, he can't believe it somehow has gotten even worse. Thinking quickly, he simultaneously tries to calm Les, while coming up with a plan on the fly.

"I'm sorry, Les. I'm really sorry. You never told me explicitly, but now I understand. So, I think you need to call your mother back right now, like you told her."

Making sure he has her attention, he continues. "She needs to have Karen let her borrow that phone for a little while and then get out of there. Have her go to a nearby restaurant and order a cup of coffee or whatever. She should stay away from a window seat, but she should be all right in public. I need to make some calls. Then we'll get her to a safe place. We can do this, but you need to trust me. Can you trust me, Les?"

No longer angry, Les nods and even pats his arm as she lifts the phone to her ear and makes the call. It's not an easy conversation, but she finally convinces her mother to do as he suggested.

When she's finished, TD points at the payphone. "As I said, I need to make a couple of calls. Once your mother's on the way to somewhere safe, we'll find a place to stay for the night and get something to eat. I'm so sorry I roped you into this Les. Can you hang in there?"

Les nods without speaking as he leaves the car. While they've been talking, he has already thought of someone close by who might be able to help. Picking up the payphone's filthy handset, he's thrilled to hear a dial tone. After punching in the number, he turns and faces the car, giving Les a little smile as he waits for the call to connect, all the while desperately hoping the person he's calling is available and willing.

⟡

Preeti Chopra works as a freelance journalist, experiencing modest success while pursuing a Master's degree in journalism. One particular newspaper, The City Express, has printed several of her articles reporting on crime in Northern Virginia. She has even had one of her pieces picked up by the Washington Post, which also owns and publishes the smaller paper.

The City Express is an advertising-laden tabloid, distributed six days a week at subway stations, bus stops, and various eateries. Despite being free, The City Express has the second largest circulation of any newspaper in the metropolitan area; it also has its own website. Preeti doesn't mind the paper's perceived lowly status. For a budding journalist, it doesn't matter where your work is published, just as long as it's published.

Preeti is a stunningly beautiful first generation Indian-American, and a great disappointment to her immigrant Bengali parents. Both are professors at one of the area's top universities. They never imagined she would study anything but medicine or law; journalism definitely doesn't please them. Like many immigrant parents, they had also hoped their daughter would marry someone from their culture. Not only has Preeti not married, she rarely agrees to meet, let alone date the men they try to set her up with. Her parents often complain to each other that she has robbed them of the joy of arranging her life.

Stuart Kurtz is the editor Preeti primarily works with at the newspaper. Always on the lookout for stories that can deliver a great headline, Stuart was drawn to the news of the shootout at the Gateway Motor Inn. The number of people killed was large by any standard; it was stunningly so for suburban Fairfax.

Yesterday morning, he had called Preeti and suggested she put together an article. After getting something to him quickly, she got lucky. Her piece not only made the cut, there was a front-page headline in today's edition leading readers to page three and the story under her byline. Never before had her work been displayed so prominently, even if it was only running in a free paper.

Stuart had called her again this morning. He wanted a follow-up piece. He liked that Preeti often included the perspective of victims in her articles and recommended providing an update on the status of the injured motel clerk. She should also explore whether there was any gang connection. His last suggestion was to include a mention of how little progress the police had made with their investigation.

Finishing, he said, "Write it well, Preeti. The paper doesn't often go with in-depth stories like this. I'd hate to see it get chopped to pieces, or even killed."

With his words providing additional motivation, Preeti spent the rest of the morning writing a draft. There was one sticking point; she knows she can't include Stuart's claim of a lack of progress with the investigation without confirming it. A call with Brenda Sherman, the Fairfax City Police media liaison yielded little new information. Learning that the Lead Detective would be in later that day, Preeti was given an appointment for a short meeting.

Brenda had set up the appointment as a delaying tactic. By the time the reporter arrived, she hoped to have an update from Roberts and wouldn't have to waste his time. Unfortunately, by late afternoon, she has still heard nothing back from the detective.

Sitting alone in a small meeting room at police headquarters, Preeti is fretting about her approaching deadline as she waits for her interview with Roberts. It's already a half hour past her promised time with the detective, and without an update, there can be no comment on the status of the investigation. She knows Stuart will be unhappy and the story will lack a key element.

Overall, she has made good progress. Her brief interview with Bobby Tomlin at the hospital was fruitful. With bare-bones medical insurance and no family savings, paying his medical bills will be almost impossible. Even if he had the money, he and his family of four face disaster. It will be many months before he works again. Preeti knows she has great stuff for the human-interest side of the story, but she needs more substance to flesh out the article. She needs answers from the police.

When he finally returns to the office, Carl Roberts isn't thrilled to find out that the appointment Brenda put on his schedule is actually for him to spend time talking with a reporter. When she explains her original plan, he understands that he put her on the spot, ignoring her many requests and leaving her in the dark. As he heads to the meeting with the reporter, he promises to get back with Brenda so she can prepare an updated statement for release to the media.

Upon entering the conference room, Carl's stern expression evaporates when he sees the attractive young woman standing up across the table from him. Briefly distracted by her beauty, he reminds himself to stay on task and keep this short. After introducing themselves, he apologizes for being late and causing her to wait.

Preeti wastes no time asking about progress on the investigation. Pointing out that there have been no updates since Monday night, she also mentions there are rumors that the police are making little progress apprehending those responsible for the attacks.

Carl takes a moment before answering, making sure he constructs his answer carefully. With a patient tone he says, "Our investigation has gained considerable momentum, but because it's ongoing, I'm sure you understand there are limits to what I can say. Though I'm not prepared to comment on the nature of the activities occurring at the motel Monday evening, I can tell you that a group of armed men conducted what appears to be a planned attacked on some visitors at the motel. All but two of the assailants died in the ensuing gunfight. Those two, along with one other individual, were seen leaving the motel immediately after the attack. Early this morning, the two men involved in the shootings were found killed at the Stafford Medical Center. That's where things stand."

In addition to recording her interviews, Preeti also takes notes. As the detective is talking, she stops writing and lifts her eyes from her notepad when he says the two men were 'found killed'. Not only is it an unusual phrase, it represents a new and potentially tantalizing direction for the story to follow.

Smiling, she says, "Thanks for the update, I really appreciate it. I noticed you said found killed. Can you tell me more about how these men died?"

Carl knows he can provide her with more information. And between her great looks and pleasant manner, it would be easy to do so. He also knows she's just trying to do her job. But he can't set a precedent of walking through a case like this, step-by-step, with just one reporter. He decides to tell her no, as pleasantly as he can.

"I'm sorry. I wish I had the time to go over all the details with you, but I'm swamped with cases. If you contact the Stafford County Police, they should have the specifics on that aspect of the investigation."

Sensing the detective is losing his patience with her, Preeti tries a different tack. "Okay, I'll do that. So, based on your summary, there's still one man you're looking for?"

"Yes, but it's our understanding that he wasn't involved with the killings. From an investigative standpoint, we look at everything, and we'll continue to do so. But in the short-term, our first priority has been on identifying and tracking down the men responsible for the shootings."

Preeti makes a note of the not so subtle point the detective continues making: three men left the motel after the attack, but only two were 'involved'. It seems a little odd, but he has delineated it that way more than once. She knows her next questions are important; with both the detective's tone and body language revealing a desire to end the interview, she may not get many more.

"Can you provide a little more information about this third man? Do you have his name? Do you think you'll have him in custody soon?"

Carl has enjoyed talking with the attractive young reporter, but he has gone on enough and said more than he intended. He has also noticed Preeti's sharp mind, always ready to probe deeper with her next question. After her last flurry, he pauses, knowing he needs to answer carefully. He also recognizes that her article could provide an opportunity.

He rapidly processes the pros and cons of giving her TD Adkins's name. Involving the press could help flush out Adkins and conserve police resources. Weighing it out though, he decides there's not a compelling reason to do so right at this moment, unplanned, with a reporter he has never met before today. For now, he'll wait; he can always contact her later.

"Currently, I would describe the third man as a person of interest. Our desire to talk with him at this time is not for the purposes of arrest. I'd also hate to link his name publicly with these terrible crimes if he weren't involved. As for when we'll talk with him, I can't say. We're deploying all available resources within the context of each case's priority. That's all I can tell you. If you leave your contact info, I would be glad to let you know if something changes materially."

Roberts has spoken these timeworn phrases plenty of times, related to plenty of cases, quite possibly in the exact same sequence. What he doesn't remember doing very often is adding the last sentence. He notices the young woman's look of surprise as she quickly fishes a business card from the sleeve of her small leather notebook, smiling as she hands it to him.

Preeti understands the interview is over, with many of her questions left unanswered. Still, she has learned quite a bit, particularly the news about the dead assailants. She also now has multiple angles from which she can approach the story. And not having every answer as to what happened might not be a bad thing anyway; it could even help her get a shot at another follow-on piece.

Denny Holmes is tempted to ignore his ringing cellphone. The call is from a Maryland area code, so it can't be his employers; they're currently away on vacation, touring some crumbling castles in Scotland, or something like that. Their absence is why he can be found relaxing in one of the Adirondack chairs on the sprawling back lawn of their riverfront mansion, several miles south of DC.

Having finished all of the work he planned for the day, Denny had just popped open a cold beer and settled in to watch the Potomac roll by when the phone began to ring. Finally answering, he smiles hearing the voice on the other end. He's glad he took the call; he hasn't heard from TD Adkins in a couple of years.

"How's it going, TD?"

"Well to be honest, Denny, I'm in a bit of a jam. And I'm sorry to call you out of the blue like this. But if you're around and available, I really need a big time favor."

"I'm available, but I guess it depends on where you need me. Right now, I'm down here near Mount Vernon. You need a boat or something? You know you can always borrow mine. The way I see it, I owe you pretty much any kind of favor after the way you saved my sorry ass."

Just listening to Denny's laid-back voice is comforting for TD.

"That's amazing," he tells him. "I hoped you were still working down there. Here it is then. If you can do it, I need you to meet up with a lady named Laura Stevens, right now. She's actually real close by to where you are. I'll give you her phone number. She needs to get out of sight fast, and stay that way for a couple of days; maybe a nice hotel somewhere nearby in Old Town Alexandria or DC. You don't need to stay with her. Just register as a couple and use your name and credit card. Don't worry about cost; the whole tab will be on me. She just needs to be able to stay under the radar for a while."

"No problem, buddy. That's easy."

After giving him the phone number and thanking him, TD says, "I knew it was a good idea to call you Denny. I'll check back in a while to make sure everything is squared away. I really owe you one."

"No way, TD, I still owe you big time. We'll talk later, man."

TD had noticed Les watching him the entire call. When he returns to the car he tells her, "I've got someone who'll be with your mother in roughly twenty minutes. He'll put her up in a nice hotel nearby under his name."

TD notices her expression soften. There may even be the faintest of smiles, or a sense of relief. "So, I'm serious about keeping our phones turned off and not using them if possible. Why don't we call your mother on your phone and let her know the plan. Then we'll turn it off."

This time Les agrees without hesitation. When the call goes through, she puts Laura on speaker so they can all talk together. After reviewing the plan, TD tries to reassure her that both she and Les are going to be okay. In only a few minutes, they're finished talking.

As soon as the call ends, Les powers down her phone. TD feels a little safer now. Getting both phones turned off, with the batteries removed is a solid precaution. Now he needs to deal with getting the bags of money secured.

"Thanks for understanding about the phone, Les. I have one more call to make. Then we'll find a place to stay for the night and I'll work on a plan."

The relief TD thought he saw on her face just moments earlier is short-lived. Returning in its place is the look of a frightened young woman, clearly unhappy with the situation.

⅄

Denny Holmes has spent a good part of his life on the water, sailing and fishing the Chesapeake Bay and its tributaries. Though he isn't wealthy, he would have been completely bankrupt if it weren't for TD's involvement a few years back. The problem occurred when Denny filed an insurance claim for the total loss of an expensive excursion fishing boat. TD was involved because it wasn't Denny's first claim. He had previously submitted a claim for the total loss of a boat just like it.

At the time, Denny was the owner-operator of a charter fishing boat, working out of Annapolis, Maryland. After years of protection, the population of Striped Bass in the Chesapeake had finally rebounded. During the legal fishing season, they were a prime target for Denny's customers. Rockfish, as they're known regionally, are a great recreational fish in addition to being delicious eating.

After a decade of hard work for other owners, Denny finally saved enough for his own boat. To differentiate himself in a competitive market, his business plan was to target high-end clientele. He purchased the largest boat the dealer would finance, and then had it further customized. Besides rigging it for group fishing, he added a wet bar amid other luxury touches above and below deck.

The total cost for the boat and upgrades tapped him for every dollar he had saved and consumed his credit cards. Fortunately, his gamble paid off. The economy was booming and the fishing his first season was abundant. He was booked solid. With his first year in business off to such an excellent start, he soon envisioned acquiring a second boat.

Denny was unaware that the contractor he used to perform the custom upgrades sometimes outsourced the work to a lower-quality outfit. Hidden from view, was an unsafe substandard job on the additional electrical wiring work throughout the boat. During a fully booked mid-season excursion, a short-circuit emitted a brief stream of sparks. A fire broke out behind the paneling in a wall between the new bar and the forward cabin. The fire quickly raced out of control. Assessing the real peril of the situation, Denny signaled a Mayday and helped get everybody off the boat rapidly and safely.

Another boat fishing nearby was able to reach them quickly, but Denny's boat was engulfed in flames and sinking. All who were aboard came though the incident without injury. With all the witnesses, there was very little to question about the claim from the insurance company's point of view.

Despite being insured, the sinking triggered a significant financial loss for Denny. He had poured a bundle of cash into the enhanced features on the boat, but he had failed to inform the insurance company about the upgrades and they would not be covered. His year ended up being a huge step backwards financially. He was idle the remainder of the season and earned only a little money working for others. When he finally received the insurance payout, it was barely enough to pay off the loan. He was able to finance another boat, though it was a lesser model, and this time there was nothing left for upgrades.

Denny soon realized how much of a lost opportunity lay at the bottom of the bay. Even though there was a bounty of Rockfish again the following season, he generated only modest results. Without the upgrades, he faced more competition and he couldn't charge as much per trip. The declining economy was also starting to have a real impact, with significantly fewer customers. He faced the real possibility that his young business would die, starved of cash.

That was when he lost the second boat.

At first, Denny hoped it was only a matter of literally losing track of the boat, temporarily misplacing it, so to speak. After a dreary week of rain, and not a single customer, he had needed two days to recover from a sustained bender of drinking and self-pity. When he returned to the public marina where he was sure he had last moored his boat, it wasn't there.

The police were barely helpful, not only perturbed with Denny, but also suspicious. Due to the weather and his drinking, he couldn't be sure as to specifically when, and in which berth he had last seen it. He could only place the time within a twenty-four hour period nearly a week earlier. Worse, he couldn't locate the ignition key.

The investigation finally determined that the boat departed the marina during a period of heavy rain, two days after Denny docked it. A security camera covering the marina recorded its departure, but due to the poor visibility and the camera angle, it could not be determined who was at the wheel. There were no witnesses.

At least he was fully covered from an insurance perspective, having learned his lesson with the last boat. This time around, he had taken out a pricier, low deductible policy, which would pay him full replacement value. Unfortunately, the insurance company was even more skeptical than the police were, particularly considering Denny's history. Suspecting Denny of attempting an elaborate fraud, the claims investigator informed him it would be take a considerable amount of time to complete his inquiry. They would also need to wait to see if the boat was recovered.

Over three months passed and the claim had still not been settled. The investigator found no provable signs of fraud, but still recommended a partial or full denial of benefits, citing gross negligence on Denny's part. When such a recommendation is made, the firm's internal policy requires a second investigator to review the case, a review that would take at least two additional months.

The second investigator saw the matter in different terms. He didn't feel the firm could prove gross negligence, not if Denny was telling the truth. Being drunk and losing your keys while someone steals your boat cannot be deemed the primary cause of the loss. He felt the firm needed to look harder at the potential fraud.

His supervisor balked at the request for the additional time and money needed to pursue another full-blown fraud investigation. Before going down that road, he decided he would solicit help from outside his group. He requested TD Adkins be brought in for a quick review.

Along with reading both investigators' files, TD conducted a face-to-face interview with Denny. During the marathon grilling, he not only asked questions about the disappearance of the second boat, he queried Denny extensively about the boat that had caught fire and sunk. Throughout the interview, TD was positive that Denny was telling the truth. Despite the long odds, he believed the man was the victim of terribly bad luck. He even told Denny his opinion at the end of the interview.

After almost a year, the claim was finally paid, with every penny of the settlement check going to Denny's creditors. Unfortunately, his business had gone under well before the claims process had played itself out. Since that time, he has gone in a slightly different direction. He still hoped to own a boat and wanted to stay near the water, but he needed steady income. Through connections in the boating community, he landed a position near Mt. Vernon, south of Alexandria. His job is to maintain, and at times skipper, two boats for an extremely wealthy couple who live there at Ferry Landing Point.

It has turned out to be a great gig for him. He lives on the grounds of the fabulous mansion, set back from the river by a large green expanse of lawn. There's also an elaborate guest villa and boathouse on the property. The owners reside there roughly six months per year, leaving Denny with generous amounts of free time. As a bonus, he resides in comfort, rent-free, in a loft apartment over the detached, brick-walled four-car garage. The arrangement is perfect. Recently, he finally scraped together enough money to buy a sailboat, a Catalina 30. With the agreement of his employers, he docks the boat along with theirs on the Potomac.

Not long after settling into the job, Denny had reached out to thank TD for believing him. TD liked the hard working but laid back waterman and agreed to meet for a beer. Surprisingly, they struck up a causal friendship, meeting twice more, always at a restaurant somewhere on the water. Each time Denny refused to let TD pay for his meal, claiming that he owed him the favor.

⚓

TD's next phone call is with the goal of securing the money and his SUV. Other than Phil and Les, there's only one person he can really trust, an aspiring young private investigator, known to his friends as Pen. TD is confident Pen will be eager to help. As the call goes through, he reminds himself to measure his words carefully. There can be no talk over the phone of bags of money, or being chased.

When Pen answers, TD can tell from the background noise that he's working one of his part-time jobs, probably bartending at one of Georgetown's classic watering holes. After a quick hello, he gets right to the point.

"I've gotten myself in a bit of a jam, Pen. If you're available, I was hoping you could do me a favor or two. Before you say yes, I need to be honest. It's all a bit sketchy."

"How many times have you've helped me out, TD? Tell me what you need."

After listening to TD explain that he needs him to pick up a vehicle, Pen quips, "I'm not sure that fits my definition of sketchy, but I'm happy to help."

"Thanks, Pen, I knew I could count on you, and I may need your help with more. I've created a real mess and I still have a few things to figure out. I'll tell you all about it as soon as I can. I guarantee you'll find it quite an intriguing situation, to say the least."

Pen smiles as he listens to TD's mysterious words. After telling him he's scheduled to be off work soon, they agree to meet in two hours, at the first gas station outside the Beltway on Branch Avenue.

⅄

Pen's full name is Franklin Pendergast III. The fancy name comes from being born into one of DC's long-standing families of note. As have three generations of Pendergasts before him, Pen will soon graduate from law school at Georgetown University. For decades on end, members of his family have rubbed elbows with those at the highest levels of power, from positions both in and outside of the government.

Despite this family legacy, Pen harbors no intention of practicing law. Gaining access to his full share of the generously funded family trust fund is predicated upon his graduating and passing the bar. With such a prize waiting, he will complete the mission, but his career as an attorney will end there.

Instead, Pen relishes the idea of becoming a top-flight private investigator. It was during his first legal internship that he learned he had scant interest in practicing law. He was particularly disinterested in the family trade, the world of corporate tax policy, government lobbying, and influence peddling that are the pillars of income for DC's wealthiest law firms. Keeping his apathy to himself, he watched as the firm's partners gorged at the trough of money swirling around Capitol Hill.

The following summer he turned down a prized opportunity at a top K Street lobbying firm. Seeking out other flavors of the law, he opted for an internship with a firm specializing in criminal defense. For three months, he supported investigators working to exonerate their clients. The job often consisted of reviewing pages of witness testimony or running down key documents, including text messages or e-mails. Sometimes the information was needed to tarnish the credibility of an accuser or potential witness. On several occasions, Pen helped unearth information that blew a gaping hole in a prosecutor's case.

That internship revealed his passion for investigative work, but he isn't content to have simply found a satisfying vocation. He yearns to be great at it. During the past year, he quickly completed the coursework and received his investigator's license. In his spare time, he loves to read about classic investigations and study various investigative techniques. He often has to force himself to set it all aside so he can focus on the work he needs to do to pass the bar. When his trust fund kicks in, it will provide him with the financial freedom to be selective with the investigations he takes on. He can even choose to work pro bono if necessary.

Pen relishes hanging out with a few investigators he has had the chance to meet, often offering to buy them dinner or drinks. Picking their brains, he acquires insights and tricks of the trade, gaining exposure to the real world skills the job requires. He thinks of it as an informal internship. He greatly enjoys hearing them regale him about how they, or a colleague, cracked some complex case. The tales of investigator folklore are told as if they are great legends. More than once, he has noticed the stories referred to a particular insurance company investigator.

Almost three years ago, paying his own way to attend an industry conference, Pen enrolled for a workshop on tracking someone who has changed their identity. The presenter was TD Adkins, the insurance in- vestigator others spoke of so admirably. Afterwards, Pen pestered TD for weeks, trying to get him to meet for lunch or dinner. When he finally ac- quiesced, TD took an almost instant liking to the determined young man.

It quickly became clear to both of them that TD found great enjoyment in sharing his knowledge. He soon thought of Pen as his protégé. Though he wasn't quite old enough to be Pen's father, there was certainly a slight feel of that to their relationship.

Contact between the two of them dropped off considerably for some while after TD's wife passed away. Pen was going through a rough pe- riod at the same time, battling with his family over the direction of his life. He twice delayed his final year of law school. Recently, he and TD had started meeting again. It was TD who convinced him to spend this summer doing something completely different, before returning to finish school in the fall.

⋏

Les gives TD a feeble smile when he returns to the car. "That was quick. What now?"

"I still have a couple of big issues I need to address, and we need to find a motel room, and something to eat. After that, I'll figure out what we should do next."

Looking across at her, he says, "One big problem is this car. We need to stop driving it around. With your permission, I'd like to have a trusted friend take it and park it near The End Zone."

After staring off expressionless for a moment, Les slowly nods her agreement. Despite her current calmness, TD can still feel her fear. Along with the sadness in her eyes, it's a painful reminder that no matter how exhilarating the last couple of days have been for him, this all must be so completely alien and terrifying for Les.

Back on the road, he ponders the nature of his ongoing problems. He needs to change the dynamic of how events are unfolding. With no control over the situation, the only thing he can do is react. He also needs some time to come up with a plan; one that not only gets him to wherever he decides to go, but will also provide safety for everyone he leaves behind.

Unfortunately, under the current circumstances, he has no idea how any of that's going to happen. He's not going to solve anything as long as he's holed up in motel rooms, dealing with tactical issues, and constantly being hunted.

⋏

Denny Holmes finds Laura Stevens sitting at a table close to the bakery counter in a Panera Bread shop. It's easy to see she her extreme nervousness as he approaches. Catching her eye, he flashes a smile as he speaks.

"Hi. Are you Laura? I'm Denny. Your daughter's friend TD asked me to help you."

Denny's smile, tousled blond hair, and relaxed manner help lessen Laura's jumpiness. Since entering the restaurant, she has been anxiously studying each customer coming through the door. With Denny now straddling the chair across the table, her fearful wait is over.

The plan he proposes is simple. Denny lives only a few minutes away, so the first thing will be for Laura to follow him there, where they'll garage her car. After that, he'll drive her to the hotel of her choice, and help her check-in and get situated. She'll probably need to stay there a couple of days before they have a better idea of how to move forward.

Hearing no mention of Les triggers questions from Laura about her safety. She also wants to know if Denny knows more about what's really going on. Anticipating her concerns, TD had instructed him what to say, assuring him it's the truth, just neatly packaged.

"I was told your daughter witnessed a fight at the bar involving some bad characters. She decided to get out of there, but evidently, someone is looking for her. She thinks it's safest to stay out of sight for a few days and that you should do the same thing. She's going to call you later."

Despite Denny's relaxed manner, Laura isn't thrilled with what she's hearing. And it's obvious no one is telling her anywhere near the full story about what her daughter is involved in. She's also concerned that her own path to safety starts with her following a man to his home; a man she only met minutes ago. She wishes she knew so much more; more about who Denny is and more about what is happening with Les.

Overcoming her misgivings, she quickly determines that the little she understands is still enough. It's enough because she can easily recall the nearly paralyzing sense of dread that engulfed her as she watched the two men prowling her driveway. Just thinking of that feeling makes her decide to trust Denny.

After they leave the restaurant, Laura doesn't know what to expect as she follows him through the increasingly wealthier neighborhoods approaching the river. With their final turn, he leads them through an ornamental gate into some woods and onto a driveway that begins to wind slowly through the trees. With the branches forming a thick canopy, for a moment it feels as if they've entered a dense forest.

They soon emerge into a broad clearing and Laura catches her breath. Off to the right, an impressive white two-story mansion sits atop a small rise. With an unobstructed view of the Potomac in both directions, the entire scene evokes images of centuries-old southern grandeur.

Instead of approaching the large colonial style home with its colonnade of pillars, they veer to the left, heading toward a lesser, but still substantial two-story brick home with dormer windows. It's only as they come around to the rear of that building that Laura realizes it's actually an ornate, four-car garage.

After stopping, Denny hops out, ushering her toward a now opening garage door on the far left. Inside, she sees three cars. One is a smoky gray Rolls Royce sedan; the other two are sleek vintage sports coupes; one easily identifiable as a Jaguar.

When she reemerges from the garage, Denny is grinning as he gestures to the large riverfront estate.

"How do you like my place?"

"It's magnificent. I must say I didn't expect something like this."

"Yep, this is where I live."

For a moment, Laura is amazed. Denny doesn't strike her at all as someone with this kind of wealth. Then she begins sensing something, like there's a joke she isn't getting. Finally grasping some hidden meaning in his last words, she smiles back at him knowingly.

"Yep, this is where I live, right here," he repeats.

This time as speaks, he swings his arms back toward the garage and upward to the windows jutting from the roof. He then explains he's responsible for the owner's two boats, as well as being the caretaker for the estate when the owners are absent. One of the perks of his job is that he lives on the property full time.

"I keep my own sailboat here as well. I'd love to show it to you. If it's possible, the view of the river is even more magnificent down by the dock."

Suddenly feeling more comfortable, Laura surprises Denny and herself when she says, "You know what, that sounds nice."

As they near the water's edge, she sees the sailboat tied alongside about half way down the long thin dock. It is a wonderful view, and Denny's ever-present smile and pleasantness briefly allow her to forget how she came to be there. But something distracts her, and her anxiousness quickly returns. She stops walking and looks back over her shoulder towards the garage and Denny's car, wondering if they shouldn't be leaving now, instead of strolling along the river.

Seeing her hesitation, Denny says, "Look, forget about the boat. The important thing is you're safe. And no one's going to be looking for you here. Chill out for a moment and enjoy the view. Then we'll get on the road and get you tucked away somewhere."

She has to admit it's relaxing here, and definitely beautiful. With only a few residential properties interrupting the tree-lined shore, the view along this bend of the river is nearly the same as it has been for hundreds of years.

After a few minutes, Denny breaks the silence. They should probably hit the road, and they need to choose a hotel. Based on his recommendation, Laura selects one in Alexandria. He then surprises her with another option. If she wants, they can get there by sailing up the Potomac and docking right in Old Town.

Laura is intrigued by the idea, and she has never been on a sailboat. She'd love to do it some time, but she's pretty sure right now isn't the best choice.

Trying to sway her, Denny says, "I know one thing. No one's going to be looking for you on the river."

"How long would it take?"

"Well it is upriver. But there's a light breeze and we have the boat's small motor. I'd say an hour, no more than an hour and a half."

Laura remains hesitant, but Denny is so likable, and he's right about nobody looking for her on the river. "Okay, there's one condition. I need to call my daughter and tell her what I'm doing"

Sensing it's non-negotiable, he says, "Okay. But TD told me their phones might be turned off. At worst you can leave her a message."

⅄

Steve Czarniak spent his afternoon with the roundtrip to Stafford. The hospital had yet to produce a final lab report, but there was a clear injection site in Raffi's neck and his death is being investigated as a homicide. They also have security video of an unidentified doctor entering Raffi's room not long before he was found dead.

The young man they found in the parking garage with his throat slit open matches the video images of the person who picked up Raffi at the bus stop car crash. His body was found on the ground next to a Monte Carlo registered to Flores.

For Czarniak, there's no longer any doubt they have located the remaining assailants. And he's not the least surprised Flores was killed. The public nature of his death is likely intended to send a clear signal that justice has been rendered, though far more brutally then if the police had apprehended them.

On a call with Roberts during the ride back, Steve commented on how quickly those who were seeking revenge found the two men. Even though the police had done a decent job, locating the assailants less than forty-eight hours after the attack, somehow, someone else had beaten them to it.

After hearing Czarniak's report, Roberts decides to call Richter. He can no longer avoid confronting the man directly. From the beginning of the call, the county detective is defensive. Frustrated, with Richter's vague responses to his initial questions, Roberts cuts to the chase.

"Why did you tell the Stafford Police the man they had at the hospital didn't match who we were looking for?"

After a notable pause, Richter responds, sounding affronted. "I don't know if you're implying something with that question, but I already told you. It didn't sound like a match to me. Not the way he described it."

Before Roberts can say anything, Richter continues, "So this is how it is? After helping you guys out in a jam, the thanks I get is you calling me up to bitch about my results? Is there anything else you would like to interrogate me about, or are we done?"

Roberts finds himself unsurprised by the man's sudden insolence. There was always something a little off about him. Refusing to take the bait, he ends the call.

Over the next couple of days, he'll put some thought into the conversation he plans to have with Richter's boss, Frank Aldretti. Carl needs to prepare and make sure he uses the right words. He needs to express his concerns about Richter, but do it without coming across as ungrateful for the help the county provides. There's definitely no upside to burning that bridge.

⚔

As he scouts for a place to stay for the night, TD considers the accelerating pace of events. Initially, it seemed he had plenty of time to think through his options. Though he procrastinated and made only a few decisions, at least it felt like he controlled his own destiny. Now he's in full reaction mode, driven by the motives and actions of others. More than anything else, that needs to change.

The motel he selects is not much different from the one he left that morning. It may be a little nicer, but it's still on the low-end. After paying with cash, he makes a glancing inspection of the adjoining rooms before suggesting they get a cup of coffee or something to eat at a local restaurant adjacent to the motel.

On their way inside, he watches as Les grabs a free newspaper from a rack next to the entrance. Sliding into the booth across from him, she raises the paper and begins slowly folding through the pages. TD is pretty sure she's less interested in the news than erecting a barrier between them. As he glances at the menu, he searches his mind for something to say that might elevate her mood, if only a little.

Looking across at Les, TD is suddenly rocked by the headline on the tabloid she's holding. The newspaper is The City Express, with Preeti Chopra's initial article on Monday night's events. Having not noticed when she first lifted the paper, it's now right in front of him, in inch high newsprint: *'Seven Slayed in Motel Shootout'*.

As if on cue, Les begins reading snippets from the story aloud. Lowering the paper when she's done, she begins to stare blankly at some point across the restaurant. She finally speaks as her eyes turn back to him. "I'll never understand people senselessly killing each other. What could possibly be worth taking someone's life?"

TD can see she's watching him closely for a reaction. Is it possible she has put everything together? Though he doubts it, he can only guess where she's going with this. Quickly deciding that saying nothing is his safest course, he ignores her rhetorical question.

Clearly upset, Les tries again. "It's just so scary. How can people behave that way?"

Again, her eyes stay on him. Finally, she pushes the paper aside. With an over dramatic "Excuse me", she leaves the table, heading towards the restroom.

TD can feel his optimism about the future rapidly ceding ground to inklings of fear and doubt. Real problems are arising. His relationship with Les is terribly damaged, possibly beyond repair. And the men who are pursuing him not only know his identity, they've proven they're quite capable of tracking him. They've also demonstrated they won't hesitate to use violence against anyone who gets in their way.

Given these stark realities, TD realizes it all boils down to a couple of critical questions he must ask himself. If given enough time, is he smart enough to construct a plan that lets him hold onto the money while keeping everyone safe? And just as important, even if the answer is yes, is it credible to believe he could capably execute such a plan?

Feeling comfortable that he's properly framed the issue, he realizes there's one other major aspect to the problem. What's the alternative, if the answer to either question is no?

With Les soon to return, TD leaves his thoughts. Grabbing the newspaper, he quickly scans the article. At least there's no mention of specific suspects seen leaving the scene. Looking up, he sees Les is almost back to their booth. Quickly folding the paper in half, he places it on the seat next to him. Though she must have seen him reading it, she says nothing about it when she returns.

Les had seen TD calmly ditch the paper and wondered why he was making the effort to hide it. She also notices his face is flushed, as if he's blushing. Several things bothered her about the newspaper article she just read, some she isn't even aware of at a conscious level. But now, a faint notion in her mind is solidifying into a terrible thought. Could the trouble TD is involved with somehow be related?

Her first reaction to the idea is to tell herself to calm down; she's far too jumpy. Besides, it simply can't be. There's no way TD is the kind of person who could be involved with all that death. She tries looking at the menu to get her mind off the horrible concept, but it doesn't work. With her emotions left raw from the constant fear, she's having trouble thinking things through. In the end, she's going to have to hear it from him.

"TD, please tell me you weren't involved with something like I just read about."

Hoping to hear his indignant denial, Les watches as he stares back at her with a hurt look. Before he can respond, her phone rings.

As she answers the call, TD realizes the significance of the moment. At some point, Les had decided to turn her phone back on, and to do so without telling him.

Les is thrilled. It's her mother calling and she sounds much better than expected. She's no longer in a near panic and feeling much safer since TD's friend found her. Right now, he's taking her to a hotel in Alexandria. Les is a little confused by an odd reference to a sailboat, but she brushes the remark aside. They agree to talk again later, after Laura is settled in safely at her destination. At that point, Les hands the phone to TD so Denny can speak with him.

TD can hear Denny's smile through the phone when he tells him they're taking his sailboat up the Potomac to reach Old Town. After TD tells him to spare no expense taking care of Laura Stevens, Denny chirps, "By the way, that's not a bad looking woman, TD. And she's a real nice lady, to boot."

"I'm sure she finds you charming as well, Denny. Thanks again for everything. This is a real tough time for her and some other people around me, and she needed help fast."

"Hey, that's cool. I understand she's someone important to you."

"She is important, but the fact is I've never even met her. I sure am glad you could help though."

As he ends the call, TD can see that Les is obviously more relaxed knowing her mother is now in safe hands. After giving her a little time to absorb the good news, he decides he cannot ignore the issue of her phone being on.

Gently, he says to her, "We really need to keep our phones turned off, Les. We don't want to show up on everyone's radar. I promise you soon we'll figure out how to manage regular communications with your mom."

Without saying anything, without even a nod, Les removes the battery again and puts her phone away. Having heard from her mother, she can finally comply with TD's request. She also doesn't resist when he hands her back her menu, along with a friendly reminder that they should try to eat something.

At least for the moment, she forgets about the assurances she was seeking from him when her mother called. Or that he had failed to say a word in response.

ᛉ

Denny's Catalina is perfect for the river. With a draft of just under four feet, the boat handles the shallows along the shores of this tidal section of the Potomac quite well.

Once on board, it takes him only minutes to get them under way for the trip upriver. To help her relax, he encourages Laura to tour the boat. He soon has her moving about, guided by his voice as he works the sails. Only twenty-five feet at the waterline, Laura is surprised by the amount of room below deck, including the multiple berths.

Next, he tells her to take the helm. Showing reluctance, she explains that it's her first time on a boat, other than a rowboat on a lake. Denny doesn't care. He soon has her smiling as she steers, soaking in the new experience and forgetting how it is she came to be sailing the Potomac this evening.

▲

Jim Richter is pissed off. He's pissed at Carl Roberts for unmasking his deceptions and at himself for being discovered so easily. Most of all, he's pissed at Keach for getting him caught up in this pile of shit. If he isn't careful, it could cost him more than his already tarnished reputation. It could cost him his job, and even his pension.

Besides being angry, Richter is done. He's calling Keach to tell him there'll be no more moves on his part. He did his job, helping lead them right to Adkins. And he doesn't need Keach to let him know that his men blew it and let their prey slip away. He heard all about the incident at the nightclub on Route 1. A police report is inevitable once a shot is fired and Richter had learned all the details.

When Keach answers his call, Richter immediately recounts his conversation with Roberts. He finishes by emphasizing that he's now cut off from any new information the investigation gains. Hearing no response from Keach, he moves on to his second reason for calling. With as much backbone as he can muster, he attempts to end their relationship.

"So, that's it for me. I'll continue passing on any call data as it comes in, but other than that, I'm afraid I'm done. It's too risky. Besides, I put you on Adkins. I think you'll agree that I've done everything you've asked. From my point of view, I consider us even."

Richter stops himself at that point before saying something he regrets. With every passing second of silence, he waits to hear Keach's telling response. Finally it comes.

"We wouldn't be where we are on this without your help, Jim. Thank you. As to whether we are even, as you choose to describe it, or whether I call and request your help again, well, let's just say we'll cross that bridge when we come to it."

⋏

The boat trip to Alexandria took under an hour thanks to a mild breeze. If they had been forced to rely solely upon the boat's small twenty-five horse-power engine, it could have taken a lot longer.

Laura is surprised when they arrive at the hotel Denny had recommended. A short walk from the dock had led them to a trendy, upscale boutique property overlooking the river. While they're registering under his name, Laura quietly protests the exorbitant room rate. Whispering, she says, "That's too much. Tomorrow I want to move to some place more reasonable."

Ignoring her until they've left the front desk, Denny says, "Don't sweat it. Les's friend is on the hook for all this. Now, before you go up to your room, I suggest a little shopping trip. We need to get you some toiletries, along with a change of clothes or two. And there are some great places for dinner close by here. Oh yeah, I almost forgot; we also need to stop at an ATM and get you some cash."

Her unease rising again, Laura objects. "I don't need any of that, really. I'm just planning to stay in the room and keep out of sight. And there's no way I'm taking any money from you."

Denny is having none of it. She arrived here with no possessions and TD had made it clear that she might need to hide out for several days. The more he can help her with now, the easier it will be going forward.

"First, this isn't costing me anything. And besides, I'm happy to help. I know you're scared, but you're safe now. I'm telling you, the odds of someone following us here are astronomical. There's no reason you can't go out for a little while and get what you need to be comfortable. And in my opinion, that includes a nice dinner."

Laura knows he's right. And it doesn't hurt that along with his sun-bleached hair, Denny is genuinely pleasant company. She also feels that she shouldn't appear ungrateful; he has been her protector today. Managing a smile, she agrees to the shopping and a quick dinner.

As they head down the cobblestone sidewalk, she reminds herself to thank her daughter's friend for taking care of things so quickly and pleasantly.

⚓

TD and Les had finished their time at the restaurant with almost no talking, hurriedly eating once they're food came. That was fine with TD. He was particularly uninterested in resuming the conversation they were having when her mother called. He's just not sure how he'll handle the situation if it comes to the point that Les demands he tells her everything.

On the short walk back to the motel, he explains that he has to leave. "I have to take care of a few things, but I won't be gone long. You're welcome to come with me, but if you're comfortable waiting here, that would probably be best."

After Les assures him she'll be fine waiting at the motel, TD immediately leaves to rendezvous with Pen. On the way to the meeting point, he wrestles with how much he should involve the young man with his problems. He knows Pen will be eager to assist, but that's not the point. The bigger question is how much information he should share. What he's asking Pen to do isn't risk free. Is it fair not to fully disclose what is going on?

Pulling into the gas station where they agreed to meet, he can see Pen is already there, parked off to one side. When the two men shake hands, Pen razzes him for arriving in the brightly colored VW Beetle.

"Well, I had to borrow this in a pinch. Maybe you can buy me a car you approve of when you get your trust fund."

When they finish laughing, TD gets to the point. "So, this is the way it is. I was working on a case, a nothing case really, absolutely one hundred percent routine. Then, Monday night, everything went completely off the rails. Foolishly, I'm now in the thick of some things that aren't that good. I could use your help if you're willing."

"Sure, you know I'm always interested in working with you, TD. What's up? Who's the client?"

Hesitating before he responds, TD finally says, "Well, before I get into all that, the first thing I need is my car. There's probably more you can help me with, but to be straight with you, I haven't figured out too much past getting the car back."

TD is coming across tense and worried. It's also clear he's not sharing any details at this point. Despite that, Pen remains willing to help. Sounding as supportive as he can, he says, "You don't have to tell me anything you don't want to, TD. As long as it's plausibly legal and I won't get hurt, then I'm okay; I'm in. I can get the car first thing in the morning. Where do you want to meet up? Here?"

TD winces. "I really need it tonight Pen. I don't know where I may be tomorrow."

Pen is a surprised by the ominous tone of TD's answer; it's not like him to be melodramatic. Thinking quickly, he says, "That's cool. I'm scheduled to work tonight, but there's plenty of summer help. I'm sure someone can cover for me."

Pen listens as TD tells him that he 'ditched' his original car. He then describes the location and model of the SUV he purchased. TD would like him to drive the VW, swap it for the SUV, and then return here; all the while ensuring he's not being tailed.

Pen is becoming increasingly concerned and unsure if he should say something. Though TD is obviously in enough trouble to have called for help, he remains unwilling to say anything about what's going on. And there's clearly much more to this than merely picking up a car or TD would have done so himself. Having already agreed to help, Pen finds himself wishing he had much more information.

Looking TD straight in the eyes, he says, "Okay, it all sounds easy enough, but I have to admit you have me a little worried. Like I said, you don't have to tell me about the case, but I've never seen you wound tighter. If it would help you to talk about anything, I'm willing to listen."

Measuring the young man in front of him, TD decides to trust him with everything he needs to know. Besides, it's not right to put him in harm's way without giving him sufficient data to work with. Going forward, he'll have to let Pen decide when to back away if things become too risky.

As TD starts in on the sensational story of his last forty-eight hours, Pen works hard to keep his expression blank. It rapidly becomes an impossible task, particularly when TD describes taking the bags of money and going on the run. Pen can hardly believe it all, especially coming from a man he has always known as intelligent and calculating. He would have never guessed TD would make such an irrational and risky choice, or get himself in such hot water.

"Wow, that's some deep shit you stepped in, TD. What are you going to do about all that money?"

Watching TD look down and hesitate with his answer, Pen suddenly understands the situation. "Wait a minute, I get it. You're going to try to keep it aren't you? And you're going to try to disappear. Oh man, that's sick. Do you really think you can pull it off?"

TD is thrilled with Pen's reaction. He didn't expect to be told what he's attempting is a great idea; he just didn't want to hear about how stupid he's being. Sensing he has an ally, TD tells Pen that he's worried he has already blown the possibility of succeeding. With Les involved as a reluctant participant and her mother temporarily in hiding, there are massive hurdles to overcome. What he needs most right now is time; time to figure out his next steps. If Pen is willing to get involved, TD can definitely use his help with buying that time.

Pen doesn't hesitate, agreeing to help without any further consideration. Before they part, TD mentions his biggest logistical problem is communications. He explains his strong suspicion that he's being tracked via his cell phone, and that he has turned their phones off and removed the batteries. The problem is how to coordinate everyone's activities without leaving an electronic footprint.

"Problem solved."

As Pen says this, TD watches him point across the road at a small, independent cell phone shop. Once they cross the highway, they can more easily read the fluorescent orange poster in the store's window touting dirt-cheap pre-paid cell phones.

Pointing at the sign, Pen says, "Just what you're looking for. We need to grab a handful of burners."

TD chuckles, both surprised and a little disappointed with himself for forgetting about the inexpensive phones, popular with people who have bad credit or who prefer keeping a low profile. After a quick needs assessment, they go inside where Pen requests four phones, using his ID for the purchase. When he chooses only one month of pre-paid service, with no credit card for auto-renewal, the clerk warns him that the phones will cost more than advertised. They couldn't care less. TD's communications problems are solved.

Before leaving for Route 1, Pen takes one of the phones with him. He'll call as soon as he has swapped the vehicles and is on his way back. As TD watches him pull off, he's reminded of how much he enjoys working with the young man. He also begins thinking of other ways Pen might be able to help.

Driving back to the motel, TD feels his fortunes are on the upswing. At a minimum, for the first time in hours he has gained back a small amount of control over events.

⚓

As soon as he's back at the motel, TD checks in on Les. He thinks he notices a faint smile when she answers his knock, but he can't be sure. As he enters her room, she quickly turns away, flopping onto the bed. The television is on, but the volume is muted and it's clear she's not actually watching anything. Instead, she's distractedly flipping through the channels, stopping for only a second or two on each one. She's also not acknowledging him, though he senses something is different. If anything, she seems less angry.

Suddenly, she turns off the television and sits up on the bed, folding her legs beneath her as she faces him. "Before I say anything else, I want to thank you again for helping my mom. You said that you would, and you made good on your promise. I also want to apologize for being so bitchy."

"Don't Les. I'm the one who should be..."

Holding up her hand, she cuts him off. "Please, let me finish, TD. And don't misunderstand me. I'm not going to pretend that I'm happy about being dragged into this. I'm definitely not. I'm scared and I'm upset. But my being angry doesn't help us. And I can also see that you're trying to make things better, so I wanted you to know that I appreciate that."

Pausing, she sighs and takes a deep breath. When she continues, the tiny smile TD thought he might have spotted earlier is there again. "I know you couldn't have possibly planned things to turn out this way. And you must be under a ton of pressure. So I thought you should know that if there's some way I can help, then I'm willing to try. But please don't take too long to get us out of this. I really hate feeling scared all the time."

Touched by her heartfelt speech, TD is almost brought to tears as he offers another apology. He's quite impressed with the strength and caring Les is showing, though he's not a bit surprised. Those very characteristics are a big part of why he's so fond of her.

He also thanks her for her continued patience, before saying, "I wanted to let you know that I'm not going to be in my room for a while. It's like you said, I need to get us out of this mess, and if I'm going to do that, we need a plan. I thought I'd take a walk out back behind the motel and do some thinking. I promise I'll come up with something soon."

TD's spirits are soaring as he leaves her room. Les is willing to help and that's huge. Does it mean she wants to leave with him? Of course not. But it does remove a huge distraction, allowing him to focus more on the problems at hand instead of worrying that she's back in her room, trembling in fear, and hating him. And who knows, there's always a chance she could change her mind later about going with him.

In the small overflow parking area behind the motel, he begins to pace steadily in a large oval. TD likes to walk while he thinks, finding it mentally stimulating. He also paces ceaselessly whenever he's on the phone. Now, briskly circling the lot, he considers the choices facing him.

First, he must revisit a prior decision; one on which everything else is predicated. It's a question he has asked himself repeatedly, but one he must answer again. Despite the worsening odds against him succeeding, does he still intend on trying to keep the money?

Refreshed by Les's support and understanding, TD is once again feeling better about himself. He's also confident he can make the right choices. All it should take is a little rational thinking, followed by some solid planning. Unfortunately, rational thought isn't easy for him to come by at the moment, not with the raw excitement of the chase and the large amount of money involved, or the intrigue of disappearing and starting a new life.

Soon, the joyous thrill of it all is governing his mind and there's no more consideration. Having come this far, he owes it to himself to make a genuine attempt at keeping the money and disappearing. Besides, any other choice would be an admission that everything he has done until now, and all that he has put his friends through, is a colossal and thoughtless blunder.

Recommitted to his goals, he knows he must stop underestimating what it will take to plan and execute a successful disappearance, and everything that means for those he leaves behind. He also knows it will be no easy task. And having people hot on his tail only complicates matters. Every minute he's forced to divert time and attention to his short-term survival is a minute he's not planning his escape.

A perfect example of the problem he faces is that he doesn't even know whose money he has. Without that critical information, pulling off an effective vanishing act will be even more difficult. And he'll never be comfortable that he has fully eluded them. Yet spending the time required for the necessary research will only delay his other preparations. As he ponders the dilemma, the speed of his steps begins to slow, before coming to a halt.

For some reason, a case from many years back has popped into his to mind. One on which he wasted months chasing down several false leads, each purposefully and expertly planted by the man who had perpetrated the fraud. And that's exactly what he needs to do now. He needs to create a false trail and lead his hunters away from him, providing him with the time he needs.

He needs them to pursue a phantom.

Pen can see The End Zone is open for business as he passes by. The lot is full of cars and there's no overt sign of police. At the nearby shopping center, he easily locates TD's Pathfinder, parked between two other vehicles. Passing it without stopping, he makes two full laps around the lot. He's unable to spot any surveillance, neither there or across the highway, but he's not completely satisfied. Pulling back onto Route 1, he checks to see if anyone follows. A few minutes later, he doubles back, again seeing nothing suspicious as he passes by.

When he returns a final time, he parks only two spots away. Not hesitating, he immediately exits the VW and walks directly to TD's car. Moments later, he's on the road. When he's sure no one is following, he pulls into a gas station and tops off the nearly full tank. At the same time, he fulfills the real reason for the brief stop. Opening the hatchback, he quickly confirms the three gym bags are still there amidst the rest of TD's luggage.

His next task is a quick fact-finding mission at the apartment complex where TD abandoned his original car. When he arrives at the location, he sees the situation is exactly opposite of the one at the shopping center minutes earlier. Here, he easily spots two suspicious vehicles; one is parked at the far end of the lot, another is closer to TD's car. He can see someone sitting behind the wheel in both vehicles, but neither has its engine running. TD had been right when he had guessed they might have his car staked out, waiting for his return.

His objectives achieved, Pen decides to have a little fun before leaving. Having noted a street name two blocks away, he stops directly in front of the car at the end of the lot. Rolling down his window, he shouts to the guy sitting inside, asking if he knows how to get to the other street. Receiving only a shrug and a dismissive wave, Pen thanks him anyway and drives off.

As he begins the trip back to meet TD, he lets out a hearty laugh. Even though he may only be shuttling cars for a friend, at least he's done it with a little flair. If that guy in the car really was on the lookout for TD and the cash, Pen wonders how he'd react to learning that for a brief moment, the money had been right in front of his nose.

Now it's time to call TD to let him know he's returning, mission ac-complished. Grabbing the cheap cell phone from the car seat next to him, he also reminds himself to make the case for being involved with any more plans his friend is hatching.

⋏

After checking in on Les and saying goodnight, TD returns to his room and is soon fleshing out a plan. Over the past few hours, he has locked in on the premise that he was tracked by the calls he made on his cell phone, not the phone itself. It's the one theory that fits all the facts. Since he seriously doubts they were tracking his phone by its active location on the network, and he's positive that he wasn't personally tailed to The End Zone, then it can only mean that they followed Phil. And the only connec-tion with Phil that could have been discovered so quickly is through their calls. If he's right, and TD feels strongly that he is, then he should be able to exploit this to his benefit.

The first move he hopes to make is easy enough. He wants to put some real distance between himself and Phil by having Phil go on the move. The men pursuing him can't have unlimited resources. Providing them with multiple targets to follow, moving in separate directions, should work to his advantage.

At the heart of his plans is a much grander diversion. Using his legiti-mate cell phone, his credit cards, and anything else he can come up with, he plans to create the illusion that he is also on the move, leaving the area and soon to be out the grasp of his pursuers. If he can execute the ruse, luring them into chasing his phantom, it should relieve the pressure and give him the precious time he needs.

Having hoped to have heard from Pen by now, TD is relieved when one of the new phones begins to ring. Pen sounds like he's having fun, enthusiastically telling him about picking up the car with the money, as well as spotting the surveillance at the apartment complex. After accepting TD's thanks, Pen urges him to give him something more to work on when he returns.

Chuckling, TD knows Pen will get a kick out of his response. "Sure, why not. Let me ask you this. How would you like an all-expenses paid trip to…let's see…how about Atlantic City?"

Laughing, Pen responds, "Alright, I'm all ears. But I must admit that's not exactly what I expected to hear."

After TD finishes explaining his idea, he tells Pen to drive toward Baltimore. At the end of their conversation he says, "If I can make this happen, it's going to be a long night for you. Rest up as much as you can, and I'll see you here in the morning."

TD hates to turn on his phone, but he needs the number for the forger he encountered years ago. At the end of it all, they'd reached an understanding and the man had been quite gracious. Hopefully the number is still good and he's willing to fulfill TD's request tonight. If he does, his services will no doubt come with a steep price tag.

TD almost uses his own phone, but remembers to turn it off and use one of the cheap spares. After waiting anxiously though several rings, his call is not only answered, but the ensuing brief conversation yields an agreement. Within a couple of hours, Pen will be in possession of a brand new Virginia Driver's License bearing his photo and physical description, accompanied by the valid license number, name, and address of TD Adkins.

TD's next call is to Phil, who is currently enduring his wife's wrath. Initially, Anne was shocked and sympathetic when he arrived home from the emergency room with his nose broken and stitches over both eyes. Unfortunately, under the effect of the pain medication he was given, Phil guilelessly answered her questions about the what, where, and why of his injuries. Anne's caring manner had vanished instantly and she had hardly let up on him since.

When his phone begins ringing, she declares, "If that's TD, then just hand me the phone. I need to talk to him."

Shushing her as he stares at the Caller ID, Phil doesn't recognize the number. When he answers, he's both relieved and anxious that it's TD. Stepping into his home office, he closes the door on Anne's repeated inquiries about who is calling.

After thanking Phil profusely, TD commiserates over his injuries and his wife's anger. He then tells him what he's planning. At the end, he says, "I'm sure you know I wouldn't ask you to do this only because it works for me. Putting some distance between us has to be safer for both you and Anne. So, what do you think? Can you take a long weekend? Let her pick the destination. Maybe it'll help her calm down."

Phil quickly agrees. Leaving the immediate area for a few days makes a lot of sense. There are several spots on Maryland's Eastern Shore that Anne really likes. When he mentions the area to TD, they agree it would be perfect.

TD is happy that Phil injuries aren't worse. He's also glad his close friend is still willing to help. "By the way, thanks for the info on the cars at the motel. I haven't had a chance to look at it yet, but when I do, I may have some questions or need a little more data. I hope it'll be okay to call you?"

Phil assures him he'll help in any way he can. Even if they leave in the morning, he should still have online access to his firm's resources. There just might be a little delay.

After his call with Phil, TD's confidence bumps up another level. He now has the outlines of a decent plan and he's beginning to build some momentum. In just a few hours, he has assembled a small team of friends willing to help. If he can just catch a few breaks, then it's possible he could actually pull this off.

Just after ten o'clock, Jon Stark calls Dan Keach with an update. Though they've had no additional sightings of Adkins, there is some news to report.

To this point, the surveillance on Adkins's car has yielded them nothing, but one of the men did make a discovery. Rotating off a long shift patrolling the area around Route 1, he had decided to check out The End Zone on his break. Finding the parking lot full, he headed to the shopping center down the street. It was there that he spotted the yellow VW Beetle. Unfortunately, neither Adkins nor the girl was with it. Stark tells Keach that they'll regularly check out the car, but if he wants continuous coverage of the growing number of vehicles associated with Adkins, they're going to need more men.

Even without its occupants, they agree the presence of the car is noteworthy for several reasons. For one, it suggests Adkins might still be nearby. It could also be that the girl came back, after dropping Adkins off somewhere close by, though he hasn't been back to his car, and she's not at either the bar or her home. Either way, it further lowers their estimate of Adkins. Why would he risk returning to the immediate area? And why leave the VW sitting there, out in the open? None of it makes much make sense. As they finish talking it over, Stark remains optimistic, predicting Adkins will soon make another mistake.

On a different front, Keach tells him that they've gained access to more of Adkins's personal information. They should soon also be able to track him via his credit footprint, though with him knowing the chase is on, they might not get much of anything.

Having finished his update, and with no current leads on Adkins's whereabouts, Jon Stark decides to speak bluntly. "Dan, I understand you have a mandate to resolve this quickly, but if we're going to make that happen, then it's probably going to require additional resources. I'm sure you're aware that this kind of effort can get quite pricey."

Keach has been considering that very fact while waiting for this latest report from Stark. He had been on the phone throughout the afternoon and evening with Richard Wilkins and Robert Owen, both who were anxious for updates. One result of their discussions is that they now have a clear view of the firm's current financial situation. The bottom line is that they have enough cash on hand to meet one payroll cycle and most of their immediate credit obligations. The firm can make it through the coming weekend, but that's about it.

As a possible source of relief, they had discussed accelerating the next cash consolidation. Unfortunately, they quickly understood that wouldn't be a short-term solution. With Eddie and the others gone, a new team will have to be assembled. Additionally, the entire consolidation process, as well as a new pick-up location, will need to be fully vetted by Keach.

Robert Owen had then laid out a timeline for accessing any newly collected funds, either from getting the consolidation process back up and running, or from some other source. He explained that any fresh cash would have to move through at least some portion of the laundering process. All told, it would probably be at least a week before any significant amount of money would be available.

Keach had been anxious to hear what Owen would say on that topic, knowing the man is desperate to generate cash flow. He had regained a little respect for the CFO when he didn't suggest overly aggressive shortcuts for moving any new cash they might bring in onto the corporate books.

At one point, Richard Wilkins came close to losing his composure again. Tired of listening to Owen's gloomy scenarios, he had interrupted, instructing his CFO to start squeezing every penny out of their affiliate company accounts, using any method possible.

Owen's retort had been quick and sobering. "We've done that already, Richard. You should remember; it was late last year. I need to be clear, gentlemen. There are no more liquid assets to fall back on."

By late evening, they had agreed on a short-term plan of action. They may incur certain costs with their creditors, due to being late with a major payment or two, but the company will stay afloat. Richard will not allow that to be an issue. Keach will remain focused on recovering the cash, but if he fails to accomplish that in the next couple of days, Richard will meet with their lender of last resort, his friends in Philadelphia.

Keach is determined to prevent them reaching that point. He's confident he'll eventually find Adkins and recover some portion of the money. It just has to be sooner than later to avoid the exorbitant cost of having to borrow from the Mob. It would also eliminate the embarrassment and risk from exposing the vulnerable state of Wilkins's operations to such predators.

Now, as he ends his call with Jon Stark, he offers encouragement. He reminds him that Adkins is looking more like an amateur than they'd initially thought. And he agrees that they'll soon catch a break. Brushing off

Stark's warning of the costs, he tells him to keep the pressure on and continue the search.

⋏

It had taken her well into the evening, with her deadline rapidly approaching, but Preeti Chopra had finally finished her next article. As she wrote, she had occasionally paused, briefly reliving the feelings of pride she had experienced when her editor told her how many column inches she was getting. It was a generous slot, but even then, there had to be cuts; she had written considerably more than she was being allotted.

After a brief recap of Monday night's events, the article follows with the brutal deaths of the two shooting suspects in Stafford. It then segues from that hospital to the one in Fairfax, where it shifts its focus to Bobby Tomlin, a hard-working random victim of gangland-style violence. This terrible event has left his family without any source of income, mounting medical bills, and no relief in sight. The article closes with information related to the sub-headline tease: *Mystery Suspect Not Actively Sought By Police.*

She had tried not to embarrass the pleasant and certainly handsome Lead Detective, Carl Roberts, and had made sure to mention his department's limited resources and tight budget. Despite that, she clearly intended for the article to leave the reader with the suggestion that someone may have gotten away.

⋏

After setting an alarm on the clock by the bed, TD also sets a backup on one on the new cell phones. He sets both alarms for five in the morning. That should give him enough time for some needed rest, but also have him up early enough to get a jump on his pursuit.

Still fully clothed and lying on top of the bedspread, he props himself up with the pillows as he continues to think of little twists he can add to his emerging plan. Soon his thoughts shift to Les, and the best options for taking care of her over the next few days. Is it safe to try to bring her and her mother together somewhere? Or would continuing to hide out with him be safer for now? Is there really any hope she could change her mind and decide to leave with him?

Despite the many questions and problems, the fatigue from an unbelievably stressful day quickly overwhelms him. Within just minutes of lying down, TD falls soundly asleep.

THURSDAY

TD is becoming quite irritated and it's getting worse. He can't seem to shake a strange snippet of digitized music that's repeating itself in his mind. Finally, he's awake enough to realize it's the alarm on the new cellphone. Annoying as it is, it did the trick. He's also glad that he used it as a backup; apparently, he fumbled setting the alarm clock on the nightstand, which wasn't going to go off until five PM.

Despite the early hour, he feels ready to work. He also senses a renewed enthusiasm for what lies ahead. Unlike before, there'll be no more fantasizing about the future while postponing key decisions. Today is about coming up with a plan and getting it done.

The first item he tackles is creating a list of diversionary tactics for Pen to execute on his trip. He wants to ensure Pen leaves an obvious trail pretending to be TD Adkins. Every resource his pursuers divert to chasing a phantom should give him more time to move forward with his own designs.

Next, TD opens the large envelope containing the information on the cars involved at the motel Monday. Determining who owns the vehicles should go a long way to helping understand who's chasing after him. He can see from a quick check of the envelope's contents that Phil has printed the data for each vehicle on a separate page. He has also clipped them all together, except for one. A yellow sticky-note is attached to the main stack: *All owned by one company!! CCVS*

The note reminds him of Phil's remarks when he handed over the envelope yesterday. It's not a huge surprise to TD that one company owns most of the cars involved. But what's far more significant is that Phil not only wrote the policy for the leasing firm, but also for the owner of the other vehicle. Phil doesn't sell a lot of auto insurance to begin with, so the odds of that occurring randomly are extremely high.

Now that he has more time to consider the information, TD begins to grasp its importance, as well as the increasing likelihood of a direct connection between the two firms; something that he hopes is the case. If he can link Wilkins Investment Group and CCVS, then he'll know exactly whom he's dealing with.

Hoping to find something online that might connect the two companies, he reaches for his laptop. As it powers up, he wagers that the big Mercedes was the car owned by Wilkins. A quick scan of the page Phil kept separate from the others proves TD is wrong; it's Slick's car, the Cadillac coupe. Disappointed that he guessed incorrectly, it makes some sense to him, though he finds the reasoning unclear. Instead of dwelling on it, he puts it in the back of his mind as he navigates his way online via the motel's free, but severely low-powered, Wi-Fi connection.

When he finally has internet access, his searches yield an abundance of information about Wilkins Investment Group, though it's an entirely different matter regarding CCVS. There's absolutely nothing about the leasing firm except a barebones single-page website displaying a few pictures of heavy-duty trucks and construction vehicles. The webpage contains almost no written content, with only two brief sentences about the company's services, a phone number, and a post office box address. Additional internet searches yield nothing. From what TD can determine, CCVS isn't a member of the Better Business Bureau, nor has anyone posted a single online review or article about the privately held business.

After working through a good portion of the information on Wilkins Investment Group, TD can tell that most of it will be of little help in answering the questions he's now asking. Why would a longstanding real estate development firm be involved in what was happening Monday night?

And if they weren't, why was one of their vehicles there? Slick certainly appeared to be running the show; did he work for Wilkins in some capacity? Was he there just moonlighting? That's about the only scenario TD can envision, if the Wilkins firm isn't directly involved.

Knowing that he has to learn much more about both companies if he's going to prove a connection, TD makes a note to talk with Phil. Hopefully something can be gleaned from the insurance angle. Unfortunately, it's all going to have to wait. It's time to meet with Les, and then he needs to send Pen on his way.

Before heading out, he runs one last online query in search of any fresh coverage of the shootings. He finds several short items on the websites of two local broadcast news stations, but neither has anything new. The Washington Post's site has a short article that he hasn't read, but it's only a few paragraphs rehashing Monday's events. The last link he clicks takes him to the online version of the article Preeti finished last night.

He's most fascinated by what he reads at the end. It appears the police are not actively pursuing any suspects. It could be a ruse on their part, but if true, it eliminates a major source of pressure. On top of that, the article presents multiple concerns. For some reason, he finds the desk clerk's injuries and his family situation deeply troubling. He promises himself that when he gets the time, he'll come up with a way to help the young man and his family. Another issue is the very existence of the article. Les could easily stumble on it and become upset all over again.

But most troubling, is one other conclusion that can be drawn from the piece; one that renders almost meaningless the fact that the police may not be actively searching for him. As the article indicates, the slaughter hasn't stopped. As of now, except for the injured motel clerk and himself, everyone that was in that motel courtyard Monday night has been killed.

⋏

Dan Keach has also started his day early, and like TD, one of the first things he did was run an online search for any fresh news about the shootings. After reading Preeti's article, Keach also has concerns regarding Bobby

Tomlin, though much different from TD's. From the beginning, he has questioned what the desk clerk might know about their operations at the motel. It's certainly plausible that he could have tipped someone off about the deliveries. Keach decides he can't take any chances; he needs to be sure. And he wants Bobby Tomlin to stop talking, not only with the police, but with the press as well.

Keach makes a note to call Richter. He'd like to know if the police think Bobby was involved in any way. His own take is that Bobby is an innocent bystander. He just needs to confirm the 'innocent' part. As for deterring Bobby from giving any further interviews, he'll delegate that to Jon Stark.

Keach is soon surprised to receive a call from Richard Wilkins, noting it's a rare day when the man is awake this early. Richard is calling because he has just read the same article. Though he's remaining relatively calm for now, he's becoming spooked by the ongoing media coverage. He also has his own suspicions about the motel clerk. As the volume of his voice increases with indignation, he says, "And the goddamn police aren't even searching for the guy who stole our fucking money."

Keach spends the next few minutes reassuring his employer that he's on top of the situation. He also points out that it's not a bad thing that the cops are no longer interested in Adkins; it leaves the field wide open for their men. As they end the call, he makes the not so subtle suggestion that Richard focus on managing the firm's financial issues with Robert Owen. He'll manage the problem of retrieving the cash.

⚔

As they had planned the night before, TD finds Les waiting for him when he leaves his room at seven-thirty. Unfortunately, she appears to be on edge again, maybe as much as her worst times yesterday. On the walk to get some breakfast, he can sense the tension as if it's radiating from her. He can hardly blame her for being wound up again. They're in a difficult situation and it was probably a long night for her.

While they wait to be seated, his eyes are drawn to the newspaper rack near the diner's front door. He can't be sure if it's the latest edition, but the tabloid's front page is different from the one Les had yesterday. Worried that she might see it, he considers a maneuver to block her view. Luckily, the need passes as the hostess returns and leads them to a booth.

Sitting in silence, they quickly scan the menus. After the waitress takes their order, Les waits a moment before looking across the table at TD. Once again, she's wrestling with warring emotions. Late last night, she remembered that he had never answered her question about being involved with the shootings at that motel. It was a sobering reminder of how little she understands about what is going on. She had continued to worry over it for some time after that and had never really slept well.

She was up almost as early as TD this morning, and from the instant she was awake she could feel the pressure from the stress and fear that she knew would be there all day. She absolutely hated it. She also knew she couldn't stay cooped up in the cramped motel room until it was time for them to meet. She had gone alone to the restaurant for a cup of coffee about an hour ago. While she was there, she had grabbed the paper and read Preeti's article. Now she wants some answers.

With a pleading tone, she says, "I'm so confused, TD. I hardly know what to think about everything that's happening. Please be honest with me. I need to hear that you're not the other suspect they were talking about in an article I read this morning."

Realizing that Les must have already seen the newspaper, he isn't surprised that she has resumed this poisonous line of questioning. Staring at her with a pained expression, he tries to determine how to best respond. As he begins to speak, he slowly reaches across the table towards her hand.

"Les, I need you to understand something…"

Before another word leaves his mouth, she pulls away, abruptly standing. As she leaves the table, he hears her mumble, "Damn you, TD."

Watching through the restaurant window, he can soon see her crossing the parking lot. When she comes to a stop on the shoulder of the busy road, he knows he'll have to run out after her if she goes any farther. Instead, she turns around and begins to move through the lot with no apparent destination. Her pace has dropped to that of a slow meandering stroll as she weaves between the parked cars. Clearly distraught, there are a few times he can see her lips moving as she talks to herself. At a certain point, she stops and gazes off into the distance.

As he wonders how long he should let her stew out there alone, she begins to move again. This time, she's making a beeline for the restaurant. Once inside, she doesn't stop until she slides into the booth across from him, her eyes cast down at the table. When she finally speaks, her words leave him with nothing to say.

"I think we should just eat our breakfast and head back to the motel. Then you and I are going to have it out."

Once they're back in TD's room, Les opens fire, berating him for all the danger and anxiety she and her mother are going through due to his 'absurd and reckless choices'. More than once, she uses the phrase 'living nightmare'. She pauses twice during the tirade, leading him to think incorrectly that she has finished. Both times, she starts up again, saying, "I can't believe this is happening."

TD says nothing until he's sure she's spent. He wants her full attention, knowing that how she views him going forward will be forever changed after she hears his story.

Slowly, he describes what happened Monday night and what he was thinking. Though she shakes her head with disdain several times as he's speaking, she displays no other reaction, and says nothing. He then covers what he best can determine has occurred the past two days. Overall, what he gives her is a highly edited, but truthful version of the events; a telling of the story that he hopes will neither disgust nor terrify her. It's also carefully crafted to put him in the best possible light, despite there being almost nothing to commend his behavior.

With Les continuing to staring at him in silence, he has no way of knowing how she's handling what she just heard. At least she let him finish without interrupting, or overt displays of anger. Unable to handle her silence, he adds, "What I most regret is that my actions have harmed people that I care about deeply, and also put them in danger. But I promise you, I'm doing my best to resolve things."

Les found herself in shock as she listened, unable to respond as TD talked, but this last small speech is too self-serving for her taste, and finally triggers a reaction. With tears appearing as she speaks, she snaps at him, "Resolve things? What do those words even mean? Why don't you just give the money back? Or give it to the police. Why don't you just end this lunacy?"

Catching her breath, she continues, "You know, right now, I feel like I'm some kind of escapee on the run. And because of you, my mother is hiding out in a hotel. How long will all this go on before you *resolve things,* TD? Who else has to get hurt?"

Again, TD waits before he answers. He knows he can't possibly blame her for anything she's feeling, and her questions aren't simply rhetorical. Les isn't stupid. He's sure she's starting to see how high the stakes are, and she can't comprehend why he would want to continue playing such a dangerous game.

To ratchet down the tension, he sits on the edge of the bed and purposefully lowers the volume of his voice. Looking up at her, he slowly and methodically goes over why the situation is far more complex than simply being able to end things if he wanted to. As he talks, he can see she's closely following his words, trying to understand.

Finishing, he says, "So as you can see, giving the money to the police comes with its own set of problems, and might very well make the situation even worse. I do hope you appreciate that I understand your fears, Les; and your frustration with me as well. I just need some time to find a way forward."

After giving her a moment to absorb everything being thrown at her, he decides to address a key issue. "There is something we should talk about before we do anything else. I need for you to make a choice. If you want, we can get you into hiding today, just like your mother. We can even put the two of you together if that makes sense. Otherwise, you can continue to hang out with me while I look for a way through this."

No longer crying, Les has been sniffling and blowing her nose while he talked. Seeing how upset she is, a surge of sympathy spurs him to console her. Standing, and moving a little closer, he says, "I'm so sorry, Les. Once I took that money, I don't know what happened. Somehow, I got fixated on leaving with it; just going off somewhere and changing my life. You would've never been involved if I had only left right away. Instead, I waited to leave until I could talk with you face to face. I wanted to tell you I was leaving, and maybe see if you were interested in coming with me."

As the last words leave his mouth, he immediately realizes their importance and his mistake in saying them. There's no way they'll fail to draw a reaction from her.

Wearing a look of confusion mixed with anger, Les pushes past him. As she pauses at the door and turns back to face him, he anticipates another outburst. Instead, both her demeanor and her words surprise him.

Looking at him sadly, she says, "I always thought you were one of the smartest guys I knew. Now I can't believe how wrong I was. I'm going outside for a walk. When I get back, I'll tell you what I've decided."

As she slams the door behind her, TD realizes just how badly he has been at understanding her thoughts and moods lately. He has been wrong nearly every time he has tried to gauge her feelings, or anticipate her reaction, sometimes way off the mark. Could all the stress he's under somehow be eroding his vaunted skills for reading people? And at the worst possible time?

Preeti's latest article is making the rounds with the all principals. Carl Roberts read it over his breakfast, recalling the attractive reporter at the same time. He wonders if he noticed a small connection between them. Or was it just his imagination?

The article reminds him of how helpful Bobby Tomlin was; he hopes the kid has a full recovery. It was Bobby's insights that helped him solidify his theory about Adkins not being mixed up with the killings. But even if things played out the way Carl believes, he still feels a little guilty over not having done the work to close out the case by definitively excluding Adkins from any involvement with the homicides.

Unfortunately, they don't have the resources available for that right now. Last night, a college student was assaulted in the city's small downtown area. Such incidents are extremely rare, but generate a ton of bad publicity. On top of that, they've had two home burglaries in the past forty-eight hours. Add in the standard ration of court appearances for prior cases, and his team of detectives is totally underwater.

Briefly questioning his decision to release Richter back to the County, Carl chooses to stick with his plan to put the motel case on the back burner for the short-term. As soon as he has the resources to pursue Adkins, he'll go after him. That's just not likely to happen over the next couple of days.

⅄

After storming out, Les ends up walking around the same area behind the motel that TD circled the night before, miserable as she works through her anger. She didn't ask to be involved in this, but now that she better understands how he got himself in this situation, she finds herself feeling a little sympathy for TD. There's no doubt the man has been a complete fool, and she certainly doesn't feel any romantic attraction to him, but she considers him a dear friend and cares about his well-being. She'd hate to see him come to harm if she could have helped him in some way to avoid it.

Right now though, she needs to focus on doing what's best for her. She knows the choices she faces. If you boil the problem down to its essence, it's either hide or help. Hiding and waiting for things to reach a resolution may be safest, but it holds little appeal for her. It's not very productive either. After mulling her choice a while longer, she returns to TD's room.

With both hands on her hips, she tells him her decision. "I want to be crystal clear, I'm not running off somewhere with you, if that's what you stupidly end up choosing. That's never going to happen. And I'll absolutely have nothing to do with guns. If I see one, I'm out of here. But if there's some way I can help you, then I'm willing to stay and try, at least for a while."

TD can't believe it. Once again, he has completely misread the choice she would make. He was sure she would ask to join her mother. It's troubling that his deductive skills are failing him so badly. The only other time he erred at such a critical level was during Elizabeth's last days. He wishes he had more time to consider the issue, but Les is standing in front of him with her stunning news and Pen should be arriving any time now.

Her pronouncement certainly has its pros and cons. If she stays with him, her safety will continue to be directly intertwined with his, elevating their risk. But there is a bright side. Spending more time together gives him a chance to rehabilitate their relationship, and there's clearly hope for that. Why else would she help if she doesn't care for him?

Thanking Les for her help, he immediately begins to fill her in on his plans. Using the remaining time before Pen arrives, he outlines his ideas for a diversion to help buy him the time he needs. Though he doesn't tell her about it, at one point during his planning, he had conceived a way to fit her into the scheme. Having discarded it, he now considers resurrecting the concept, but before he can say anything, she interrupts, beating him to the punch.

"I've got an idea," she almost shouts. "Those guys looking for you, they know you left The End Zone with me. So, I'm thinking maybe it makes sense for me to go with your friend on his trip. I forget his name. Sorry."

Les pauses, feeling slightly confused. TD's face shows a faint smile, but there's no other sign that he agrees with her idea. Maybe he doesn't understand. Trying to clarify, she says, "I just think that if you want them to follow someone they believe is TD Adkins, it might help the illusion if I'm by his side."

After another pause, and still no reaction, she mumbles, "I don't know. Sorry. I guess it's a bad idea."

TD is thrilled, but not because Les wants to go with Pen. It's because almost magically she's herself again. Standing in front of him is the bright, thoughtful, earnest young woman he finds so endearing. For the first time since yesterday, she's animated and engaged, no longer in glum denial of the situation.

Clearly smiling now, he says, "Why don't we talk it over with Pen when he arrives? He just texted to say he'll be here in two minutes."

Pen agrees enthusiastically with the idea of Les joining him on his trip to the Jersey shore. Besides the potential to enhance the illusion, he believes there's another reason the idea makes sense. Looking at Les, he says, "Even if it does nothing to help, at least it'll put some distance between you and the real TD, just in case our diversion fails."

TD has been waffling on the topic, but finally takes a position. "To me, the safest option is getting Les into hiding somewhere with her mother. And as for your point, Pen, if the diversion is successful, and Les is with you, it's possible that could actually put her at greater risk. And I won't be there to help."

As the ongoing discussion over her safety begins to waste valuable time, it ends up being Les who calls a halt to the debate. "We need to stop going around and around on this. I'm going along with Pen. That's my decision."

When no one says anything to the contrary, Pen breaks the tension of the moment by showing off his new counterfeit Virginia Driver's License. It bears his picture, but TD's name and address. Inspecting it closely alongside his own, TD can see that it's a top-quality fake. He's sure no one will give it a second look.

He then leads them through a final review of the diversion plan. Pen will make an overnight trip to Atlantic City, posing as TD, with Les by his side. As they travel the two hundred miles by car, they'll light their path to the coast leaving digital footprints. From there, they'll extend the illusory trail to New York, and ultimately JFK International Airport, even as Pen and Les double back to DC.

As they prepare to leave, TD empties his wallet of every credit card he has, giving them all to Pen. He then hands over his original cellphone. "I'm pretty sure they're tracking this phone, so use it frequently. But only make calls to Phil or The End Zone, and of course the travel reservations, but nobody else. As for the credit cards, put them in play. You know how to do this, Pen. Every digital breadcrumb you leave along your path will just add more texture to the illusion that I'm on the move."

The last items he hands Pen are several straps of cash totaling $25,000 and a player rewards card for the casino hotel where he has already made a reservation. Pen tries to stifle his smile, seeing the expression on TD's face.

Before Pen can crack a joke, TD says, "Try not to lose it all too fast. As for the player's card, I had to get one when I entered a poker tourney there a few years back. So you can wipe that smirk off your face. Besides, if you're going to pretend to be a high roller, then I might as well earn some comp dollars."

Not knowing how to react to his last comments, Pen and Les stay silent. Then all three start to laugh when TD flashes a big smile.

"Seriously, use the comp card," he says. "Who knows, it might help with the ruse. Whatever you do, create the illusion that I'm up there having a grand time with my newfound cash. Play the five-dollar slots, buy tickets for a show, whatever, just have some fun. Then get the hell out of there."

♠

With Pen and Les on the road, TD tries connecting with Phil. It's early, but to his surprise, his friend answers on the second ring. Sounding clear-headed and relatively upbeat, he tells TD that they've just finished packing the car. Though Anne has yet to settle on their destination, he's sure it will be somewhere on the other side of the Chesapeake Bay Bridge. Phil adds, "She's in charge, and I've gotta tell you, I'm not getting much sympathy here."

Getting down to business, TD shares his theory about being tracked by his cell phone traffic. He also believes that it was Phil who they followed to The End Zone. He adds, "Be sure to pay attention today, they may still be on your tail. But even if you're followed, don't worry. I seriously doubt they'll bother you and risk exposure, at least as long as I'm not around."

After telling Phil a little more about the diversion, TD asks him if he can search for other possible connections between the two firms that insured the cars. "There's just has to be a link. If I can prove it, it should make things a lot easier for me."

"No problem. With the meds I'm on, Anne is going to be doing all of the driving anyway. I should have plenty of time during the trip to look into it online."

Even after they're on the road, Phil notices Anne continues to wear an expression he believes is intentional, and one that clearly conveys her annoyance with him. Understanding that she's still upset, he decides to makes another go at explaining what happened, while also sprinkling in a few more apologies. Despite his intentions, she isn't interested in hearing what he has to say.

Jumping in before he gets far at all, she declares, "I get it. TD is more than just a friend to you; he's like a brother. And I know that asking you not to help him would be fruitless. I just can't handle seeing you hurt again."

After a short pause, along with a brief look over at him, Anne says, "I'm actually happy we're heading out of town, Phil, but this had better not last much longer. Friend or not, TD needs to end this so we can feel safe again."

Staring out the side window, Phil is smart enough to say nothing more than, "I agree."

As they ride along listening to a cycle of news, traffic, and weather on the radio, Phil waits before taking out his tablet computer. When he finally does, he first volunteers to run a search for possible destinations and lodgings. Only after they settle on a spot and he books a reservation, does he access his company's system.

Once he's logged in, he heads for the customer and billing data repository. His plan is to start his research for TD by following the money. Along with pulling up all of the associated customer information, his first queries will provide the billing and payment history for the various policies and each associated invoice.

⋏

Over the next several hours, Pen and Les begin their masquerade. With Pen behind the wheel, Les makes frequent calls using TD's cellphone. At a highway rest stop in Delaware, they use two of his credit cards to purchase

gas and some snacks. Back on the road, Les works her way through a cho-
reographed sequence of calls from a list TD had drawn up. The script includes calls to a travel agency, several airlines, and occasionally to Phil, who
is intentionally letting the calls from TD's old phone roll over to voice mail.
On one call, Les puts Pen on the phone with one of the airlines. Using TD's
credit card, he books a one-way flight from New York to Los Angeles, for
departure in three days.

Next, Les calls a few hotels adjacent to JFK airport, eventually booking a guaranteed room for two nights, starting the next day. TD was
quite enthusiastic about this part of the diversion. He called it laying out
'a future trail'. Even if they aren't tracking his credit cards, he's leaving a
record of phone calls. Any decent investigator should be able to interpret
that he's on the move, heading to New York, and then on to somewhere
else. Catching enthusiasm for the game, Les adds some polish of her
own, booking two nights at a hotel in Los Angeles to coincide with TD's
phantom arrival there.

In between their diversionary maneuvers, Pen and Les talk about
TD. She can tell from the stories, that in his own way, Pen is as fond of
him as she had been. Despite understanding that, she's still not thrilled
with his unadulterated enthusiasm for helping TD now. It's obvious he
doesn't get how stupidly TD has behaved. Maybe it's a man thing. And it's
not that she now hates TD; it's just that she has become extremely disil-
lusioned. Besides, Pen is involved in all of this by choice. He wasn't suddenly thrown into a chase, fleeing in fear of his life with no knowledge
of what's going on.

It does help though, for her to hear Pen echo many of the same opin-
ions of TD that she has held for some time. When she asks which of his
qualities Pen most admires, she finds his answer reassuring.

"It's not just that he's intelligent," he says. "There are plenty of smart
people in the world. But TD's also thoughtful, and he has great insights.
Some of the stuff he comes up with is simply amazing."

Les watches as Pen gazes down the road. She can tell he has more to
say and waits for him to go on. Pen is about the same age as she is, but she

can tell he thinks of TD in a fatherly way, just as she has at times. When he starts in on another story, Les carefully places her questions, hoping to learn things that have only been hinted at.

For example, Les is aware that TD is a widower, but knows nothing more about it. When Pen mentions having helped TD follow-up on some issues connected with his wife's death, she asks to hear the full story. Overcoming Pen's reluctance, she finally convinces him to relate a condensed version of the events.

Saddened deeply by what she hears, at least it helps her understand why TD would avoid sharing any details. The story also triggers thoughts about the plan she had been preparing to hatch on him. In a way, what she has learned only reaffirms her original thinking about the now abandoned idea.

After a break in the storytelling and a few more calls, Les asks, "What do you think about this mess TD is in? You don't think there's any way he was part of the killing, do you?"

"I've only known TD for a few years," he tells her. "But never for a minute have I felt he could be involved in anything like that shootout. I believe him. I think he stumbled onto this and acted impulsively. He definitely took something that didn't belong to him, and that turned out to be major league stupid, but I'd bet any amount he never planned a single bit of it."

With a more reflective tone, he continues. "The funny thing is I don't think he completely regrets it. Sure, he's torn up about Phil getting hurt, and I know he deeply regrets the impact this has had on you and your mother. But I have to tell you, he's more alive than I've seen him since his wife's death. And it's more than the excitement of the money, or being chased. Something has awakened inside him, for better or worse."

Understanding his last words might sound less than comforting, Pen tries to reassure her. "I do know this. In the end, TD will do the right thing, whatever that may be. And of course, he's very fond of you. He thinks the world of you. I'm sure he would never intentionally put you in danger."

Les can feel a swirl of emotions rising from Pen's speech. His unsolicited comments about TD's affection for her are flattering, but at the same time a little embarrassing. What is important is that Pen so admires TD and believes in his innocence regarding the shootings. That's critically important to her. But despite feeling better about certain aspects of what's happening, the fact remains that TD is on the run, and somehow, horribly, she and her mother are involved. At some point, when this is all over, and hopefully they're safe, she'll work on forgiveness. Until then, she'll reserve any further judgment on TD's fine character.

Refocusing on the script he prepared, she reminds Pen to tell her when they make their final turn east, towards Atlantic City. At that point, she'll turn off TD's phone. They want their trackers to follow them north, first to the shore, and then on to New York; but they'd also like to keep their head start, and continue with the diversion before their pursuit is upon them.

⋏

During a brief status call, Dan Keach and Jonathan Stark both acknowledge how difficult their task of finding TD Adkins is becoming. They remain confident they'll eventually track him down, though the challenge of accomplishing that quickly enough to save The Group from even greater pain is growing larger.

Keach knows he can't allow anyone to rip them off like this without a response, but he'll soon have to make a decision whether to continue searching for Adkins with such intensity and manpower. It's going to reach a point where it would no longer make financial sense unless they recover all of the money, and with each passing day that grows increasingly unlikely. At a certain point, they'll have to cut this way back, maybe even down to just one man searching for him.

Still, he's not ready to give up, and when he gives the go ahead to stay at it for another day, Stark responds positively. "If you ask me, I think soon he's going to make another mistake, and when he does, we'll get him and the money. We can also deliver the retribution he deserves."

Stark then reminds Keach that in the next hour or so he'll be sending over the background file his firm has produced on Adkins. It contains all of the publicly available information on the man, and some not so public. It should help them generate some fresh leads. The file also includes Adkins's credit card numbers, but Stark points out that getting real-time access to his recent activity is both problematic and costly.

Dan decides they'll hold off on tracking the credit cards for now, but raises one last topic before ending the call. "I'd really like the noise level on this to taper off," he complains. "We can't control the media, but they'll soon move on to another story. The problem is this motel clerk in the hospital, Bobby Tomlin. He needs to pipe down and stop giving interviews. And I'd still like to know for sure if he's involved in any way. While we have nothing going on with Adkins, I'd like you to put one of your guys on Tomlin. Find out what he knows and provide him with a little incentive to clam up."

After talking with Stark, Keach calls Richter, telling him he wants an update every two hours on the cell phone activity for both Adkins and Madrigal. Richter is upset with himself for answering the call. When he begins to protest the overuse of his phone company contact, Keach cuts him off.

"Look, this is only for another day or so at the most. Figure out a way to take care of your contact and learn to roll with things, Richter. And while you're at it, why don't you stop the constant whining."

⟡

While crossing one of the long causeways linking the mainland to Atlantic City, Les turns on TD's phone. She quickly fires off a call to The End Zone and another to Phil's voice mail. She'll repeat these same calls a little later, but turns the phone off again for now.

Pen explains that the illusion they hope to create has TD staying at one of the casino hotels located by the marina. But before they check-in there, they'll first get two rooms at one of the older, cheaper hotels, a block off the boardwalk, and a little more than a mile from the marina. Paying for those rooms with cash, they'll return there to spend the night instead of staying where TD made his reservation. The extra rooms will add a layer of personal security for Pen and Les. It should allow them to sleep safely, particularly in case their diversion works so well that the pursuit shows up by tonight. In the morning, they'll make their final moves before driving back to the DC area.

Using one of the public lots near the beach to park, they walk another block away from the ocean before getting two rooms at The Sea Breeze Hotel. Blocked by larger buildings on three of its sides, guests at the aging turquoise building have no view of the water, and almost never catch very much of the ocean air its name suggests.

Instead of driving from there to the Marina Club Hotel and Casino, TD's plan now calls for them to take one of the public jitneys. Similar to airport rental-car shuttles, the jitneys serve a circuit of stops along the long boardwalk and over to the marina. Though slow, the shuttle provides them an unobtrusive way for getting around Atlantic City.

While they're waiting at the jitney stop, a block off the boardwalk, Pen notices Les looking around and acting jumpy. Before he can ask what's bothering her, she speaks.

"Is there a beach at the marina? Or a boardwalk?"

Pen shakes his head, "Sorry. It's just a cluster of hotels around an inlet that hosts several marinas."

Les looks disappointed. "I need some time to think, Pen. I want to look at the ocean and take a walk on the boardwalk. Alone. I promise not to run off. Do we have time? Can we meet back here in a little while?"

Les has taken on a discouraged look and Pen knows they're ahead of schedule. Weighing and rejecting the risk of her running off, he agrees to her request. They'll meet back here in exactly an hour and then make their way to the Marina Club.

⚓

Taking only a few breaks, Phil had worked most the morning examining the insurance company's records as Anne drove them east. Slowly working his way through the data, he felt a rising sense of excitement over what he was learning. When he finally completed a review of the payment histories, he thumped the dashboard with his hand, at the same time nearly shouting, "I've got you!" Even Anne cracked a smile at his enthusiasm.

Phil had known there was some type of connection between the two firms all along; he had just never gotten around to telling TD. It was all related to the Cadillac owned by Wilkins Investment Group. Of course, he couldn't prove it, but that shouldn't stop him from telling TD what he knew, he just never had the chance yesterday at the bar before the fighting broke out. And it had slipped his mind again this morning when they talked earlier, no doubt due to the painkillers he was taking.

When he had first seen the printout back at his office, he quickly remembered when the Cadillac had been added to Wilkins's business policy. It was over a year ago, and up until that time, the policy had never covered more than two cars, one each for Richard Wilkins and Robert Owen. When they wanted to add a third vehicle, Robert Owen had called Phil directly to make the change to the policy. That had never happened before either. All prior changes had been handled by one of Owen's assistants and rarely involved Phil at all. He also remembers Owen listing himself as the only driver of the new car.

It had been many years since Phil sold Wilkins their initial policy. He had closed the deal with Robert Owen directly. That was probably the last time they had talked prior to Owen calling to add the Cadillac. Phil had expressed surprise that the company needed to insure so few vehicles, but Owen had explained that they leased the remainder of their fleet from a small firm specializing in the industry. That company also handled the insurance for those vehicles, which he described to Phil as being predominately heavy trucks and construction equipment.

Thinking back on those conversations had triggered another memory, this one related to his acquisition of CCVS as a client. These days, he successfully sells a wide range of commercial insurance products, but early in his career, most of his earnings came from selling business auto insurance. What he now remembers is that he had never personally called or contacted CCVS to make a sale. They brought their business to him unsolicited, telling Phil he had been highly recommended. He's sure he wrote it down at the time, but right now, without seeing his old files, he can't remember who had made the referral. Even without his notes, he's willing to bet it was Robert Owen.

Regardless of his suspicions, his research had initially yielded nothing to prove any type of connection between the two firms other than his recollections. Still, as he pored over the billing records, there had been bits of information here and there that stood out. Whenever he encountered one of the odd pieces, he'd leave the trail he was on to follow where it may lead.

It was while he was working his way through the leasing firm's payment history that things began to look strange. In the early years of the policy, the company had frequently changed their method of payment, something that's quite unusual. Once a company establishes a source of remittance, they seldom change it, and certainly not as many times as CCVS had. Over the years, they had rotated through a variety of payment sources, paying their premiums using several different credit cards. When they had paid by check, they were drawn against a number of bank accounts.

Surprisingly, he also found multiple sources of payment when he reviewed Wilkins's history. Not nearly as many as with CCVS, but during one calendar year they had used three different bank accounts to pay consecutive quarterly invoices, something Phil doubted he could replicate if he looked at the records of any other company he worked with. Clearly, both of these firms were playing games with their accounting and cash management practices.

He finally found exactly what he's looking for within the tangle of payments. It hadn't been easy, but it was there. After listing and comparing each of the bank and credit card account numbers the two firms had used, he found two matches. They occurred several years ago right after the recession hit bottom, and coincident with a flurry of switched payment methods at the leasing firm. CCVS had twice paid an invoice with a business credit card also used by Wilkins Investment Group.

After first confirming that he hadn't made an error copying the information, Phil considered its importance. No matter what scenario he envisioned, he was unable to come up with a single logical rationale for two supposedly unrelated companies to share a credit card account. It would only make sense if they were directly connected. He had his link. Now he needs to contact TD.

When they pulled off at the next highway rest stop, the car had barely come to a halt before Phil was running to the pay phone to call his friend.

"I knew there was connection," TD tells him when he hears the news. "Now I just have to figure out how to use it to my advantage. I'll let you know if I need anything else, but I think I'm good for now. Thanks, man. I hope you feel better soon. Enjoy the weekend, and don't forget to send me the bill."

After sharing a laugh, Phil can't let his friend go without one last question. With a far more serious tone, he asks, "Are you sure you know what you're doing, TD?"

"Hell no," TD replies heartily. "I'm making it all up on the fly. But don't worry, I'll figure it out. This is definitely the most fun I've had in years, if the stress doesn't kill me."

⋏

Les uses one of the long access ramps leading up from the street to reach the boardwalk and her first clear view of the Atlantic. As she moves down the promenade, she passes the old Steel Pier jutting out from the boardwalk. Facing the ocean, long rows of shops offering tacky tee shirts, cheap souvenirs, and French Fries seasoned with Old Bay line the nearly four-miles of wooden planks. One grand old shop claims to have sold saltwater taffy at the same location for over eighty years.

But Les hasn't come to the boardwalk to sightsee. She's here to gaze at the ocean while she tries to organize her thoughts, and ultimately to consider her ongoing participation in TD's schemes. Passing up an empty bench, she climbs up on the boardwalk railing until she's balanced on the top rung. Perched facing the sea, for a while she's content to watch the light surf roll up and back across the thin strip of sand.

Throughout the morning, it has become increasingly difficult for her to stay calm and continue to suppress the level of fear she's experiencing.

Everything about her situation tells her to run and get away. It may even have been a mistake coming here with Pen. TD was probably right; if they're being closely followed, she may be no safer here than back with him. She also can't stop worrying about her mother. Feeling her thoughts starting to race out of control, she steadies herself by watching the small groups of beachgoers enjoying the sun and light breeze along the shore.

Listening to Pen talk about TD on the drive here was both fascinating and confusing for her. In different ways, each of his stories illustrated his admiration for the man. But Pen's enduring respect also puzzles her. Even if he's sure TD wasn't directly involved, it doesn't change what happened Monday night. Men were gunned down fighting over money. Innocent bystanders were killed or injured and lives were ruined.

In Les's mind, it has to be wrong to be associated with any of that, in any manner. And yet, Pen and her are both involved in the aftermath, putting themselves at risk to help a man who took something that wasn't his. And his actions since then have resulted in additional violence and injuries, putting more innocents in harm's way.

At one point, just before their arrival in Atlantic City, Les had articulated her confusion. She asked Pen how he reconciled his admiration for TD with this man now on the run with someone else's money, leaving a trail of havoc in his wake.

Pen nodded at her question, smiling faintly, but he didn't answer her right away. It wasn't until they had passed through the last tollbooth, once again paying with TD's credit card, before he finally responded.

"TD's a good man," he said. "He's a kind, intelligent man. He's also a friend who has helped me in the past, and right now, he needs my help. You know, he had a really tough break a couple of years ago. And he'll admit that he didn't handle it as well as he might have. But he has been getting better. And it's like I said; he made a mistake doing what he did Monday night. Maybe it was some kind of delayed reaction to what he had let his life become. Regardless, it's done, and he can't erase what happened. If we choose to help him, we have to accept the situation as it is."

After a brief pause, he added, "I know one thing for sure. He definitely made it worse by hanging around DC. In my opinion, that was his biggest mistake."

Les had already learned TD's reason for staying in the area and now Pen had referred to it as well. Unable to resist, she wanted to know if his thinking matched what TD had told her. Looking away, almost as if she didn't want to hear his answer, she asked, "Why do you think he stayed around?"

Pen began to laugh, but quickly stifled it. He then stared over at her briefly, his expression a bit sad. Turning his eyes back to the road, he spoke. "Well, even though I haven't known you too long, I'm guessing you're smart enough to know the answer to that question."

There had also been some surprising information gleaned from their conversations. It was clear Pen viewed TD as some kind of legendary fraud investigator. Evidently, he used to be a real all-star in the insurance industry, but she had never heard a single word about anything like that. When she asked about it, and why he no longer did it, Pen shared the few things he knew about how TD's career had ended. It was all bundled together with his wife's sudden death and the way his company had handled paying a life insurance benefit. He believed it was TD's choice to quit, and it hadn't been pretty at the end.

Now, sitting here at the beach and having gone over it all again, Les finds she has become more sad than angry; sad she and her mother have become entangled in this mess and sad for TD. Maybe Pen's right. Maybe TD's actions this week are partially some response to the difficult times he has gone through the past few years. One of Pen's offhand remarks still echoes in her mind. He said, "If anyone can figure his way out of this, I believe TD can. Hopefully it can be a catalyst for getting on with his life. He definitely needs to find some happiness again."

Les liked that part. She cares for TD, and it would greatly please her to see him truly happy. She had been laying her own plans for something she thought could result in exactly that. Unfortunately, the ugly genesis of what is happening now, as well as the question of her ongoing involvement continues to weigh heavily on her.

Checking her watch, she sees it's time to rendezvous with Pen. Her time alone at the boardwalk has definitely been helpful. She may not be happy about things, but she's a little less conflicted. Going forward, her priority will be protecting herself and her mother. As far as helping TD, she'll have to revisit that on a day-to-day basis.

As she leaves the boardwalk, she can see Pen is already waiting for her. When she finally reaches him, he smiles and says, "Well, at least it's a nice day. Did you figure out what you needed to?"

"Not completely," she tells him. "But I'm here and still willing to help."

Robert Owen's sense of entitlement, combined with sloppiness on his part, is the reason Eddie's King's car is covered by the company's insurance policy. For years, the firm has financed a luxury sedan for him, but he craved more. In addition to his Lexus, he wanted a second, sportier ride. Choosing almost every available option, he custom ordered the Cadillac CTS-V Coupe, along with its 556- horsepower V-8 and $80,000 price tag.

Richard Wilkins vetoed the extravagance the moment he saw it, but it was already too late. If they tried to sell it right away, they'd take a huge loss on the purchase. Determined not to let Owen have the car, he finally decided to award it as bonus to a top employee. Dan Keach suggested Eddie King, touting the great work he was doing with the consolidations. When they gave the car to Eddie, Owen was supposed to have the ownership and insurance transferred to CCVS. Feeling deprived, and petulant over how the matter had been handled, Owen never completed the tasks.

Dan Keach knows nothing of Owen's omission, but he's currently thrilled, having learned of someone else's sloppiness. Over the course of the morning, Jim Richter had called with multiple updates on Adkins's cell phone usage. It's a huge break. The man has made the mistake that both he and Jon Stark had hoped for and anticipated.

Not only is Adkins using his phone again, he's on the move. Based on the location of his calls, it appears he drove to Atlantic City this morning. Besides continuing to communicate with Madrigal, he also called several airlines, and a number of hotels in New York and Los Angeles. Keach marvels at the man's stupidity. Without him continuing to use his phone, and using it to make his travel plans, they'd have no idea where he currently was, or where he planned to go.

After he shared the news with Jon Stark, Keach reminded himself to keep things in perspective. Though he's happy to have a fix on Adkins's location again, there's much to be done before they have their hands on him and the money.

There's also an aspect of the news that gives him great concern; the possibility that Adkins has gone to Atlantic City to gamble with their cash. As he considers that prospect, Keach becomes angry, visualizing Adkins wagering huge stacks of chips at the blackjack and roulette tables. Making a promise to himself, he swears that if he finds out the man has lost one penny of their money gambling, he'll personally deliver the retribution, whenever the chance for that ultimately comes.

TD has spent most of the day mapping out potential next steps and taking them to their logical conclusion. The largest portion of his work went towards fleshing out two different relocation scenarios to a considerable level of detail. Having completed that task, he feels more confident that he can not only effectively disappear, but also do so without living with the constant fear of being unmasked.

Despite the forward progress, a huge problem lingers unsolved: ensuring the safety of those directly affected by his actions. Phil and Anne are both exposed to ongoing danger, and the situation with Les and her mother is problematic as well. Despite spending no small amount of time circling the issue of their security, he has yet to envision a viable solution.

Late this morning, he met face-to-face with Denny Holmes for the first time in years. When TD called to set up the meeting, Denny was preparing to do some sailing. To avoid ruining his plans, they agreed to meet at the marina of the gleaming new National Harbor complex. Rising above the Maryland shore of the Potomac, it sits just downriver from DC and Alexandria. It would be a short drive for TD and Denny could come by boat.

The main reason for the meeting was to give Denny one of the clean cellphones. He had also been considering stowing the bags of cash with him for safekeeping. TD was rapidly tiring of constantly choosing between leaving the money somewhere unprotected, or keeping it in the car where it was also left unattended at times. Before he reached the marina, he had decided it was a lame idea. Though Denny is quite likable, and TD knows that he feels indebted to him, he isn't willing to trust their limited relationship with a million dollars.

Denny was in a typically sunny mood when they met, ready to help in any way he could. Along with taking the phone, he agreed to confirm Laura's safety a couple of times a day and keep TD informed.

As the brief meeting ended, TD said, "Thanks again for your help, Denny. I hope it wasn't too difficult for you getting here. This was really convenient for me"

"No problem, it was real easy," Denny replied, "It's not that far at all from where I live, and it actually takes about the same time whether you go by car or boat. If not for this inlet here at the marina, you'd be able to see well downriver, past Ferry Landing Point and even to Mount Vernon."

For the second day in a row, Stark's most lethal operative enters a hospital with a job to do. Using a public restroom on the same floor as Bobby Tomlin, Samuel removes the athletic warm-ups he was wearing, leaving him again dressed in surgeon's garb. Checking his image in the mirror, he carefully tucks his blonde hair under a light-blue paper cap. He then dons a surgical mask, adjusting it to hang loosely near his chin, obscuring a small part of his face.

Once he leaves the restroom, he moves quickly down the hall and into Bobby's room. As Bobby looks up, Samuel speaks clearly, but quickly.

"How are you feeling?" he asks, as he moves toward the bed. "Are you having any chest pains? A closer look at your x-rays indicates you have a broken rib near your left lung."

Bobby begins sitting up slowly. He doesn't remember this doctor, but so many have been by. Along with the nurses, it's been a non-stop parade of caregivers dealing with his concussion, the multiple fractures, and preparing him for surgery on both legs. There's no reason in the world to be alarmed by a new face.

Unwinding a stethoscope from around his neck, Samuel leans in saying, "Here, let me listen to your breathing."

Bobby is sitting up completely now. As the doctor holds the cold instrument below one shoulder blade, he asks him to take a deep breath and then slowly let it out. As he exhales, Bobby suddenly feels uncomfortable; the doctor has moved his face to within inches of his ear.

"If you lie to me, I will kill you," Samuel hisses. "Do you understand? Now, tell me. What was your role in the hit at the motel Monday night?"

Sensing he should just keep staring forward, Bobby shakes his head ever so slightly and whispers, "Nothing. No way. I knew nothing about it."

Samuel can sense Bobby's mortal fear; and it's just that, nothing more. The trembling young man is scared for his life, but he's not lying.

"You need to stop talking with everyone about what happened," Samuel continues whispering. "You need to forget that you ever met Eddie King. And you need to shut up. Do you understand? From now on, you just tell people your memory is hazy. If you don't, it'll be a huge mistake for you and your family."

The last threat is more than Bobby can take. Still shaking, he turns to get a good look at the man. Instead, he's violently shoved forward, bent over in half at the waist. Before he can sit back up, the man has spun away. With two strides, he's out of the room.

Bobby is disappointed; he never got a decent look at the man's face. If he were asked for a description, he'd be unable to give one. He had quickly understood what was happening. He was even planning to keep his mouth shut. That was until the guy threatened him and his family. Lying back on his bed in pain, he thinks about calling the nurse, but hesitates. Then he remembers the business card Detective Roberts gave him. The detective had been so polite; maybe he should let him know what has happened.

After considering it for a few minutes, he picks up the bedside phone. Bobby had held no grudge about anything that occurred Monday night. He even felt a little guilty about his own small role helping Eddie. But now he's furious. That guy should have never threatened his family.

♠

Pen and Les are relatively relaxed knowing they have some time before any pursuit would arrive if they were being followed. When they reach the Marina Club Hotel's front desk, Pen presents his fake ID along with TD's credit card. After checking in, they forego a trip to the room and immediately begin gambling. Moving around the casino, they spend brief stints at various table games and high dollar slot machines. Pen does the gambling whenever they play, always making sure he presents TD's casino comp card.

TD had reminded them that surveillance cameras would be recording their every move on the floor of the casino as well as the public areas of the hotel. They would also be tracked by the casino's computers, which monitor all transactions involving a guest's casino card, credit card, and room key. Their objective is to portray themselves as a young couple enjoying some gambling and entertainment. Pen is wearing a cheap fedora and a loud beach shirt he had purchased on the boardwalk while waiting for Les. The outfit is not really a disguise, but it serves a small purpose that might help later.

Initially, Pen found it stressful placing the large bets TD had prescribed. He was particularly nervous playing blackjack at two- to three-hundred dollars a hand before he eventually relaxed enough to enjoy it. Surprisingly, he was winning. They soon gave back all of the profits at a five-dollar slot machine. Playing multiple combinations, at twenty-five dollars per spin, they had lost over five hundred dollars before hitting a small jackpot. When they finally cashed in their remaining chips and slot machine receipts, they were surprised to find themselves over a thousand dollars in the black.

After the flurry of gambling sessions, they eat an early dinner at one of the hotel's celebrity chef restaurants, charging the meal to their room. In total, they spend several hours at the Marina Club before departing via the main entrance, where they grab a taxi. Their ride is less than a half a mile, taking them to another of the hotels at the marina and frustrating the cab driver with both the short distance, as well as Pen's insistence on paying the small fare with TD's credit card.

Once inside, they proceed directly to the hotel's box office, where Pen purchases tickets for that night's show at the comedy club. After a slow stroll through the casino, and a little more gambling, he leads them off the casino floor in the direction of the hotel's luxury shopping arcade.

Instead of entering any of the shops, they execute a pre-arranged maneuver. Now walking briskly, they pull a U-turn and separately enter the restrooms they had just passed. Waiting just inside, they each count to ten and then re-emerge, this time moving away from the shops. As Pen had explained earlier, an effectively executed stop-and-go maneuver can be an excellent way to spot a tail, though not foolproof. When he's positive that no one has reacted to their moves, they again change course, heading for the exit closest to the jitney stop.

Forty minutes later, they're back at the Sea Breeze where they started their day in Atlantic City. At the door to their rooms, Pen says goodnight, reminding Les to stay in her room, as well as the time of their early start the next morning.

Though she is finished with her role, Pen is heading back out immediately. As agreed by all, only he will be involved with the next, far riskier activities.

⟁

Jon Stark was pleased to hear Adkins was using his phone again, but he had expressed several concerns when he initially received the news from Dan Keach. With both Adkins and Madrigal on the move and communicating again, they needed to consider whether to resume the tail on Madrigal.

Stark believed it would only make sense if they thought the two men were attempting to hook up again.

A brief discussion led to them agreeing that the odds of a second rendezvous were fairly low. It appears Madrigal is travelling south on the eastern shore of Maryland, and is hardly any closer to Adkins now than if he had never left the area. And the call data suggests Adkins will be leaving Atlantic City tomorrow, apparently heading to New York and possibly on to Los Angeles.

Stark's primary concern was the overall trustworthiness of the new leads. As clear as Adkins's plans may seem, they remain hypothetical, based only on a series of phone calls. The only thing they can be sure of is that the calls were made from Adkins's cellphone, which has traveled to Atlantic City. There's no proof the man is physically with his phone and anyone could be making the calls. Stark had not implied that they should ignore the information; he just wanted his client to understand the possibilities.

After acknowledging his concerns, Keach told Stark that he was giving Adkins too much credit. He also reminded him that it was the same call data analysis that had led them to the man the first time. It was his opinion that the calls are a solid lead, and with nothing else to go on, it's the lead he wants Stark to run down.

The credibility of the new information had continued to bother Stark well after he finished his call with Keach. He doesn't mind catching a break, but this one feels just a bit too fortuitous. Adkins's phone had been silent for an extended period before lighting up like a Christmas tree. Why? Was the battery dead and he had finally recharged it? Had he figured out the phone was being used to track him and had turned it off, only to later decide he could risk making calls again? Stark had learned yesterday that Adkins had been a top-flight insurance fraud investigator, and not too long ago. Any competent investigator would know that using your cell phone announces your location to the world.

In addition to his misgivings, he needs to deploy his limited resources wisely. He had hesitated for the better part of an hour before finally dispatching two men to Atlantic City. He sent Drew Waters along with a less experienced operative. Stark hopes his indecision doesn't end up burning him. Waters hadn't gotten underway until after two PM, and it will probably take him close to four hours to get there in the late afternoon traffic.

At least when they arrive, he may have some fresh information for them. He had just called an old friend, also ex-military, and now the chief of security at one of the Atlantic City casinos. Even though Adkins doesn't have a reservation at his hotel, it didn't mean he couldn't help. The Atlantic City security establishment works closely together and Stark's friend promised to make a few calls. If Adkins has a reservation, or has registered at one of the casino hotels, they may soon know exactly where he's staying.

⚔

With the underlying stress continuing to take its toll, TD is already feeling fatigued and it's not even that late. He has talked with Pen several times, confirming that the diversion was going as planned. He also spoke with Les once, though they talked for less than a minute. For now, he has no idea whether the effort put into the diversion will bear fruit. At least it has given him the day to focus on research and planning. Understanding who is after him is critical to engineering his escape from their pursuit.

TD is worried that the work he and Phil have completed today will be wasted if the conclusion he has reached is wrong. If that's the case, then he still doesn't know his enemy, and finding a path forward will continue to be highly problematic. In fact, his situation will have grown worse, with him still lingering in the area and nobody really any safer. His intuition tells him he's right, but he has only limited proof, and his instincts have been alarmingly inaccurate the past few days.

As he researched Wilkins Investment Group, TD had looked for things that stood out from the norm. There wasn't much. At first glance, the company seemed just like one of the many large development firms in the region. But it was that fact itself that he found interesting. The firm's founder, Richard's father, had passed on a solid record of accomplishment and growth. With such a legacy, the company should now be bigger, stronger, and better positioned then it is, with a far better track record than it has recently demonstrated.

One likely cause of such a result is that the son lacks his father's skill for running and growing the company. It happens more often than not with second-generation family businesses. But when he also considered the evidence linking the firm to what he observed Monday, TD soon realized there's another possibility; one with a different take on Richard Wilkins's business acumen. Maybe it isn't his goal to grow the firm. Maybe the company's primary purpose these days is to act as a front for the illegal activities, and the vehicle for processing the cash being generated.

By early evening, he had decided it was quite probable that a corrupted Wilkins Investment Group is behind it all. Thanks to Phil, he can link the company to every vehicle involved in the operations at the motel. He also knows that what he witnessed Monday wasn't something new, or a one-time event; it was a practiced routine. He can only guess at the frequency, but even if it occurs just every month or so, then huge sums of money are being generated on an annual basis.

Confident with his analysis, TD knows he must test his theory. He needs to design an effective probe, something that will trigger a response and leave no doubt. Only then can he be sure he has locked down whom he's dealing with and begin to act upon that knowledge.

Jon Stark was thrilled with the response he received when the hotel security chief finally got back with him. Adkins has checked in at the Marina Club Hotel and also purchased show tickets at the hotel next door. A guy named Dave Bonner is the number two man on the security team at the Marina Club, and Stark is told he'd be happy to take his call.

The information he receives when he connects with Bonner is rich with details. Adkins had checked in earlier that day, paying with his credit card and presenting a Virginia driver's license. Utilizing the hotel's surveillance system, and aided by the fact that Adkins had used a casino rewards card, Bonner was able to tell Stark even more.

Accompanied by a young woman, Adkins had spent a couple of hours gambling. They weren't throwing money to the wind, but they had played at a level considerably above that of the average customer. They then ate an early dinner at one of the hotel's better restaurants, before leaving the property by taxi.

After the call with Bonner, Stark still feels something isn't right; it all seems a little too easy. And why is Adkins making no effort to hide his identity? Regardless of his behavior, disputing the fact that they've found their man again makes little sense. Bonner's description of Adkins's companion matched perfectly with the young woman he had fled the strip club with just yesterday.

Quickly calling Waters with the news, Stark marvels at Adkins's stupidity. "It's really unbelievable. You'd think that after nearly being caught at the bar yesterday he'd lay low. He must believe he shook us off and is in the clear."

As they talk strategy, Stark emphasizes the warnings he was given. "We have to be careful making any overt moves up there; Bonner was emphatic. Not only will his men not steer us directly to Adkins, but if we're going to take him, we need to grab him somewhere else. Nothing can go down at the Marina Club or any other of the big hotels in Atlantic City. Their security guys were glad to help, but it was a professional courtesy. They're not going to tolerate any rough stuff on their watch."

Armed with the update from Stark, Waters decides not to take a passive approach and simply wait for Adkins to return to his hotel. He sends his partner to wait near the theater where Adkins purchased show tickets. Maybe he can spot him leaving at the end of the performance. Meanwhile, Waters will cover the guest room elevators at the Marina Club on the theory that eventually he will return to his room.

Before taking up a post, Waters decides to alert the security staff at the Marina Club of his presence. He knows they'll quickly spot anyone lurking around looking suspicious and he wants to avoid any difficulties. When he checks in with Bonner, the man's response is rather cool, but Waters had expected nothing different.

ᛜ

When he goes back out for the evening, Pen is wearing a light colored suit with a crisp white dress shirt and tie. He had laughed when TD suggested the wardrobe change, but now it makes more sense. Hopefully, the transformation helps him appear to be a different person from the casually dressed guy wearing the hat and cheesy shirt.

He has to work quickly if he wants to be back at the theater before the show he's supposedly attending lets out. Before heading to the marina, he enters the closest boardwalk casino. Once he's atop a stool at one of the bars, he orders a drink and inserts a twenty-dollar bill into the counter-top slot machine. His actions are all part of an effort to add an additional layer to his new cover.

He's approached just moments after receiving his drink. Tall and attractive, the slim young blonde looks nothing like Les. With an eastern-European accent, she asks him if he's looking for 'some company'. Nodding yes, he offers to buy her a drink, and takes the next several minutes to explain exactly what he wants. After she agrees to his request, they're soon in a taxi on the way to the marina.

Dressed sharply, with a working girl on his arm, Pen blends easily into the casino nightlife. Casually moving though the gaming area, he finally positions them at a bank of slot machines with a clear view of the theater's entrance. While the girl plays the slots, Pen furtively checks the area around him. It doesn't take him long to spot the man Waters sent to look for TD. He's also sitting at a slot machine, two aisles over. Rarely playing the machine, his attention is almost exclusively on the theater.

The guy stops feigning any interest in gambling when the theater doors are pushed open and the show lets out. Instead, he stares intently at the faces of the emerging crowd. Drawing no notice, Pen and his date leave the area and are soon in a taxi for the short ride to the Marina Club. His 'disguise' really needs to hold up now. Though he's no longer carrying the fake ID, or pretending to be TD, he's still nervous about being back at the scene of his masquerade of just a few hours earlier.

Just as they had done at the previous casino, they take seats in front of a bank of slot machines. This time, his view is of the gaming area and atrium fronting the guest room elevators. Unfortunately, even after a second sweep, he has failed to identify anyone who looks suspicious. Did he guess wrongly about the man lurking near the theater? Have all his efforts failed to draw a tail?

Knowing TD believes instinct and intuition are a big part of the job, Pen checks his gut, which is telling him he's right about the guy at the theater. If that's the case, then he should soon find the same guy, or someone like him, looking for TD here at the Marina Club. The key is not being spotted first.

Keeping the girl close to his side, they change slot machines a few times. At one point, they leave the area completely, waiting ten minutes before returning. Occasionally, he cuddles with the girl, or plays a few spins himself. To further meld into the scene, he orders a round of cocktails from a passing waitress. Another ten minutes of growing doubts pass before his patience is rewarded. He spots the guy from the theater approaching the elevators, before he stops and pauses to look around.

Making another slow scan of the area, Pen finally identifies a second man. He's standing close to the end of a row of slots, along a broad aisle running through the casino. After seeing the two men make eye contact, he watches as they separately weave their way through the slot machines. They soon end up sitting one seat apart from each other, pretending to study the video poker displays in front of them.

Though tempted to leave that moment, Pen wants to see if there's any indication that they're on to him. After a brief conversation, one of them stays in place while the other moves toward the casino's main bar. Pen quickly loses sight of him, but it doesn't matter. He has learned all he really needs to know; TD's pursuers have followed him to Atlantic City.

He and the girl soon leave together by the hotel's main entrance. After a short wait at the taxi stand, he adds a generous tip to her fee as he puts her in a cab. Riding separately back to the boardwalk, he calls TD, confirming their ruse is working.

In the morning, he'll lay out one last piece of bait.

⋏

Turning out the bedside lamp in her Alexandria hotel, Laura Stevens feels a little safer than yesterday, though she remains unsettled. She had forced herself out of her hotel room for a morning walk around Old Town, but found herself feeling uncomfortable being alone outside. After picking up paperback novel from a small bookshop, she retreated to her room and spent most of the afternoon reading.

Despite her efforts to relax, she worried constantly about Les. Even though Denny checked in with her twice, assuring her that Les remained safe, she won't find any comfort until she sees her daughter again. She has also begun to wonder if they'll ever be able to return to their home without fear.

Two hundred miles away, Les is experiencing many of the same thoughts and emotions. The day's events had certainly been interesting, keeping her busy as well as enlightening her. She had learned things about TD that stayed on her mind throughout the evening. At one point, she abandoned the television show she was watching to sort through her conflicting thoughts.

The one constant throughout her day was a strong desire to return home and resume working at the club. She knows that until that happens she has little control over her life.

⋏

Stark's latest status report to Keach is a mixed bag. Obviously, the good news is that they're once again hot on Adkins trail. The bad news is that his men arrived too late to find Adkins on the casino floor. They've yet to lay eyes on him, but everything points to him still being in Atlantic City.

Currently, they have the elevators staked out at the hotel where he's staying, as well as the main entrance. The problem is the Marina Club is a large property and his men have already been on post for a long time.

When Keach urges him not to let Adkins slip through his hands a second time, Stark agrees to deploy more resources. A half hour later, he has two additional men on the road, heading for New Jersey.

⚔

As he turns in for the night, Carl Roberts thinks about the call he had received from Bobby Tomlin. When he learned the young clerk had been threatened, he offered to arrange for him to be moved to a different hospital. Bobby immediately refused and Carl decided not to press the matter. Though he has concern for the young man's safety, he's not too worried. Carl believes that if they actually intend to hurt Bobby, they would have done so when they were there earlier.

Thinking about Bobby and the case brings to mind the attractive young reporter, Preeti. He should give her a call and suggest they meet for coffee. He'd enjoy seeing her again and he can use the case as a pretext. He'd also like to convince her to turn down the publicity on an investigation that will soon lay dormant if nothing new surfaces.

Preeti has also been thinking about the case as she ends her day. Brimming with pride that another of her articles was published that morning, she reminds herself not to be overly happy. People have died, and lives and families have been ruined by the events she has been covering. And even though the story has been a nice break for her, it's now pretty much at an end. If she wants to continue making a name for herself, she'll need to find something fresh to report on.

⚔

As he succumbs to his almost total exhaustion, even the sunken motel mattress feels good to TD. For the past few days, he has sustained himself with the excitement of making a fresh start with his life. Unfortunately, most of that feeling is gone now, replaced with a growing fear that taxes him heavily.

Sure, he made some good progress today with his planning and research, and he's definitely gleaning plenty of intellectual satisfaction from this game of hide-an-seek, but how and when does it all end? Identifying his pursuers is one thing, but stopping them is an entirely different problem. How will he possibly be able to disappear while ensuring the safety of the friends he leaves behind? What happens if he grows weary of the chase before he solves that problem?

As he looks ahead to tomorrow, the first thing he must do is confirm his theory about who is pursuing him and come up with a way to turn that knowledge to his advantage. Only then can he finalize his plans. A number of loose ends are bound to remain, but it's time for him to stop hesitating. Tomorrow he must take action.

He must also deal with one chronic problem; something he alone can solve. Every night this week has ended the same. Each night he has committed himself to leaving the area the next day and kicking off his disappearing act. Sadly, the following night, he finds himself in the same place, facing the same problems.

Tonight, as he turns off the light, the only commitment he makes is to breaking that cycle.

FRIDAY

Soon after Les silenced the alarm clock on her phone, Pen called to remind her of their departure at six AM. They have one last trick to play before heading back to meet with TD.

Despite the early hour, she feels as clear minded as at any time the past two days. Maybe she benefitted from the break in all the running and scheming, or having finally slept deeply for a few hours before her alarm sounded. But neither is the true source of her newfound sense of clarity. Before going to sleep, she had come to a total change of heart about helping TD.

No longer would she be a reluctant and terrified participant in whatever TD is trying to achieve. It's time for her to get out. It had taken her a couple of hours to reach that conclusion, but now that's she's slept on it, she feels even better about her decision. Even if she ignores the ethical questions raised by TD's choices, the danger of her being involved with any of it is too real. She can no longer support his endeavors, nor will she stay on the run with him.

She had also realized that she wouldn't feel secure until she's together with her mother, preferably somewhere far away from him. Whatever the cost that might entail, TD is going to have to finance it for as long it takes this storm to pass.

Sometime on the ride back to DC, she plans to call and let him know how she feels. For now though, she's keeping her decisions to herself. She'll probably tell Pen after they've left Atlantic City. It might be helpful to hear his advice on the best way to break the news to TD.

Drew Waters is having difficulty remaining optimistic. They've yet to lay an eye on either Adkins or the girl, even with the arrival of reinforcements, and the man's phone has gone silent once again. Added to the total lack of progress since arriving in Atlantic City, is the fatigue of almost twenty-fours on the move.

His team has been positioned carefully and Waters remains confident his men will spot Adkins if he tries to leave. They're watching the elevators and stairwells leading from the guest rooms, as well as the main entrance to the hotel and the exit from the parking garage. For Waters, surveillance isn't the issue. The question is whether Adkins is still at the hotel, or even in Atlantic City.

With the casino nearly deserted overnight, it had become more difficult for his men to blend with the dwindling number of gamblers. That forced them into changing positions frequently while still coordinating coverage. Maybe Adkins had slipped past them during one of their rotations. It's even possible he made it back to his room before his men were all in place. In either case, Adkins could be sleeping and it might be hours before he emerges.

Waters knows he can check with hotel security to learn if Adkins ever returned to his room. The security monitoring system logs all room entries and they can easily determine if he entered since he was last seen leaving the hotel. Despite the critical value of that information, Waters has yet to contact Dave Bonner. That's because he knows his next request could be his last. There's surely a limit to how much help they can request and he senses they're approaching it. If the roles were reversed, he could easily see himself shutting things down and requesting they leave the property.

With several hours before his next scheduled status report, his plan is to check with hotel security just before calling Stark. Waters is dreading that point in time. If Adkins isn't in his room, it means they've have let him slip away once again.

While Les waits in the car, Pen enters the bus station in Atlantic City, pulling a piece of carry-on luggage behind him. At the counter, he inquires about the bus line's baggage service and the time of the next departure for New York City. Within minutes, he has completed the transaction, paying cash to ship the bag to the bus line's luggage office in New York for pick-up by a designated individual. Pen knows no one will ever make a claim.

Inside the bag, TD's cell phone lies nestled among some socks and underwear. The phone's ringer and vibrate are both turned off. With the battery fully charged, it should have enough power for a couple of days. Once the bus for New York departs at seven-fifteen, they'll begin making periodic calls to the phone throughout the day and into tomorrow. To anyone tracking the phone, it will appear that TD is moving toward New York. Within a few hours, it will place him in downtown Manhattan.

Returning to the car, Pen sends a brief text message to TD: *All tasks completed successfully. Heading back.*

⅄

TD starts his day feeling edgy and irritated for the second morning in a row, though this time his alarm going off is not the cause. In addition to a pervading feeling of physical and mental fatigue, something feels wrong. Something has changed. He can't articulate it yet, but it's definitely there, hiding behind a rapidly rising tide of self-doubt.

The uncertainty was bound to show itself. How could it not, with so many of his instincts and deductions either faulty or outright wrong over the past few days? Right now, he must determine if this is some kind of emotional reaction, or if it's his rational brain calling for him to take heed.

If he's going to succeed, he needs to rely on his intuition with a level of confidence that he currently lacks. And that must be fixed before anything else.

⅄

Instead of sharing her thoughts with Pen, Les spends the first hour of the return trip pensively gazing out the window. Once again, she's wrestling with her decision to stop helping TD. A choice that at first seemed clear-cut has ended up being not so straightforward.

She knows she can make a rational case for helping him. Even if they find a safe place, she and her mom can't hide out indefinitely. And though it may be emotionally satisfying for her to refuse to help, assisting TD might actually shorten the time she'll spend living in fear.

However, it's that very fear which sits at the heart of the problem. It's always present, even when she's hiding like last night in her hotel room. And it's so much worse whenever she's in public. She did her best all of yesterday, but that kind of stress is more than she can handle. If every moment in public requires constant vigilance and acts of deception, then she would rather just hide somewhere.

In the end, she decides to stick with her choice from last night. Though she feels badly for TD and the jam he's in, she's not responsible for it in any way. She needs to protect herself and her mother. She can't involve herself with his stupid impulse to take that money and disappear.

As they leave New Jersey, Les turns from the window and faces Pen.

⋏

It's called an epiphany, a moment when you suddenly see things from a strikingly different perspective. It's not just a variation on a theme, but a wholly new understanding of the essential nature of something. It's also a feeling TD is about to experience.

Once again methodically pacing behind the motel, he has been trying to formulate ways he can exploit the information now at his disposal. No longer are there any doubts regarding how he's being tracked. The speedy arrival in Atlantic City of his pursuers confirms his cell phone is the lure, though that also raises other issues.

To track him by his phone means he was identified during the first twenty-four to thirty-six hours after the events at the motel. How that identification came about remains unclear, but somehow it was accomplished quickly. Once they knew who he was, obtaining his cell phone number would be no big deal.

Yet that's where things get problematic. Identifying him is one thing, but rapidly setting up live tracking of his phone takes time, as would accessing his call data. If it were being undertaken by law enforcement, it would require a variety of approvals and the issuing of a warrant. Even assuming those hurdles had been cleared, and with surprising quickness, the men who showed up at The End Zone were not the police. Neither were the men who followed Pen and Les to Atlantic City.

But that aspect also troubles TD. It just doesn't seem plausible that the men who fumbled their attempt to take him at The End Zone are part of a team with the hardware and technical expertise to track his phone. And they would have to possess a rapid strike capability to have deployed those resources in such a short timeframe.

Slowly, TD works through a few alternatives; solutions to the puzzle that are less black and white. One possibility is that he's facing a two-headed threat. The organization he's tangling with wouldn't have to be technically adept if someone in law enforcement was providing them with access to his call data or location.

He quickly decides he likes the concept; it feels right to him. Someone on Wilkins's team has a back channel to the police. It doesn't even have to be access to someone formally on the investigation, though that seems more likely. Regardless of the source of the data, the theory answers many questions.

Contemplating the ramifications of such a scenario, TD quickly recognizes the increased level of danger he faces. If he's right about the police helping his pursuers, even if that help is coming from only one bad cop, then his situation is suddenly far more perilous and unpredictable. And that's when it him, his epiphany. An icy realization of how badly he has been deluding himself since Monday night.

Instantly swamped by a wave of guilt and remorse, TD shakes his head. Speaking loudly to no one but himself, he says, "What were you thinking?"

Reexamining what he has done, with all the delusion and fantasies stripped away, there's nothing left for him to feel but shame. As the result of his having taken a significant amount of money that isn't his, the rightful owners have deployed men who are fiercely determined to get it back. Not only have they proven to care nothing for legal niceties, they're quite possibly receiving assistance from a corrupt cop.

And worst of all the things he now comprehends is how carelessly he has involved his friends in this debacle. Now that he grasps the extreme danger of the situation, it seems inconceivable he would be able to execute a disappearance without living in constant fear. And his friends might never be safe.

Breaking away from his thoughts, TD checks the time. There's still roughly an hour until Pen and Les return. Accompanying his awakening is a renewed sense of energy and optimism. And at least the diversion achieved its goal, gaining him valuable time that can still be used for planning. Planning that will occur under a radically different mindset now that he's no longer preparing a vanishing act.

With ideas exploding in his mind, he immediately starts in on a new approach, one that results in ending his possession of the money as soon as is feasibly possible. Simply abandoning the bags of cash won't work. The money would still be lost to its owners, with no one but him to be held responsible. Handing it over to the police would have the same effect.

What he needs to come up with is a strategy for returning the money to its owners. At least that should prove to be easier than trying to disappear with it. He simply needs to figure out how to do that without anyone else getting hurt, including himself.

⅄

Pen noticed Les become increasingly distraught as she explained her thinking to him. He could tell she truly cares about TD, but it's also obvious she doesn't have it in her to keep going. He can't blame her. It takes more than a small dose of craziness to play the kind of games they've become involved in, particularly with such dangerous competitors on the field.

Mostly he had nodded while listening, occasionally commiserating. When she finished making her case, both to him and herself, he convinced her not to dump the news on TD with a phone call.

Les agreed to wait. She hopes to use the remainder of the drive to try to relax, if even just a little. She knows it's not going to be easy telling TD her news.

⚔

When Drew Waters reports in at ten AM, Jon Stark works hard to contain his frustration with his team's continued failure to find Adkins in Atlantic City. Keeping his voice steady, he reminds Waters they're going to be speaking with their client on a three-way call. They need to provide an update and decide on their next steps. As Stark prepares to connect them, he issues a final instruction. Once their client is on the line, Waters is to avoid conjecture; his job is to report the facts.

Dan Keach greets them with a friendly, "Good morning, gentlemen", but he does not introduce himself by name. Stark then announces that Waters is also on the call, and says, "Alright Drew. Will you please bring our client up to date as to what we've learned since yesterday?"

As instructed, Waters delivers a fact-based report. "We know Adkins was at the Marina Club Hotel until late yesterday afternoon. He checked in midday and presented his credit card and driver's license at the front desk. He was accompanied by a young woman who matches the description of the woman he was last seen with on Wednesday. They spent several hours gambling, while using a casino player's card, and charged a meal in one of the restaurants to the room account. From the time of their arrival until they departed by taxi, they were observed by multiple surveillance cameras. I was not given access to the video, but we have no reason to doubt it was Adkins. Since they left the hotel, we've been unsuccessful in spotting either of them. We also learned that he purchased tickets for a comedy show at a neighboring hotel. Despite having a man there when the show let out, we were unable to confirm whether they actually attended."

After fielding a few questions from Keach, Waters continues. "I spoke with hotel security just prior to this call. The room is booked through tonight, but no one responded when the hotel staff tried to deliver a room service breakfast that had been ordered for this eight this morning. Card key access records and hallway security video indicate they entered the room only once, yesterday afternoon. No one has been in the room since, and there have been no further sightings of the couple since they left the hotel."

Waters had forgotten to tell Stark that his team had been told to vacate the property by the chief of security. As he considers mentioning it, Dan Keach asks, "Do either of you think Adkins is still in Atlantic City?"

Waters is tempted to reply during the short silence that follows. Instead, he holds back, remembering Stark's warning against conjecture. It's a good move.

Immediately before this call, Dan Keach had talked with Jim Richter. They had reviewed the most recent report of Adkins's call data, updated as of nine that morning. Apparently, the man has once again ducked away from his pursuit.

Breaking the silence, Keach says, "Gentlemen, I just received some interesting news here, right before we began. Based on the latest call data, it appears Mister Adkins left Atlantic City early this morning. Would you like to know where he's heading?"

Without waiting for an answer, he continues, "It looks like New York City."

After a brief pause to let the news sink in, Keach asks drily, "Based on your track record, Jon, do you think it makes sense for me to continue employing your team to chase around after this guy?"

Waters is more than a little embarrassed at his own failures, and it's only made worse by having to listen to his boss respond to their client's pointed question.

Remaining polite and business like, Stark says, "If Adkins decides to invest any effort in hiding, it will be extremely difficult to find him in New York City. And I would never recommend trying anything at the airport. I know it's not what you want to hear, but we might be better served by letting this guy continue to run until he thinks he's safe. Then we can come up with a plan to take him."

Following a brief discussion, the call ends with Stark and his men being asked to stand down. When Keach is off the line, he thanks Waters for his efforts. He knows there's no benefit to be gained from treating the man roughly. Besides, if he hadn't hesitated before sending him, Waters might have arrived in Atlantic City smack in the middle of Adkins's little gambling jaunt.

⋏

From Dan Keach's point of view, the information that Adkins is heading to New York is just one aspect of a larger problem. Robert Owen had already stopped by his office this morning. After spending Thursday exhausting every option, he and Richard Wilkins have reached a conclusion. Without an infusion of funds in the next two to three business days, Wilkins Investment Group will begin to go under.

⋏

Once he begins thinking about how to return the money, TD quickly realizes one of his assumptions is wrong. Returning the cash may be just as challenging as trying to disappear with it. An hour of strategizing has yielded only two viable alternatives. Unfortunately, one doesn't solve his biggest problem and the other remains vague, involving a high level of complexity and considerably more risk.

Obviously, he can approach the police. He can hand over the money and tell them what he knows. Along with the video he made at the scene, his signed contract with Julia Crane to follow Tim will absolve him of any involvement with the shootings. As for his taking the money, from a legal standpoint it's unlikely he'd face even minor charges.

The glaring flaw in this alternative is it deprives his pursuers of their cash. And the chance they would seek revenge at some point is certainly high. If he chooses this path, he'll live with constant fear and he wouldn't even have the money.

The other solution involves him directly contacting the owners and negotiating terms for the return of the cash. That requires him to determine its owner beyond any doubt. Right now, he's unable to say with one hundred percent certainty that it belonged to Wilkins Investment Group. He has a strong working theory, but that's all it is.

Even if he proves ownership, he'd face another hurdle: convincing his adversaries that once their property has been returned they should consider the matter settled, no harm, no foul. He must be able to walk away without fear of reprisal, and that's not going to be easy; executing this strategy will expose his knowledge of their activities. At the same time, that knowledge might be the very leverage he needs.

His thinking is interrupted by a text message from Pen; he and Les will be arriving in a few minutes. Looking for something to distract him from the massive problems at hand, TD begins folding through one of the day-old newspapers lying around the room. Discovering little of interest, he soon finds himself re-reading the story on the shootings.

Thinking about how little the reporter knows about the real story suddenly triggers an idea, leaving his mind racing through the possibilities. He would need some help making it work, but that shouldn't be a problem. Pen has shown he's willing and Denny Holmes would probably pitch in. Still, his quickly developing plan would require at least one additional and potentially unwitting accomplice.

As Pen and Les arrive, TD opens the door to his room. Even from where he's standing, he can see Les is wearing a stern expression. Hopefully she'll brighten up when she hears that he's planning to get rid of the money. When she gets out of the car, he's surprised to see her walk away with nothing more than a nod.

"Where's she headed?"

Shaking his head, Pen says, "I'm supposed to tell you she wants to talk about something serious. She just needs a minute or two to get her thoughts straight."

"That's fine, because we all need to talk. It's over, Pen. It's all over. I'm going to give the money back just as fast as I safely can; maybe in a day or two."

With Pen staring at him in surprise, TD continues, "Hey, before I forget. Thanks again for running that little diversion. It gave me the time I needed to figure things out."

"No problem, TD. When she hears your news, I think it's going to be well received. She can't take much more of this. I bet you've already guessed that's what she wants to discuss."

As he watches TD turn toward his room, Pen catches a glimpse of the anguish he knows his mentor is feeling over what Les has had to deal with. "You're doing the right thing," he says. "I hope you'll let me help you run this out. You know you can count on me."

Turning back to face him, TD manages a slight smile. "Thanks. I hoped that was the case. I'm sure I can use your help."

"Like I said, I'm here."

After asking Pen to keep an eye on Les, TD closes the door to his room and calls Denny Holmes. "Hey. I might need some help moving Laura Stevens again today. I was wondering if you're up for that."

"No problem, today's wide open. And I already told you, I owe you big time. Wait a minute, is everything cool with her?"

"Thanks, Denny, yeah, everything's fine, it's just precautionary. I hate to ask you for even more, but what about this weekend? I'm working on an idea and I might need one last huge favor."

"The weekend is fine too. Whatever you need, man."

Les had spent the last two hours of the trip convinced she must separate herself from TD and the dangers that surround him. But seeing him standing there waiting when she returned had caused her to waver. Now, after a few more minutes of thinking, and nearly changing her mind again, she chooses to stick with her plan. Regardless of her feelings of guilt over not helping him, her desire to protect herself and her mother wins out.

Turning back towards the rooms, she catches a glimpse of Pen quickly retreating around the corner of the building. She had already seen him once and assumed he was sent by TD to make sure she came to no harm. Calling after him, they're soon walking together. When she tells him she wants to talk with TD alone, she notices a little smile. Laying a hand on his shoulder, she says, "Thanks for watching over me. I appreciate it."

"No problem. He's in his room waiting for you."

Once inside, Les begins immediately. "We need to talk."

Before she can continue, TD says, "Let me say something first. I think I know what you want, but even if I'm wrong you should hear me out."

After debating with herself for hours, Les is determined not to let him derail her thoughts. Plunging forward, she says, "I think it's time for..."

"Stop, Les. Please let me talk. I want you to know that I'm ending this, all of it. We're going to get you and your mother away from here for a few days, and after you're safe and I've finished arranging some things, I'm going to give the money back."

Les is thrown completely off kilter by TD's unexpected declaration. Instead of welcoming the news, she's overwhelmed with fear and skepticism. Raising her voice, she sarcastically asks, "So this is all going to suddenly end? Just because you've changed your mind? You'll give them their money back and everyone's going to be happy again?"

TD can't believe her reaction. After staring at her for a moment, he says, "I don't think you're being fair. And isn't this what you want? I might not have managed things perfectly, but the last time I checked everyone is still in one piece. And yes, after thinking it all through, I've changed my mind. I've come up with something that I believe just might work."

Les is instantly embarrassed by her outburst. She came here to tell TD that she wants out and that she needs to feel safe, and here he is telling her he wants exactly that. Why did she end up yelling at him?

With tears welling in her eyes as she fights back the urge to cry, she says, "I'm so sorry; I don't know why I reacted like that. It's what I want too. Why don't you tell me what you're planning? Maybe I can help."

"Thanks, Les, but that's not happening. You're not going to be involved in any way going forward. We both agree the best thing is to get you somewhere you can feel safe, and where I don't have to worry about you so much. If we're lucky, this will all be over in a few days."

Breaking into tears, Les moves toward TD, reaching out to hug him. Wrapping her arms around his shoulders, she says, "Thank you. Just tell me what you want me to do."

After calling Pen inside to join them, TD announces the first item of business is moving Les and her mother out of the immediate area. As they discuss possible locations, Pen volunteers one of his family's properties. They own a luxuriously furnished cabin in the mountains of West Virginia near Berkeley Springs. It's only a few hours' drive. He can take the two of them there, help them get situated, and be back by late evening.

Even as he's telling them about it, Pen regrets making the suggestion. If they agree with his proposal, it means at least another six hours of driving. It seems like that's all he's been doing for days now.

Seeing the expression on Pen's face, TD reads his thoughts. "I know this means another road trip for you, but it's going to take me some time to get things rolling. Nothing I'm going to need you for is going down today."

After discussing a few details, they all agree. Pen and Les will pick up her mother in Alexandria and head to the cabin. Once they're settled in, Pen will return to hook up with TD. With no reason to wait, Les calls her mother with the news. TD also calls Denny, waving him off from helping with Laura Stevens. Ten minutes later, Pen and Les are back on the road.

With Les heading toward a safe haven, TD experiences a mix of emotions as he begins plotting his next steps. There's no escaping the fact that part of him rues his surrender. For four days now, he has tantalized himself with the thought of disappearing and starting a new life. It might have even happened with Les by his side. Fortunately, the rational part of his brain is in control and he quickly pushes that folly from his thoughts.

Pulling out his notepad, he rapidly scribbles item after item, creating a list of tasks. When he's done, he sorts through it, prioritizing the work.

The first job he must tackle is critical and he's ready to take it on. Picking up the one cell phone he has yet to use, he punches in a number he looked up earlier and puts the phone to his ear.

⋏

After his call with Jon Stark, Dan Keach heads directly to Richard Wilkins's office to rejoin a meeting with Wilkins and Robert Owen. Having convinced themselves of the firm's imminent financial implosion, the two men have been scratching around for solutions that don't involve the firm declaring bankruptcy. So far, they've come up with only one.

As he often prefers, Wilkins is standing with his back to the room, pondering the view. He has reached the point where he can hardly bear the presence of Robert Owen, let alone feign interest as the man prattles on about the problems they face. He knows Owen is in no way responsible for the robbery, but the severity of the liquidity crisis they're confronted with is very much his charge.

Before Keach had stepped out for his call, Owen had grimly recapped the situation. Without quickly receiving a large infusion of funds, they're effectively broke. They can meet payroll by scrounging up all of the cash on hand throughout the firm's subsidiaries, but that's about it. There would be nothing left to conduct business or pay bills, and every one of their creditors will have to be stiffed. The situation would remain that way until a significant amount of funds could be brought in from the field and processed.

Owen was talking about dealing with the firm's bankers when Keach returned. "I may be able to hold these guys off for a short time, but to do that I to need to warn them that we're going to miss our next loan payment. Even then, it will probably be the end of the line for a couple of them. And I seriously doubt anyone is interested in loaning us more. We're currently overdue on all of our notes, which in most cases have already been refinanced at least once. I need to call our primary lender Monday, and then make similar calls over the next week to the remaining holders of our debt."

Wilkins continues to find it difficult to believe they've been cutting things so closely. Despite hearing about it from Owen for days now, he still refuses to accept what is happening. Turning away from the window to face them, he growls, "I still don't understand why things are so goddamn tight. Losing one month's income can bring this company to its knees?"

Owen finds it's infuriating that Richard is posturing as if he's hearing about this for the first time. "I don't think it helps to go over that right now.

You know the company hasn't been profitable for several years. And even then, we never maintained large reserves of cash. We needed that money that was stolen; and we're not talking peanuts. Roughly how much were we expecting this month, Dan?"

Keach knows exactly to the dollar how much was coming in. The control processes he and Eddie King put in place allow them to back-check the receipts from the various operations. Still, before answering, he pauses as if to think. There's no reason to let Owen believe he can snap his fingers and Keach will instantly respond. When he's satisfied he has made the man wait long enough, he says, "We were bringing in eight hundred and fifty-two thousand."

"Doesn't seem like that much," Wilkins mumbles. "That's all that's standing between us and staying afloat?"

"For now," Owen responds tersely. "But we also need that every month. I'm sure you're capable of doing the math. We'll net almost ten million dollars on the side this year, tax-free, and that would have been pure gravy if the company were otherwise profitable. As it is, we need every penny of it."

Hearing the number summed up like that reminds Richard why they got into the business to begin with. But he doesn't need to hear Owen's commentary on the lack of profits. He also finds it disgusting that they're barely able to keep things afloat, even with the extra millions rolling in. Are they really losing that much on the real estate development side, or is Owen mismanaging the firm's finances as Wilkins strongly suspects?

Once again, he queries his CFO, "You didn't really answer my question. I still don't understand why we require so much cash to stay in business?"

Owen looks over at Dan Keach as if to apologize for the impending lecture. Turning back to Wilkins, he says "Do you want me to list the projects we have that are completely underwater, or that we've had to mothball until the economy heats up? Because I can do that, except I don't think it's going to help us right now. You know as well as anyone, our situation is the result of making bad decisions in a bad economy. If we're lucky, a year from now we might start seeing some legitimate income again. Until then, we have to rely on the off-the-books operations."

"Man, I hate this bullshit," Richard barks, unwilling to hear any more. "So, what you're telling me is I have no choice but to call my friends up north and make some arrangements."

Turning back to face the window, he gives Owen no time to answer. "Goddammit! Once I do that, I'm going to owe them forever. Aren't there any other options? Daniel, can you please remind me why we can't at least get some cash in here by next week?"

"It's going to take some time to repair the damage to our organization," Keach tells him. "Bringing the money in securely and covertly would be a real challenge on such short notice, particularly with the police snooping around. Even if we managed replacing the lost personnel, and set up a new procedure, I doubt the amount we could collect this soon would be enough to solve our short-term problems."

Nodding toward Owen, Keach also reminds them that any cash coming in would still have to be run through the various subsidiary businesses and the accounting processes they've set up to launder the money. Shortcutting that regime would greatly increase their risk of detection and eventual scrutiny from the IRS.

Wilkins has been working hard to control the rage building inside as he listened to Keach's response, though his anger is directed at Robert Owen. He would have fired the man already if they didn't need his help working through the upcoming financial issues. As he's formulating a verbal put down to humiliate him, there's a knock on the office door.

Poking her head through the doorway, his assistant says, "I'm so sorry, Mister Wilkins. I know you said no interruptions, but there's a man on the phone who insists you would like to speak with him. It's a Mister Adkins."

⋏

Having called the main number for Wilkins Investment Group, TD was transferred to Richard Wilkins's executive assistant, who was adamant about not putting him though. A determined roadblock, she informed him that Wilkins was in a meeting and had left instructions not to be interrupted.

Unruffled by his repeated requests to speak with the firm's namesake, she told him he was welcome to leave a message.

Trying to be persuasive, TD makes one last effort. "I understand you have your orders, but I assure you that the matter I'm calling about is not only critical to your company, but also Mister Wilkins personally. I'm quite sure he would be very disappointed, even angry, if he learns that I called and he was unable to speak with me."

Not letting her put up another objection, he continues, "Here's an alternative. There's no need to put me through unless he wants to talk. There's certainly no harm in checking on that. Please tell him Mister Adkins is on the phone and has the items he's seeking. I'll gladly hold while you give him the message."

The waiting seems like an eternity. At one point, he checks his watch, but it has been less than thirty seconds. He decides he'll wait one more minute before hanging up. Though he believes it's highly unlikely they're set up to track his call, he's packed and ready to leave the motel. Just as he's about to give up, he hears the on-hold music stop.

"Thank you for holding. I'll put you through to Mister Wilkins."

The three of them were in total shock when Wilkins's assistant broke in with the news that Adkins was on the phone. When she had finished delivering the full message, Richard looked at Dan Keach and asked, "How do we want to deal with this?"

Keach quickly responded, saying, "Let me handle the call until we determine what's going on."

With them gathered around Wilkins's desk, hovering over the speakerphone, Keach holds up an index finger signaling them to wait. Having never anticipated Adkins would call, ne needs a moment to consider the ramifications. He wonders what has changed that would cause Adkins to contact them now. Is there any risk associated with taking the call? Letting his mind spin through the multitude of possibilities, he's suddenly frozen by a question with potentially grave implications. How did Adkins figure out to call here and ask to speak with Richard Wilkins?

The brief time it takes Keach to work through his thoughts is too long for Richard's threadbare patience. Frustrated by his inability to shape events, he refuses to wait any longer. Pushing the button that puts the call on speaker, he says, "This is Richard Wilkins. It's so nice of you to call, Mister Adkins. And I must say it's about fucking time you came to your senses. So, are you calling to tell me you're returning my money?"

Dan Keach cringes at Wilkins inability to restrain himself. He also thinks he knows what's coming next. Unfortunately, he's immediately proven right as they hear the dial tone emanating from the speaker. Adkins has hung up on them.

▲

The call couldn't have gone better from TD's perspective. Wilkins's reaction leaves no doubt the money is his. It was also interesting to learn the man has trouble controlling his anger; that could prove to be an advantage at some point. He will definitely call Wilkins again, but not until much later in the day. That will give him plenty of opportunity to stew about how the call ended, as well as lessen the time he has to react to what TD is planning.

Moving on to his next task, he sets up a new, randomly named e-mail account. He then composes and sends a message to Preeti Chopra, the author of the articles in the City Express. The brief message states only that it's urgent that they talk about 'yet to be released and highly newsworthy information concerning the motel shootings'. After emphasizing that only he possesses this information, he provides the number of one of the cell phones he has been using, along with a request for her to call him as soon as possible.

The last thing he does before leaving the motel is to destroy the cell phone he used to call Wilkins; the only call he made with it. After removing the battery, he snaps the clamshell in half and throws the pieces on the floor, stomping on them several times. When he's finished, he tosses the fractured pieces into a large trashcan at the end of the row of rooms. He also makes a mental note to purchase a couple more of the cheap phones.

As soon as he's back on the road, he calls Denny Holmes.

⋏

Richard Wilkins's anger rapidly morphs into embarrassment when he realizes the result of his behavior. Mumbling a half-apology, he asks Dan Keach for his thoughts.

Avoiding any commentary on his employer's lack of self-control, Keach says, "I don't know what to think. It doesn't make a lot of sense that he would contact us to begin with. And even though he called and hung up, I don't think he's taunting us. Maybe he can't take the pressure. Maybe he's trying to cut some kind of deal."

Wilkins explodes, yelling, "What kind of deal? There's not going to be any goddamn deal. He either gives us our money back or he's fucked."

"Can we strive for some rational discussion here, Richard? I must admit my opinion of this man is beginning to rise. And I wouldn't exactly describe his situation as 'fucked'. I'd like to suggest we take a minute or two to rethink how we're viewing things."

Keach can feel the fear and anger in the room, but he's starting to think they should be feeling optimistic instead. Having absorbed the shock of Adkins unexpected call, he's now focused on the initial message the assistant delivered. Adkins wanted them to know he 'has the items' they're seeking. Clearly, the game has changed.

With renewed urgency he says, "Richard, I think you should consider postponing your call for an emergency loan. I believe we have a real chance at getting the money back and I agree with what you said. Requesting such a favor is something you won't be able to undo; you will owe them forever. Let me ask you this. What would happen if you personally call the bank Monday and request delaying payment for another week or two? Robert, is that at all feasible?"

Over the next few minutes, Keach listens as Owen and Wilkins discuss the possibility, including what Richard could say or promise that would keep their creditors at bay. There isn't much, and Owen is only able to come up with a couple of ideas.

Wilkins doesn't like any of them. Losing interest in the topic, he says to Keach, "Look, before I agree to call the bank, you need to convince me that we're not simply postponing the inevitable. The problem I have is this guy is already in New York. What makes you think you can find him any time soon and get our money back?"

"I agree that's an issue," Keach answers. "If this guy really wants to hide, it's going to take a long time to find him. But I'm not so sure he's in New York. The only thing we know for sure is that his phone is there. And his call today came from a different number. Regardless of where he is, I'm far more interested in understanding why he called. And there's one more thing, since I'm sure your name wasn't attached to any of those bags of money. How is it that he figured out to call you directly, Richard?"

Keach immediately holds up a hand to stop Wilkins from responding to his rhetorical question. "Look, we don't have to understand everything this moment to know that he has figured out it's our money. Whatever the reason for his call, I doubt it was to blow us a kiss as he disappears."

Having paused briefly to make sure he has the full attention of his colleagues, Keach continues, "Whether you want to believe it or not, I'm sticking with my first reaction. Adkins wants to cut some kind of deal and I think we should be preparing for that possibility. I also predict he's going to be calling back soon."

⋏

The first thing TD wants to address when he calls Denny is the perception that the man is somehow in his debt. TD reminds him he had only been doing his job when he supported Denny's claim for the loss of the second boat. Had he not believed his story, he would have recommended against him.

After Denny reluctantly agrees, TD tells him what he needs. He wants to lease Denny's boat for part of a day, as well as his services as captain. It will probably be tomorrow or maybe Sunday. It will also involve Denny holding a few bags for him, before delivering them to a pre-arranged location at a specific time.

Denny protests when he hears the request. "Come on, TD. I'm not going to charge you for something like that. For one thing, it wouldn't even be much. I insist you let me do this for you as one last favor."

"Okay," TD agrees, "But before going forward, I need to be honest with you. There's some level of danger to all this. A lot will depend on finding the right location."

After a brief moment of hesitation, Denny says, "Okay. What kind of danger are we talking about? And what sort of place are you looking for?"

TD tells him, "The bags are someone else's property and I need to deliver them, but the situation isn't so straightforward. And since the men I'm meeting aren't the nicest guys, there's the possibility something might go wrong. You shouldn't have to worry, because I'll be handling the final leg of the delivery. But since you'd be involved, even indirectly, I felt like I should mention it."

After pause to allow Denny to object, TD continues, "The location is key. I need something isolated. I was thinking somewhere along the Potomac that you can approach from the water, with limited access from the land."

By the time TD finishes describing what he has in mind, Denny is laughing softly into the phone. "Well, as long as I don't need to carry a gun, then I'm not too worried. As for the location, well, you just described where I live."

"I'm not going to use your home, Denny. This is going to be some serious business."

"Yeah, well I'm being serious. The place is perfect."

Denny quickly describes the layout of the extensive and currently vacant riverside property where he's the caretaker. TD agrees it sounds promising, but before they can explore the idea further, he receives a call. Though he doesn't recognize the Caller ID, the only person with this number, other than Pen and Denny, is the reporter he e-mailed earlier.

Asking Denny to hold, TD tries to answer the call. Unfortunately, between driving and handling the phone, he fumbles the task and both calls end up being disconnected. Pulling off the road, he takes a deep breath and gathers his thoughts. He may have just found a location that fits his plans. Now, with an opportunity to talk with the reporter, he has a chance to ratchet up the pressure on Wilkins.

When he calls the number back, Preeti Chopra answers immediately. After stating he can't disclose his name due to concerns over his personal safety, TD tells her he was an eyewitness to the shootings at the Gateway Motor Inn. More importantly, he has evidence and unreleased information about what was being contested that night. He finishes by asking her, "Is that something you'd be interested in writing about?"

Preeti is stunned. The anonymous e-mail had certainly intrigued her, but she had cautioned herself until she was sure she wasn't dealing with some crank claiming special knowledge. Now that she's talking with him, the man on the phone sounds calm and serious. She needs to proceed carefully as she establishes his authenticity. She doesn't want to spook him and lose a potentially huge lead if he happens to be legitimate.

"Of course I'm interested, sir. And I understand about your name. Is there an alias we can use for the short-term?"

When he doesn't respond immediately, Preeti says. "Also, if you're willing, I'd be glad to meet somewhere for a cup of coffee so we can talk face to face."

TD gathers his thoughts before answering her, reminding himself that what he tells her must be as close to the truth as possible for it to have the impact he needs. He also must gain her cooperation quickly if she's going to serve his purposes. He needs her to write an article before they can get together, preferably today.

Ignoring her offer to meet, he begins by telling her she can call him 'Tom'. Over the next few minutes, he leads her through his story, relating how he was at the motel for other purposes and was positioned to witness the incident from start to finish. He doesn't think it was some drug deal turned violent. Instead, it was a planned hit on what he believes was one component of an extensive money laundering operation. At the end, he gives her his most tantalizing piece of information, nicely dressed up in a partial lie.

"I have good evidence that a large real estate development firm, one based right here in the District of Columbia, is directly involved with the money laundering. It's a well-known downtown firm, and I think this could be a great story for a reporter."

TD had used the phrase 'District of Columbia', and put a subtle emphasis on the word 'downtown' for a reason. He doesn't want to lead her too close to Wilkins Investment Group, headquartered fifteen miles outside of the city. He just needs what she writes to be enough to scare the hell out of Richard Wilkins.

Preeti found herself holding her breath as she listened. If what he's saying is true, this could be the ultimate break for her career, but she's going to need more than just some anonymous innuendo. And the caller obviously has both a motive and an agenda he's pursuing, otherwise why would he be contacting her.

"Tom, I assume you're telling me all this with the goal that I'll write something. And though it's quite fascinating, and you sound credible, I'm sure you understand it's a very rare event when the paper publishes anything based only on an anonymous source. Again, is it possible for us to meet? Do you have concrete proof to support your allegations?"

TD knows things are going his way with the reporter already talking about writing a story, now he just needs her to do so quickly. "I'm glad you're taking me seriously, Miss Chopra. Unfortunately, I can't meet with you until sometime tomorrow, maybe in the morning. Please trust me when I tell you that the lives of others continue to be in grave danger because of these events. I believe a news story that gets this information out there will make those people much safer."

Pausing briefly, TD moves to close the deal. "Here's what I'm offering. If you want to meet and receive a copy of the hard evidence I possess, then you need to write an article covering what I've told you. And it must be published in tomorrow morning's paper."

Preeti's excitement immediately turns to disappointment. Until the last moment, she was feeling okay with what she was hearing. But there's no way she can approach her editor with a story like this, based on a call with an anonymous tipster. She tells Tom she appreciates the seriousness of the situation, but what he's asking is quite unlikely to occur.

TD can hear the disappointment in her voice, but he believes he'll have her after he drops a few more bombshells. "Miss Chopra, I won't lie, I need help. And I'm serious about lives being in danger, including my own. But I also understand that you need some proof to believe in me, so please listen closely. In the next hour, I'll send you several photos by e-mail. They're still frame shots, taken from a video I recorded during the shootout."

After intentionally pausing for effect, he continues, "As a further incentive, here are a few nuggets of information not released by the police. One of the victims, Tim Crane, was at the motel cheating on his wife. He was using room one-fourteen. To his grave misfortune, he stepped outside for a cigarette at the wrong moment; he was killed in the crossfire. I'll also include an image of a courier handing off a bag of money to another of the men who was killed. You should know there was a lot of money involved; hundreds of thousands of dollars."

Preeti doesn't know what to say. Whatever this man's agenda may be, he's spinning quite a tale. And he's offering proof as well. Before she can respond, he's talking again.

"I need to hang up now. I'll send you those images soon so you can get started. Then I'm going to call you back in three hours. If the story is a go, we can set up a meeting for tomorrow morning where I'll give you much more."

"Three hours is too short a timeframe for me to know if there will be a story tomorrow," Preeti protests. "There are others involved with making that decision."

TD waits to respond. He wants to sound unthreatening, even as he does just that. Removing all emotion from his voice, he says, "I understand. However, if that's the case, then I'll give the same offer to your competitors over at the Washington Post. I'm sure they'd love to jump ahead of you and your paper's coverage of this story."

The last thing TD hears as he ends the call is a soft gasp from Preeti. He feels confident the story will run. If that happens, tomorrow morning he'll meet with her and determine if he can trust her with any more information.

⚔

Preeti didn't tell Tom that the Washington Post isn't really a competitor, or that she's a free-lance journalist. None of that is important. Besides, she doesn't want to push him toward another paper and lose the story. After jotting down a few notes to summarize her conversation with him, she calls Stuart Kurtz.

Considering her source is anonymous, Preeti is surprised to hear Stuart's enthusiasm for the potential story. More so than her, he's motivated by her informant's threat to give the information to another paper. He wants her to start working on it immediately, though she'll have to wait on a promise as to when and if her article will run.

"Let's get a look at the content and quality of the photos," he tells her. "If they're good, and you can verify a decent portion of what he told you, we may very well run with it."

Next, they discuss how to approach Tom's claim that a major DC developer is involved. Short of receiving another unexpected break this afternoon, it's highly unlikely she'll be able to confirm such an allegation by the newspaper's deadline. Despite that, unless he's overruled, Stuart agrees she can keep it as one of the major aspects of the story.

He warns Preeti to limit the assertion to a stripped down version, with no speculation as to which firm it might be. She must also indicate that specific aspect of the story remains unconfirmed. Even in a watered down form, it's going to take some work on Stuart's part for it to pass a final editorial review, but that's his job.

Preeti promises to forward him copies of the photos when she receives them. She again has to contain her excitement when Stuart ends the call by saying, "Who knows. If this story pans out, you might be right back on the front page."

⋏

For the first time in days, TD feels a sense of satisfaction. His new plan is progressing nicely, and now that he's thinking clearly, it also feels like he's doing the right thing; right for both him and the friends he has involved.

Back on the phone with Denny, he apologizes for dumping their earlier call. After a few more questions, TD agrees that the property at Ferry Landing Point sounds like the perfect spot. If the layout matches Denny's description, then that's where he'll return the bags. For now though, he's not planning to tell Denny they're loaded with money. He does tell him there's likely to be one other person involved, a trusted friend named Pen. He then asks Denny if he can have his boat ready by first thing in the morning, or if that's too soon.

"Man, what kind of sailor do you think I am? My boat is always ready to go."

It's clear from Denny's light-hearted tone that he's not offended. Following a little more banter, they agree to meet at the property in a few hours. Only by seeing the place can TD be sure, and begin to finalize his plans for how he hopes things will transpire.

⋏

The accumulating stress of the past few days has left Richard Wilkins feeling tired and disgruntled. He has never had less control of his company or events. In addition to his disdain for Robert Owen and his mismanaging of the firm's finances, he's also growing increasingly unhappy with Dan Keach.

The thing that causes the most resentment is the manner in which Keach rejects or ignores the majority of Richard's suggestions. And even though they're facing exactly the type of situation he keeps Keach on the payroll to handle, he can hardly stomach the man's I'm-in-charge crisis-management attitude. One of the last orders Keach issued was regarding

Adkins calling again. If that occurred, Wilkins's assistant was to put him on hold until both Keach and Wilkins were on the call. Keach had also staked a claim to managing any future calls with Adkins. Richard bristles every time he thinks about that.

Unable to focus his attention on anything of detail, he decides to take the rest of the afternoon off. On the way out, he stops at his assistant's desk and countermands Keach's instructions. Any call from Adkins should be forwarded directly to Richard's cell phone. She is not to include anyone else. He will take the call alone.

His assistant immediately protests, sheepishly telling him that Keach had called her just a few minutes earlier, sternly reminding her to include him on any calls from Adkins. Is Richard sure that he wants her to ignore that order?

Staring at his assistant dourly, he says, "Mister Keach is employed here at my will, as are you. If you'd like for that arrangement to continue, I suggest you do as I ask."

Turning toward the elevators, he adds, "And there's no need for you to mention this to him. Let him think he's in charge. Understood?"

⊥

While organizing her notes, Preeti decides to follow-up on Bobby Tomlin's status. From the start of the call, it's clear that something is different. Unlike their prior conversation, he now shows no interest in talking, particularly after she mentions her upcoming article. When she tells him that she's considering including an update on his status, his response is polite, but terse.

"Thanks for your concern ma'am, but I'd appreciate you not writing anything more about me and my family."

Preeti has encountered people who are reluctant to talk with reporters, even after having first been more open. There are plenty of benign reasons for such a reaction, but Bobby's sudden reticence suggests a different possibility, particularly with Tom's warning of peoples' lives being in 'grave danger' still fresh in her mind.

"Is everything okay, Bobby? I know you're badly injured, and you certainly face a lot of hurdles, but you seem different from when we talked the other day."

For a moment, neither of them says a word. Bobby is scared. The reporter seems nice enough, but he doesn't owe her anything. And after being threatened in his hospital bed, he can't imagine how talking with her could possibly help him.

Breaking the silence, he whispers, "Please leave me alone. And please leave me out of your article. It's too risky for me."

Preeti could hear Bobby's voice trembling as he ended the call. Worried about him, she briefly considers calling Detective Roberts. Instead, she turns to her laptop and starts to work on the article. Maybe her informant's warning is true about lives being in danger. If it is, then maybe it's also true that publishing the information he's giving her could help change that.

Writing with an elevated sense of purpose, she finishes her first take with surprising speed. It's still a draft though, with space potentially reserved for something to tie in with the photos; photos she still hasn't received.

⅄

TD has been editing and working with a copy of the video he took at the motel. During a couple of short sessions over the past few days, he has created over a dozen still frame shots of key events and individuals. He also created two shorter video clips. One shows two full delivery cycles occurring back-to-back, though he has intentionally pixelated the images of the couriers' faces and the license plates on their cars. The second clip begins as the attackers arrive, and ends when the first shot is fired.

Having stopped at a coffee shop to use the free Wi-Fi, TD sends off a series of e-mails to Preeti Chopra. The first message contains images of two different couriers handing bags to Slick, though you cannot see the couriers' face in either shot. Another message contains images of the attackers, including one firing his gun into the backseat of the Mercedes. TD follows with two more emails, each with one of the shorter video clips attached.

After leaving the coffee shop, he purchases a few items he needs at the adjoining shopping center. Back in his car, he lays out his purchases on the seat next to him. Along with two more of the cheap cell phones, there are four thumb-size digital flash drives, and a roll of masking tape.

Working as he sits in his car, he copies a set of files from his laptop onto three of the thumb drives. Each now contains a copy of the original unedited video, along with the shorter video clips, the still shots, and a written summary he created of the information Phil provided from the insurance billing records. The last thumb drive receives only a copy of the complete original video, edited to censor the faces of any couriers and their license plates. Removing it from the laptop, he puts a small piece of masking tape on the cover to mark it separately from the others.

With enough time having passed for the reporter to receive his e-mails, TD calls her back. After she answers on the first ring, he says, "This is Tom. Did you receive the information I sent?"

When she confirms she has all of the messages, he says, "Good. I think the attachments will greatly underpin my credibility. Have you talked with your editor about running the story?"

Preeti is unwilling to answer him without seeing what he has sent. She quickly opens the first message, and then each of the attached still frame shots.

As she's doing this, he says, "The photos and video clips should provide you with ample documentation of what I told you earlier. And I promise you there's much more hard evidence."

Preeti finally tells him, "My editor thinks the story will run as long as the photos are good."

"Well, they're real images of what took place. You're welcome to use them with your article, but personally, I think the risks are too high. Obviously, there are some very dangerous men involved with all of this."

Preeti knows there's no chance the photos will run, at least for now. Not wanting to let him off too easily, she asks, "What about us meeting and the additional proof you promised?"

"Can you meet first thing tomorrow morning? National Harbor at eight-fifteen?"

"Okay, I can make that, but where at National Harbor?"

"Just get there and I'll call you with the final details. And don't arrive early. One last thing Miss Chopra; please come alone. If you're not alone, there will be no meeting."

⚓

After watching the video clips, Preeti can barely contain her enthusiasm as she forwards Tom's e-mails to her editor. She has never covered a story anywhere near as exciting as this, but she also knows she must keep things in perspective. There's a lot of information to verify, and more to gather if this story is going to have legs. On the upside, Tom's claim that he possesses additional 'hard evidence' now appears much more credible.

Stuart Kurtz is also excited when he calls, but he confirms her earlier guess; he doesn't plan to use any of the images with the article. After they discuss several potential changes to her draft, he ends the call, saying, "You better get back to work, Preeti. You may be writing another front-page story."

As soon as he hangs up, Preeti realizes she forgot to tell him that her informant had agreed to a face-to-face, first thing tomorrow. Picking up her phone to call him back, she hesitates, and then changes her mind. If she tells him, he might not want her to go, and certainly not alone. And Tom had been clear about that aspect. She's going to have to fly solo on this one.

For a brief moment, she considers whether she's ignoring her own safety. So far, nothing about Tom has seemed threatening in any way. She makes a conscious decision not to worry about it; besides, he may not even show; she had arranged a meeting with an anonymous source once before and that didn't pan out. She must admit it though; Tom has certainly come through so far.

⚓

TD has placed an inch-long strip of masking tape on the back of each of the three cell phones in his possession. As he begins to label them, he writes *OLD* on the phone he has been using. From now on, it's only for talking with the reporter. The first of the unused phones he marks with the word *HOT*. The second he labels *SAFE*; that one is now dedicated exclusively for communicating with Pen and Denny.

Before he makes two critical phone calls, he intends to move well away from his current location. He's too close to National Harbor, where things will really start rolling in the morning. He knows his risk of being detected right now is fairly low, but it's a reasonable precaution.

Almost an hour later, after having driven through downtown DC and re-crossing the Potomac, TD pulls into a parking garage in Arlington. He used the time during the drive for a mental walkthrough of his rapidly emerging plans. Though there are still some holes to fill, he believes his overarching idea is solid.

With a sense that his chances for success are improving, he grabs his notepad. Flipping back through several pages, he finally finds the information he's looking for. Picking up the phone marked 'HOT', he punches in the number from his notes.

Kenny Clarkson handles the overwhelming majority of his duties from his squad car, rarely spending much time at department headquarters. Today, he's working another evening shift, but he came in a couple of hours early to deal with a rising backlog of paperwork. In addition to several other tasks, he has yet to write up the report Pete Czarniak assigned him on Tuesday's visit to the private security firm.

Before he makes much progress, he's interrupted by a call from the main switchboard; a man is requesting to speak with him specifically. When the caller is put through, he can hardly believe what he hears.

"Officer Clarkson, my name is TD Adkins. I'd like to have a quick conversation with you. Do you have a moment?"

Kenny hardly knows how to react. Slightly flustered, he responds, "Sure, go ahead Mister Adkins, but I should warn you before you say anything. You are a person of interest in the investigation of the homicides at the Gateway Motor Inn and I ..."

After losing his train of thought, Kenny finishes, "…and I would like to advise you of your rights."

Kenny had paused because he's slightly confused. He has never Mirandized anyone over the phone, and though it sort of makes sense, he's not even sure if it applies in this case, with Adkins not really a suspect and calling in on his own. Still, he doesn't want to compromise the investigation if the man suddenly begins confessing. Unfortunately, before he can start, Adkins is talking again.

"I get it officer, I understand my rights. I just want you to know I'm innocent of anything to do with those shootings. I'm preparing to exonerate myself by providing you with concrete evidence, as soon as…"

Clarkson is getting nervous, particularly at the mention of evidence. Interrupting, he says, "Please Mister Adkins, I need to advise you of your rights. And I strongly encourage you to turn yourself in. Where are you at this moment, sir?"

TD chuckles, "Which is it officer? Do you want me to turn myself in, or are you planning to read me my rights over the phone?"

Giving him no time to respond, TD says, "Don't answer me; just listen. I'm planning to clear my name, but it needs to be on my terms, and at the time of my choosing. According to your department's website, the lead detective there is Carl Roberts. Is that correct?"

"Yes Sir, But…"

"Fine. Please tell Detective Roberts that you spoke with me and that I declared my innocence. Tell him that I'll be in touch again soon, maybe even tomorrow."

"Yes Sir, will do. But…"

"And Officer Clarkson, if I were you, I wouldn't share this information with anyone but Roberts. There's someone rotten on your team or somewhere over there. Don't forget to tell that last part to your boss. Have you got all that?"

"Yes Sir. But as I've been trying to say, if we could just meet, I think…"

Clarkson stops when he realizes Adkins is gone. After quickly scribbling notes of everything the man said, he heads for Roberts's office as fast as he can move without running.

⋏

TD isn't ready to talk with Richard Wilkins, but when the time comes, he's going to want to call him on his cell phone and he doesn't have the number. An experienced investigator has several of methods for obtaining such information, but he decides to try the potentially easiest method first. Still using the phone marked *HOT*, he calls Wilkins Investment Group. As with the last call, he's routed to Richard Wilkins's assistant.

"Hello. This is TD Adkins again. Mister Wilkins expects me to call him later, but I'm embarrassed to say that I've misplaced the number he gave me for his cell phone."

TD is a thrilled when she provides the number with no hesitation. As each element of his plan drops into place, he has to remind himself to stay focused and avoid overconfidence. Things may be going well so far, but he'll soon be skating out onto same pretty thin ice.

⋏

Pen has been on the road nearly the entire day. After picking up Laura Stevens, he had obtained a rental car in his name so she and Les could follow him to his family's cabin. Before making the return trip, he spent some time helping them settle in, including a stop at the closest grocery for some fresh food.

When he had finally handed over the keys to the cabin, he told Les, "Try to relax. No one is going to find you here. You're well stocked and shouldn't have to go out for several days. I promise that TD or I will call you soon and hopefully everything will be cleared up."

Near the end of his return trip, Pen checks in with TD. He wants to meet at eight o'clock at a place named Ferry Landing Point. After giving him directions, TD tells him they'll be meeting there with Denny Holmes. Together, the three of them will walk through the game plan for returning the money the next day. Pen should also plan to be at the same location tomorrow, possibly early in the morning. He needs to be set up in advance to covertly record everything that happens with sound and video. Pen will also be coordinating communications and backing up TD if something goes wrong.

"Well, at least you don't have me chauffeuring again," Pen remarks. "It'll be good to be part of the action."

Though he had sounded enthusiastic up until then, TD's last words belie his mood. "The last thing I'm hoping for tomorrow is action."

Carl Roberts is astonished. Kenny Clarkson is in front of him, bearing the news that their mystery man from Monday night has called and declared his innocence. That Adkins chose to reach out to Clarkson is probably linked to the patrolman's interview of his client, Julia Crane, the wife of the dead bystander. Overall, Adkins didn't say much, except that he would be in contact again and clear his name. Kenny can't remember whether Adkins would be calling him or Roberts.

If Clarkson ends up being the man's preferred contact, Carl wants him better prepared for any subsequent calls. Coaching the young officer, Roberts reminds him that Adkins will probably want to keep the duration of any call short. To avoid wasting time, Kenny should forget about trying to read him his rights; besides, he doesn't appear to be confessing to anything. Most importantly, he should be in listening mode. He should let the man have his say, and focus on obtaining as much information as possible.

"What about his reference to something rotten?" Kenny asks.

"Yeah, that's definitely not good," Carl replies, shaking his head as he answers. "Let me think about that. In the meantime, let's play this straight and follow his advice. Don't talk with anyone else about this. Nobody. You got that?"

After leaving the office, Richard Wilkins stopped for an early dinner, polished off with several drinks. A second call from Adkins, so confidently predicted by Dan Keach, had never come. Now at home, he feels bitter and defeated. Having been at the helm for less than a decade, he has run his father's business into the ground. Worse, with his tottering firm nearing collapse, he's probably going to have to ask for an emergency loan, or risk compromising the front for his myriad illegal activities.

From his perspective, little of the blame for what has happened lies at his feet. Ignoring the impacts of the recent economic nosedive, along with his own greed, Richard sees Robert Owen as the primary villain. His CFO clearly ran the firm's finances too close to the edge. Any remaining fault for their current situation lies with Dan Keach. He obviously hired and promoted men who were so incompetent, they couldn't avoid being taken down by a bunch of immigrant punks, not even connected guys.

The whole situation is a train wreck and he's just getting angrier continuing to think about it. One thing is certain, Robert Owen is finished. He'll be gone as soon as this is all over, fired without notice. Maybe Dan Keach as well, though pulling that trigger will require careful planning.

Ever since arriving home, Richard has been completely distracted, mindlessly roaming through the house from room to room. Finally, after fixing another drink, he tries watching television. Hopefully it can divert his attention for a while and help him relax.

⚔

TD has purposely arrived at Ferry Landing Point well ahead of when he asked Pen to meet him there. He wants some time to talk with Denny alone, face to face. He can no longer avoid being more open about what's happening. Only after he's sure Denny understands the risks involved will he proceed.

While TD reviews the main events of the past few days, he also watches Denny faces as he listens in amazed silence. A key aspect of his plan involves Denny holding the bags of money for a period of time. TD knows that if he's going to trust this man with a million dollars, as well his personal safety, then he needs to be damn sure about it.

After several minutes of talking and fielding questions, TD is happy to see Denny's reaction appears quite normal. Of course, he's astounded hearing the whole story. Who wouldn't be? But to TD's practiced eye, Denny showed no detectable reaction as he learned the aforementioned bags are full of cash. Based on his instincts, he decides to trust the man.

Finishing, he says, "I've been a complete fool, Denny. I thought I could pull it off without hurting anyone. My biggest mistake is that I didn't think things all the way through. At least now, I know it has to end. I'm hoping to do that here tomorrow."

With Denny reassuring him that he's still willing to help, they begin a tour of the property. At each point of interest, Denny proudly indicates various features of the estate as if he owned and designed it all. And one thing is clear: the place fits TD's needs perfectly.

There's only one way to approach the property by car. After passing through an imposing iron gate, a paved driveway snakes through a hundred yards of woods. Along with a six-foot-tall wrought-iron fence, the thick trees border the property on three sides. The woods end in a neat line, surrounding a large clearing roughly two hundred yards deep and running over a quarter of a mile along the Potomac. A lush green lawn covers the entire expanse.

A little ways past the tree line, the driveway forks as the pavement ends. From that point forward, it consists of light-colored pea-sized gravel. Up a small rise to the right, the driveway circles in front of the mansion's white-pillared portico. The left branch passes the large two-story colonial garage, before ending at a sizeable guest villa set away from the other buildings. Footpaths from both the villa and the main home lead to a boathouse perched over the river's edge. They also connect with a spindly wood-planked dock, jutting out over the water, thirty to forty yards from the shore.

Viewing the layout as they stand next to the garage, TD quickly envisions ways he can use the terrain and its features to his advantage. As he talks through a few possibilities with Denny, a loud buzzer sounds briefly inside the garage. Stepping though a side door, Denny checks the security camera before pushing a button to open the front gate.

TD watches as Pen's car emerges from the woods. Almost immediately, it slows to a brief a stop as it reaches the fork in the drive. TD had done exactly the same thing when he arrived. Something about the way a driver would naturally pause at that point gives him an idea.

Once Pen has joined them, TD begins outlining his plan. Talking as they walk, he leads them onto the stretch of grass between the broad forks of the driveway. As they reach the middle of that section of the lawn, they're almost equal distance from the mansion, the garage, and the start of the dock, with each roughly fifty yards away. Coming to a halt, TD tells them that this is the spot. This is where he plans to conduct his transaction with Richard Wilkins.

TD explains that his plan calls for Denny to deliver the bags of cash by boat. That way, if Wilkins doesn't agree to his side of the deal, the money isn't already there, at risk. When he arrives, Denny will stay with the money after tying up at the far end of the dock, nearly a hundred yards from where they now stand. Before that, he needs to be waiting somewhere on the river, as close by as possible, but out of view from where they now stand.

Denny tells them he can bring his shallow-draft sailboat close to the shoreline at a nearby bend in the river. He has done it before. The spot is completely blocked from their view by trees. Even with TD reminding him that the timing of this aspect of the operation is critical, Denny remains confident.

"Don't worry. I can be here in just a couple of minutes from the spot I have in mind."

Satisfied by Denny's assurance, TD tells them that when he's ready for the money, he'll signal Pen, who'll be observing everything from the windows on the upper level of the garage. Once he sees the signal, Pen will alert Denny to get under way.

Slowly moving back towards the garage, the three men frequently stop to discuss some aspect of the plan as TD walks them through it again start to finish in close detail. When they're done, he insists on one more pass, this time with each of them articulating their individual roles as they come into play. When he's confident they're all on the same page, he sets a tentative rendezvous time for the next day, subject to a final confirmation in the morning.

Before they leave, Denny takes them to his apartment above the garage. The sight lines are excellent, with an unobstructed view of the spot on the lawn where they had just stood. A window on the end of the garage offers a view of the entire length of the dock.

Back outside, TD hands Pen his video camera, an envelope, and two of the flash drives. "Everything is there that you'll need to take these guys down if this turns out badly or I go missing anytime soon. The original documentation is in the envelope, with digital copies on the flash drives. And there's the video of course. You'll also find contact info for a newspaper reporter. If anything goes wrong, she deserves to break the story. Give her one of the drives. Everything else goes to the police."

Looking closely at his mentor, Pen says, "Think positively, TD, it's a good plan. What about a weapon? Do you need a gun? I wasn't planning on carrying, but I'm not sure I'd parade around out there on that lawn unable to defend myself."

"No. No gun, Pen. That could only screw this up even more, but thanks."

Looking towards the spot where he'll stand tomorrow, he says, "I appreciate you're optimism, Pen, but I'm not so sure. Nothing about this has worked out so far. Not for the punks who started it back at the motel, not for the guys they attacked, and definitely not for me. And you know, my instincts have been really off several times lately; and on major things too. I may have lost my touch."

The two men say little after that. After shaking hands, they drive away; Pen first, soon followed by TD. Before pulling off, he waves to Denny, who's already heading toward his boat.

⅄

Despite the early hour, Richard Wilkins had nodded off sitting in his living room, the effect of a half dozen drinks finally taking its toll. It wasn't a deep sleep, and he woke soon after his phone began ringing. Clearing his mind, he had barely said hello before his caller was talking.

"Mister Wilkins? TD Adkins here. I would like to…"

Briefly startled, but quickly becoming lucid, Richard decides to take control of the conversation. "Listen here, I…"

"Mister Wilkins, please be quiet for a moment and let me speak. I need to be sure you completely understand what I'm telling you."

Indignant at being interrupted, Wilkins barely contains his temper. "Okay, fine. Let's hear what you have to say?"

"What I would like to do is to give you your money back. Then I want be left alone. That's all. You get your money back and you forget about me. Permanently. I plan to return it to you tomorrow morning. Do you understand?"

Richard is fully coherent now and wary of a trap; it all seems a little too easy. He and Dan Keach both believe Adkins is legitimate, but they also agreed that there's a considerable risk of some kind of a sting by law enforcement. Keach had already warned Richard several times to make sure he was extremely careful about admitting anything, or agreeing with any assertions Adkins may make, particularly over the phone.

"Listen, I'm not completely sure what you're referring to, Mister Adkins. I think it would be better if we met somewhere to discuss this."

TD had prepared for this possibility, and had already decided not to waste time with any contrived dancing around. Waiting for a second before responding, he says, "I was afraid you might start playing games. If you choose to go that route, it will certainly be your loss. Do you realize your men have no idea where I am? If it weren't for me calling you, you wouldn't have an ice cube's chance in hell of getting your money back before I disappear and spend every penny. If you want to play stupid, go ahead. It sounds to me like you'd be damn good at it."

Pausing only to catch his breath he says, "Now, let's try this one more time. Are you prepared to call off your men *AND* forego retribution in exchange for the immediate return of your money?"

Wilkins waits before answering. He knows he has very few options, but he detests this man dictating to him. "Yes. I believe that can be arranged."

"Excellent. Then please be prepared to meet tomorrow morning. I'll call you sometime early with the location. Who knows, maybe we'll meet where you lost the money to begin with."

⅄

TD had waited until he was back in Maryland before calling Wilkins. Now he just needs to hide out one more night for what is sure to be a stressful day. He has already paid in advance for his room, including tonight, but at the last minute, he changes his mind. He doesn't need to risk staying at the same place.

When he has finally checked-in at another cheap motel, it doesn't bother him at all that the room smells, or the bed is old and uncomfortable. He knows he won't be sleeping much tonight anyway.

SATURDAY

Richard Wilkins had endured two difficult phone calls with Dan Keach before he could sleep last night. The first was generally a monologue, consisting almost entirely of Keach blasting Richard for his "amateur hour antics" and "screwing everything up". The second call started no better. Richard found himself close to firing Keach right then over the phone, no longer willing to listen to his highhandedness. When he reminded his security chief of the significant failures that could be laid at his feet, they finally agreed to halt the recriminations and call it a night, setting a meeting at the offices for six in the morning.

Upon pulling into the garage, Richard sees a car parked beside Keach's in the firm's reserved spaces. Once inside, he meets the driver, a man introduced to him as Jonathan Stark. It's clear to Richard that Keach and Stark know each other and probably have similar backgrounds, though Stark seems to have a rougher edge.

Richard finds Keach's bearing even more imperious this morning, if that's possible. As the meeting begins, it's obvious that Dan believes he's in charge and wants to ensure the others share his perception. There's a slight military affectation to both his posture and the tone of his voice, as well as his choice of phrases. When Richard asks about Jonathan Stark's presence, Keach responds, "Jon is here to assist with our operations this morning on an as needed basis."

Continuing to take the lead, he says, "Before we discuss dealing with Adkins, we have another problem here."

Keach had brought a newspaper with him to the meeting and left it on the glass coffee table. Now he retrieves it, dramatically plopping it onto Richard's desk with two hands. At the same time, he says, "There's another headline story about the shootings in this rag newspaper. This reporter, Preeti Chopra, keeps churning out articles and she's turning up the heat. Though some of her allegations are inaccurate, this kind of publicity can quickly lead to no good."

Richard grabs the paper and scans the first several paragraphs of the article, occasionally reading the most inflammatory sentences aloud. During the ensuing discussion of the potential ramifications, and how they might respond, Wilkins proposes they consider threatening the reporter.

Keach quickly tries to shoot down the idea. "I don't know, Richard. Lots could go wrong with that, and it could easily act as an incentive for her to dig deeper. I was thinking that we should prepare…"

"I don't fucking care," Richard shouts. "She needs to understand the risks associated with pursuing this. You know, there are reasons why you don't see many news stories about organized crime. I'm just saying, maybe someone should point out to her the benefits of proceeding very carefully with such allegations."

To Richard's surprise, he finds his argument bolstered by encouragement from Jon Stark, forcing Keach to reconsider. When he changes his mind, they agree that Stark will deal with delivering a warning, though not too heavy-handedly.

Switching their focus to Adkins, Keach reiterates the importance of not fumbling their next contact with the man. Resuming a lecturing tone, he suggests that they position themselves closer to the Gateway Motor Inn, based on Adkins's mentioning it as a possible location for their meeting. Though he doubts it will actually take place at the motel, it could easily occur nearby. They can also continue to discuss their preparations on the drive over there. Once they receive the exact location, they might even have a chance to scout the site in advance, an advantage Keach would love to have.

Suddenly, out of context, Richard blurts out, "I want the man killed. If not today, then god damn soon."

With an unusually friendlier tone, Dan Keach responds, "I don't necessarily disagree, Richard. That's one of the reasons I asked Jon to join us today. If required, he can provide, shall we say, specialized services. But before we act, we need to understand where Adkins is coming from. Remember, he's offering to return the cash in exchange for no retribution. If that's truly the case, then we should at least go through the motions."

Looking from Wilkins to Stark, and then back again, he says, "Once we have the cash we can better assess the situation. Then we can decide if any further actions are needed, either right then, or sometime down the road."

⋏

While waiting in line to get a bagel and coffee, Carl Roberts thinks about the call Kenny Clarkson received yesterday. He can't remember an investigation quite like this. Instead of hiding and staying clear of the police, a man they weren't even actively pursuing is voluntarily communicating with them. Carl had considered discussing the situation with the Chief, but decided to wait until Adkins makes contact again. Hopefully that will be soon. Of additional concern is the remark he made about something being rotten. He definitely wants to learn more about that.

Thinking about Kenny Clarkson reminds him to find some time to write a commendation for the young officer. Having stepped out of a squad car and into an investigative role for the first time, the young patrolman has done an outstanding job.

As he's leaving the coffee shop, Carl grabs a free newspaper from the rack near the door. The headline immediately catches his eye: *Big Money Behind Motel Shootings?*

Quickly reading the article, he finds himself puzzled by the suggestion that a downtown DC firm is involved. Nothing in their investigation has pointed in that direction. Maybe the writer got their wires crossed and is thinking about Wilkins Investment Group. Regardless, it suggests an inter-esting possibility and merits some follow-up. He also wonders where the reporter is getting their information. Checking the byline, he sees Preeti Chopra wrote the piece.

By the time he reaches his car, the article and the investigation have left his mind. Instead, he's busy with thoughts of the alluring young reporter.

TD had slept poorly, earning little rest from a few fitful sessions. At a certain point, he gave up trying to sleep. Instead, he immersed himself in another step-by-step review of his plan. He also added an item to the top of his to-do list; before kicking things off today, he needs to talk with Les.

Arriving at National Harbor a little after seven-thirty, he then turns around and drives back almost a mile before pulling off the road. From there he calls Les. The phone rings several times before she answers, but it doesn't sound as if he woke her. After confirming she and her mother are okay, he tells her the main reason he's calling. If things go as he hopes today, they should be able to return home tomorrow.

"That would be great, TD, but I don't want to come back to a situation that isn't safe. This is a nice isolated place. My mom and I feel comfortable here."

"I'm glad to hear that, but please don't worry. I may have really screwed things up before, but I would never have you return if I wasn't sure you were out of danger."

Continuing, he says, "I can't believe it all turned out like this, Les. I hope that one day you'll forgive me. Hey, before I forget, will you please apologize to your mother for me?"

Les takes a moment before she answers. "I know you didn't mean for all this to happen, and I know you didn't plan it this way. But I sure wish you had thought about how things might turn out before you started all this. That's what you didn't do. As for apologizing to my mother, I think you should probably do that yourself."

Checking the time, TD sees he needs to end the call. "Okay, I just can't do it right this moment. I'm sorry, but I have to go. I promise you I'll apologize to her, even face-to-face if that will make you happy."

"Alright," she replies. "But I'm going to hold you to that promise."

After his call with Les, TD spends some time thinking about how he might be able to repair their relationship, but soon realizes it's time to call Preeti Chopra. When she answers, he first has her describe the vehicle she's driving before giving her the final directions to the meeting place. Instead of National Harbor, he's sending her several miles further south to a restaurant he selected the night before. To get there, she'll have to drive right past where he's now sitting.

When he pulled over to call Les, he had parked on a service road adjacent to the main drag. With the lighter morning traffic, it should be easy to determine if the reporter is travelling solo. When her car passes a few minutes later, he waits briefly before following. As if to confirm his suspicion, two cars pass just seconds later, travelling in the same direction. Despite their speed, he was able to see that both vehicles carried multiple passengers. He hopes she isn't being tailed, or has lied to him about coming alone.

TD quickly maneuvers onto the main road and floors it to close the gap. He's soon able to fall in behind the trailing car at a comfortable distance and determine there's no problem. A man and a woman are in the front, accompanied by a child riding in a booster seat behind them. Changing lanes and accelerating past them, he turns his attention to the second vehicle.

This one is a bit more worrisome. As it keeps pace with Preeti's car, he can see there are two men occupying the front seats. Up ahead of them, Preeti's car is slowing to make the turn into the restaurant. Seconds later, he goes on full alert when the car in front of him also begins to slow and signals a turn.

Instead of pulling into the restaurant behind them, TD makes a sudden left-hand turn at a gap in the median. Scooting past the oncoming traffic, he slides into the parking lot of a convenience store on the opposite side of the road. With a clear view of the restaurant, he can see Preeti has remained in her vehicle as he instructed. Unfortunately, he can no longer see the other car. When the two men emerge from behind the building and enter the restaurant, he assumes they must have parked in back. Not yet convinced that Preeti is travelling alone, he decides to move the meeting to another location.

The news of the change of venue draws a polite protest from the reporter, but moments later, he watches as she begins driving toward the secondary meeting point, a fast-food restaurant three miles further south. When no one follows her out of the parking lot, or crosses over with him from the northbound side, he's finally satisfied there's no tail.

Minutes later, he pulls into an empty space immediately to the left of where Preeti is now parked. As he stares over at her, she finally feels his gaze and turns her head. Making eye contact, TD lowers his passenger-side window and waits for her to lower hers.

Speaking only loudly enough for her to hear, he says, "Hi, I'm Tom. We can go inside for a cup of coffee if you'd like. Though to be honest, I'd prefer to sit in one of our cars and talk for a few minutes."

With a slight smile, Preeti says, "Please forgive me if I appear overly cautious, but why don't we start inside? If we need more privacy, we can always come back out to the car."

TD immediately agrees, knowing he'd make the same choice if their roles were reversed. Once they're sitting across from each other sipping cups of steaming coffee, he breaks the ice with casual questions about her tenure with the paper, and if she has experience covering stories like this. Measuring the young reporter, he watches her closely as she answers. He needs to assess her trustworthiness right here and now, particularly in light of the fact that he'll soon be disappointing her.

The thing that most impresses him is her patience. She had to drive to three locations this morning before meeting him. And then, when he queried her with somewhat mindless questions about her career, she pleasantly answered without hesitation, showing no hint of restiveness. Sensing a genuine earnestness in her, he decides to trust his judgement. Besides, she held up her end of the bargain. Hopefully, she can be trusted with the responsibility he plans to give her today.

Committed to moving forward, he says, "I'm afraid you're going to be disappointed with me. I've lied to you."

Guarding her reaction, Preeti tries to avoid glaring at him as she says, "I'm not sure I understand. Are you saying you made this up? The images are fakes?"

"No. I was there and I witnessed everything. And the pictures and video are definitely legit. I took them at the Gateway Motor Inn Monday night. What I lied about is something that's not going to happen. I told you I'd be giving you more information today. I'm sorry to say that I won't. But please, let me explain."

After pausing to confirm that Preeti is willing to listen, he says, "Honestly, I intended to provide you with more. Unfortunately, I came to realize that I couldn't do that. It would put too many people at risk."

Finishing, he says, "Look, I feel badly about deceiving you, but I'm faced with limited options for solving of a huge problem. And I have not been exaggerating when I told you that lives are in danger. I also think we both got a fair deal. I needed that article printed, and you received valuable information for a great story. Information you would have never received otherwise."

TD hopes Preeti will not react too negatively. While he was talking, an obvious look of disappointment never left her face. At least she listened to everything he had to say before she responded.

When she finally speaks, it's with an even tone. "Okay. I can accept most of that, but not everything. Like why did you have to drag me out here this morning and run me all around? It seems a little over the top if you ask me."

"I understand, but I had to meet you and talk with you to determine if I can trust you."

"And...?"

"I do. And I want to explain. But before we continue, I want you to know my real name. It's TD Adkins."

Preeti immediately perks up, realizing that she's at least learning a little something more. "TD? Is that short for something?"

Chuckling at the familiar question, he replies, "No. Seriously, that's my given name. The letters T and D, both capitals. It's a long story."

Watching her smile at his response, he continues. "The reason I'm giving you my name is in case you ever hear about something bad happening to me."

Pausing to confirm that she understands the seriousness of what he's saying, TD continues. He tells her he has set things up so if anything ever happens to him, everything he has learned about what was going on Monday night will be forwarded to both her and the police. But for now, and possibly forever, he must hold back critical pieces of that information. It's the only leverage he has over people who may want to do him grave harm.

"I took something from them. It was wrong and it was a mistake, and I plan to return it today, in fact. When I do, I'm hoping they'll consider the matter settled. Just in case they don't feel that way, or change their mind, I have to have something to hold them at bay. That's why I can't give you everything I know. I also can't give it to the police, which I anticipate might be your next question."

At the mention of the police, Preeti remembers something from her interview with Detective Roberts. He mentioned a third suspect seen leaving the motel. Now she realizes that it's probably this man sitting across from her. The detective had been clear that the third person wasn't involved in the shootings, and the photos Adkins sent her certainly support that.

Having taken a moment to absorb everything, Preeti says, "I think I understand things a little better now, Mister Adkins, but I can't say I'm happy about being led here under false pretenses. I'm also concerned that you might have been involved in the commission of a crime, or have special knowledge that might help the police. Being aware of those issues makes me quite uncomfortable."

"I get where you're coming from. You should know that I'm going to be in touch with the police today, I promise. You're welcome to follow-up with them to confirm that has happened. Hopefully that eases your conscience somewhat, at least on that point."

Preeti is surprised with his last response. She has to admit the man doesn't lack courage. And he appears to have a plan.

With more urgency, TD says, "I have to go now, but I do have one last request. I've trusted you with my name and given you information that can harm me as well as others. Those people are innocent of any involvement with this besides helping a friend escape from imminent danger. Please don't put their lives at risk by publishing a story about our meeting today."

Before she can respond, he's standing in front of her with his hand extended. After they shake, he walks to his car without looking back.

⋏

Once he returns up the road a distance, TD pulls off and takes a few deep breaths. He's already feeling the weight of what he's about to do and can see his hands are again trembling a little as he selects one of his cell phones. Checking his reflection in the rearview mirror, he sees someone who appears far more relaxed then he's actually feeling. Of course, it would be strange if he weren't nervous. Who wouldn't be unsettled as they initiate a course of action from which there's no turning back?

His next move is a call to Detective Roberts. While he waits to be connected, he glances at a piece of paper he has pulled from his notepad. Scrawled on the page is a short checklist of the items he wants to make sure he covers with the detective. It will also help him minimize the duration of the call, even though it's unlikely it's being traced.

When Roberts answers, TD identifies himself and immediately starts in on the message he wants to deliver. "I called to make sure you're aware of the reason I was at the motel Monday night, though I think you probably already know. I was hired by Julia Crane to follow her husband. I also wanted to tell you that I'm completely innocent of any involvement whatsoever in those killings."

As Roberts tries interjecting a question, TD speaks over him, saying firmly, "Please just listen to what I have to say, Detective. Otherwise I'll have to hang up."

He then tells Roberts he has a full video recording of the shootings and will be sending him a copy. He doesn't mention that it has been slightly edited. "After viewing it, you'll have no questions about who was responsible. It should also eliminate any doubts you may have about my involvement. I've also provided a portion of the same evidence to a newspaper reporter."

Ignoring TD's warning, Carl interjects, "So that was you. But why are you doing this?"

"I'm trying every trick I can to escape from a huge problem I created. As for contacting you, besides clearing my name, turning over this evidence is my own small effort at being a good citizen."

"I appreciate that Mister Adkins, but I must inform you that you remain a person of interest in this case. You were observed leaving the motel with property that may not be yours. At a minimum, you have removed evidence from a crime scene. Though I can't promise you won't face charges, I think the smart thing for you to do is to come in and tell us what you know."

"Well, that's not going to happen. At least not in the short term," TD quickly responds. "If I'm alive after today, then maybe we can talk. And you can throw the book at me with whatever charges you dream up. As for the shootings, I think you'll find the video is pretty damn conclusive. Now I need to go, Detective."

Almost shouting, Carl says, "Hold on one last moment."

Looking at his own set of notes, he sees underlined at the bottom of the page: _What is Rotten???_

"You mentioned to Officer Clarkson that you thought something was rotten here. Can you at least tell me what that's about?"

"Someone is hunting me. They tracked me by my cell phone and they tracked me fast. Real fast. And there's no way these men were with law enforcement. Whoever it is, they're obviously receiving frequent updates on my location. If I was you, I'd be wondering how they keep finding me so quickly if it isn't with information coming from inside your investigation."

Letting his words sink in for a second, TD says, "I have to go now, Sir. Good luck."

Roberts had anticipated a call with Adkins would be interesting. Even still, he's intrigued by the claim of video evidence and the allegation of a leak. He can't wait to see what Adkins is sending him. He also noted the remark 'If I'm alive after this'. At least Adkins understands the risks he faces. Carl hopes the man can handle himself, because whatever is going on, nearly every person in that motel courtyard Monday night has turned up dead.

As for the possibility of a leak on his investigative team, Richter is the obvious candidate. It also means there is plenty to think about over the next few days. It's probably time to discuss this development with Chief Simmons. Together, they can decide whether to talk with Frank Aldretti, Richter's boss over at County.

⅄

TD removes the piece of tape from the thumb drive he had marked separately before slipping it into a padded envelope addressed to Detective Roberts. He had driven past a post office earlier, and now, on the way back, he pulls in and drops the envelope into a curbside mailbox. Though it's still only mid-morning, he has completed each of the preparatory steps in his plan. Now it's time to close the deal.

He's soon back at National Harbor and this time he enters the rapidly growing complex. After parking in one of the public garages, he heads down the hill to the marina. To his right rises the new Capital Wheel, the huge fourteen-story observation wheel offering distant views of the Capitol and Washington Monument from its gondolas. Making his way onto the main marina pier, he finally spots Denny waving at him from among the many boats.

He can see that Denny now owns a classic sailboat, considerably different from the excursion fishing boats he lost. After thanking him for coming, TD says, "I still have to make two quick phone calls. Then I'll get the bags from my car and we can get going."

Walking to the far end of the small grid of docks, TD looks downriver. If not for a broad bend in the shoreline that blocks his view, he might be able to see as far as the waterfront at Ferry Landing Point. He has already talked with Pen earlier this morning when he arrived at the property. Now it's time for a final call to make sure he's ready to go.

As soon as he's on the line, Pen confirms everything is set. His car is out of sight inside the garage and he has taken over Denny's second floor apartment. He set up TD's camera there, along with two of his own. When TD finally runs out of questions, he reminds Pen that even if everything goes as planned, he's not to leave the garage until an hour after everyone departs, just in case they have someone watching.

When he finishes the call, TD puts the phone in his pocket, exchanging it for the one marked *HOT.* It's time call to Richard Wilkins.

⅄

Wilkins and his team have been puttering around for close to three hours waiting for Adkins to call. They have changed locations multiple times, though always staying within a close radius of the motel. Coincidentally, they stopped for coffee and a bathroom break at the McDonalds from which Raffi had launched his attack. Right now, they're parked in the lot of a Wal-Mart.

Robert Owen has been doing all the driving so far this morning, with Wilkins in the passenger seat, and Dan Keach nestled in back along with an assortment of communications gear. As they've circled the area, Richard has at least derived some small pleasure from the seating arrangement. He has particularly enjoyed watching the sour expression that appears on Owen's face each time Keach barks out the next set of driving instructions.

At Keach's request, they have linked Richard's phone to the car's speakers via Bluetooth, enabling them to take the call from Adkins together. Wilkins noticed Keach's smugness when he made the suggestion, but he didn't mind. For the moment, he has his ego in check, cognizant that the stakes are too high to handle the call on his own.

Several times this morning, he has caught a glimpse of Jon Stark in his side view mirror, riding in the car directly behind them. The same vehicle is now parked the next row over. The driver is a blond-haired man wearing sunglasses, with Stark riding shotgun. Richard finds the men's presence reassuring. If they need some muscle this morning, it's clearly ready and available.

⚔

TD checks the time and notes that it's now ten AM as he makes the call to Richard Wilkins. Denny projects it will take no more than twenty minutes for them to get under way and reach the property downriver. On top of that, TD still has to complete a couple of last minute tasks before they can leave.

Once he determines Wilkins's current location, he can decide on a meeting time and give him the address. If Wilkins is near Fairfax, as TD expects, then he'll set the rendezvous for eleven, leaving him enough time to make the drive, but with only a little to spare.

⚔

As the call rings loudly over the car's speakers, Richard lets it go a second, then a third time, before nodding at Dan Keach as he answers.

Skipping any pleasantries, TD immediately starts in, speaking at a measured pace. "Before we go forward, I want to review our pending transaction. I will return the money today, but only by delivering it into your hands. This needs to be a deal between us personally. In exchange, you guarantee that you and your associates will leave me alone, completely and permanently. That also includes my friends. Once you have the money, any issues between us are settled. If you don't agree, then the only thing I can promise is that you'll never get your money back."

After a short pause, TD asks, "Do we have a deal?"

As he waits for an answer, it's as if he can feel the man's seething anger coming through the phone. He's concerned that Wilkins might accept, but insist on sending someone in his place to collect the money. That won't do. Part of TD's future safety net is having connected Wilkins directly to the cash.

When Wilkins finally agrees, adding no conditions, TD is thrilled. "Excellent. Now, I just need to be sure you understand the ramifications of any…"

Wilkins interrupts TD with a blast, unwilling to be lectured any further by a man he detests. Leaning towards the windshield, he yells, "Who do you fucking think you are? I'm sick and tired of listening to your condescending…"

Dan Keach quickly ends Richard's rant by grabbing his shoulder and firmly pulling him toward the seatback. Speaking loudly enough for all to hear, Keach says, "Why don't we listen to what Mister Adkins has to say?"

Hearing a second voice on the call neither surprises nor bothers TD. Based on the number of men deployed to recover the cash, he wouldn't have expected to find Wilkins suddenly flying solo. It might even prove to be a good thing having someone more self-controlled to deal with, particularly considering Wilkin's proven volatility.

"I just want to be crystal clear," TD resumes. "Any attempt to harm me or my friends will go very badly for you, including threats or intimidation. If such a thing occurs, even once, I've arranged for detailed information about what was happening at the motel to be provided to the police and the media. That includes a video recording of all the deliveries that took place before the shootings, as well as independent information directly tying your firm to what occurred."

Before anyone can interrupt, TD says, "I also don't want you to think I'm bluffing. When I return the money, I'll give you a copy of everything I have. Review it closely. There's no doubt your company will come under considerable scrutiny if it's ever released. I sure wouldn't want to be you at that point."

Richard Wilkins hates being threatened. Worse, this is straightforward blackmail. Red in the face and starting to shake with a renewed fury, he's ready to erupt again. Luckily, before he goes off, Dan Keach speaks from the back seat.

"What assurances do we have that you won't do such a thing anyway?"

"Because it's the only thing I have to keep you from coming at me in the future. I don't want to be constantly looking over my shoulder. I want to be able to live openly, without fear, maybe even in this area."

"Then you shouldn't have taken something that didn't belong to you and now try to blackmail me," Wilkins shouts at him.

This time TD uses a harsher tone. "Look, I'm giving you your money back. And I don't intend you any harm in the future. I've been hoping you would consider this a big misunderstanding, but I've got to have an insurance policy in case you don't see it that way."

Pausing only briefly, he continues. "You need to understand that this is all in your hands. If you're able to restrain your desire for revenge, the information I have will never see the light of day. Just don't force my hand. Maybe you've seen the latest City Express newspaper. If not, then you should check it out. I was the source for that article. Clearly, I'm capable of feeding the media a variety of story lines. They can be partially true, like they've been so far, or they can be explicitly factual. Or it can all stop. It's up to you."

Wilkins responds immediately, surprising everyone by not yelling. "Just shut up, okay. It's time to end this. I've already agreed that we have a deal and I prefer not listening to any more of your bullshit, you fucking weasel. And I'm warning you. If you don't return every goddamn dollar, you're going to suffer some dire consequences."

His vitriol spent, Wilkins turns toward Robert Owen and loudly asks how much money was taken. After a brief silence, TD hears a third voice say, "eight fifty two". Before he can internalize what that means, Wilkins is speaking again.

"Eight hundred and fifty two thousand dollars, Mister Adkins. And by the way, I know about your little jaunt to Atlantic City. I hope you were a winner, because there's going to be holy hell to pay if you don't have each and every fucking one of those eight hundred and fifty two thousand dollars to hand over today."

TD is confused by the figure that Wilkins keeps citing. Though at the moment he can't remember the exact amount he counted out, he's certain it exceeds a million dollars. He's going to have to process this information later. For now, he simply ignores it and asks where Wilkins is currently located.

"I'm near the motel, like you suggested."

When TD provides him with the address for the meeting, Wilkins remarks, "That doesn't sound like it's anywhere near here."

"It's not, so I guess you had better hustle. The meeting is at eleven and I won't stay there forever. And don't enter the property ahead of time if you arrive early. Just be on time and come alone."

Listening carefully, Dan Keach has already typed the address into his phone's GPS. With the app now displaying the location on the Potomac, he leans forward and speaks. "Mister Adkins, I'm Mister Wilkins's associate and I'll be accompanying him today. That's non-negotiable. We won't agree to the meeting otherwise."

TD had already decided it would be highly unlikely that Wilkins would agree to come alone, or even tell the truth about how many men would be with him. Hopefully, the property's layout and his game plan should counter any disadvantage.

"Okay, I'll agree to two of you, but that's it. Now, last items. There's going to be a fork in the driveway as soon as you come out of the trees into a large clearing. That's where I want you to stop your car. From there, you'll walk to the center of the clearing to meet me. You should see me walking to the spot as well. Second, this phone number is no good after this call and you'll have no way of contacting me. That means now's the time for any final questions."

Hearing nothing, TD ends the call, saying, "See you at eleven, gentlemen."

While they were talking, he had been pacing back and forth along the dock, oblivious to all else. Now it's time to get moving. Before heading back to the parking garage, he looks out over the Potomac. After reaching into his pocket to retrieve the phone he just used, he pulls his arm back behind his head. Then, with a mighty heave, he sends the phone flying well out into the river.

During her drive back home, Preeti has been trying to sort out her thoughts. She wants to discuss what she learned with her editor, but she also needs to prepare for him being upset with her. He's not going to like that she met with her informant alone, certainly not without telling him.

For several minutes, she has been holding her phone as she drove, debating whether to tell him anything at all. Before she can decide, she receives an incoming call with the designation 'Private Caller'. She considers ignoring it, but decides to answer.

Though Jonathan Stark uses a pleasant tone, his words are quite threatening. "You need to curb your interest with those motel shootings. Whoever is giving you information is feeding you crap. Or maybe you're just getting the facts wrong. Either way, a lot of people were badly hurt that day. If you keep writing about it, the list is going to get longer. Do you understand?"

Preeti's pulse is pounding but she's concentrating as best as she can, focusing on remembering every word and the voice as well. Refusing to respond, she feels her fear slowly turning to anger during the long silence after his question.

When Stark speaks again, he says, "Good. I think you get it."

Those were his last words. Looking up, Preeti is stunned to see she is parked on the shoulder of the road. Without thinking, she had pulled over and stopped driving during the short call. Now that she's back in the moment, she's instantly reminded of TD Adkins's warning.

With a rising indignation at being threatened, she quickly calls his number to let him know what happened. Unfortunately, he doesn't pick up. After leaving a brief voice mail, she pulls back onto the road, shaking her head in amazement at the twists and turns of the story she's covering.

⋏

While Adkins was giving them his final instructions, Dan Keach was already putting his men in motion, sending a text message to Stark with the meeting location and the order to get on the road. Once they're finished with Adkins, he gives Owen directions for how to get them there, before calling Stark to strategize.

Keach wants Stark and Samuel to use all haste. Once they arrive, they should attempt to approach the property indirectly, with two objectives. First, they should quickly scout the immediate area to determine possible paths of exit. Additionally, Samuel is to get himself into a concealed position from which he can take down Adkins if given the order. They also agree on the signal Keach will make for such an action. Finally, they discuss how they will follow Adkins away from the location if that becomes necessary.

Looking at the satellite view on his GPS, Stark comments, "That shouldn't be too hard. The entrance to the place is at the end of a dead-end street. And it's at least a quarter of a mile through the woods on either side to reach another street or road. The rest of the property borders the river. If he drives out, we can follow him easily. It'll be a little tougher if he leaves on foot, but we should be able to cover that as well."

Relieved that the waiting is over, Keach chuckles as he ends the call with a wisecrack. "Sounds good Stark, but you didn't mention if the bastard tries to swim his way out."

Laughing as he responds, Stark says, "I'll check with Samuel, though I bet he's equally effective at his job in the water."

⚔

TD stands frozen in a moment of panic at the end of the dock, having realized that he didn't check the label taped to the back of the phone before pitching it into the river. As he stares out at the spot where it entered the water, he stabs a hand into his pocket and extracts his one remaining phone. Flipping it over, he sees the word he's hoping for: *SAFE*.

With an audible sigh of relief, he re-pockets the phone and quickly heads for where the boat is berthed. He then follows the narrow walkway alongside until he sees Denny working near the stern. Calling out, TD tells him the only thing he has left to do is to fetch the bags. He should be ready to leave in ten minutes.

"Great," Denny shouts back. "I'll go ahead and get underway. I'll tie up at the end of the dock and wait for you there. It should save us a little time."

As he jogs back to the parking garage, TD shifts his thoughts to the last call with Wilkins and the amount of money he's demanding. He repeated the same figure several times. It was $852,000; a total that TD knows is considerably less than is in the bags. As he tries to figure out why there would be such a large variance, and how it could affect what is about to happen, he also wonders if it might conveniently solve a last minute problem that has arisen. He no longer has all of the cash he started with.

Earlier this morning, he remembered that he had never asked Pen for what was left of the $25,000 he gave him to use in Atlantic City. And there's the $20,000 he spent on the car. He has been working on the problem in the back of his mind, but so far has come up with nothing that looks good. At this point, the only thing he can do is to offer to make up the shortfall in a couple of business days and hope that doesn't blow up the transaction. Now, all of that may be unnecessary. If Wilkins is dead set on receiving $852,000, because he believes that's how much cash was taken, maybe TD should deliver exactly that amount.

Back at his car, he pops open the hatchback and begins rummaging through each of the bags, removing the accounting slips he discovered earlier. Adding them together in his head, he comes up with a total of $1,088,000. That's the number he now remembers from when he counted it Monday night. Looking at each of the pages again, an idea strikes him. Laying them out next to each other, he examines each of the totals. Selecting just two, he adds them together and knows he has it solved. To insure against his stressed out mind making an error, he uses the calculator on his phone for a final check. The result is the same. If he only includes two of the bags, the total comes to $852,000.

TD considers whether Wilkins is playing some kind of weird game by asking for less money. Maybe it's a test, with severe consequences if you fail. After a little more thought, TD jettisons the idea. He simply can't fathom a scenario where it would make any sense. At the same time, there's still one problem. This all can't be a coincidence.

Thinking back, he remembers that two of the accounting sheets were identical in format, with the third possessing several small differences. A quick glance indicates it's also the matching pair that total up to the magic number. That's when he figures out the last part of the puzzle. The third bag came from the trunk of the Cadillac. It's the only bag Slick never took inside with him.

TD immediately begins refining his overall theory of events. He concludes that Slick was running his own operations, off the books and out of sight from Wilkins. That would explain why the cash in the third bag isn't included in their total. The money could be Slick's personal take from a variety of activities. Regardless of the source, it would lead to the same result. Wilkins failed to ask for the money because he doesn't know the third bag exists.

TD likes the way his revised theory fits together. As he considers the possible ramifications, he puts the accounting slips back, making sure he returns each to the correct bag. He also sees that he has caught a little break. Over the past few days, he had purposefully removed any cash he needed from only one bag. By luck, he had chosen the third bag. That means he doesn't to have to shuffle any cash around to come up with the right total for Wilkins.

As he prepares to leave, he notices a few subtle differences with the third bag. Though it has the same color and manufacturer as the others, this one has a small zippered side-pocket and a few other minor variations. Still, it's hard to tell them apart if you're not looking closely. He considers marking it more clearly to avoid any possible confusion, but then decides there's no reason to do so. He's not taking it to the meeting; he's planning to hand over the exact amount Wilkins is asking for. Pushing the extra bag to the side, he shoulders the straps of the other two and steps back from the car.

Shutting the rear hatch triggers something in TD. Despite an earlier commitment to proceeding more thoughtfully and deliberately, he realizes he hasn't invested a single moment of serious thought into his snap decision to leave the third bag behind. After pausing for a few seconds to think it through, he now reverses course.

If his theory about the third bag is wrong, he could be facing some gravely serious consequences. And right now, there's no way that he can be sure. It could be as simple as one of Wilkins's people having made a mistake when they quoted the total. And if Wilkins were to arrive at the meeting point and make a revised demand for the full amount, then TD needs some options. He's certainly not planning to bring the matter up for discussion, but at least as a precaution, the third bag needs to come along.

By the time he makes it back to the marina, he has grasped another of the possible outcomes of having more money than Wilkins has demanded. Laughing aloud, he ponders the prospect of netting almost two hundred thousand dollars as a result of his little adventure.

⅄

As they race ahead of Wilkins and the others, Jon Stark and Samuel will be arriving with plenty of firepower. Along with four handguns, there's a collapsible scoped rifle in the trunk. They're also making very good time, with Samuel pressing their speed as much as possible.

Stark has continued studying the satellite view of their destination, while relating what he's seeing to Samuel. As they ready themselves for what they're about to encounter, he describes the large mansion with several out buildings, set slightly off-center in a broad riverside clearing. A relatively dense layer of woods surrounds the property, running at least a hundred yards deep. Backing to the woods on every side is a prosperous neighborhood of large homes on half-acre parcels. When they hit a stoplight, Stark passes his phone to Samuel so he can look it over as well.

The two men fall into a rhythm as they continue the drive, addressing the pros and cons of attempting to take down Adkins at such a location. Though he has selected a seemingly isolated spot, and one that's out of view of unwanted attention, it still presents several problems for them. On a Saturday morning, there will be plenty of people at home in the nearby residences, with some likely to be out in their yards. Noisily tromping through the adjacent woods could easily draw attention. It's also obvious that the sound of even a single gunshot could generate multiple calls to 911.

There is also only limited access to the property by vehicle. After turning off a heavily travelled road, you have to pass through a residential neighborhood to reach the main gate, which sits at the turn-around point of a long dead-end street. If shots are fired, getting everyone out of there quickly and unseen will be a real challenge.

Stark checks in with Dan Keach when he and Samuel finish their assessment. After hearing Stark's report, Keach agrees with his advisory against gunfire. They will be armed and ready for any circumstance, but unless the situation takes an unpredictably dangerous turn, they will not discharge their weapons.

Based on the limitations facing them, Stark outlines a plan for physically neutralizing Adkins and quietly removing him from the spot if needed. That way they can then deal with him in whatever manner they desire, at a place of their choosing. Keach agrees with his suggestion to taking Adkins, but only if it's required.

As they end the call, he reminds them that no action of any type with be pursued without his signal. And it will be his signal alone. Daniel Keach, not Richard Wilkins, will be running today's show.

⅄

Before he reaches Denny's boat, TD notices his cell phone beeping. It's also not the first time he has heard the chirping sound the past few minutes. Has he missed a critical call? He doesn't want to stop, but only a few people have this number and they're all important to the events at hand.

Reluctantly, he puts down the bags and checks his phone. Preeti Chopra has tried to call him and he also has a new voice message. Hesitating for just a moment, he decides he can't spare the time to talk. Without listening to the message, he slings the straps of the bags back over his shoulders and continues forward.

Suddenly, he again freezes with panic. The marina berth where he stood just minutes earlier lies empty; Denny and his boat are gone. Then, as quickly as it arose, his confusion evaporates when he remembers the plan. Looking to his right, he sees the boat tied up at the end of the main dock. He can also see Denny puttering around on deck, unaware of the constant tension and fear that are nearly overwhelming him.

Just downriver, Pen sits ready in Denny's garage apartment. After setting up the equipment, he had conducted a walking inspection of key points around the grounds. During the tour, he regularly broke stride to gaze back at the windows of the garage. Each time he was unable to detect any of the three cameras now situated there. Even knowing exactly where to look, he could see nothing that betrayed the existence of any surveillance.

Two of the cameras are positioned to track Wilkins and anyone with him. From the moment they exit their car, every step of their walk to the meeting spot and their interaction with TD will be recorded. The third camera, facing out from the far end of the garage, is dedicated to the area around the boathouse and dock. He has also planted two miniature ground-level microphones. Their excellent sensitivity and wide area of coverage should capture anything said between the parties.

With time on his hands, Pen checks the status of each piece of equipment a final time. A software package installed on his laptop provides him with the capability to adjust and control each individual camera and microphone remotely. From the comfort of Denny's sofa, he'll be able to visually monitor and record everything going down, while staying completely clear of the windows.

Pen is finally starting to enjoy himself. This type of work is much more in line with what he prefers and it's definitely a unique case. And there's the added bonus of helping a friend. Satisfied that he has everything ready, he confirms his status with a text message to TD.

TD can hardly catch his breath as he reaches the boat. He has been relying on a seemingly endless supply of adrenaline-fueled energy for days now, but this morning he's running on empty. On top of already feeling completely exhausted, he's now experiencing some light-headedness. To steady himself, he leans against one of the large wooden pilings at the edge of the dock.

Already at the side of the boat, Denny sees TD isn't look that great. "You okay buddy? Why don't you hand up those bags and then climb aboard? We need to get underway if you want to stay on schedule."

Denny's words help TD refocus. Pushing away from the piling, he slowly hoists each of the bags into Denny's waiting hands. Again, even the limited activity nearly depletes him, causing him to feel faint. Shaking it off, he mumbles to himself, "You need to settle down and get with it. You have a job to do."

When they finish with the bags, Denny again reaches over the side, extending a hand to help a clearly wobbly TD. Once he's on deck, Denny looks him over closely. "You don't look so well. Are you all right? I hate to see someone talking to himself like that. You sure you want to go through with this?"

Drawing some refreshment from the breeze moving across the water, TD is beginning to feel like himself again. As he looks in the direction of where they're heading, he forces a smile and says, "Yeah, I'm fine. Let's go. I need to finish what I've started."

⅄

In addition to being worried about her safety, Preeti has been thinking about the need to debrief her editor. She can't keep him in the dark and then expect his help in the future. She also needs to let him know about the threat to her safety and get his take on it. The problem is she's just not ready to make the call.

Right now, she feels it's more important to let TD Adkins know what happened, particularly since he told her he was dealing with these people today. She decides to make one more attempt at contacting him. Then she needs to find a safe place to hide for a few hours. Once she has made some notes about everything that has happened she'll call her editor.

⚓

Denny cheerfully explains that they're going to make excellent time as he moves the boat out into the main channel. Riding with the river's strong current, and the breeze that just picked up, he should have them off Ferry Landing Point in less than fifteen minutes. It's easy for TD to see the great enjoyment and energy Denny derives from being on the water. Unfortunately, with his thoughts on the events about to unfold, he's unable to share the enthusiasm.

Several minutes after they get underway, TD's phone rings with another call from the reporter. He's reluctant to take it, but her persistence might mean she has critical information for him. Having not listened to her voice message, he decides he can't risk ignoring another call.

Answering tersely, he says, "I have one minute to spare Miss Chopra. And I'm sorry, but I haven't had a chance to listen you your message yet."

TD is glad he answered when Preeti tells him about the threat she received. It lets him know that Wilkins or someone close to him saw her article. Right now though, he needs to reassure another frightened young woman.

"I'm sure everything about this is starting to scream danger to you, but the whole matter should be dealt with and over by Noon. After that, I believe you'll be left alone."

As a simple precaution, he suggests that she stay on the move for the next hour or two. It shouldn't matter after that. He also recommends turning off her phone and removing the battery. Trying to sound upbeat, he says, "Don't worry, I'm confident things are going to turn out alright."

"And what if you're wrong?"

"Then you're going to have one helluva story."

"That won't do me much good if I'm dead or beaten to a pulp," she protests. "You should know that I'm considering calling the police."

TD can see they're already running close to the Virginia shore and Denny has just yelled out 'five minutes'. He needs to end the call.

"Please try not to overreact, Miss Chopra. I don't mean to sound flippant, but when is the last time you heard of a local journalist being harmed because of a story? I truly believe this threat is nothing more than hot air."

Hearing no response, he adds, "I'm sorry this has happened to you, but please give me a chance to take care of it. If anything like this occurs again, I promise I'll accompany you to talk with the police. Right now though, I have to go."

With the call finished, TD watches the passing shoreline as he works to keep his growing anger from taking over his emotions. He hopes he's right in telling her that they wouldn't hurt a reporter. The idea really makes little sense to him. It seems you'd instantly motivate a swarm of journalists to investigate even further.

Still, the threat angers him, and adds another name to the list of those he's putting at risk with his actions. He's also disappointed with himself again. He never even considered the possibility they would threaten the reporter before he involved her. If he is consistently failing to think things through, what else has he missed? Is he on the verge of making a huge, potentially fatal mistake?

With doubt threatening to overcome him, TD battles a strong urge to call off the whole thing. Finally able to contain his warring emotions, he reminds himself it should be no surprise that his adversaries are playing hardball. Not only did he already know that, but it also doesn't really matter; it's not as if he has many choices for moving forward.

He soon catches sight of the dock and boathouse, but quickly finds them blocked from view as Denny steers them out of the main current, moving them in much closer to the shoreline on their right. With their speed dropping off rapidly, TD wonders how much longer it will be before they arrive. At the same time, he hears Denny calling out to him from the helm.

He tells TD that this is where he'll return after dropping him off at the dock. As they move past an inward bend in the shoreline, Denny slowly waves his arm back and forth, pointing at a small inlet running for about thirty yards. He explains to TD that he will lie in as close as possible to the river's edge while waiting for the call from Pen. Even though the water is not very deep closer to the shore, he'll still be able to maneuver the shallow-drafted Catalina. The weaker current there, will also allow him to keep the boat in place with a light anchor.

TD thinks the spot is perfect. Just ahead, the tiny cove ends with the shoreline pushing back out into the river. Until that point, the same thick stand of trees that surrounds the property also lines the shore here. There's no way that anyone at the meeting point will be able to see the boat.

Denny tells him it should take about three minutes to reach the dock from the inlet. TD makes a mental note of the timing. He's going to need something to talk about to cover the period from his signal to Pen until Denny returns with the money. The situation will be tense enough without leaving everyone standing there silently staring at each other.

As they come alongside the end of the long dock, TD realizes that somehow, every aspect of his plan has worked out perfectly to this point. Trying not to jinx himself, he erases the thought, instead focusing on his only remaining objective: returning the money without anyone else getting hurt.

⯅

Samuel and Jon Stark have arrived early enough to execute the quick reconnaissance they planned during the drive there. When they reach the small cul-de-sac, the only indication of the property is the presence of two short stone markers standing on each side of an asphalt driveway leading into the woods. Just past the tree line, the driveway narrows as it passes through a black ornamental wrought-iron gate, currently sitting wide open.

Instead of entering, Samuel makes a U-turn, driving them back up the street some distance before parking. From there, they quickly return to the entrance on foot, before splitting up as they move into the trees. As they begin flanking the property, they initially follow the line of a seven-foot tall iron fence running away from the gate in each direction. Both men are now wearing a wireless earpiece connected to their phones, and networked with

Dan Keach. They're also armed. Each has a high-powered semi-automatic handgun nestled in an armpit holster, and Samuel is also toting the collapsible rifle, inside a long black vinyl bag slung over his shoulder.

As Stark circles to the right, the thickness of the undergrowth along the line of the fence is making it difficult for him to make much headway without making a lot of noise, particularly considering the close proximity of the neighboring homes. He had anticipated some type a fence, and now he's either going over the top or turning back. As he makes the decision to return to the main gate, Samuel checks in with an update.

Samuel had initially encountered the same tough going and quickly made the decision to scale the fence. The undergrowth was dramatically thinner on the inside and he was able to pass swiftly and relatively noiselessly through the belt of woods. He soon found exactly what he was after, a nicely concealed position well into the property.

Describing his location to Stark, Samuel tells him he's currently twenty feet back from the internal tree line. He's elevated about four feet off the ground, having braced himself between the forked trunks of a large tree. Though his view of the river is partially blocked by a garage and the woods to his left, he has a full perspective of the house and the driveway. Most importantly, he has an unobstructed line of sight covering the clearing where the meeting is to take place. Based on the layout, he's about as close as they could hope. Since climbing into his perch, there's been no activity at the property, with no vehicles in sight and no sign of Adkins.

To some extent, Samuel's final observation surprises Stark. Based on their instructions, and the wide-open gate, he had assumed Adkins was already here. Checking his watch, he sees it's less than fifteen minutes until the meeting. Adkins must be waiting inside the house, or maybe the garage. As Stark begins moving back toward the gate, Keach reports that he and Wilkins are no more than five minutes out.

⋏

When they reach the end of the dock at Ferry Landing, TD disembarks unsteadily, his frayed nerves on full display. Even with both feet planted firmly on the planks, his legs are visibly shaking and it feels as if he has vertigo. When he tries taking a step, he has to throw his arms out to the side just to keep his balance and not fall over. Worse, Denny is laughing at him.

That's when he realizes it's the pier that's wobbling, not his legs. Unlike the newly built marina, the aging wooden structure is weathered and unstable, particularly at its far end. Simply shifting his weight causes the last few sections to list from one side to the other.

Smiling broadly, Denny shouts, "Sorry, man. I forgot how bad it is this far out on the dock. We're having some problems with these last couple of pilings. Just relax; it only sways a little. It's not going to collapse."

Placing one hand on the side of the boat for stability, TD manages a faint smile as he waves for Denny to come over to him.

A

Keach instructs Robert Owen to pull up alongside Jon Stark, who has just emerged from the trees to the right of the driveway. He then tells Owen to go wait in Stark's car for further instructions. Offering nothing more than a sigh in protest, Owen sullenly climbs out.

As Stark replaces him behind the wheel, he says, "I think I should drive you guys from here. I didn't find a good spot myself, but Samuel is in excellent position on the north side of the property. That'll be on our left when we get inside. If you end up needing my help, I need to be able see what's going down."

It makes sense to Keach. For a brief second, he considers Adkins's condition of only one person coming besides Wilkins, but then quickly decides it doesn't matter. "That's fine, but I want you to stay behind the wheel when we get there."

Before they get moving, they check in with Samuel and put him on the car's speaker. After Stark fills everyone in on what they've learned about the immediate environs, Samuel provides a quick debrief on his position. Keach then follows with a terse reminder that he's in charge during the meeting. No one is to take any action unless he calls for it. He continues with a final review of their strategy.

"Our number one priority, gentlemen, is recovering the cash. As we do that, I'll be assessing the reliability of the man we're dealing with. I don't like it all that he traced the money to us so easily, and I'm concerned that he may know too much. If I sense he represents an ongoing threat to Richard or our operations, or if the meet goes sour for any other reason, then I'll signal for action. Look for me to reach behind my back, and then quickly open and close my fist twice. Once we've restrained Adkins, we'll remove him from this location and determine his fate later."

After re-emphasizing the need to avoid gunfire except in self-defense, Keach reviews the plan for taking Adkins. Stark will first draw his attention by jumping from the vehicle with his weapon drawn and aimed. That will be the cue for Richard to hit the ground. Simultaneously, Keach will move toward Adkins, also brandishing a weapon. By that point, having already left his sniper's nest in the trees, Samuel should be closing on them rapidly. His mission is to physically restrain Adkins, and if necessary, temporarily incapacitate him. Then they'll move him into the vehicle and depart.

Wrapping up, Keach says, "After we…"

Samuel interrupts; his voice restrained but clearly audible. "Heads up, boys. Our target just appeared from behind the garage. He's walking toward the clearing."

Looking at his watch, Keach says, "Okay. He's here. We'll wait one minute for any last Intel, and then we roll."

During the river crossing, TD had carefully positioned the bags of money on deck, near the front of the boat. The two bags holding the $852,000 are pushed next to each other. The other sits to one side, a couple of feet away.

Now looking up at Denny, TD says, "When you return, grab those two bags that are next to each other and put them here on the dock. Then look for me and watch closely as I get near. If I hold up three fingers, then go ahead and put the third bag on the dock. If there's no signal, then it's just the two. Either way, be ready to shove off the moment I'm back on board."

Wearing a look of confusion, Denny says, "I get the whole two bag, three bag thing. It's just that they look an awful lot alike. What if something happens and they end up being moved? It would be easier for me if could I just stow the third one close by, separately."

Agreeing to the idea with a nod, TD watches as Denny grabs the solo bag and stuffs it into a locker along the rail. The act triggers an image from Monday, one of Slick believing he was safely stowing the same bag in the trunk of his car. It also reminds TD of how many people have already been killed or injured because of those damned bags.

With his mind back in the present, he thanks Denny again as he reaches up and they shake hands. At the same time, he takes one final measure of the man about to sail off with all that money.

As the boat moves away, TD heads along the dock, walking more briskly as he nears the shore. By the time he steps onto land, his countenance has turned grim. His pace also begins to falter as he moves up the low rise into the clearing. Then he stops completely as he looks back over his shoulder. Out on the water, he can see Denny's boat circling back upriver to its hiding spot.

Once again, a wave of doubts rushes over him. Why didn't he just hide the money somewhere close by, right here on the property, instead of trusting someone he doesn't even know very well? Has he increased his risk by not having it at hand? Minutes ago, he had taken satisfaction at how well his plan was going, but now he finds himself questioning its complexity.

Whatever the answers, it's too late now. Hopefully, he's not walking into a trap; one he possibly set for himself.

⚔

Even though he's about a hundred yards away, Samuel whispers as he updates his colleagues with the news that Adkins is carrying nothing with him. For now at least, it appears that he's alone, but without the bags. Adkins had stopped walking at one point, gazing back as if he had changed his mind or was looking for someone, but he's on the move again.

Samuel is now aware that his position has a critical blind spot. Hopefully, Adkins was waiting in the garage and came out of a door on the opposite side, blocked from his sight. Maybe that's where the bags are. With the goal of improving his view, Samuel briefly considers changing positions, but decides it's too late. Besides, Stark just reported that they've passed the gate and are almost through the trees. In a moment, they'll be able to see everything for themselves.

⋏

For TD, it feels like it took forever to cover the last fifty yards to the center of the clearing. At least he's able to take comfort knowing that Pen is watching his progress from the garage. He also knows that it's certainly possible Wilkins has someone here as well, tracking him from a distance.

They should be here soon if they're on time, but he has no way of knowing if they've even passed the gate. Pen would know, but other than calling him or physically coming out of the garage, they have intentionally omitted any other method for communicating. TD doesn't want to risk reacting to any kind of signal that could potentially expose Pen's presence.

Turning back toward the river again, he can still see Denny's boat. Moving slowly against the current, it's almost out of sight. TD again feels a slight wobbliness in his legs as he takes in the panoramic view from the crest of the low grassy hill. This time there's no rickety dock to blame; it truly is his nerves.

Suddenly, he hears the crunching sound of tires on gravel. Pivoting in that direction, he sees they've arrived, but ignored his instruction to stop at the end of the pavement. He can also see that there are three men inside as their vehicle comes to a halt a short distance onto the right fork of the driveway.

With anger adding to his tension, he watches as the two passengers exit the vehicle and begin walking toward him while the driver remains behind. He recognizes one of the men as Richard Wilkins from a picture he found online. The second man from the call is probably the one to his left. He didn't bargain for a third man though, particularly not one sitting just out of his immediate field of vision.

Corralling his emotions, TD quickly adapts. Though he prefers not to waste time negotiating peripheral issues, he needs to establish who is in charge. Looking at the man alongside Wilkins, he shouts, "This won't do. We agreed on just two of you. Your man needs to get out of the vehicle and close the door. He should stay back, but have him step far enough away so I can see all of you at the same time."

Keach is instantly disappointed with himself. Having hoped to manage and control the meeting, he now realizes it was a tactical error bringing Stark along. By violating their prior negotiation, he has given Adkins the opportunity to raise an objection and start setting terms. Added to that, he can feel Wilkins next to him, already bristling as they listen to orders from a man he holds in contempt.

After Keach relays Adkins's demands, Stark subtly adjusts the weapon holstered under his jacket as he gets and out and steps away from the vehicle.

⋏

Pen is growing increasingly concerned. TD is unarmed and outnumbered three-to-one. And even though he commands the situation now, the body language of the men he faces suggests they're anxious to reverse that.

From Pen's perspective, the driver represents the biggest threat. Twice already, he has reached across his body to touch something under his jacket. He did it as he was leaving the vehicle and again when he got to the spot where he's now standing. He's obviously checking the position of a weapon. TD has constructed his plan to counter such a possibility, but Pen is still tempted to warn him. Unfortunately, there's no good way to do that.

⋏

Whenever he envisioned how the meeting would transpire, TD was always standing face to face with Richard Wilkins. This is completely different.

With the driver hanging back and the two men approaching him, he's at a clear disadvantage. Considering the current dynamic, he decides to keep some distance between them. Just before he determines they've come close enough, they stop on their own, about ten feet away.

He first thanks them for arriving on time, and then looks directly at Richard Wilkins. "I don't think I've made it clear that I regret what has happened. I want to apologize for taking the money and any inconvenience it may have caused."

Wilkins is struggling to control himself, but he appears to relax a little when Dan Keach rests a hand on his shoulder. At the same time, Keach nods at TD for him continue.

"I know this may seem tedious, but I think it would be a benefit to us all if I reiterate the deal we've made. I'm returning your money, and you're agreeing to leave my friends and me alone. That also includes the reporter you threatened this morning. To be clear, that's no more tailing anyone, no more ransacking people's homes, and no more threats. It all stops as of now. You walk away from here with your money and the whole matter is done with and settled."

It's obvious that Wilkins is trying hard not to lose his temper. When he responds, his words are delivered steadily, but with plenty of attitude. "You know what? I'm already sick of hearing you talk. What I really want to know is where my fucking money is? You obviously like to run your mouth. Why don't you talk about that? Because, what I don't see is…"

TD interrupts, hoping to prevent Wilkins from imploding the meeting in a fit of anger. "Please remember that there's more than just the money you're receiving today. We need to go over that first. When we're finished, and after you've confirmed your agreement with our deal, then I'll give you your money."

Wilkins's response is an irrational, profanity-laden rant; a clear sign that he's spinning out of control.

Forced to raise his voice to talk over him, TD adds a threatening edge to his tone. "You need to calm down and listen to me. If you can't control these outbursts, then you will *NOT* get your money back. And you'll be lucky to stay out of jail."

Pausing long enough to let his perfectly timed thunder strike home, he continues. "The way I see it, I've done you a huge favor. If I hadn't come along and taken your money at the moment I did, it would be in police possession as we speak."

TD can see that they're stunned by his logic. He's also pretty sure that neither man would consider him as their benefactor, yet that's exactly how things stand. Using the moment of silence to shift the topic, he tells them why he was there Monday night and describes the video images he recorded. He follows that with the various bits of information he has unearthed and tied together since then, all pointing directly at the involvement of Wilkins Investment Group, and ultimately Richard Wilkins.

Holding his hand open as he puts it out in front of him, he says, "It's all here on this flash drive. Remember, it took me only a matter of days to figure out whose money this was. Given all the information that's on here, it won't take any time at all."

Looking directly at Richard Wilkins, TD finishes, saying, "Call it blackmail, or whatever you want, but I need to walk away from here today feeling optimistic about a safe future. If I don't, then this information is going public. And if that happens, I can assure you it's not me that's going to be doing any prison time."

⋏

For Pen, it's like watching a movie he downloaded. Riveted to the laptop's screen, he's totally engrossed in the drama in front of him; and now it's the crucial moment. If Wilkins agrees and they move forward, TD's bold plan has worked. Otherwise, things could turn ugly.

As he watches, the man standing next to Wilkins again touches his shoulder. This time the two men talk using short whispered sentences. With the volume turned up to the max, Pen hears Wilkins say, "Okay. I agree."

And suddenly, with that, it's over.

Glued to the monitor, Pen watches as Wilkins stares down TD with an expression of total contempt. When he finally speaks, it's with the most calm he has displayed.

"I'm not going to pretend that I like this at all. But as long as you return the money right here and now, then we have a deal. You and your friends will be left alone."

The moment the last words are out of Wilkins's mouth, Pen sees TD flash the signal to call Denny.

⅄

It has taken Denny far longer than he planned to return to the spot where he will wait. The breeze from earlier had completely died, and even though it would have been in his face, he could have used it to tack across the river's strong current. Without it, he was forced to rely almost exclusively on the boat's light motor.

Having finally reached the tiny inlet, he again encounters conditions he didn't anticipate. The current is considerably faster than he thought it would be this close to the shore. To avoid the strong flow, he moves even closer to the river's edge, nearly bottoming out in the shallow water. After maneuvering into a decent spot, he kills the motor and drops a small anchor to maintain his position.

Pen's call comes just thirty seconds later. Moving to the rail, Denny meets stiff resistance when he tries to pull in the anchor. A second attempt confirms his incredibly bad luck; the anchor is snagged on something heavy on the river bottom. Following the anchor line after it enters the dark green water, he thinks he can make out a tree trunk or large limb lying in the muck. Giving the motor a little power only sets the anchor more firmly.

Failing to see the obvious course of action, his mind begins racing through ways he can swing the boat free. Spinning around frantically without purpose, he looks first to the bow then up to the rigging. Then he's back at the rail for another attempt to unsnag the line.

⅄

Several times now, TD has swiveled his head from watching the men in front of him to scan the Potomac. He made the signal to Pen twice to be sure he didn't miss it, but he didn't note the time. He now realizes there's no way to know if Pen actually saw it. If he did, then Denny's boat should have at least appeared around the bend in the river by now.

His chest is pounding after another fruitless look over his shoulder. He can feel his pulse throbbing in his neck and even hear it in his ears. Was it a colossal mistake to trust Denny, or is this just some glitch in his plan that he failed to account for?

⅄

Denny slowly shakes his head, gripping the boat's rail with both hands as he hangs over staring into the water. Even after losing two boats, this is shaping up as his biggest screw-up ever. He needs to do something; every second of delay is putting TD's life at risk.

Lifting his head to the sky, he suddenly lets loose a wordless scream, filled with amazement at his own stupidity but also with his sudden relief. Spinning away from the rail, he opens a deck locker and quickly unsheathes a large knife stowed there. Seconds later, he has cut the line and the boat is free.

⅄

TD is worried that the men across from him will detect his skyrocketing fear. His hands are shaking again and he's trying to keep them out of sight enough that they won't notice.

When Wilkins confirmed his acceptance of their deal, TD told them a colleague would be delivering the money within minutes, though he said nothing about him coming by boat. Now, under the impression that another vehicle will be arriving at any time, Wilkins and Keach have turned to the side, regularly eyeing the break in the tree line where the driveway emerges.

During the wait, Keach has been intermittently talking with Wilkins. Once again, he leans in close, holding a hand up to hide his mouth and speaking at a volume too low for TD to hear. "As far as pursuing anything against this guy, I'm recommending we let it go. We can't risk the scrutiny and I think he's playing it straight with us. Besides, our hands are certainly going to be full cleaning up our organization after this train wreck. With what we've learned, it's clear that I put my trust in men who have displayed extremely poor judgment."

Keach's failure to acknowledge his own accountability further darkens Richard's already dour mood. At least he has his anger under control and is thinking clearly again. He also agrees with his security chief; they need to forego retaliation. He detests the man for stealing from them, and now compounding that with blackmail; but their desperate need for the money, along with the knowledge Adkins holds, trumps Richard's desire for vengeance.

TD is relieved to see that the men across from him don't yet appear to be overly concerned about waiting. Still, he's badly outnumbered, and if the money isn't here soon it could be a catastrophe. He knows he should be focusing on what to do if Denny fails to show, but he's having trouble shaking the image of him sailing off with all that money.

Deeply disappointed with having concocted such a daft plan, TD's thoughts suddenly shift in a radically different direction when he realizes there may be an issue with the video he's about to give them. He can't remember if he was already recording when Slick stowed the separate bag in the trunk of his car. He's fairly sure that occurred before Tim arrived, but the question is whether out of curiosity or boredom he had started recording at that point. He definitely has done that on prior investigations.

Battling the increasing tension, TD is no longer positive about much of any of it. Wilkins knows the exact amount of cash from the two bags, and the video definitely shows Slick carrying those bags out of the room, so that's good. But if his taking delivery of an extra bag is on the video, they'll be sure to notice. Even if it isn't there, what if they have access to the police investigation, as he suspects? Could there be video from another source showing him carrying away three bags? Or witness statements? That's certainly possible.

Another quick glance towards the river yields the same result: no sign of Denny. Along with worrying about Wilkins running out of patience, TD realizes he must decide about disclosing the existence of the third bag. He won't be able to influence their response if they learn about it later. They would quite probably feel duped and could unilaterally decide the whole deal is off. That's far too great a risk.

In an attempt to stall for every possible minute, he decides to give them the flash drive now. Holding it out toward Keach, he says, "Let me go ahead and give you the information I promised. Don't forget, there are copies of this. And they're teed up to go to the police and the media if I'm ever harmed in an even remotely suspicious manner."

As Keach steps toward TD and takes the drive, Wilkins complains loudly, "I still say this is blackmail, goddammit!"

TD responds in a calm matter of fact tone. "If the roles were reversed, it would definitely feel that way to me. But this is the only way I can see for both of us to achieve our goals. You want your money back and I want to live without fear of reprisal."

Sensing his words have struck the right chord, TD decides to push his luck. "There's one other piece of information you may not have and I want to be as open as possible."

With their full attention, he says, "There was a third bag of cash at the motel. Since I'm making you whole *AND* repaying exactly what you've asked for, I can only assume you have no knowledge of this other money; and also that it's not yours."

"Wait a minute. Do you mean to tell me that...?"

TD was certain Wilkins's temper would flare when he heard the news. Cutting him off, he says, "Please remember; you're getting every dollar that you demanded and expected. You're also gaining valuable knowledge about serious breaches in your firm's security and the honesty of your men."

Finishing with a white lie, TD says, "Besides, we're not talking about a lot of money in the whole scheme of things."

He had considered calling it a 'recovery fee', but felt that would be too inflammatory. Now, gauging their reaction, he believes he might just get away with this last gambit. Though Wilkins is visibly affected, his colleague showed little emotion during the exchange. His only reaction was to put a firm grip on Richard's shoulder as TD finished talking. He then hurriedly whispered something in Wilkins ear.

Dan Keach had immediately understood the situation. If cash was being generated and collected that they didn't know about, it had to be Eddie King's. That means he was probably taking business from them. And Adkins is right; gaining that information has considerable value, though it's unlikely to be worth as much as what was in the bag.

After receiving a begrudging nod from Wilkins, Keach looks over at TD and says, "As long as there's nothing else you should be telling us, then we remain in agreement with your proposal."

Sneering as Keach finishes, Richard Wilkins stabs a finger into the air, pointed at TD. "Let's cut the bullshit. You need to stop fucking around and turn over the money before I change my mind."

A

Denny's heart leaps as Ferry Landing comes into view. There, on the crest of the clearing, he can see TD with two men immediately opposite him. Another man is behind them, standing off from the group, away from their vehicle.

One of the men is now pointing at TD and the situation looks far from friendly. Denny considers ringing the ship's bell, or maybe just shouting out, but there was nothing like that in his instructions. TD had been very explicit about what he was to do and he's hesitant to stray any further from the plan; being delayed is bad enough.

A

Standing there with nothing to give them, TD realizes the magnificence of his failure. He had control of the money until the point he truly needed it, and then he gave it away. Now he's clueless about what to do next. No longer in control of events, he hopelessly turns his head towards the river one last time.

In that moment of pure elation seeing the sailboat gliding toward them, he wonders why he ever worried. And there's Denny, smiling and waving as the boat closes on the dock.

Turning back to Wilkins, he says, "I'm sorry for the delay, gentlemen, but the money has finally arrived. If you would please wait here while I walk to the dock, I'll leave the money for you there and you can…"

"Right," Richard shouts. "And watch you sail off? Leaving us standing here hoping there's even five bucks in those bags. No way."

While he listened to Wilkins irrational rant, TD kept his focus on the man next to him. When Keach locked eyes with him and gave a slight nod, TD knew it was over. He had done it. Somehow, his plan had worked.

Looking at Wilkins, he says, "Yes sir, that's precisely what's going to happen. And every dollar you demanded will be there waiting for you. You can come and get it as soon as I'm on that boat."

From there, it all went exactly as planned. Denny put the two bags on the dock before TD's foot hit the first plank. He spent the remaining time watching for the signal to put out the third bag. It never came.

Pen can finally relax. He had been hovering over the laptop, practically holding his breath since Wilkins's first tirade. And TD, well he can hardly believe TD. He knows the man has an instinctual ability to read people and situations, but that wouldn't have been enough today. Today also required a lot of guts.

Even though Denny had called Pen to tell him he was running late, it did little to relieve the pressure; there was no good way to let TD know. The most amazing part was watching his mentor maintain his cool under what must have been incredible stress. It was a tough situation, and a couple of times Pen thought it could have easily spiraled toward violence. Yet somehow, TD had managed to pass every test and keep things moving forward.

For TD, it was as if the walk from the clearing to the boat had never happened. Before he knew it, Denny was reaching out a hand to help him climb on board; seconds later, they were underway.

He had felt it was important to appear steady and confident after leaving Wilkins and his men standing on the hill. He had never looked back as he walked briskly to the boat. Had he done so, he would have seen that both Wilkins and Keach had followed him for several paces before stopping and honoring their end of the deal.

Jon Stark had never moved off his spot during the entire proceedings, but by the time TD had reached the dock, he was back behind the wheel and ready to roll. The moment TD was on board, he picked up Keach and Wilkins and drove them directly across the lawn to the riverside. Keach then trotted down the dock and quickly rifled through the two bags waiting there.

⋏

Pen shut everything down and began packing up once the men had retrieved the money and left the property. Things had gone almost perfectly from a technical standpoint. He had lost part of the audio feed right at the end when their car drove over one of the microphones, but by then it no longer mattered.

He had been surprised by the late appearance of another man. While the others fetched the bags from the dock, a fourth had entered the clearing from somewhere behind the garage. He carried an elongated backpack that looked like it held a weapon. Pen watched as he came to a halt when he reached the gravel driveway. He soon joined the others when they slowed to pick him up on their way out.

Pen looks forward to telling TD that both sides had a man in reserve, though their opponents' extra was obviously on hand for a much different purpose.

At the end of it all, he feels great about what transpired today, particularly being able to help TD. It was really something watching his plan come to fruition. Having witnessed the encounter from start to finish, Pen knows today's outcome was in no way assured.

▲

The fastest way for Denny to put distance between them and Ferry Landing Point was to ride with the current and head downriver. After sailing several miles, he brought them about and began the slower journey back to the marina at National Harbor.

Other than giving Denny a heartfelt 'thank you' when they first lost sight of the dock, TD had spent the outbound trip in silence. Denny wanted to congratulate him on his success but decided to let him be with his thoughts. The man had been through a lot.

TD began to unwind on the return leg and they were soon joking about Denny's delayed arrival with the money. When they finally reach the marina, TD removes $25,000 from the remaining bag and holds it out to Denny. "Please take it. I couldn't have done this without you. A lot of people are much safer now because of your help."

Denny knows he'll be unsuccessful trying to refuse TD's offer so he takes the money, but immediately begins to insist on giving some of it back when he sees how much there is. He soon stops protesting altogether, when it's clear that TD is determined for him to have it all. Besides, who is he to dispute the value put on his services?

As TD heads off with the bag of money slung over his shoulder, Denny sets out onto the river once again. By the time he finishes the short trip back to Ferry Landing Point, he's wearing a broad smile, already thinking about whether he should use the money for some nice upgrades to his boat or maybe parlay it into something larger. `

▲

By the time he reaches the parking garage, TD can feel his energy rapidly ebbing. During the trip back upriver to the marina he had slowly embraced the sense of accomplishment washing over him, justified in his pride. He had achieved everything he set out to do. He had returned the money, no one else was hurt, and Wilkins had agreed to call off his hounds. And there was a nice red cherry sitting atop it all: the bonus of a couple of hundred thousand dollars to show for his efforts.

But even as he had watched the riverside scenery passing by, joking with Denny and enjoying his success, TD knew there was another side to the story. Once he was back in his car, he sat there thinking for some time, dwelling on the negative aspects of his ill-conceived decision to take the money. When he reckons in the toll on his friends' lives, any sense of victory vanishes.

As he starts the car for the drive home, he can feel the fatigue wearing him down. His own bed will never feel better after five nights of sleeping on a variety of lumpy motel mattresses. Desperate for some real rest, he may even take a nap. Before he does, he needs to check with Phil and let him know what happened. TD hopes he's in less pain and feeling better. He also needs to thank Pen again and set up a time to meet so he can compensate him for his help.

Most importantly, he needs to call Les and let her know it's safe for her and her mother to return. He desperately hopes she doesn't completely hate him. He understands that from her point of view, he's probably someone to be avoided in the future, but losing the close friendship they built is going to be the toughest thing for him to deal with.

Thinking about it triggers a wave of sadness. As he feels his mood rapidly sinking, there's even a taste of the emotions he experienced after his wife died. He's sure part of it is simply exhaustion. He also needs to adjust to a completely different mindset now that he's no longer on the run, facing constant stress.

Regardless of the cause, instead of descending into a funk, TD immediately commits to fighting it off. Whatever happens moving forward, there will be no returning to those dark days.

A Few Weeks Later

Recovering the money was one of several critical efforts needed to save Wilkins Investment Group from the wreckage left by Raffi's attack. Robert Owen also delivered a much-needed win two days later, convincing their bankers to give the firm a short extension to meet its debt obligations. In parallel, he used a somewhat abbreviated laundering process to channel the recaptured cash more rapidly through the appropriate accounts.

Dan Keach's organization-wide security audit had unmasked several vulnerabilities. Embarrassingly, some of the problems were clearly due to his own laxity. Enlisting Jon Stark again, they quickly determined the scope of Eddie King's rogue operation after identifying his former deputy. One conversation with Dan Keach was all it took for Eddie's man to agree to have his late-boss's business taken over by The Group, giving the organization a nice boost in revenue. Keach had been quite persuasive, though it obviously helped to have Jon Stark and Samuel sitting with him when he confronted the terrified deputy.

Keach hadn't resolved his thoughts on the matter of Eddie King. Technically, Eddie hadn't been skimming or stealing from them. And he certainly wouldn't have been the first guy in this line of business to try to set up on his own. Keach found himself wondering how he would have handled the situation if he had learned about Eddie's activities in a different manner, while he was still alive.

While he personally designed a new consolidation process, Keach tasked Marty Carpentier with executing a one-man roving collection of the cash accumulating in the field. He had to place his trust in someone in the organization and Marty had impressed both him and Jon Stark with his demeanor and work ethic during the recovery attempts.

Through it all, Richard Wilkins regularly fumed at his immediate subordinates over the near destruction of the firm and their failure to prevent it. Despite his strong desire to do otherwise, he accepted Keach's counsel to wait several months before firing Robert Owen. Keach convinced him that Owen's knowledge of the firm's finances and accounting gimmicks was essential to restoring the company's fiscal stability. Besides, they'll need some time to identify a qualified and willing replacement.

Wilkins would also like to fire Keach; what occurred was just as much his failure as Owen's, if not more so. But he also knows that terminating the firm's association with its security consultant will be a delicate matter. Angering him with an unexpected firing would be accompanied with considerable risk. Richard has decided to wait to execute this personnel decision as well. When everything has settled down, six months or so from now, he'll solicit the help of his friends in Philadelphia to deal with the removal of Daniel Keach.

⒜

Preeti Chopra had waited several anxious days after her rendezvous with TD before talking with her editor. To her great relief, she had received no further threats. As anticipated, Stuart Kurtz was upset with her for meeting with Adkins alone, though he wasn't overly worked up. Having been a reporter himself, he understood the choices Preeti made.

Stuart's interest had cooled regarding any follow-on article covering the money-laundering angle. Though the information provided by the informant was intriguing, he's not really in a position to use it. The City Express isn't about investigative reporting, and there's no way the newspaper would fund it. If Preeti wanted to press forward, she would be on her own, working free-lance.

Given some time to think about it, Preeti decided it was unlikely she'd pursue the story. Continuing to investigate the matter, particularly on her own, would entail personal risk; TD's warnings and the threat she had received left little doubt about that. And even if she was able to uncover enough to move from speculation to fact, there was no guarantee it would be published.

Despite her decision, she didn't want to lose track of the story completely. She decided to call Detective Roberts to learn if the investigation was continuing.

⋏

The motel shootings case proved to benefit both Kenny Clarkson and Sean Landry. Carl Roberts had let them know that he appreciated their excellent work that night and had noted his praise in their personnel files. When the two got together for a celebratory beer, Kenny shared more good news. Roberts had asked him to stop by his office that afternoon.

Roberts told him that he had received buy-in from Chief Simmons to expand his team of detectives over the next couple of years and that he needs to develop a pipeline of qualified candidates. He wants to schedule Kenny for the investigative course work and training the department share's with the county. If he keeps his nose clean and does a good job with the training, Kenny will have a shot at making Detective within a year or two.

Roberts had also met several times with the Chief to discuss the status of the case. Of primary concern was the allegation Adkins made about a leak. They also needed to decide whether to pursue any additional investigative work based on what has come to their attention since that night.

They reached two decisions. The first was that Roberts should definitely call Frank Aldretti over at County and provide his take on Richter's performance. Simmons counseled Carl to tread lightly and not state an opinion that Richter was dirty. He should stick to the facts, point out the performance issues, and share Adkins's allegation. Aldretti was a seasoned veteran. He could draw his own conclusions and take it from there. He certainly didn't need Carl's recommendations for a course of action.

The second decision was more difficult. After a discussion lasting almost an hour, Roberts had reluctantly agreed not to expend any further resources on the case unless requested by the Commonwealth Attorney's Office. Together they had reviewed the files, including the information Adkins had sent them, and considered the allegations of money laundering made in the newspaper.

Clearly, something was going on at the motel that night, but Simmons couldn't be persuaded to go further. The city simply doesn't have the resources to pursue such an open-ended investigation and there would be complex questions regarding jurisdiction. He suggested Roberts contact the Virginia State Police or possibly the FBI, to see if either agency might have any interest.

⋏

Roberts refused to stop working one angle related to the investigation. In response to Preeti Chopra's inquiry as to its status, he had suggested they meet for lunch. He could have easily given her the information by phone, but lunch meant an opportunity to see her again. He'd like to see if there really was a spark between them, or if he had just imagined it the first time they met.

Preeti had a similar motive when she agreed to meet, choosing not to press him for an answer when he returned her call. There was something very likable about the detective, and she suspected he was interested in her as well. If he asked her out socially, she might just say yes.

⋏

Jim Richter was convinced that working on the case had been a real boon for him; particularly when Dan Keach called and delivered the news he had been hoping to hear: his gambling debt was erased.

The reprieve had come with a warning never to show his face again at any of their poker games. Richter cared nothing about that as long as he was out from under what he owed. Keach had also instructed him to stay clear of TD Adkins and not to discuss the case with anyone, ever. That seemed obvious to Richter.

Then, this past week, Frank Aldretti called him into his office. The discussion did not go well. Aldretti told him that Carl Roberts had called, thanking him for the resources the county had provided. Unfortunately, he made a particular point of expressing disappointment with Richter's performance. Roberts had also mentioned that they suspected a leak on the investigation.

When Richter began to protest, Aldretti cut him off. "Save your breath Jim, we both know your career has been stagnant for some time. I need people on my team who strive to do their job well. Even when I put you on simple straightforward assignments, you fail to excel."

Aldretti had paused, looking away for a moment before continuing. "You're going to be faced with a choice, Jim, and I hope you make the right one. The County is preparing an early retirement offer for you. It's not generous, and there are no financial incentives for you to accept it. Indeed, your pension will be reduced considerably by the fact that you're leaving early. Despite that, I strongly recommend you take the offer."

Aldretti had also told him that effective immediately he would be office bound, handling administrative tasks. If he refused to 'retire', he'd be assigned to nothing but the most undesirable duties. There'd be no overtime and he'd pull exclusively night and weekend shifts. Most importantly, Aldretti would call Roberts and offer him any assistance he might need in pursuing the possible leak.

It was obvious to Richter that it was time to move on.

The past few weeks were about starting life over again for TD. Fighting off a second period of depression was not an easy battle and there were many periods of deep introspection. He had made huge mistakes and harbored an abundance of regrets.

Occasionally, he found himself contemplating where he might be right now if he had just taken the money and run that first night. If he had only recognized that it was an absurd fantasy that Les would want to join him, Phil would be unharmed and Les and her mother would have never been so badly scared that they were forced into hiding. His daydreams usually ended with the same sobering reminder; there was also no chance that any of that would have occurred if had simply left the bags of money untouched.

He also reached a clearer understanding of how badly his life had remained adrift, even the past few months. Despite believing that things had been improving, the truth was that his progress was minimal. Other than his visits to see Les at The End Zone, he had continued his isolation from any other social setting. Professionally, he had taken very few cases. Closely examined, his life the last two years consisted of very little that could be considered positively.

To foster the process of self-healing, TD committed to making amends for the trouble he had created. Unsurprisingly, even contemplating the effort improved his overall outlook. Slowly, he began thinking about the future again. He even created a short list of career options that he might pursue. He wasn't on a mission to reinvent himself. He just needed to fashion a version of TD Adkins that he could respect and enjoy living with again.

When TD first returned to his apartment, he was pleased to find that the condition of the place wasn't nearly as bad as it might have been. He had always assumed Wilkins's men had broken in. Someone had covered the broken sliding glass door with a piece of plywood, but other than that, the damage was primarily superficial. Unexpectedly, the small safe in his office was gone. Even though it was obviously too small to hold all the money, they had taken it with them, simply cutting out the section of flooring that it had been bolted to.

He found the photograph of Elizabeth on the bedroom floor amid the disorder left by the intruders. After removing the shards of shattered glass from the frame, he stowed the picture in the bottom drawer of his dresser. He knew that displaying it would be a constant reminder of a chapter in his life that he is determined to leave behind.

By the end of his first day back, he had decided to sell the condo. He'll lose some of the money he put into it, but that doesn't matter. His current plan is to rent some place until he determines what his next undertaking will be. Wherever he ends up, it's definitely not going to be a basement apartment. He'd like to find a place with plenty of windows.

⚊ ▲ ⚊

Early on, TD insisted on treating Phil and Anne to a nice dinner. Based on a tip from Phil, he took them to her absolute favorite restaurant. TD had prepared himself for an icy reception from Anne, but that wasn't the case. He could tell that both of them were concerned over how he was faring.

The meal passed pleasantly and there was no talk of the recent events. Earlier that day, Phil had called to let TD know that his firm had notified Wilkins and CCVS that their auto insurance policies would not be renewed at the end of the coverage period. TD couldn't tell which of them had laughed harder when Phil gave him the news.

He was glad to see his friend's nose was healing quickly. Despite the initial swelling and ugly bruises, the damage had not been too severe. It was also clear that Anne had gotten over her anger towards him. Phil had told him that she recently commented how well TD had handled things in the end.

As the evening wound down, Anne asked him, "Do you have any ideas for what you'd like to do next?"

After assuring her that he was hard at work on the problem, they all laughed when Phil said, "Whatever it involves, if you happen to come across any bags of money, please just leave them there for someone else."

⚊ ▲ ⚊

Seeing Phil's broken nose reminded TD of Bobby Tomlin. He had read about his injuries but had heard nothing more. Hoping she might know something about Bobby's recovery, he contacted Preeti Chopra. He also wanted to confirm that she hadn't been threatened again, as Wilkins had promised.

Preeti was surprised and delighted that Bobby's situation was of interest to TD. She had honored Bobby's request not to mention him in her last article, but she still worried about him. She had slowly regained his trust by continuing to reach out to him and they now talked every few days.

Bobby had been released from the hospital only the day before TD called her. He'll be able to walk again, but the injuries to one leg were so severe he's not allowed to put any weight on it for three months. His difficult and painful rehab will take even longer. It's quite possible he'll need additional surgery and it's unclear when he'll be able to work again.

TD learned that Bobby and his family are in a real tough spot. He and his wife have two young children and Bobby needs constant help; at this point, he's barely able to walk using crutches. Insurance will cover most of the hospital bills, but their high deductible and out-of-pocket costs will erase their meager savings. With no apparent source of income for many months to come, Preeti has been helping them identify government assistance and charity programs that might provide some support until Bobby is literally back on his feet.

Despite his efforts to help everyone that night, bad luck had punished Bobby severely. Whatever his future, it would not be the same. Upon hearing about the young man's condition, TD knew exactly what he wanted to do. A few hours later, he called Preeti back. She was quite impressed with what he intended. It was totally unexpected and she agreed to help.

TD waited a couple of days before calling and it was Bobby's wife, Kristen, who answered. She already knew that TD wanted to meet with them in person and offer some assistance. Preeti had talked with her and Bobby and had vouched for TD. Kristen gave him the address of their apartment and told him he was welcome to visit the next day at Noon.

The visit was a short one. After the briefest of introductions, TD expressed his sympathy for Bobby's injuries and thanked him for his help at the motel that night. TD seemed a little uncomfortable, almost embarrassed. He then pulled an envelope from his pocket and held it out for Bobby.

"I want you to have this. I know you don't know me, and I can't really articulate why I'm doing this, but you need it far more than I do. Use it to help take care of your family until you can work again. Maybe you can go to school full time for a semester or two. I don't know, but please take it."

The young couple was moved by the short speech, delivered with obvious sincerity and emotion. When Bobby took the envelope, TD quickly turned and left the apartment. He said goodbye as he reached the door but he didn't look back. He didn't want them to see that his eyes were beginning to tear up.

As he got in his car, he felt wonderful. For the first time in a long while, TD was positive that what he was doing was right. Inside the envelope he had given them was a cashier's check for $75,000.

⋏

TD continued to refine the list of possible jobs he might pursue. Initially, he forced himself to include at least one complete career change, though he soon realized that he really loved what he had been doing before he abruptly quit. His list currently focuses on jobs related to fraud investigation. All of the choices involve work that he's sure he'd enjoy and would leverage his skills.

He had not anticipated that the best idea would come from Pen. They had talked very little since TD left the bags of money on the end of the dock and sailed off. Despite intending to meet, they had been unable to get together. Pen's schedule had been packed for two weeks, primarily the result of taking four days off from work to help TD.

When they finally arrange a lunch meeting, TD takes his checkbook with him. He plans to compensate Pen for his help, paying him the same amount as Denny. His plan is for Pen to keep whatever remains of the $25,000 he was given for the trip to Atlantic City. TD will then write him a check to cover any shortfall from the gambling, as well as his expenses.

At the restaurant, the two men are clearly happy to see each other. They talk for quite a while before ordering and continue to spend much of the meal deep in conversation. After they finish a full recap of the final faceoff with Wilkins, Pen says, "By the way, I've got some money out in the car that belongs to you. I'm sorry I didn't return it sooner. The good news is we actually turned a small profit. There's just over twenty-six thousand."

TD is happy that Pen raised the topic on his own. Smiling, he says, "That money is yours to keep. I insist. I want to thank you again for your help, and most importantly for being there when I needed you. It definitely means a lot to me."

Pen isn't surprised at TD's generosity. He has demonstrated that plenty in the past, sharing so much of his time and knowledge with Pen. Instead of putting up a futile protest, he moves on to the second topic he intended to address.

"I don't know what your plans are for work, TD, but I want you to consider an idea. Please don't reject it out of hand."

Pausing to convey his sincerity, Pen says. "I think you should take me on as a partner. We'll launch DC's newest investigative agency and call it Adkins and Pendergast. Doesn't that have a nice ring to it?"

TD knows it's not a bad idea and not a real surprise either. Pen had suggested something similar once before, though it was during one of TD's darkest periods when nothing would have interested him. Now the idea has genuine appeal.

Instead of responding positively, TD balks, intent on curbing his impulsive decision-making. Self-doubt tempers his enthusiasm as well. "I tell you what Pen, it's an idea that could work for me, but I need to think it over. And you should do so as well. I'm not sure it would be such a great deal for you."

TD's upbeat mood has vanished. With a regretful tone, he adds, "I think my deductive skills are gone. Or maybe they were just highly overrated to begin with. Look at a couple of the magnificent failures I've had the past few years. I completely missed what was happening with Elizabeth, and I just did it again with Les. This time I imagined something that was never there. Partnering with someone capable of such huge blind spots could be a real career mistake."

Pen snaps back, "That's bullshit and you know it. I hate speaking so bluntly, but you need to drop the self-pity act, TD. I'm sorry to tell you this, but it's time to move on."

Pen watches TD closely, trying to gauge whether he has gone too far. Proceeding with a conciliatory tone, he says, "And forget about losing your skills, we all make mistakes. But the way you thought your way through that situation was awesome. You figured out that you had to return the money and then you went to work. Look how quickly you linked Wilkins to it all. And then you read exactly how he and his colleague would react to your offer. Watching all that tells me you haven't lost a step."

Finishing on a lighter note, he says, "You know, maybe it's just women you haven't figured out. As for the rest of it, well, if you ask me, you've still got it."

Smiling at Pen's last remarks, TD looks away for a moment before responding. He knows his young friend is right. "I tell you what; I'll sleep on it, so to speak. There's still one matter I need to address before I start working again. Let me see how things go and where my head is at after that."

"No hurry; take your time. Whenever you're ready is fine."

TD hopes he reaches that point soon. The more he thinks about it, the more he knows Pen's idea is solid. Combining his experience with Pen's energy and skills would make a potent team.

⋏

Though he has been dealing with his personal issues in a healthier way, TD's biggest challenge remains. He still needs to address matters with Les. He also knows Pen's comments were on target about learning to move on. It will be a terrible blow if their friendship can't be salvaged, but whatever becomes of his relationship with Les, he has to accept it and go on with his life.

As each day passes, he feels a growing urgency to resolve things. The worst of it is that they haven't talked since he gave her the news it was safe to return. He has tried multiple times, but she never answered his calls or responded to his texts. He even resorted to a schoolboy ploy, having Phil stop by the bar to encourage her to contact him. The result was the same: silence.

He's reluctant to go to The End Zone to see her. Though they've shared many personal conversations there, this is completely different and much too important. Unfortunately, he has no other options. When he finally decides to go, it's only to make a final plea for them to set a time to talk soon at a different location.

He visited on what would have been one of his regular days and arrived just as the bar opened. By the time he reached his table, Les had come over to meet him. Though she greeted him with a pleasant smile, he senses something uneasy in her manner.

Despite having prepared a few things to talk about to break the ice, he's unable to stay on script. Without even sitting down, he blurts out, "I'm so sorry about what happened. And I know I messed things up between us. I'm just hoping that you can forgive me and we can go back to being the good friends that we had become."

Though it came out a little faster than he would have preferred, it wasn't too bad. And at least it was coherent. As she turns her head away towards the empty bar, he can tell his words have had an effect.

Les is on the verge of tears. Turning back to him, she says, "I don't know, TD. I appreciate your apology, and I'm grateful you kept us safe, but a lot has happened. You acted stupidly, and I'm not just talking about you taking the money."

"I understand that," he responds. "And I don't blame you at all for how you feel. I wish none of it had ever happened."

TD can see he's upsetting her. Abandoning his effort to salvage things for now, he changes the subject. "Listen, I feel terrible about the damage to your home. I have a present I'd like to give you and your mother. Let me take the two of you out to a nice dinner and I can give it to you then. That's all I ask. Will you at least do that for me, please?"

Again, Les looks away. This time she takes much longer than before. When she finally turns back to him, her tears are evident.

"I think you should leave now. Seeing you here is more upsetting than I thought it would be. I'll think about what you said, but for now I'd like you to go."

TD quickly leaves the bar without another word. As he returns to his car, he's already battling the emotions that he knows must be beaten back if he's going to avoid hitting a new all-time low.

ㅅ

Several days later, Les sent TD a text message agreeing to meet. The decision to do so wasn't an easy one; she still cares about him as a person and a friend. But any reminder of the killings at the motel and his taking the money continues to upset for her.

That TD had misunderstood their relationship and asked her to leave with him is a different matter. Not only has she been unable to sustain her anger about that, she also believes that she shares some culpability for what happened.

Though she has decided to meet with TD, she isn't going to bring her mother along. She and Laura had recently argued over Les's repeated refusals to talk with him. Les also resents her mother's conciliatory words about TD. She finds it quite frustrating that her mother isn't as upset with him as she is.

There are reasons Laura's opinion of TD hasn't so easily soured. For the past few months, she has often listened to her daughter talk about her wonderful friend from the bar. It has been a steady stream of chatter about how thoughtful and understanding he is. Laura had also heard nothing but praise from Denny Holmes as to TD's character.

Not only did Les not tell her mother that TD had invited them to dinner, she even chose not to mention that she was going to meet him.

⚔

Arriving at the restaurant alone, Les makes an excuse that her mother is unable to join them, claiming she isn't feeling well. TD allows it to slide, though he's sure it's a lie. What he cares most about is making amends with Les and saving their friendship.

As her reticence slowly thaws, they ease into the shared rhythm of conversation between close friends. TD is elated over how things are progressing. He couldn't have hoped for more. When he senses the timing is right, he slides an envelope halfway across the table.

Tapping it with his hand, he says, "Les, I want to give you this check for twenty-five thousand dollars. It's to pay for the damage to your home and possessions. Please don't say it's too much, I put you through a lot. Take it and buy yourself some nice things."

Les had prepared for this exact situation. She knew he was bringing some kind of present and had guessed that he might try to give her money.

She had also considered letting him help, but was leaning against it. Now, seeing how much he wants to give her, she knows she can't take it.

Pushing the envelope back towards him, she makes sure that she smiles as she speaks. "Thank you, this is so generous, but I can't possibly accept it."

"Come on, Les. I'm the reason those men showed up at your home. I saw what they did and you shouldn't have to pay for it. Please let me take care of this."

Les can feel the compassion behind his plea and begins to waver. She knows what this means to him and he also happens to be right; he's to blame for what happened. She also knows the financial impact will not be small. Almost every piece of her furniture is ruined or needs repair, and her landlord has threatened to hold her liable for the cost of any damage not covered by insurance.

Sure, he's trying to salve his conscience by overpaying for her troubles, but it's only partly about the money. Les knows TD genuinely cares for her and wants to help. With a happy sigh and a smile, she decides to make a concession.

"Okay, I'm willing to let you help, but let's try a different approach. There's no way I'm taking all that money from you. When I get a repair bill, or replace some of my furniture, then you can pay for it."

"That's perfect, Les!"

"I should also tell you that we're thinking about moving. We're staying in the area but we just don't feel safe living there anymore. So you can help pay for that as well."

TD is thrilled with her typically practical solution. Most importantly, she's opening up to him again, sharing her feelings and plans.

They continue talking long after their meal is finished, almost as if nothing had happened between them. They talk only about the future. TD even mentions his potential collaboration with Pen.

At evening's end, they're both quite happy that their relationship is on the mend.

🙟

Les felt better that night than at any time since fleeing the bar in fear of her life. Her friend was back; the kind and considerate friend she had grown so fond of, not some crazy man with fantasies of running off together with stolen money.

Before falling asleep, she made a major decision. Changing her mind, she resolved to press forward with her plan for TD; a plan she had been hatching for some time.

The next morning she called both Pen and Phil to get their take on it. It was important that they didn't think she was crazy. She was happy to find that they both loved the concept; Phil was particularly encouraging.

Later that day she called TD. She asked him to meet her at The End Zone the following Monday at two PM. She told him she wanted to talk about something she has been considering for a while.

That evening, she told Laura about her dinner with TD. She talked about the large check he offered and their agreement over how he would pay for the damages. Then, finally, she told her mother about her idea.

⚔

Over the next few days, TD tries to predict what Les wants to talk about and whether it involves him in some way. He decides she's facing an important choice and wants his advice. It's probably something about a job or a new place to live. Regardless of the topic, he's quite excited. He's also as happy as he can remember feeling in a very long time.

That weekend he bought a new vehicle, trading-in both his original car and the SUV he had purchased while on the run. He was lucky that the SUV hadn't broken down at a critical time. While assessing its value, the dealer found several significant problems requiring immediate repair. TD ended up getting less than half of what he had paid for it just a few weeks earlier.

After earmarking funds for Les's repairs and his own upcoming home move, there's not a significant amount left from the money he took. He has decided to start the new firm with Pen and that will eat up the rest, which is fine by him. He's in the prime of his life, has plenty of assets, and no doubts that the firm of Adkins and Pendergast will be a great success.

⋏

TD is in a remarkably good mood on the drive to The End Zone and it's not only because he's on his way to see Les. Before leaving, he had talked with both Phil and Pen about his plans. The conversations reminded him of the great value of their friendship and everyone is pleased that he's finally focusing on the future.

Monday afternoons are the slowest time at the club and when he arrives there are only three other customers. As he takes a seat at what was his usual table, Les waves from near the bar. Wearing a smile that's almost a grin, her eyes are bright with excitement as she brings him a beer. With her customary wink, she tells him she'll be back to talk in a minute. She just needs to check on the other patrons.

As she moves away, TD notices another person has entered and taken a seat just a couple of tables away. Looking over, he's surprised to find an attractive woman, close to his age. Other than some dancer waiting for a tryout, he can't remember the last time he saw an unaccompanied woman in the bar at this time of day. Considering her age and modest attire, he doubts she's a dancer. She's probably here to interview as a bartender or waitress.

He finds himself briefly embarrassed when she catches him staring at her. When she returns his look with a welcoming glance and a smile, he nods and quickly turns away. As he does, he's struck by a strong sense of something familiar about her. Determined not to look over again, it feels as if she's still staring back at him.

TD keeps his eyes on Les, who is now headed his way. As she passes close to the woman's table, he notices Les give her the slightest of nods before taking the seat next to him. He finds it odd that Les didn't speak to the woman or offer to take her order. That only solidifies his theory that the she's not here as a customer. He bets with himself that at any moment the owner will emerge from the back to conduct a job interview.

Turning his attention to Les, TD finds himself distracted by how close-ly she's sitting to him. As she puts her hand on his arm and leans in even further, he tries to understand what is happening.

Speaking softly, she says, "I've been thinking about something that involves you for quite a while. I even started working on a plan, but it was interrupted by your little escapade."

Smiling sweetly, Les continues. "Despite what happened, I've decided to go ahead with the idea, particularly after I learned more about you. I've also discussed it with Pen and Phil and they think it's a great idea."

TD's mind is spinning as he leans away from her. What could she have been planning 'for quite a while' that involves him? And since when did she seek advice from Pen or talk with Phil? He can see that she's flush with anticipation over what she's about to tell him, yet he has no idea what's coming next. Once again, his legendary instincts are failing him.

"Please forgive me for presuming to tell you this, TD, but everyone agrees. You've spent enough time alone since your wife passed. It's time for you to get out there and meet someone. I think you're the kind of person who needs somebody to share your life with."

TD is confused, even a little perturbed. He certainly can't understand why Les thinks he needs dating advice from her. She may be right, but is this really what she asked him here to discuss? He definitely thought it would be something more important. As he tries to formulate a response that won't sound too impolite, he notices Les is now smiling and looking directly at the woman at the nearby table.

Returning her attention to him, she says, "There's someone I think you would enjoy meeting. Maybe you can spend a little time together and find out if you have anything in common."

In was during those last few seconds while she was speaking, that TD finally figured it all out. He knew for sure when she leaned back and once again looked over at the woman who was now standing, having tentatively moved a step towards them.

Even knowing what was coming, he was hardly prepared for Les say-ing, "TD Adkins, I'd like to introduce you to Laura Stevens."

Author Biography

G. S. Rock lives with his family in northern Virginia, where he grew up and lived most of his life, except for a memorable five-year stint in The Netherlands.

After a twenty-year career in IT management consulting, writing is one of his new pursuits. He also enjoys road trips, having logged over thirty-five thousand miles since 2007 and driven through all of the forty-eight contiguous states.

The author is also an avid poker player, participating in dozens of tournaments each year.